Glen Petrie was b brought up in the L service in Singapo 1949–51 Emergency Leslie Thomas's 'virgin soldiers') and was educated at Balliol, Oxford, the University of Exeter and London University's Institute of Historical Research. After teaching in London for ten years he became a full-time writer in 1977. He has published (1971) a biography of the Victorian reformer and feminist Josephine Elizabeth Butler and eight novels, largely on historical subjects, including *The Fourth King*, based on the tragic marriage and death of Alexander Pushkin, and *Alma*, the story of Alma Mahler.

Glen Petrie lives in North London with his wife, the psychologist Pat Petrie. They have four sons.

THE DORKING GAP AFFAIR

A MYCROFT HOLMES ADVENTURE

Glen Petrie

CORGI BOOKS

All the characters in this book are fictitious, and any
resemblance to actual persons, living or dead, is purely
coincidental.

THE DORKING GAP AFFAIR
A CORGI BOOK 0 552 13594 1

Originally published in Great Britain by
Bantam Press, a division of Transworld Publishers Ltd

PRINTING HISTORY

Bantam Press edition published 1989
Corgi edition published 1990

This book is set in 10/12 pt California
by Colset Private Limited, Singapore.

Corgi Books are published by Transworld Publishers Ltd.,
61–63 Uxbridge Road, Ealing, London W5 5SA, in Australia by
Transworld Publishers (Australia) Pty. Ltd., 15–23 Helles Avenue,
Moorebank, NSW 2170, and in New Zealand by Transworld
Publishers (N.Z.) Ltd., Cnr. Moselle and Waipareira Avenues,
Henderson, Auckland.

Printed and bound in Great Britain by
BPCC Hazell Books
Aylesbury, Bucks, England
Member of BPCC Ltd

For Brenda and Dennis

Prefatory Note

Until very recently little has been known of the life and career of Sir Mycroft Holmes KBE except that he played an active role in two of the cases investigated by his more celebrated younger brother, Sherlock, and that, following the Reichenbach Falls incident, he was granted power of attorney over his younger brother's affairs. Because of this general ignorance, when Professor Gordon Z. Finegold stated in his monumental work *From Nadir to Nemesis: an account of the deterioration in Anglo-German relations, 1871 – 1914* that but for the untimely death of Sir Mycroft Holmes in the *Titanic* disaster of 1912 Britain could have avoided participation in the First World War, the proposition was greeted with incomprehension, not to say critical derision.

Even Finegold's many friends and admirers at Oxford and elsewhere felt that he had been more than rash in making such an assertion at a time when circumstances did not permit him to present the evidence which had caused him to reach such a conclusion. A quarter of a century later, however, under the Ninety Year Rule exercised by the Foreign Office, the papers relating to the work of Sir Mycroft Holmes have now passed into public domain. It is the belief of the present editor of these papers that serial publication of all or even part of them will more than confirm Professor Finegold's view of the role played by Sir Mycroft in the history of diplomatic relations between the governments of Great Britain and Germany's Second Reich.

Prologue

Clutching his carpet valise under one arm and clinging to the rail with his disengaged hand, Jean-Christophe Thibault climbed the companion-way from the saloon on to the deck. The steam-packet had been pitching and rolling ever since it had headed out of the mouth of Boulogne harbour. Then he had wondered whether the master might not decide to turn back to await a more favourable wind and tide: the thought of having to disembark only to embark again under the alert gaze of agents of the *Sûreté* and the military's Statistical Bureau was intolerable.

Now, however, the steam-packet was approaching the mouth of Folkestone harbour. Immediately ahead the grey sea-walls reared up and fell away in a noisy spray of white spume. To the west the English cliffs were still in daylight, while in front the acetylene lamps swinging on their chains above the pier-heads glowed in the deepening twilight, and seemed to come no nearer. Several seamen ran past where he was standing to mount the rigging and furl the sails, with apparent unconcern at the

9

rolling and pitching of the vessel. Smoke and sparks belched from the soot-blackened stack as the packet battled towards the harbour entrance on steam alone.

The sailors dropped down on to the deck, slipping down the ropes. At last the packet, battling almost side-long against the waves beating off the massive curved stone bastions fronting the harbour walls, nosed into the calm waters of the inner basin. The quays reared up in the increasing darkness; the wind-driven rain came gusting over them, while above the piers the swaying lamps hissed. Longshoremen in gleaming oilskins and sou'westers looked down on the boat deck from the quay, shouting to the crewmen and waiting to receive the mooring ropes. Thibault stared up at them, fearful lest even among these English working men there might be agents seeking to intercept and apprehend him.

The packet's bulkheads bumped and jolted against the quayside, causing the deck to shudder violently. Ropes coiled upwards into the swaying lamplight and were seized by the shouting, swearing longshoremen. Passengers were pouring up from the saloons; they swayed into one another as they tried to maintain their balance on the slippery, sloping deck, clutching at their hand-luggage. Husbands endeavoured to support wives who in their turn struggled to hold in the billowing, wind-caught spread of their skirts, while children clung on to any scrap of their parents' garments they could reach.

The gangplank was lowered down from the quayside and secured on the deck. The passengers began to stumble up it on to the rainswept platform of the quay. Pulling his hat low over his eyes and clutching his collar about his face, Thibault followed the last of the passengers to the gangplank. About halfway up it the toe of his boot struck one of the raised treads and he stumbled, falling forward and dropping his valise as he did so. A seaman came running down from the head of the gangplank and reached out to assist him to his feet. Fearful that the fellow might use his accident as an excuse to drag him back on to the boat, Thibault waved him away with an unnecessarily violent gesture. He saw the look of surprise on the man's face, and mumbled an apology. The man glanced contemptuously at him and shrugged in the direction of one of his companions.

Thibault stepped up on to the quay and felt the reassurance of stone beneath his feet. Alone, he walked to the gates. Halfway along the quay he took one glance back. There was nobody following him. Two sailors were clattering down the gangplank to the boat's deck. Another was standing in the shelter of the bridge-house lighting his pipe, the flame momentarily illuminating his weather-beaten face. Crewmen shouted to each other across the wind-lapped desolation like seabirds crying. There was nothing out of the ordinary, he decided.

The last of the passengers had filtered ahead of him through the gate under the big gas lamp. Two policemen with two men in brown bowler hats and ankle-length ulsters remained there, waiting. Thibault walked up to them with a now confident step. One of the men in plain clothes was tall, middle-aged, with a thick moustache which drooped somewhat sadly at the ends in a style he had come to regard as peculiarly English. The other was a much younger man with the broad, broken features of a prize-fighter. As Thibault was about to pass through the gate the older man stepped forward, raising his hat.

'Pardonnez moi, monsieur,' he asked in clumsily accented French. 'Ai-je l'honneur à m'addresser à M.

11

Jean-Christophe Thibault, citoyen distingué de la ville de Lyon?'

'My name is indeed Thibault,' Thibault replied in English. 'And I am a native of the town of Lyon. Though in this instance I have come from Versailles.'

'Then you, monsieur, are the gentleman we have been sent to meet.' The older man bowed and replaced his hat on his head.

Thibault was aware of the younger man staring at him as if examining an item of cargo.

'If you will permit, monsieur,' the older man continued, speaking slowly and rather loudly as if addressing somebody who was hard of hearing. 'I am Inspector Greatorex of the Metropolitan Detective Police. And my colleague here is Sergeant McManus of the same.'

'Pleased to meet you, sir, I'm sure,' said Sergeant McManus, touching the brim of his bowler hat.

'Take the gentleman's bag for him, Sar'nt,' said Inspector Greatorex with a hint of impatience.

'Yes. Yes, of course!' replied Sergeant McManus, darting a cross look at his superior before he took the carpet valise from Thibault.

'We have a carriage here to take us up to the railway station, monsieur,' said Inspector Greatorex. 'If you'll be so good as to step this way. We've been h-instructed to accompany you, if you have no objection to the h-arrangement.'

'H-instructed by the Commissioner,' Sergeant McManus interposed. 'Sir Philip Doughty hisself.'

'I have no objection in the world,' Thibault told them. Far from it: after his anxieties and fears of the past forty-eight hours, already he was beginning to feel wonderfully safe.

12

Inspector Greatorex nodded to the sergeant in uniform standing by the gate, who saluted. He touched Thibault on the elbow, directing him towards the hackney carriage standing against the kerb on the far side of the wet, gleaming harbour yard. Sergeant McManus, with the valise, took up the rear.

'You are to accompany me all the way to London, Inspector?' asked Thibault.

'Not quite to London h-itself, sir. We've been instructed to h-escort you into Surrey, monsieur . . . That is, as long as you are agreeable. Only the h-Important Personage who is to meet you—' He broke off and glanced about him into the shadows – unnecessarily, thought Thibault, in view of the fact that the yard was almost devoid of traffic. Then he asked, as if there were a possibility that he had misunderstood his instructions, 'That's what you is seeking for to do, ain't it, monsieur? To have words with a h-Important Personage? At least, that's what we been told . . . ain't it, Sar'nt?' he called back over his shoulder to McManus.

'I have information I wish to communicate to a representative of your government – that is true,' Thibault confirmed.

'Very well, monsieur. H-according to our h-understanding, the h-Important Personage has decided – in view of the circumstances – it would be best if you was to meet him in a comfortable, quiet sort of a place—'

'Rather than in the 'urly burly of the – er – metropolis,' McManus intervened.

'Thank you, Sar'nt,' Inspector Greatorex called back to him. 'I don't know how Monsieur Thibault here could possibly understand what I'm a-telling him if it wasn't for your kind assistance.'

He held the door open for Thibault to climb into the carriage. He climbed in after and settled into the seat opposite Thibault. McManus threw the valise on to the narrow floor space between their feet, then climbed in beside Inspector Greatorex. The inspector leant out of the window and called up to the cab-driver to take them to the station.

As the carriage turned in the darkness to climb the long, gradual ascent to the town, Thibault asked, 'Shall I be meeting the Reverend Sir Horatio Rumbelow at this place in Surrey?'

Inspector Greatorex glanced at the disgruntled face of Sergeant McManus.

'Don't know nothing about no reverend gentleman.' McManus shook his broad, battered head.

'It was the Reverend Sir Horatio Rumbelow to whom I wrote from Versailles,' Thibault explained.

'Begging your pardon, monsieur,' Inspector Greatorex replied, 'we just receives our h-instructions from the Commissioner at Scotland Yard . . . You've a-heard of Scotland Yard, I daresay, even though you're by way of being a foreign gentleman.'

Thibault smiled. 'Of course. I'm sure the whole world has heard of Scotland Yard.'

'Then you'll h-understand that all we knows of the matter is that we has to deliver you safely – if you'll for-give my turn of phrase, monsieur – to this h-Important Personage's seat in Surrey . . . You being agreeable, of course.'

'Dare say as it'll be nice and quiet in Surrey,' said McManus, 'after all that there war with them Prooshian

14

Germans you've been fighting in France . . . not to mention them terrible Red revolutionaries in Paris, sir. Was you in Paris, sir, when all them terrible Red revolutionaries took over the city?'

Thibault shook his head. 'There was no war round Lyon,' he told them. 'And no revolution. I daresay I and my family lived as quietly as we would have done—' he hesitated for a moment – 'in Surrey,' he smiled. 'I saw nothing of the terrible events which have afflicted our poor country until I travelled north, to Versailles.'

'If you don't mind me asking, sir,' McManus continued. 'How come you speak our lingo so well?'

'Lingo?' asked Thibault.

'Tongue,' Inspector Greatorex offered helpfully.

'Lang-widge,' said McManus slowly and loudly.

'Oh!' Thibault laughed. 'I do a great deal of business in this country. Particularly in Manchester. Cotton, you know? I am in textiles myself. I have many friends in the north – many. That is why I mentioned the Reverend Sir Horatio Rumbelow. He is Rector – I think that is how you call it – of St Elphege's in Wilmslow. It is very near Manchester . . .'

The railway journey took almost two hours. Once they stopped at a fairly large junction, where Inspector Greatorex drew the curtains across the windows for as long as they remained in the station.

'We don't want nobody a-coming in and disturbing our privacy, now do we?'

But for the most part they stopped at small country stations at which nobody either got out or got on board and which seemed to consist of dark expanses of rainswept wooden platform, so that Thibault began to feel that they were travelling deeper and deeper into a deserted, dreamlike unknown.

When, finally, they stepped down on to the platform, it was that of a small but prosperous place flagged with stone rather than wooden planks, and with a well-roofed brick station house. Thibault saw the sign indicating the Dover and South Eastern Railway Company and the name of the town, but the latter meant nothing to him. Inspector Greatorex and Sergeant McManus walked to the platform gate, one on either side of him, so that the small handful of passengers who had got down with them might have been excused for believing him to be under arrest.

Inspector Greatorex handed the tickets to the man at the barrier. 'The carriage from the Hall?' he asked.

'Along the pavement,' the ticket-collector replied. 'Mr Whettam has been waiting this past half hour.'

Behind them the train, belching sparks up into the night, was drawing out of the station. In front of him Thibault saw a long street stretching between rows of uniform houses. The moon broke through the storm-wrack of the sky, shining on the slate of the steep roofs. On either side of the little town huge ridges loomed pitch black and somehow threatening so that, without rational cause, his previous anxieties began to return. A cold wind blew up the street. As his escort led him down the pavement to where stood waiting a varnished, two-horse, family brougham, he found he could not stop shivering, however much he clutched his coat about him.

The coachman who came to greet them was as small and sharp-visaged as a Longchamps jockey.

'Mr Greatorex?' he called.

'Mr Whettam,' the inspector replied. 'Begging yours

16

for having kept you and your beasts waiting this draughty night.'

The coachman peered at Thibault.

'All's well that ends well,' he announced. 'So you're the French gentleman . . .' He touched his hat with his whip. 'Bonne jewer, eh, Monsewer!'

Thibault laughed with the others, but dutifully. He was suddenly affected by a great weariness. He allowed himself to be escorted to the carriage and took his place inside with Inspector Greatorex and Sergeant McManus.

They began to toil uphill, up the slope leading to the top of the western ridge. Through the window he could see in the fitful moonlight an ever-increasing wilderness of scrub and low woodland stretching downwards to the town. The wind rattled the pane and found its way under the glass and into the carriage. Finally, after a brief trot along a level carriage drive at the top, they passed under an ancient stone gateway and clattered on to a cobblestone yard.

The carriage door was opened. A thickset stableman, his face concealed in the darkness under the peak of his tattered cap, helped Thibault down. Inspector Greatorex and Sergeant McManus jumped down after him and took their places, one on either side of him. He glanced up and around him. Gables and pinnacled turrets pointed upwards into the broken sky. A clock mounted in the small domed tower above a stable building chimed the three-quarter hour. Somewhere the wind was slapping a loose shutter against the stone of the wall.

A shaft of light shone across the yard from where a door had been opened at the top of a flight of stone steps. A neat, slight gentleman in evening dress appeared on the stone platform, a woollen muffler thrown around his

17

neck against the cold. Behind him, holding up a lamp, came a liveried footman.

'Well done! Oh very well done!' the gentleman exclaimed. 'You have brought our guest safely to us!'

He came down the steps, holding both hands out to Thibault. As he received them in his own Thibault felt revolted by their soft clamminess; it was as if the man shared his own apprehensiveness.

'Monsieur Thibault! What an adventure, eh? Was it difficult, travelling out of poor, dear France in these unhappy times? No, no! You shan't answer any of my impertinent questions until you have had a chance to refresh yourself and to take some supper, eh? Come in, my dear fellow, out of this dreadful wind. It's spring, you know, but scarcely to be believed. I'm afraid it will do nothing to improve our climate's dreadful reputation!'

The footman came down and took Thibault's carpet-valise from Sergeant McManus. The gentleman ushered him up the steps and into the house before he had a chance to thank or to tip the two detective policemen. He followed his new-found host along a candlelit whitewashed passage punctuated by ancient, twisted, medieval wooden beams until they emerged into a great, carpeted hall where, in an open fireplace the size of a poor peasant's cottage, whole branches of sturdy trees were blazing, so that the heat struck his face.

As they stood there, his host was speaking to him.

'I was asked to entertain you – you know that – for discretion's sake . . . Because the person who wishes to meet with you, and you yourself, I am sure, would not want those who are not our friends to know of the encounter. However, I would not have you think you were a whit less welcome on that account . . .'

18

But Thibault's attention was caught by the sound of a piano being played in an adjacent room. The music was classical, of the antique, Baroque kind: an exercise in graceful but cold, expressionless counterpoint. He recognized it from a previous occasion – both the piece and its performer. It had been in the Petit Trianon at Versailles, two months previously, at a reception given by Admiral Saisset for German members of the armistice negotiating committee.

He glanced around him. The great hall was empty save for the slight figure of his host and, standing well down the passage up which they had just come, the figures of Greatorex and McManus. All other doors were shut – all except that from which the music was coming.

'Yes, my dear Monsieur Thibault,' his host was saying soothingly, 'that is the gentleman who wishes to speak with you. He is a fine musician, is he not? He has been giving my wife and me such pleasure all evening . . .'

Thibault began to feel fear not like the apprehension he had felt when boarding the steam-packet at Boulogne, but as an animal feels fear. He was trembling; his legs felt weak so that he could not have run away even had there been some place of safety to run to; he was sweating, visibly sweating, he was sure. He felt his mouth hanging open, his lips and tongue cardboard dry as he shook his head and croaked, 'No! Please! For God's sake, no!'

Then the piano-playing ceased abruptly.

'Brilliant!' declared his host with a sycophantic smile. 'A true master. You'll not find a man in your country or ours to match him . . .'

Chapter One

Mycroft Holmes was finding it hard to conceal his impatience; it was only the fact that he was in the hall of Balliol, his old college, which prevented him from showing it more obviously. Up on the dais, two effete, ageing young men in evening dress, with long romantic forelocks falling over their eyes, were assaulting Beethoven's *Kreutzer* Sonata with an unnecessary vehemence. Mycroft had come down to Oxford on one of his periodic visits to his younger brother (by seven years) who was an undergraduate at Brasenose College. It was his brother who had requested that they attend the Saturday evening musical recital at Balliol, and Mycroft had felt obliged to comply.

He now regretted it. His corpulence meant that he spilled over the confines of the small, hard-seated chair. The evening was warm and the hall, like the entire university city, was filled with undergraduates, their parents, their sweethearts, their sweethearts' parents, their own sisters and their sweethearts' sisters. There was a general, rapid movement of ladies' fans like the silent flutter of moths' wings. Many of the younger sisters were casting surreptitious glances at handsome young clergymen in the hope of attracting reciprocal glances. They had good reason to hope, since there were a number of clergymen gazing with austere regard at the ranks of young ladies in the hope of selecting from their midst suitable vicarage wives.

But for the most part the audience was a study in wrapt attention, occasionally exaggerated, self-conscious attention. There was no affectation in the concentration Mycroft's brother was giving to the music, however. Mycroft would have preferred it if there had been; his brother's obsession with the intense was a cause of considerable worry to him. Sherlock, in the rusty black gown of a university scholar, was sitting erect, his lean Grecian face deeply serious. With his left hand, the heel of which rested on his knee, he was imitating expertly the fingering of the violinist on the dais.

The end of the recital was greeted with enthusiastic applause to which the performers responded with deep, hair-trailing bows, arch smiles, and self-deprecating waves of the hand. Sherlock applauded politely; Mycroft clapped his hands three or four times with all the grace and conviction of a performing seal before heaving himself up from his chair with the aid of his stick. He stared about him, paying no heed whatever to the looks of disapproval from his immediate neighbours. Then, spotting a face he recognized near the entrance, he waved his stick and pointed it, emitting an 'Aha!' which, but for its penetrating loudness, could have been taken for his clearing his throat. Lowering his stick, he made his way through the still-applauding audience. 'Spode, dear fellow!' he roared, adding to the displeasure he had already aroused among other members of the audience.

Spode, a clergyman in his mid-thirties, waited for him at the top of the steep flight of steps leading down to the Garden Quadrangle.

'Holmes, my dear boy! What brings you back to the old *Alma Mater*?' he asked.

'Duty, Spode. Duty. The sense of obligation an elder brother must feel toward a younger after the passing of our dear parents. I stand somewhat *in loco parentis*, you understand.'

He glanced over his shoulder. There was still applause ringing from the hall, but some people were beginning to make their way past them, down the steps and into the evening sunlight.

'I don't believe I've had the pleasure of renewing our acquaintance since you went down and I obtained preferment from my curacy at St Mary the Virgin,' said Spode. 'Do you follow some profession? Or did you return to your family's acres in – Huntingdon, was it?'

'Yorkshire, North Riding. No. I serve Her Majesty in a humble capacity. I have a lowly but secure desk with the Treasury. Whitehall offers the inestimable advantage of being a quarter of an hour's walk from my club and my lodgings, both of which are in Pall Mall. You, of course, have spent a considerable part of the intervening years in a foreign clime.'

'That is perfectly true,' Spode replied, taken by surprise. 'But who on earth told you so?'

Sherlock came out of the hall door.

'Ah! Sherlock!' Mycroft called him over through the throng. 'There was no call for so time-consuming a demonstration of approval. My brother, Spode, is I fear a BNC man. I would have preferred him to have followed

22

me here, to Balliol, but he'd have none of it. He's all for fencing and fisticuffs and other such reckless and hot-blooded pursuits.'

Mycroft shuddered. Sherlock stared at Mr Spode as if engaged in some assessment of his character and appearance. Mr Spode gave an embarrassed little laugh.

'I'm sure Brasenose is an admirable college,' he declared. 'A round hole for a round peg, eh?'

'It is true, sir,' Sherlock replied to Mr Spode, 'that being a BNC man provides me with opportunities to practise the athletic skills of my choice. But, contrary to my brother Mycroft's belief, such exercise does nothing to blunt my mental perceptions. Although we have never before met, for instance, I can tell you that until very recently – a week or two at the most – you have been abroad, in Lower Egypt, I surmise. You have been engaged in archaeological discovery . . . Ah!' – he raised a finger to prevent Mr Spode from confirming his statement – 'You have been at Memphis, have you not, sir? At the tomb of M'na, in the southern suburbs of the old city?'

'That is quite remarkable!' Mr Spode exclaimed. 'You must have the gift of second sight! I have indeed only just returned from Lower Egypt – last week, in fact.'

'Not second sight, Mr Spode,' Sherlock told him. 'No great powers of deduction are required when it is perfectly apparent that the coat you are presently wearing has lain folded in a press for many weeks, and has not been worn long; that your face has not merely been made brown by the sun, but has been weathered by it – something that could scarcely have been effected by the deplorable weather we endured all spring. You have been in the open, for many hours at a time, in a desert place. Your eyes are narrowed, which suggests that you have been facing into sunlight much of the day. But the left hand side of your face has been tanned darker than the right. We men of the north, when we work in hot climates, work until noon and then retire into the shade. From this it may readily be deduced that you have been working in a desert place well to the north of the equator, but facing directly toward the south. An attentive reading of the columns of the *Pall Mall Gazette* informs us that the eastern wall of the Temple of M'na has fallen, leaving no protection from the morning sun. But the sanctuary – if one may call it that – which has recently been discovered and exposed lies to the south of the archaeological excavations. So one may quite easily draw the conclusion that you have been working in the open for some months, in a northern desert, with the object of your attention to the south of you, and without protection from the sun on that side of your face exposed to the east. The Temple of M'na fits the case perfectly, does it not?'

'It does – I grant you that,' Mr Spode replied. 'But I remain astonished. Are there any secrets one may keep from you?'

'Everything that is of real significance, my dear Spode,' Mycroft intervened. 'The secrets of the heart and soul . . . Come, Sherlock. We must have you back in Brasenose before the gates are locked on you.'

As they strolled across the Garden Quadrangle at the leisurely pace which was the nearest thing to brisk exercise ever practised by Mycroft, he remarked, 'That was well done, my boy. I was quite relieved to observe that the dreadful music to which we were compelled to listen had not entirely dulled your brain. But I do regard it as my duty to point out to you that the habitual listening to such outpourings can only do harm. Beethoven's music – it cannot be said too often – plays too violently upon the sensibilities. The *Kreutzer* Sonata in particular appears to have been contrived quite wilfully to batter the emotions. I wonder how fathers can permit their impressionable daughters to be present when it is performed. The sensibilities of young women are so much more fragile than those of the stronger sex; one dreads to think how many brain cells have been damaged in those pretty little heads tonight!'

Crossing the Front Quad, Sherlock led the way up the steps to the porter's lodge and the gate.

'In that case, my dear Mycroft, you will be delighted, I daresay, to learn the topic on which I intend to address the University Aeolian Society next term.'

'A *musical* subject?' asked Mycroft. He waved his stick in the direction of the porter's window. 'Goodnight, King!' he called.

The window rattled open and the porter's head appeared.

'Goodnight Mr – er – Holmes, sir!' he recalled in the nick of time.

'On what other subject would I be likely to address the Aeolian Society?' asked Sherlock.

Gathering the skirts of his tattered gown about him in the manner of a young Roman senator, he stepped out of the gate on to the Broad. Turning as Mycroft followed him, he continued, 'I intend to offer a few of my own original observations on the polyphonic structure of the vocal music of Don Carlo Gesualdo, with particular reference to the later madrigals.'

Mycroft stopped stock still in the gateway. 'The later madrigals?' he asked.

'That was what I said, my dear Mycroft.'

A line of carriages was drawn up along the pavement outside the Master's Lodge. Some members of the audience were climbing into them, while others continued to chat in small groups, reluctant to let so beautiful a summer's evening come to an end.

'You young rapscallion!' exclaimed Mycroft, pursuing Sherlock between two of the carriages and out on to the Broad. He waved his stick imperiously, ordering a couple of cabs to stop in order to let them cross to the opposite pavement. He panted with unaccustomed exertion.

'You don't fool me, young man! I know perfectly well what attracts you to Don Carlo Gesualdo. It's the fact that he murdered his wife, the man whom he wrongly presumed to be her *inamoratus*, and the little son whom he took to be their bastard. His later music reflects the morbid delusions from which he suffered. I utterly forbid you to pursue so unhealthy a subject!' Grunting to himself, he mounted the pavement.

'You may keep me company down the Turl,' he said, waving his stick at the nearby street corner. As they continued down the pavement, he said, 'Should you wish to pursue the subject of late sixteenth century polyphony in all seriousness, I would suggest you examine the works of Orlandus Lassus. His music appeals to the most discerning critics – more so than that of Gesualdo. At the same time he was a man of a quiet, melancholic disposition, a valetudinarian who wisely sought the safe and tranquil life. There is no unhealthy freneticism to be found in his compositions; nothing to steer the listener toward the perilous shores of neurasthenia. His is a truly

26

English sort of music, even if composed by an Italian.'

'Lassus was a Fleming,' Sherlock corrected him.

Mycroft slapped his hand to his brow.

'You see? I am still the victim of that dreadful sonata. We must pray that my bed at the Mitre will not prove so uncomfortable that the damage to my psychic constitution cannot be repaired before I face the rigours of the Great Western Railway back to Town tomorrow.'

He had become short of breath so that their progress down the narrow Turl had to be interrupted several times to permit him to recover.

'You should find a sort of physical recreation which is agreeable to you,' Sherlock remarked, disapprovingly.

'My dear boy,' exclaimed Mycroft, 'I should have thought it perfectly apparent that what I need is rest, not physical exertion!'

As they came out on to the High he drew his flipper-like hand from his glove.

'There, my dear fellow! My duty's done for today at least. And you must return to BNC before you find you're too late, eh?'

They shook hands. Mycroft watched as Sherlock went off down the High. He sighed heavily, drew out a large white handkerchief and mopped his brow.

'Ah well!' he said to himself. 'What's undone can't be helped, I suppose. He'll go his own way.'

With solemn tread, he walked a few paces up the High then heaved himself up the steps of the Mitre Hotel.

'Mr Holmes, sir?'

The clerk's mode of address suggested that he had been awaiting his arrival.

'Sir?' asked Mycroft. He rested against the desk.

'There are two gentlemen, if you please, sir,' said the

27

clerk. 'Come all the way from London, sir. I told 'em as you was gone across to Balliol College; I offered to send the boots, sir, to fetch you. Only, they said it'd be best if they was to wait for you here. They're in the private drawing-room, if you please, sir.'

'Have you any idea who these gentlemen might be?' asked Mycroft.

'One of 'em said as he was a Sir James Swarthmoor, sir.'

'Not *a* Sir James Swarthmoor, man! Sir James Swarthmoor, First Secretary to Her Majesty's Ministerial Cabinet . . . Take me to your private drawing-room,' he ordered, displaying every sign of revitalization. 'Let us see what brings the Cabinet Secretary to Oxford in pursuit of his lowliest lieutenant, eh?'

He even rubbed his hands together.

Chapter Two

'Sir James!' exclaimed Mycroft as he entered the small, comfortable drawing-room. 'How very good of you to look me up here, in Oxford.'

He glanced from the mature but still handsome features of Sir James Swarthmoor to the elderly, distinguished-looking clergyman who was rising from the armchair beside him.

'You are perfectly aware, Holmes, I am sure,' Sir James replied, 'that I would not come calling at your hotel at this hour of the evening, simply to "look you up", as you put it . . . Holmes, this is Sir Horatio Rumbelow, the Rector of St Elphege's at Wilmslow. Sir Horatio is an old 'varsity friend of Lord Granville's – at whose house he is presently staying, in Curzon Street. He came up from Manchester by train this morning, to present us with a little conundrum: a somewhat disturbing little conundrum, as it transpires . . .'

'We did not like to fetch you out of Balliol—' began Sir Horatio.

'You would have greatly obliged me had you done so,'

Mycroft interrupted him. 'It would have provided me with a most welcome excuse for escaping from an ordeal – ordeal by music of the noisy, passionate sort. I was enduring it solely out of consideration for the somewhat immature disposition of my younger brother.'

'Sir James,' Sir Horatio continued, 'decided it would be best if we drew as little attention to ourselves, and what has occurred, as possible.'

'And what *has* occurred?' asked Holmes.

'We may talk tonight, on the train, without the least fear of being disturbed,' Sir James replied.

'Tonight?' asked Mycroft. 'On the train?' He was unable to conceal his discomfiture.

'We have chartered a special,' said Sir James. 'It is under steam at this moment.'

'Sir James has instructed the hotel servants to pack your valise,' Sir Horatio continued in his most emollient clergyman's voice. 'I expect they have taken it out to our carriage by this time. And the railway car is quite comfortable. One may enjoy a cigar and a glass of wine – and we have brought with us an excellent cold chicken.'

'No help for it, I'm afraid,' Sir James added sympathetically. 'This may turn out to be a very serious matter, don't you know.'

The single-carriage train rattled over the points through Didcot. Sir James's manservant cleared away the wreckage of a cold roast chicken and brought in a decanter of port. All three gentlemen lit their cigars.

'You say,' said Mycroft, 'that M. Jean-Christophe Thibault intended travelling overnight, direct from Boulogne to Folkestone and thence to your rectory near

Manchester, on Tuesday the second of May. Seven weeks ago, in fact.'

'You may see his letter for yourself,' Sir Horatio replied. He passed over the single sheet of notepaper. 'He is a substantial man of business,' he continued as Mycroft cast his eye over it. 'A sound fellow, for a Frenchman, and well respected by tradesmen of the better sort among my flock who are also in the clothing business.'

'But you did not think to communicate with anybody – his family, or anyone in a position of authority – when he failed to reach your home on the prescribed date, or shortly after?' asked Mycroft.

'Why no. Not for ten days. After ten days had passed without his appearing I wrote to Madame Thibault in Lyon, enquiring after her husband. I did not think to do so earlier. It seemed to me that there was every reason why he might have found it difficult to reach Manchester from Versailles.'

'And you have received Mme Thibault's reply?' asked Mycroft.

'Two days ago,' Sir James intervened. 'The same morning, Lord Granville received a private *bordereau* from the French Prime Minister, requesting official assistance in establishing the whereabouts of M. Thibault.'

Mycroft nodded.

'Sir Horatio, what was the gist of Mme Thibault's communication to you?'

'She said that M. Thibault had left Lyon at the beginning of April, having business in Versailles – you will recall that owing to the political situation in Paris, M. Thiers had established the government of the French Republic in Versailles. She said, also, that since the end of April she had received no word from him – and that

31

she had no knowledge of any intended visit on his part to Great Britain. She said she had written to M. Thiers about it. She is, it would appear, distantly related to the family of the French Prime Minister.'

'Quite!' said Mycroft. He sat back and drew on his cigar, listening to the steady, rhythmic noise of the train as it headed down the peaceful Thames Valley in the blackness outside. 'So the *bordereau* received by Lord Granville is the result of the private intervention of a member of the family who happens to be in a position of influence.'

'Quite so,' Sir James agreed.

'There's no question but that Thibault actually boarded the steam-packet at Boulogne on the evening of the second of May?' asked Mycroft.

'None at all,' replied Sir James. 'There is a reliable witness to his disembarkation at Folkestone Quay that night. A member of the uniformed Kent Constabulary who was on duty at the harbour gates is prepared to take his oath to a French gentleman answering to the name of Thibault and fitting his description being met by two men at the pier-head gates.'

'And what of these two men?' asked Mycroft. 'What has our observant police officer made of them?'

'They claimed to be officers of the detective branch – K Division – of the Metropolitan Police Force,' Sir James answered.

'Scotland Yard men?' asked Mycroft.

'Exactly so – a detective inspector and a detective sergeant. Needless to say there is no record of their existence in Scotland Yard.'

'So what we are confronted with is a case of abduction,' said Mycroft. He allowed his cigar ash to fall over the knee of his trousers. 'Or could it be a question of *chercher la femme*?' he continued.

'My dear fellow!' exclaimed Sir Horatio in a shocked tone.

'Saving your cloth, sir,' Mycroft told him, 'it would be a necessary hypothesis when dealing with the case of a disappearing husband – particularly when it is a *French* husband . . .'

'Of course, Mr Holmes! Quite so! I beg your pardon sir!' Sir Horatio apologised.

'Except that if it is such a matter, Sir James,' Mycroft continued, 'what are we to make of the extraordinary statement in Thibault's letter to Sir Horatio regarding "information of the utmost importance" ' – he tapped a plump finger on the bottom of the notepaper – 'which he says he wishes to communicate "to the highest in the land"? It suggests, surely, that this was the very purpose of his journey to this country? Would you say, sir,' he asked Sir Horatio, 'that your friend is of a peculiarly excitable disposition?'

'Why no, Mr Holmes! On the contrary. For a man of the south, he is a very steady, sound fellow: what in the north west some of us refer to as "a square abacus man".'

'In a word, then, a solid tradesman of the better sort, not given to extravagant utterances?'

'Certainly not, Mr Holmes!'

'Let me ask you another question, if you will, sir. Was M. Thibault a dabbler in political matters? He was not of the radical, anti-clerical persuasion? I ask because it is a weakness in men of business in France that they do not leave political matters to men of breeding and landed property as is the custom in this country.'

'I have heard him express the opinion that the Government of Great Britain should become more aware of the threat posed by an increase in the power of the Kingdom of Prussia – or the new German Empire, as we must now call it, I suppose,' said Sir Horatio.

'Your friend, sir,' asked Mycroft, 'was that commodity rare in France, an anglophile?'

'A wishful thinker, Holmes!' Sir James interposed before Sir Horatio could reply. 'I daresay there were a great many of his persuasion in France who would have liked to have seen this country take France's side in the late war!'

'Nevertheless,' Mycroft replied solemnly, 'we have here an honest, substantial man of business who comes across the Channel without informing his wife and family or his highly-placed connections in the government of France, in the hope that the Rector of St Elphege's in Wilmslow – a clergyman who is himself somewhat better connected (I hope you will forgive me saying so, Sir Horatio) than most parsons of the Established Church – will arrange a meeting between himself and "the highest in the land". And then this man – there can be no doubt about it, surely? – is abducted, and disappears utterly! One does not have to be a sensationalist to at least posit the hypothesis that there has been a conspiracy to silence him.'

Sir James Swarthmoor cleared his throat uncomfortably, but offered no further reply.

The train drew into Paddington Station, entering a bay on the extreme eastern edge. The billowing steam eddied and drifted from the window, giving way to the glare of lamplights. An assistant station-master in frogged topcoat and silk top-hat stood at the carriage door as it

34

was opened by a second top-hatted factotum. The platform, as Mycroft, Sir James and the Reverend Sir Horatio Rumbelow, Bart. got down, was otherwise deserted, save for the porter who took Mycroft's valise. They had drawn up opposite a sooty brick archway. Beyond, on the black, gleaming pavement of the Harrow Road, two broughams stood waiting with their coachmen, one bearing on its coachwork the arms of the Earl of Granville.

Raising his hat, the assistant station-master expressed the hope that Sir James Swarthmoor and the other gentlemen had enjoyed a pleasant ride. As Sir James replied, thanking him courteously for his trouble, Mycroft glanced up at the iron bridge stretching across the entire width of the station house, which was almost immediately above them. In a break in the steam which still billowed upwards from their locomotive, he caught a glimpse of a slight, youthful figure, dressed in fashionable, young man's clothing – velvet cap with polished peak clamped down on dark curls, black, scarlet-lined cape over plum-velvet braided jacket and narrow trousers in a dark plaid. Whoever it was had been standing at the rail watching, the silver knob of his black ebony cane pressed against his cheek. The moment Mycroft raised his eyes the figure stepped back so that the steam fell like a concealing curtain around him.

Mycroft said nothing to his companions. As they crossed the platform to the archway, Sir James said, 'I see Lord Granville has sent his carriage to fetch you back to Curzon Street, Sir Horatio. Holmes? I spend tonight at the Carlton Club. You lodge at the St James's end of Pall Mall, do you not? Would you care to take a lift there in my carriage?'

'That is extremely kind of you, Sir James,' Mycroft replied, perfectly aware that Sir James would wish to continue talking with him during the drive. Mercifully, he decided, it would be a relatively short one.

The staircase from the bridge formed one side of the archway. As they passed, even without turning his head, Mycroft caught sight of the small, slim figure watching from the top, only partly concealed by an iron buttress. This time he received a clear image of the face – the bright, dark eyes set almost orientally in the soft, pale complexion. There was nothing oriental, however, about the curls escaping from the peaked cap and the determined set of the small mouth and chin.

'Discretion, my dear boy. The utmost discretion,' said Sir James as they rattled down Praed Street and out into the turmoil of the Edgware Road. 'We don't want any wild notions to get loose, do you see? Nothing around which the scribblers of *The Morning Chronicle* or *The Pall Mall Gazette* can weave their fantasies about the Defence of the Realm and that sort of thing. That is precisely why I have suggested to "Pussy" Granville that we should employ you in this matter.'

'You flatter me, Sir James.'

Mycroft stared out of the window at the passing scene. The progress of the carriage was impeded by the clutter of flare-lit market stalls which pressed out from the pavement into the highway, with their compliments of shabby, ragged customers and street children, like rodents, scavanging the rubbish in the gutters for food; while on the throughfare itself, drays struggling in from the Middlesex countryside to Covent Garden market, hackney-carriages and knifeboard omnibuses were all competing for passage, their drivers bawling at each other and even threatening each other with their whips.

'Not in the least,' Sir James assured him. 'One cannot forget the invaluable part you played in resolving that dreadful business, three years ago, of the Countess of Kilgarden and the Papal Nuncio to the Kingdom of Sardinia.'

'You are too kind,' Mycroft replied.

His mind was distracted by his sighting of the same conspicuously fashionably dressed youth dodging between the market stalls in the same direction as themselves: the soft, pretty, yet determined features caught in the watery glow of the flare-lights.

'No great perspicuity was required on that occasion,' he continued, 'once it became clear who had been manipulating at least one of the parties to the unfortunate affair.'

'You refer to Prince von Bismarck's valet,' said Sir James, somewhat ruefully.

'To Carl Philipp Emmanuel Guttmann. The Prussian Minister-president's confidential agent . . .'

'Acting in a private capacity, Holmes. Let us not forget that.'

Mycroft smiled, shaking his head only very slightly. 'That was what you decided,' he confirmed.

There were still a few pedestrians strolling in Pall Mall when he bade Sir James Swarthmoor goodnight on the steps of the Carlton Club and crossed the street to his lodgings at Number 73a, on the corner with St James's Gardens. He could see, under the lamplight at the Waterloo Place end of the pavement, a pair of 'gay' women in imperial crinoline, a finery now out-dated among the respectable. Some twenty paces in the opposite direction, a young, good-looking negro, wearing the soiled, darned satin of a street acrobat, his feathered headdress on the pavement, was executing a clumsy dance-shuffle to his own strange nasal chanting:

'All dem darkies am a singin',
Singin' to de ole banjo.
All dem bells in Heben am a ringin'
To hear dem darkies singin' so.
Chicken in de basket, chicken in de pot,
Oh, all dem darkies is such a happy lot!'

One or two passers-by threw coins into the headdress.

'Mr Holmes! I thought you weren't coming home till tomorrow night. And I've nothing prepared for you!'

Mrs Turner stood at the top of the stairs, her ample ebony hair, of which she was excessively proud, tied in papers, her comfortable figure swathed in an eiderdown wrapper, for all it was a warm summer night.

'Government business, I fear, Mrs Turner, has brought me back prematurely. The Cabinet Secretary in person was sent to fetch me.'

Mycroft was convinced that his landlady's culinary zeal was stimulated by her recognition of his importance.

'Oh, Mr Holmes! It just shows, doesn't it, Her Majesty's ministers can't manage even a weekend without you to tell them what's what!'

'Something like that, Mrs Turner.' He thrust his stick into the hallway vase.

'There's some cold mutton,' said Mrs Turner. 'And I can make you a nice pot of tea.'

'I have dined, thank you. But a pot of tea would be agreeable. I hope I haven't disturbed the excellent Mr Turner.'

'Oh no, sir! Nothing ever wakes him once he's nodded off. I could toast you some muffins, sir; fresh this afternoon.'

'I believe I could manage a muffin, if you please, Mrs Turner,' he replied. 'Or even two,' he added as an afterthought.

He went upstairs and placed his valise in his bedroom. Then he went through to his study, which overlooked Pall Mall. He did not light the gas but went to the window and looked out from behind the folds of the undrawn curtain. The negro was still on the pavement below. He had ceased his song and dance and was picking up his headdress and pocketing his money. He glanced up and down the street then, with a light, agile step, crossed it. As he reached the other side the same slight, well-dressed figure as before emerged from the shadows of the tradesmen's gateway of the Oxford and Cambridge Universities Club opposite St James's Street and came running down the pavement to meet him. Walking together and talking, they passed below on the Carlton Club side of Pall Mall, the pretty, fashionably-dressed youth and the ragged negro vagrant. Mycroft dodged back behind the curtain the moment he saw their heads begin to turn to look up at his window.

Chapter Three

'Does the Almighty choose us, or do we choose him? Or shall we find that to choose and to be chosen is the same thing before the dreadful throne of Judgement?' the voice of the Rector of St James, Piccadilly, droned on. 'For has not the Almighty decreed the part we are to play in His wonderful Providence?'

Mycroft heard his own sudden, grunting snore. He stared around him like a guilty thing upon a guilty summons, murmuring 'Amen!' in agreement as he did so, and found Sir James Swarthmoor peering at him over the side of the pew. Beside him stood one of the church beadles with his wand. The beadle put his finger to his lips. Sir James whispered, 'I'm sorry to disturb you at your devotions, my dear boy. I would be grateful if you'd accompany me outside.'

'But, Sir James! Divine Service, you know?' Mycroft protested in a loud whisper.

'I'm sure God appreciates the need we have of you,' Sir James said in a low voice.

A ringletted child of indeterminate sex had climbed up

to look over the panelled rail of an adjoining stall. 'Mama? Papa?' it called. 'Why are the gentlemen talking in church? Don't they know it's very naughty to . . .'

The head disappeared abruptly. There was the sound of a smack followed by a wailing shrill enough to cause the rector to cease his droning from the pulpit. With weary resignation, Mycroft drew himself to his feet and followed Sir James from the pew. The beadle led them to the door and the rector resumed his sermon.

In the yard outside, Sir James placed his hand on Mycroft's sleeve. He pointed with his cane toward the west end of the church and the passageway to the Jermyn Street gate.

'No absolute hurry, my boy,' he said as they followed his direction. 'But you remember what you said last night, about *chercher la femme*?'

'Of course,' Mycroft replied.

'*La femme*, it would seem, has already put in her appearance.'

'Aha! So you have no further need of me!' exclaimed Mycroft. 'You could have left me to my pious contemplation for another quarter hour before telling me.'

'It is not as simple as that, I'm afraid. The lady has come from Paris in search of the missing M. Thibault. She is at this very moment sitting not four hundred yards away, in Kendall's Hotel, waiting to speak with us.'

'She is not by any chance', asked Mycroft, 'a rather young Russian lady, with dark curls and a somewhat stubborn-looking mouth and chin?'

'No, Holmes!' Sir James could not help smiling. 'I can't imagine what led you to suppose that. What makes you suggest she might be Russian?'

'The fact that we were followed on foot, last night, from Paddington to the Carlton Club, by a young Russian lady dressed as a boy. She lurked in the shadows by the entrance to the Oxford and Cambridge Universities Club while I crossed the road to Number 73a.'

'How did you know that this spy was—'

'Of the feminine gender?' Mycroft interrupted him. 'Nothing can be more simple. The organization of the female pelvis makes concealment impossible from the observant eye.'

'Russian, Holmes? How could you tell she was Russian? Did you speak with her?'

'I can't imagine you plucked me from Morning Service,' Mycroft broke in, 'simply to test my powers of observation. Tell me something about this lady who awaits us at Kendall's Hotel.'

'She is a Madame Tirard. Her husband was one of the mayors of Paris before that unhappy city was seized by the revolutionists. M. Tirard was imprisoned by some of their more extreme elements and is presumed to have been shot by them. Mme Tirard then placed herself under the protection of our M. Thibault. She is here with a letter of introduction from Admiral Saisset . . .'

'The Admiral Saisset who assisted Marshal Gallifet in putting down the Communard revolutionists?' asked Mycroft.

'The very same,' Sir James replied.

'And she has been driven to come to us, here in London, through her own personal worry and distress?' asked Mycroft.

'Why, Holmes, do you suppose it might be through somebody else's worry and distress?'

They had stepped down from the churchyard into Jermyn Street.

'You know, Sir James, I avoid suppositions wherever possible,' Mycroft replied. 'They do nag at the brain so! Rob one of one's quiet!'

On arriving at Kendall's Hotel Sir James and Mycroft went straight up to the drawing-room. The Reverend Sir Horatio Rumbelow, Bart. was already there, sitting in an armchair. A woman of some twenty-eight years was standing at the open window looking down at the well-dressed Sunday strollers on the pavement below. She was dressed not quite in mourning, but with a sombreness which both suggested bereavement and set off her handsome good looks. She was remarking in fluent English, but with a French accent which made her voice all the more attractive, 'It is strange, you know? – when one is sad oneself, to see how other people go about quite happily; to understand that, for them, the world is still a wonderfully ordinary place.'

She noticed that Mycroft and Sir James had arrived. She turned to acknowledge them, reaching one hand behind her to hold the silken bow of her bustle in place as she did so.

'Sir James! You have returned already! And this is . . .?'

'Mr Holmes, madame,' Sir James replied.

Mycroft took the tapering fingers stretching from the black lace mitten in his own podgy grasp.

Mme Tirard withdrew her hand from him almost as soon he touched it.

'Are you an officer of the police, Mr Holmes?'

'Oh dear me no!' Mycroft replied.

'We have not yet decided that this is to be a matter for the police, Madame Tirard,' said Sir James.

'I am a humble government clerk, madame,' declared Mycroft, 'who possesses a certain talent – *ex officio*, you appreciate – for recognizing the solution to problems which others of greater rank and position than my humble self may find intractable . . .' He cleared his throat. 'May I be seated?' he continued. 'I have always found *mens sana in corpore quieto*.'

Before Mme Tirard had a chance to reply, Mycroft slumped into an armchair beside Sir Horatio's, stretched his legs, and rested his stick between the toes of his boots.

'I understand you have come here in the hope of finding M. Jean-Christophe Thibault, silk manufacturer of the city of Lyon,' he said, 'a gentleman whom you have come to regard as your . . . protector? . . . since the loss of your husband.'

'My dear Holmes!' Sir James protested at Mycroft's directness of approach.

'It is not idle curiosity which makes it necessary for me to ask you to explain the exact nature of your relationship with M. Thibault,' Holmes continued.

Sir Horatio leant forward.

'I'm sure I speak for Sir James as well as myself when I assure you, madame, that you are addressing the most sympathetic and understanding of audiences.'

'Thank you, monsieur,' she smiled.

She seated herself on an upright chair by the open window, carefully arranging her skirts as she did so, then folded her hands demurely in her lap.

'My husband was Mayor of the *Deuxième Arrondissement* – which is, as I'm sure you well know, the heart of Paris, the centre of its fashion and commerce, yes?' she began.

Mycroft nodded.

'Pray do continue, madame.'

'Very well.' She cleared her throat, touching her lips with her fingertips. 'M. Thibault was a frequent visitor to Paris before this terrible war. He came on business from Lyon, you understand. When his business affairs permitted, he would take a few days *en vacances*, you know? My husband, who was acquainted with him for many years, did not object to my being his companion at least during the day. M. Thibault was a most kind and charming gentleman – you will know that, Sir 'orace . . .'

Sir Horatio grunted and mumbled, 'Yes, indeed.'

'M. Thibault told me of your generous hospitality towards him on his visits to Manchester,' she added in his direction.

Mycroft heard a subdued, second grunt from Sir Horatio. Mme Tirard continued, 'In those days, he had the time to be attentive to me in a way my poor husband did not.' She paused momentarily, running her fingertip lightly along her lower lip. She dropped her hand back into her lap. 'So he became very dear to me, *messieurs*,' she said almost defiantly.

From the corner of his eye, Mycroft noticed Sir James's nod of sympathy.

'I considered it my duty to remain at my husband's side while our poor, beautiful city was besieged by the armies of Prussia. And then, after the siege was ended and the Prussians had had their victory march down the Champs Elysées' she made the Prussian triumph sound utterly contemptible – 'the *Comité Central* formed its own government – the *Commune de Paris*, you know? A rabble of anarchists and socialists! M. Thiers sent Admiral Saisset in person to my husband in the *Deuxiéme*

45

Arrondissement – Admiral Saisset, the great hero of the defence of Paris against the Prussians, the darling of the Parisian people. He brought a message to my husband from M. Thiers in Versailles. It implored him to remain at the *Mairie*. It also said that within three or four weeks he would have assembled an army capable of crushing the Communard rebels.'

Mycroft raised himself from the prone position into which he had slumped. He was now sitting erect.

'Then commenced the most terrible events of all,' continued Mme Tirard. 'More terrible even than the Prussian siege! You will recall, perhaps, how the loyal supporters of the Republic, men, women and children, came to greet Admiral Saisset in the Rue de Rivoli and were butchered there, in the open street, in front of the *Mairie*, by the Communard National Guard . . . Forgive me,' – she drew her handkerchief from her sleeve – 'I witnessed the dreadful scene, *messieurs*,' she explained.

Sir Horatio leaned as far forward as he could. He took her hand and held it for a moment. She pressed the small lace handkerchief to her cheek. Sir James moved to her, to place his hand reassuringly on her shoulder. Mycroft waited.

'Thank you, gentlemen,' said Mme Tirard. 'You are kind. Wonderfully kind.'

She lowered her handkerchief. Having released her hand, Sir Horatio sat back. She turned, looked up, and smiled at Sir James. Then she found the strength to continue.

'My husband learnt that functionaries of the Paris Commune were coming to the Rue de Rivoli to seize the *Mairie*. He insisted that Admiral Saisset return to Versailles immediately, and that I accompany the Admiral

46

to safety. I begged my husband to allow me to stay with him, but he was quite determined I should go. Admiral Saisset and I walked all the way – he disguised as an artisan, a cabinet-maker, and I as his daughter, in service to a farmer's wife living near Chaville.

'Once I was in Versailles I was just one among many hundreds of women of all types without family or means. Then, a few weeks later, as our gallant soldiers were advancing through the suburbs of Paris, news came of the arrest of my husband at the hands of the murderous *canailles* and of his being taken to their filthy dungeons in the Menilmontant *faubourg*. I could not be certain of his fate at their hands. But I had little doubt that it was the same as that suffered by other brave spirits who remained loyal to the Government in Versailles and that he was taken out and shot in some Montmartre courtyard for the entertainment of the mob.'

Sir James patted her shoulder again. She reached up for his hand and smiled bravely.

'I found myself alone and unprotected. I had already written to M. Thibault at Lyon, telling him I had reached Versailles and safety. He came to me, *messieurs*. He came to me and took me from the tent I was sharing with twenty other women – few of them ladies, permit me to say. He procured me comfortable lodgings and provided me with the means to live. And, *messieurs* – I beg you to believe me! – he asked nothing of me in return for his generosity – he respected my bereavement, however uncertain . . .'

'What of Admiral Saisset, madame?' Mycroft interrupted her. 'Did he take no practical interest in the situation you found yourself in when you had reached Versailles?'

Mme Tirard hesitated. 'He was—' she began. The question had taken her by surprise. 'He was too busy to be concerned about one unimportant woman . . .'

'Of course he was, Holmes!' exclaimed Sir James. 'The responsibility for the putting down of a serious rebellion was his – and the reduction of a well-fortified city . . .! Mme Tirard, pray do continue. Perhaps you could tell us something of M. Thibault's decision to come here, to this country?'

'Alas, Sir James. I have little to say about it. I knew only of his intention – that he had written to you, Sir 'orace. But of what his business was – except that he thought it was important – I know nothing. I am practised in not asking gentlemen about their business or political affairs . . .' She smiled sadly. 'My husband, you know,' she said. 'He had many secrets which I had to respect . . .'

'Of course!' said Sir Horatio.

'I knew only that M. Thibault was going to travel to Manchester for a few days, and that he had said he would make sure I was provided for before he returned to his family in Lyon.'

'So you knew nothing of the statement in the letter M. Thibault sent to Sir Horatio here,' asked Sir James, 'that there was a matter "of the utmost importance" which he wished to communicate to "the highest in the land"?'

'Why no!' exclaimed Mme Tirard. She glanced about her. 'I cannot imagine—' she began.

'Gentlemen, it is perfectly obvious', interposed Mycroft, 'that this is one of those business matters which Mme Tirard – whom I am sure is the most tactful as well as the most amiable of companions – has learnt not to enquire into. From what we know already, and from what Mme Tirard has so patiently and so clearly been relating, I would have thought that there may be a very simple line of enquiry which we may now follow.'

Sir James looked across at him with an expression of disbelief.

'Oh yes!' said Mycroft. 'M. Thibault is a manufacturer – and one of some worth and standing in the world of commerce. Would you not say so, madame?'

'But certainly, Mr Holmes,' she agreed.

Mycroft tapped the toes of his boots with his stick. He glanced up again, first at Sir Horatio, whose mouth had fallen open, and then across at Sir James.

'I'm sure that amongst those we might describe as "the highest in the land", the President of the Board of Trade would be included,' he said.

'Certainly,' Sir James agreed.

'A silk manufacturer in a substantial way of business, such as M. Thibault,' Mycroft continued, 'would be anxious, beyond all other considerations, to ensure that nothing should impede the recovery of France's trade in silk following the ravages inflicted on it as a result of the war with the German states. I'm sure, Sir Horatio, you can think of one or two of your more substantial parishioners who, under similar circumstances, would be of entirely the same frame of mind.'

'Oh yes! Most certainly!' Sir Horatio confirmed.

'So what would be his chief concern regarding Great Britain in this field of endeavour?' asked Mycroft. 'Why, obviously he would be desperately worried lest Her Majesty's Government, in the belief that France's silk industry was destroyed, should allow an unrestricted flow of cheap silken goods to pour out towards European and world markets through our concessionary ports in China.'

'Perhaps . . .' Mme Tirard began. Then she said, 'I know nothing of such matters – but M. Thibault told me how worried he was about business matters as a result of the war.' She paused. 'It was heavy on his mind, you know?' She paused a second time. 'He spoke of it many times,' she concluded.

'You see?' Mycroft asked in Sir James's direction. 'And who would reap the greatest advantage from the collapse of the French silk industry? Not this country; wools and cottons are our staples in the textile business. France's two major rivals in the production and manufacturing of silk: the Chinese and the Italians. Let me ask you this. What peoples are most given to such methods as abduction, kidnapping or the elimination of rivals by means of force to further their commercial interests?'

He waited for a moment before continuing.

'What peoples have raised banditry and criminal gangs almost to the level of social institutions? Sir James, I would suggest you put it to Sir Philip Doughty and his officers in the Metropolitan Police that they investigate the warrens of Limehouse and Wapping – the opium dens and mahjong divans. Or the basements and coffee-houses frequented by the Italian clockmakers and silk-weavers of Spitalfields and Clerkenwell.'

Mme Tirard stared at him.

'They said you were a clever man, Mr Holmes.'

But she was very close to tears.

'I am sorry if I sounded untrusting, yes? – when you first came in.'

'Why should you be trusting, dear lady?' Mycroft pulled himself out of his chair in an ungainly manner. 'To be trusting in this sorry world is to be foolish indeed.'

He caught Sir James's eye. He said to Mme Tirard, 'Others may advise you differently. For my part, I cannot see that there is anything for you to do now but to remain here, in the safety of this excellent hotel, and rely on the thoroughness of our police in their search for your friend.'

Chapter Four

'Excellent! Your fellow here does a most excellent Sunday lunch!' Sir James exclaimed.

The Reverend Sir Horatio had brought them to the Athenaeum Club as his guests.

'We stole him – or perhaps "poached" would be *le mot juste*, eh Holmes? – from the Hotel Meurice in Paris,' Sir Horatio replied. 'In happier days, of course.'

They had just completed the meal with a rarebit. The waiter removed the plates. Sir Horatio beckoned over the head waiter. He ordered brandy and cigars to be brought to the smoking-room.

'I must say, Holmes, I found your explanation for poor Thibault's disappearance most ingenious,' he said, as they placed their used napkins on the table. 'I truly believe that Mme Tirard found it quite reassuring – better, I suppose, than a complete mystification. Gives room for some sort of hope.'

'But you, sir, were not convinced,' Mycroft replied, rising with the others from his place. 'Any more than Sir James was.'

52

'No. I was not,' Sir Horatio admitted.

Mycroft went the short distance to the window and looked down on to the street. The negro was still below on the pavement, as he had been when they came in: still with his feathered headdress in front of him, still shuffling his feet and no doubt still chanting his absurd rhyme about

All dem darkies am a singin',
Singin' to de ole banjo . . .

There was still the organ-grinder playing to his small audience of ragged female urchins and dolly-mops on their Sunday afternoon out.

'As I tried to tell you,' Sir Horatio was saying, 'I don't believe the wording of his letter regarding the importance of what he wished to communicate bore the construction you wished to place upon it.'

'Of course it didn't,' Sir James agreed.

'But Mme Tirard was satisfied,' said Mycroft.

'Mme Tirard had not actually read it,' replied Sir James.

'Nor must she,' said Mycroft. He placed his finger across his lips. Sir James nodded discreetly, and led the way across the hushed landing to the smoking-room. There they settled in the comfort of armchairs and tobacco smoke.

'No, my boy,' said Sir James. 'I did not find it at all a plausible theory.'

'It was the best I could manage on the spur of the moment,' Mycroft replied. 'And she, as Sir Horatio has remarked, fell on it greedily – but not, I think, for the reason he supposes.'

'You believe that the initiative for her coming to London is somebody else's – not her own?' asked Sir James.

Mycroft carefully trimmed off the end of his cigar. He rolled it in the flame of the vesta before lighting it. He drew on it several times before finally settling back in the leather of his chair and saying, 'Well, gentlemen? Would you say she was a truthful sort of woman?'

'She said something I found a little strange,' remarked Sir Horatio.

'She said that Thibault told her he had stayed with you on previous occasions,' Mycroft said. 'I noticed you were a little taken aback.'

'This would have been the first time on one of his visits to Manchester he had been my house guest,' said Sir Horatio.

'Quite so,' Mycroft told him. 'She said it to ingratiate herself with you, of course. Not the worst of sins.'

'So why do you suppose she was eager we should believe your theory for Thibault's disappearance?'

'Because she does not want us to know the real reason – or because her instigator doesn't,' Mycroft replied. 'Just consider this. Jean-Christophe Thibault disappears on the second or third of May. Today is the eighteenth of June. Yet all this time, his mistress – no, Sir Horatio, I appreciate the obligation you feel toward the virtue of charity, but that is what she proclaims herself – and his dependant for at least the time the revolutionists held Paris, remained silent.'

'Perhaps out of a womanly sense of shame,' suggested Sir Horatio.

Mycroft looked at him, took the cigar from his lips, caught the expression on Sir James's face, replaced the cigar between his lips and drew on it once more.

'Perhaps,' he agreed at length, but without conviction. 'If so, she has performed a wonderful *volte-face*. No sooner has Mme Tirard heard about her lover's disappearance than her womanly modesty is miraculously overcome and she arrives post haste in London, complete with passport issued by Admiral Saisset.'

'Are you by any chance suggesting that Mme Tirard is, in effect, an agent of the French Government?' asked Sir James.

'I am presenting it as a possibility – the possibility that the information of the utmost importance which Thibault wished to convey to our government emanated from the French Government, and that *Messieurs* Thiers and Saisset are most anxious that he, or at least it, should not reach its destination.'

'You do not think, then,' Sir James asked, 'that agents of the French Military Bureau of Statistics or the *Sûreté* are responsible for his disappearance?'

'On the contrary,' Mycroft replied. 'If they had been, the lady would not be here with a *laisse-passer* from a senior military figure in the government of the Republic.'

'And you have no genuine theory as to whom the abductors might be?' Sir James asked.

Mycroft shook his head.

'Well,' said Sir Horatio with a sigh, 'I fear these matters are becoming too deep for the head of a humble parson such as myself. It is just as well I shall be taking the night train from Euston back to my parishioners; at least I'm allowed to feel of some use to them.'

'I'm sure your concern for M. Thibault's safety – if we can still ensure it – will prevent you from speaking to

55

anybody about what you have heard us discuss these past two days,' Mycroft told him.

'Not even to Lord Granville?' Sir Horatio asked Sir James.

Sir James coughed. 'Perhaps it would be best if we apprised the Foreign Secretary of our findings at an appropriate time – by written memorandum, don't you know?' he suggested.

'If you think it best, Sir James.'

Sir James Swarthmoor and Mycroft bade the Reverend Sir Horatio farewell and Godspeed in the hallway of the Athenaeum. They stepped down on to the shady side of Pall Mall and began to stroll down it toward the Carlton Club.

'You were not trying to give that good man a fright, were you, Holmes?' asked Sir James. 'I mean, by suggesting that the government of France may be implicated in this business.'

'No, Sir James. I was not.'

The organ-grinder was gone. So was the negro and his feathered headdress. There was only one ragged little barefoot girl holding a splintered wooden hoop in one hand and swinging herself round the lamp-post with the other.

'I tell you frankly, Sir James,' Mycroft continued, 'I believe there to be deeper matters here than you supposed when you decided to bring me back from Oxford, last night.'

'But you do not intend explaining further at the moment?' asked Sir James.

'I intend to pass the remainder of this very warm afternoon in the stillness and shade of the Diogenes Club.

Some hours of absolute quiet and repose are essential if I am to prevent the feverish activity of these past two days from wrecking the delicate equilibrium of my mental and physical constitution.'

'I know the bees which fly in your particular bonnet, Holmes. Would I be wrong in surmising that already you are playing with the notion of a Prussian hand in this game?'

'I propose, Sir James, during the hours which remain between now and half-past eight this evening, when the excellent Mrs Turner will have prepared my evening meal, to void my mind of all hypotheses and intellectual constructs. The fakir's begging-bowl will not be as empty as my intelligence in a quarter of an hour's time.'

Across the street the ragged little girl swung aimlessly in the sunlight, and even the two nursemaids who pushed their bassinets toward the scarlet sentries in front of St James's Palace moved silently in the summer heat.

Chapter Five

Mycroft had his own conception of what Paradise would be like. He would be suspended in a void apart as if on a gossamer thread as weightless as a spider's, over a chasm without light or sound or breath. The brain would cease operation and the mind would become emptied of all thought. Physical sensation would drain away like the oncoming of sleep, and all that would be left would be a last remnant of awareness – an awareness of an eternity of calm.

In the same fashion that the Gothic masters had built their cathedrals to provide themselves and their contemporaries with some little figure of the glory of God and their place in that glory, so Mycroft with several like-minded acquaintances had devised and founded the Diogenes Club as a place where men (a woman would have found it easier to enter the Monastery of Mount Athos than the Diogenes Club) could sink into the nearest thing to a condition of supernal vacuity that could be devised in the centre of a great, bustling metropolis. Such had been the determination of one of the founder members of the club, a *Tunku* from Johore Bahru whose wealth was inexhaustible, that he had had the street outside the windows of the principal rooms paved with rubber tiles for twenty yards on either side, to obviate the grinding of carriage wheels and the footsteps of passing pedestrians.

Mycroft now reclined in one of the sancta of this temple – the smoking-room. He had passed · several hours in the most delightful coma, which was now being rudely disturbed. A new member had entered with a newspaper under his arm. He had taken only a few paces when the senior waiter's attention had been drawn to his presence by another waiter. The senior waiter moved across the room to intercept the newcomer, rapidly and silently. But not so silently that the utter peace was not disturbed. He guided the member out on to the gallery.

'Begging your pardon, sir,' he whispered. 'I'm afraid you're not used to our rules yet, if you don't mind me saying, sir. The reading of newspapers and journals, sir – in the smoking-room. Expressly forbidden. The noise – the rustling of the pages, you see, sir? Some of the gentlemen find it most distressing to their nerves.'

'Of course! Of course!' the new member whispered back apologetically. Fearful that, even now, he had spoken too loudly, he glanced into the smoking-room. He caught Mycroft's fixed, angry stare coming at him from the black leather depths of a deep-winged armchair, and turned away instantly.

'There is a reading-room, sir,' the senior waiter was whispering. 'It's in the closet, sir. Behind the main library.'

'I'm obliged to you, er . . .' The new member spoke in a voice so low he could scarcely catch the words himself.

59

'Thompson, sir.'

'Much obliged to you, Thompson.'

Mycroft despaired of returning to his approximation to Nirvana. He signalled to the waiter to bring him a flame with which to light his cigar. The waiter took a wax taper from a jar on the whatnot by the door. Above the screened hearth the single flame of a gas-mantle was kept permanently alight. Going to it to light the taper, the waiter passed a gentleman who had begun to snore gently, his ribboned pinces-nez rising and falling rhythmically on his broad chest. The waiter removed a small pencil from his apron pocket. He stooped over the sleeper, holding the pencil horizontally under his nose. The snoring stopped immediately. The waiter replaced his pencil in his pocket, went to the gas-mantle and lit the taper, then brought it silently to Mycroft, who lit his cigar with it.

Mycroft smoked in silence for a few minutes. Being restored to full wakefulness, he got up and trod softly over to the window, looking down on to the street from behind the leg of the curtain. Long evening shadows fell across the pavements. A hansom-cab trotted noiselessly past; a couple of silk-hatted clubmen strolled by opposite, smoking black cigarettes. Otherwise, the street appeared to be deserted. In a moment of decision he left the smoking-room, cigar still between his fingers, and went down to the hall. The porter emerged without being summoned and handed him his hat, gloves and stick.

'I shall leave by the back,' Mycroft informed him.

He went past the main staircase which he had just descended and through a door into the secret bowels of the building, past pantries, kitchens and the wine-racks at the cellar doors. He went out into the low sunlight of the gardens behind Carlton House Terrace and turned into Pall Mall by the messengers' arch of the London Joint Stock Banking Company. As he had expected, he found the negro standing at the corner of St James's, lounging against the wall and looking in the opposite direction. Without the negro turning to see him he walked down the pavement with a rapidity which would have surprised his acquaintances, back in the direction of the front entrance of the Diogenes Club and his own lodgings. There was a closed gateway entrance at the War Office Building down a raked incline from the level of the street. As he reached it he stopped abruptly, pointing the ferule of his stick into the shadows and removing the cigar from his mouth.

'*Syeyichaz, dyevushka moya!*' he called in a stern voice. '*Kto viy khotyeye? Pochemu viy stoyayetye na menya?*'

The slight figure moved, a stir in the obscurity after the sunlight.

'Do not trouble yourself to speak Russian, Mr Holmes.' The girl's voice rang clear, with a pedantic absence of foreignness. 'My spoken English is quite perfect; though I am told I sometimes have trouble with my syntax when I write.'

She stepped up out of the gloom.

'Well, Mr Holmes!'

She looked straight into his eyes. Then she smiled, and very gently pushed the point of his stick aside.

'I am surprised you do not know that in my country, the daughters of noble families learn English from the cradle – even before their own language. But then, even Mr Holmes can't know everything, can he?'

61

There was scarcely the least pretence about her boy's clothing: if anything, it enhanced rather than concealed her feminine good looks.

'Certainly, he can't,' replied Mycroft. 'He can't know why he should be pursued and spied on by a strange young woman – a young woman who should know better than to be wandering alone about the night streets of any great city.'

He looked into her eyes, gazing up at him from under the polished peak of her cap. Her hair was a disorganized mass of dark brown curls bundled under her cap, but her eyes were a luminous blue, set above high, slavic cheekbones and with the hint of a steppe-dweller's Mongolian slant. As she gazed at him, challenging him, the small, narrow mouth gradually stretched into a smile. But there was no suggestion of coquetry on the small, determined face. Though she was strikingly pretty – perhaps the prettiest young woman he had ever encountered – there was no trace of flirtatiousness about her.

'How did you know I was Russian, Mr Holmes? Since I am supposed to be a stranger to you.'

'You *are* a stranger to me, young lady. But there are some things you cannot keep hidden from me – such as the fact that you and your minions, such as they are, have had me under observation since my return to Town last night.'

'My minions?' she asked.

'Followers?' suggested Mycroft.

'Ah yes!' She glanced up the street toward St James's Palace. Mycroft followed her gaze. The negro was standing watching them from some fifty yards off. 'He attached himself to me in the same way a piece of muddy straw attaches itself to a boot. I have not scraped him off because, as one of your poets put it, he has proved himself "a wonderfully necessary man." ' She shrugged slightly. 'I do not require his protection,' she explained. 'I can protect myself.'

Mycroft glanced at the slim black cane she carried.

'It is simply that I find he has his uses,' she said. 'Now, Mr Holmes. It is you who have addressed yourself to me. I had no intention of addressing you in the street. I would have waited until you had entered your lodgings over there, at Number 73a, and made yourself comfortable. I do not address gentlemen in the street, least of all when I do not know them.'

'But you have been spying on me, madam!'

'No, Mr Holmes. I have not. I am Sophie Trubetskoy – and the Trubetskoys do not spy on anybody!'

'You are the Princess' – Mycroft paused, recollecting – 'the Princess Sofya Sergeyevna Trubetskoy?'

'Yes, Mr Holmes. My father was Prince Sergey Trubetskoy.'

'My dear young lady!' Mycroft was both surprised and scandalized. 'Princess! You can't remain out in the street' – he let the cigar which was still smoking between his gloved fingers fall into the gutter. He pointed at her with his outstretched hand held palm upwards – 'dressed like this!'

'I dress like this because it is comfortable and convenient if I wish to walk freely about the streets. I have no wish to remain caged up like one of your little Miss English Mouses – Mice, I mean. I was awaiting a suitable occasion to speak with you, Mr Holmes. That is all. I knocked on your door yesterday afternoon – or early evening, at about this hour, you know? But you were gone to Oxford – I heard your housekeeper say so to two gentlemen who had also come to call on you. Then this fellow' – she flicked the point of her cane in the negro's direction – 'overheard one of the gentlemen say he would go to Oxford immediately to fetch you back. I went to Paddington to await you there; but when you got off the train it did not seem – well – *convenable* to speak to you. And then, when you did reach home, you were obviously concerned with important matters; the hour was late; I did not wish to disturb you. And my own apartments are not so far away from here – in Bruton Street, you know? I promise you, Mr Holmes, if you had simply walked across the road just now and gone in, I would have knocked on the door and called on you as properly as you could have wished.'

'Since there is no help for it,' Mycroft told her, 'I had better ask you to come in with me now. We can't have you loitering about Pall Mall dressed like this any longer. Good heavens! You could have been taken up by the police! I can't think what Mrs Turner will say!'

'Perhaps you would prefer to return with me to Bruton Street?'

The thought of being seen crossing Piccadilly with a young woman in boy's clothing was too much for Mycroft.

'I would not put you to the trouble, Princess.'

'What trouble, Mr Holmes? Since I have to return there anyway . . .'

But Mycroft had already taken her by the arm and was steering her across the street. The dreadful possibility had occurred to him that Sir James might come down the steps of the Carlton Club and see him; or, worse still, one of his fellow-founding members of the Diogenes. Already, he had his passkey in his hand as they reached the front door. He opened it, assisted her across the threshold with more than welcoming zeal, and gratefully closed the front door behind them.

Mrs Turner came out of her front parlour as he was thrusting his stick into the hallway vase. She stared at Sophie Trubetskoy in astonishment, as if trying to work out in her mind the nature of the phenomenon before her. Quite rudely, Mycroft pushed Sophie Trubetskoy to the foot of the stairs. 'Tea, if you please, Mrs Turner,' he called over his shoulder as they went up. 'You take tea black, I expect, Princess. With a slice of lemon and lump sugar. You do have a slice of lemon, Mrs Turner?'

'I will have tea in the English manner, if you please,' said Sophie Trubetskoy. 'I drink tea the way you describe it only from a samovar.'

'And toasted muffins, if you please, Mrs Turner,' Mycroft called down.

'I don't want muffins, thank you, Mr Holmes,' said Sophie Trubetskoy. 'They make one fat.'

'*I* want muffins,' said Mycroft. 'I *need* muffins – to soothe a digestive system which has been profoundly agitated by the events of the past two days.'

'What you mean', she told him as they continued up the stairs, 'is you *think* you need them to soothe your brain. Single gentlemen are the same the world over. When their little world is the least bit upset they long to run back to the nursery, where a loving *nyanya* will toast muffins for them.'

Mycroft opened the door of his study for her.

'If it is not an impertinent question, Princess – may I ask how old you are?'

'I'm twenty-three.'

'You look younger . . . and sound older. Will you come in?'

She looked around her at the furnishings, which were designed with consideration for nothing save male comfort.

'Please sit down.' He indicated the armchair which stood by the hearth, opposite to and in better repair than the one in which he habitually sat. Then he indicated the heavy Windsor chair at the table littered with copies of *The Times*, *The Morning Post* and *The Pall Mall Gazette*. She shook her head.

'May I stay here, by the window?' she asked. 'I love the daylight. I always linger in it for as long as I may. There was so much darkness in my childhood.'

'You spent your childhood in exile in Siberia with the Prince, your father?' Mycroft asked.

'Until I was eight years old. My father died when I was eight. My mother took Kathy, my sister, and me back to St Petersburg after he died . . . Mr Holmes, before I tell you the business which has brought me here, will you tell me – if you truly did not know who I was – how you knew me to be Russian?'

'May I be seated?' Mycroft asked.

'Of course.'

She remained standing at the window, bathing her face and chin in the dying sunlight. He slumped down into the armchair. It creaked under his weight.

'You should take more exercise, Mr Holmes,' she observed, 'and refrain from eating muffins.'

Mycroft ignored the remark.

'First let me tell you that your male attire no more conceals your estate than it does your sex. You are

66

marked by your deportment and inbred *hauteur*. You carry none of the stigmata of a life of toil: there is no coarsening of the complexion, and no stoop of the shoulders which indicates drudgery. At the same time you present no trace of the mouselike gentility which, as you yourself observed a few moments ago, is the hallmark of the unmarried female of the more prosperous *bourgeoisie*. This, of course, might be true of a young noblewoman anywhere – even here in England. I recall that the Princess Trubetskoy, your mother, is French.'

'Yes. She is.'

'But there is a quality recognizable in you which sets you apart from young ladies of occidental Europe. There is a boldness – but a boldness which has nothing of the hussy in it. It is an air of confidence, of ingrained authority. You carry weapons, and I know that you would not be afraid to use them if necessary. Your cane, for instance, is admirably crafted; there is no hint of the division between hilt and scabbard. But you have given away its true function by the manner in which you hold it, extending your index and forefingers to conceal the spring-release. I notice that you are also carrying a small firearm in the skirt of your jacket – a derringer, I suppose. With a man, the fullness of the tailoring might provide concealment. The pelvic organization of the female anatomy, alas, prohibits it.'

Sophie Trubetskoy smiled and nodded.

'Please continue, Mr Holmes.'

'Not everybody would have noticed either that you are carrying a swordstick, or the pistol, of course. In fact, very few people . . . In fact almost nobody . . .'

'Except Mr Mycroft Holmes?' she suggested.

'Quite so, Princess. I do not boast, you understand. I

67

am merely replying to your question. This boldness to which I refer has nothing of defiance in it: it is the boldness of a young woman who has been brought up to believe that she has as much right to freedom and independence of action as her brothers – who has been brought up in the same way as her brothers, to ride and to shoot like them. Only in Russia are the daughters of the nobility so brought up. And then, finally – if you will forgive me for saying so – there is the unique cast of features. You have that Asiatic shape of the eyes set in a face which is pure Viking. Where is that to be found save in Russia?'

'Circassian blue eyes and dark curly hair. My mother says it is because I am half Russian, half French. You make it sound very easy, Mr Holmes.'

She left the window and sat down on the arm of the chair opposite his, one hand resting on the knee of her close-fitting plaid trouser, the other on the handle of her cane.

'And now! I wonder if you have . . . deduced—?'

'That is the right word, Princess. Very good!' Mycroft told her.

– 'why I have come to you?'

'I have an idea. Not a guess – but an informed notion . . .'

'Yes, Mr Holmes?'

'One moment, Princess, if you please.'

There was a light tap at the door and Mrs Turner came in with the tea things and muffins in a covered dish. She placed the tea-tray on an occasional table which she then placed by Mycroft's chair. She removed the silver lid from the muffin dish.

'There you are, Mr Holmes. Just as you like them,' she

announced, and cast a disapproving glance across at Sophie Trubetskoy, who was swinging one foot gently to and fro.

'Thank you, Mrs Turner,' Mycroft said pointedly.

Mrs Turner left the room with the silver lid. Mycroft waited until the door was closed.

'Princess?' he said. 'There is only one thing – perhaps person would be more accurate – who could possibly be of mutual interest to us two.'

'Yes, Mr Holmes?' She was very serious.

'Carl Philipp Emmanuel Guttmann?' Mycroft asked.

'Yes?' she asked in turn, seeking an explanation.

'Shortly before your sister, the Princess Orlov, died so tragically in Torquay, in the cholera epidemic of 'sixty-nine, she was visited by Carl Philipp Emmanuel Guttmann – perhaps the most evil man alive today.'

'Do you really think so? That C.P.E. Guttmann is the most evil man living?' she asked.

'It would be hard to conceive of anybody more wicked,' Mycroft replied calmly. 'In the same way that it would be hard to imagine any single individual who has been responsible for so much human misery. Not, at least, since Attila the Hun or Genghiz Khan. I sometimes wonder whether the Four Horsemen of the Apocalypse are not lying in wait to do his bidding.'

'Then, Mr Holmes, you will be interested to know that C.P.E. Guttmann is here, in England, at this moment.'

'Now? When did he arrive?'

'On the afternoon boat-train from Dover, yesterday.'

'My dear young woman!' For a moment he sat silent. Then he exclaimed, 'It is not possible! I say that it is not possible!'

'What is not possible, Mr Holmes?'

'That it is coincidence that Mme Tirard and C.P.E. Guttmann should arrive in London on the same day, by the same boat!'

'Who is this Mme Tirard?' Sophie Trubetskoy asked.

'A man has disappeared – a French gentleman who is well connected in his own country,' said Mycroft. 'We fear he has been abducted. Mme Tirard is his close friend. She says she has come in the hope of assisting in finding him. Perhaps there has been no communication between her and Guttmann. Perhaps she is his pawn, as other unfortunates have been before her. Perhaps she is as wicked a woman as he is a man. But it cannot wholly be coincidence that they arrived together in England.'

Chapter Six

'Have you ever met Herr Guttmann – I mean, face to face?' asked Princess Trubetskoy.

Mycroft shook his head.

'I had the privilege of restoring in some measure the reputation of a poor, kind-hearted Irish lady living in Florence who had, quite innocently, become the instrument of his machinations. Alas! I was unable to prevent the conflict between the Papacy and the Kingdom of Italy which was the goal of his plotting and conspiring on that occasion!'

'I have met him,' said the little princess. 'In St Petersburg, when I was nine years old.' She shuddered. 'He held me by the hand! The Prussian Minister-president was then Prussian Ambassador to His Imperial Majesty, the Tsar-emperor. Herr Guttmann was his *valet de chambre*.' Her voice was filled with angry contempt.

'He was always something more than a mere valet,' Mycroft suggested quietly.

'You mean that he is a musician? That Prince von

Bismarck employs him to play the piano to him after dinner to comfort him during his attacks of flatulence?'

Mycroft winced. He was not accustomed to young ladies referring openly to such physical discomforts.

'He plays extremely well, I believe,' he said.

'Mr Holmes! In the olden days, before he was sent into exile, the Prince, my father, employed *serfs* to play to him after dinner – serfs whom he had sent to Italy to learn music.'

'Carl Philipp Emmanuel Guttmann has for some years now been Prince von Bismarck's confidential secretary – the agent of his more obscure designs. It does not do to underestimate such a man, however socially contemptible he may appear.'

'I do not underestimate him, Mr Holmes. He is my enemy. We Trubetskoys do not underestimate those whom we honour by regarding as enemies!'

'What has he done', asked Mycroft, cautiously suppressing his amusement, 'to merit this – er – elevation?'

'Don't you know, Mr Holmes? You who know that he visited my sister shortly before her death?'

'You hold him responsible for her death? I was in Tuscany then – on government business,' he added on an apologetic note. 'I do not enjoy travel,' he added yet again, in extenuation.

'He murdered my sister. If you are willing, I shall explain the circumstances. You will then understand more fully why I have come to you to offer you my assistance.'

'To offer *me your* assistance?' asked Mycroft, taken by surprise.

'Of course. There is nothing you can do for my poor Kathy. But I regard it as my duty to my family's name as

72

much as my personal satisfaction to assist the Englishman who alone recognizes, and has set himself to oppose, the evil which is Carl Philipp Emmanuel Guttmann.'

'How did you find out . . .?' asked Mycroft.

'I have many friends and acquaintances in many places. It is what happens, I suppose, when one has no real home; my mother lives in Nice, but I am not *Niceoise*, nor even French; and we have been gone from Russia now for many years. So I lead a nomadic life, encountering many people. One such person is a gentleman employed by your Foreign Office – a Mr Colton?'

'Frederick Colton? Ah yes! He was our Second Secretary to the Pitti Palace during the Kilgarden affair. So he told you about me?'

Sophie Trubetskoy nodded. She moved off the arm of the chair on which she was seated and settled into the chair itself.

'Your sister – Katerina Orlov – she was considerably older than you?' asked Mycroft.

'Oh yes. I think that was part of her tragedy, you know? She spent so much more time in prison in Siberia with our father than I did. I was eight when we returned to St Petersburg – I still had some of my childhood left. But Kathy was nineteen. Did you ever see my sister, Mr Holmes?'

'I don't recall having seen her.'

'You would not have forgotten her. She was so very beautiful! When we were in St Petersburg I would be allowed to sit and watch her being dressed to go to the opera or the ballet. I was so envious of her looks, I'm sure I sinned against the Commandments!'

'If so it was an unnecessary sin, I assure you, Princess.'

'Mr Colton did not tell me you were a ladies' man, Mr Holmes . . .'

'Who? I? Oh, my dear child!' Mycroft laughed in awkward embarrassment.

'You are not eating your muffins,' the little princess observed. She pointed to the dish. Obediently, Mycroft took one.

'Then, quite suddenly, she married Prince Nikolay Orlov,' she continued. 'I was terribly shocked. To me, he seemed so dreadfully old. But I suppose it must have seemed a grand thing for the daughter of a Siberian exile to become the wife of one of His Imperial Majesty's closest advisers. And my brother-in-law is a charming and learned man, I have to admit.

'Shortly after the wedding Prince Orlov was posted as Imperial Minister to the Court of Brussels and Kathy, of course, went with him. It was while they were on holiday in Biarritz – this would have been the summer of 'sixty-one – that she met von Bismarck. Mr Holmes, I truly believe that my sister loved her husband, and that she would never have deserted him. She had met von Bismarck before, in St Petersburg. But it was now, when they were on holiday together . . .' she broke off for a moment.

'And von Bismarck had become Minister-president of Prussia,' Mycroft gently suggested. 'An even greater man than her husband?'

'Von Bismarck became infatuated with Kathy,' the princess retorted angrily. She paused. 'I'm sorry,' she said. 'It isn't the picture most people have of him, I know. But it was always he who begged her to leave her husband's side and go on holiday with him whenever he could escape from Berlin and politics. You see, Kathy was one of the few people who could calm von Bismarck when his nerves became overwrought. He sleeps badly, yet he slept as peacefully as a child when she was beside him. He said so in his letters to her. She could ease his dyspepsia by playing the piano to him and singing.'

'Guttmann would not have liked that!' Mycroft observed. He picked a napkin off the tea-tray and wiped the butter from his fingers. 'It was precisely because of his ability to sooth von Bismarck's nerves that he wormed his way into his confidence.'

'Exactly, Mr Holmes.'

She watched with evident distaste as he screwed up the napkin and dropped it on to the plate.

'I suppose,' said Mycroft, ignoring her disapproval, 'that it was Guttmann's task to arrange these holidays – these week-long *tête-à-têtes*. With discretion, of course. It's the sort of thing the man was born for.'

'My sister was convinced that he was jealous of her,' the princess replied. 'She told me about it, latterly. I thought she was exaggerating, seeing things that weren't there . . .' She lowered her eyes and shook her head. Mycroft waited.

'Because she was feeling guilty?' he suggested quietly. 'Because she was genuinely fond of her husband?'

The princess nodded. 'Kathy said that he was always courteous,' she went on. She raised her head and looked across at him, but her voice had become harsh and dry. 'She said she thought he wore his courtesy like one of those masks that are worn at the Venice Carnival – the ones that are so varnished they shine . . .'

She paused again. Then she said, 'She told me that there were times when she thought that the eyes behind the mask were those of a dead man – empty . . . hollow?'

'The eyes of somebody without a soul,' Mycroft stated.

'You would have believed her?' the princess asked. She sounded ready to be grateful.

'Most certainly,' he assured her. 'I have heard another lady, in another place, say almost exactly the same thing.'

'In the summer of 'sixty-nine,' the little princess continued, 'Kathy and von Bismarck were supposed to be meeting in Biarritz. Up till then, I suppose my brother-in-law had been complaisant about their friendship. But things were a little different in 'sixty-nine. Everybody was saying that there was going to be a war between France and the north German states. Prince Orlov had just been appointed the Tsar-emperor's Ambassador at the Tuileries, so naturally he was anxious to keep a safe distance between himself and the Prussian Minister-president. Because of this he refused to let Kathy go to Biarritz. Instead he arranged for her to cross the Channel, to stay in Torquay for the summer. My mother and I were sent to keep her company. The house we rented was a very pleasant one, with a beautiful and well-kept garden such as Kathy loved, set among the pines on the cliffs overlooking the town. But for my sister, of course, it was like a return to exile.

'One afternoon, when we were sitting at the bottom of the garden in the shade of the pines, looking out over the sea and watching the ships passing, our English parlourmaid came from the house to tell us that there was a German gentleman come to call on us, a Herr Guttmann. You can imagine how disturbed we were at this! One thing was certain: Kathy mustn't be allowed to see him. So mother decided that she would receive him in the drawing-room by herself while Kathy and I waited in the garden.

76

'I suppose Prince von Bismarck had sent Guttmann only to try to persuade Kathy to return with him to Biarritz. It's my belief, however, that Guttmann saw a providentially-sent opportunity to destroy her once and for all.'

Mycroft nodded his agreement.

'For two reasons,' he said. 'Firstly because he saw in your poor sister a rival for his princely master's affections. But also because von Bismarck's infatuation for your sister was politically dangerous. One must give C.P.E. Guttmann the credit due to him. He is the true disciple of the Prussian philosopher, Hegel, who preached that love of the State is one and the same as love of God.'

'My mother told us', said the princess, 'that he told her Prince von Bismarck was very disappointed at finding Princess Orlov absent from Biarritz. He declared that it was his master's greatest hope that the princess would change her mind about staying in England and would return to France to join his master. He said that his master had commanded him to offer Princess Orlov his protection on the journey to Biarritz.

'My mother told him that we were all going to stay there, in Torquay, at least until the autumn. Guttmann then began to talk about the friendship between Princess Orlov and his master. He told her what pains he had gone to over the past eight years, making sure there shouldn't be a breath of scandal about the affair. My mother knew exactly what he meant. She dismissed him with all the scorn of which she is capable – I have seen grand-dukes wilt under her contempt. But according to her Guttmann stood up to take his leave and bowed, not a whit disturbed. He simply remarked that he was afraid the story could not be kept out of the public journals much longer . . . Unless, of course, Princess Orlov was prepared to act under his advice. He would remain, he told my mother, at the Grand Hotel down in the town for a further twenty-four hours, so that we could consider more carefully what he had said.

'None of us doubted what he meant. My poor darling Kathy knew that she had been trapped. If she went with Guttmann to Biarritz, she would be declaring her disobedience toward her husband and also betraying the best interests of our motherland at a most critical time. If she did not go with him, Guttmann would ensure that our families' names – and possibly that of his master – would be publicly dishonoured. I am certain the monster had calculated how a Trubetskoy princess would resolve the terrible dilemma with which he had confronted her.'

'I'm sure of it,' Mycroft agreed.

'She had not been sleeping well since arriving in Torquay,' the Princess continued. 'A local physician had prescribed chloral as a sleeping draught. The servants had bought tincture of arsenic before our arrival – to rid the cellars of vermin. The bottle was a small one, and there was scarcely enough left to cover the bottom of it . . .'

'More than enough for the purpose,' Mycroft murmured.

'As you know, Mr Holmes – there was cholera in the town.'

'And the symptoms of arsenical poisoning are – at least to a superficial examination – identical with those of death from cholera,' said Mycroft, 'so your medical adviser did not think an autopsy was called for.'

The princess nodded her assent.

'My mother and I found the bottle. We buried it at night, under the cliff's edge; we wished to ensure that our darling was laid to rest with the full rites of our Orthodox Faith. And it *was* murder, Mr Holmes, not suicide. We committed no sin.'

'Princess, it was murder indeed – and of the most loathsome kind,' said Mycroft. 'There is no fouler form of murder than the procurement of a self-slaughter by the use of blackmail.'

'Mr Holmes, this evening I have told you something known only to my mother and to me – and guessed at, I imagine, by the creature, Guttmann. I have placed my confidence entirely in you.'

'I shall not betray it, Princess.'

She sat forward in her chair.

'Since my sister's death, Mr Holmes, far from underestimating C.P.E. Guttmann, I have made it my purpose, while God gives me life, to hound him as he hounded poor Kathy – to thwart his schemes, to protect those whom he seeks to injure and, if possible, to bring him to the same self-destroying wretchedness which he inflicted on my darling.'

Staring into her face, Mycroft felt something like fear at the strength of purpose contained within the small, delicate features. Then, quite suddenly, she relaxed and sat back. Waving her slim black stick at the tray, she said, 'The tea – and your muffins – will be getting cold.'

Chapter Seven

'I wanted to reach you the first time Guttmann came to England,' said Sophie Trubetskoy.

'The first time?' asked Mycroft. 'Do you mean to say he has been here earlier this summer?' He held out the muffin dish to her. She shook her head.

'Mr Colton sent to me by telegraph to tell me that he himself had seen Guttmann here, in England, earlier this summer,' she said as Mycroft returned the dish to the tray.

Mycroft stopped, still holding the tray. 'When exactly?' he asked.

'Oh,' she shrugged. 'The first week in May, I think.'

'You *think*?' Mycroft asked.

'Know, then – if you insist. It was very shortly after May Day. The second of May probably . . . Yes, the second. Yes, it was. I remember because my mother always rises early for the *Trimazo*, you know? Mr Colton had told me about you: how you alone in English government circles regarded Guttmann as somebody *extraordinarily*' – she gave full weight to each syllable –

'dangerous. But I was in Nice with my mother. And I did not know where you were.'

'The gentleman I told you about, Princess – the French gentleman – vanished on the night of the second and third of May.'

He carefully put down the muffin dish.

'Do you remember where it was Mr Frederick Colton saw Guttmann?' he asked.

'It was in Sussex – or is it Surrey?' She uttered a self-deprecating laugh. 'I can never remember which is on top and which is on the bottom!'

'Surrey is to the north – closer to London.'

'Then it was Surrey, I think. It was a place with one of your funnier English names: God-al-ming?'

'Godalming,' Mycroft nodded seriously. 'In Surrey.'

'It was in the high street there,' the little princess continued. 'Mr Colton was passing a draper's shop when Guttmann stepped out from it, holding a new pair of gloves. Guttmann was so concerned with staring up and down the street that he did not look where he was going, and almost knocked poor Mr Colton down. He didn't apologise, even when Mr Colton called after him by name . . .'

'Particularly when he realized that Mr Colton had recognized him?' suggested Mycroft.

'That is correct. Mr Colton said that he hurried so fast he was almost running to a dog-cart which was waiting with its driver round a corner in a lane. It was as if he thought if he could get away fast enough Mr Colton might think he had made a mistake.'

'I'm sure that was exactly what he was hoping . . . It is a pity Mr Frederick Colton is now at our legation in

Buenos Aires. He's a sound young fellow, with all his wits about him.'

'He is a very beautiful man,' said Sophie Trubetskoy. 'Oh!' she exclaimed, putting her fingers to her mouth. 'I forgot. You do not say "beautiful" about gentlemen. Not in England.'

'I'm sure Mr Colton would not care to hear himself so described,' said Mycroft.

'He *has* heard himself so described, Mr Holmes. As you say, he did not altogether approve of the description . . . But to the point of my being here with you, this evening,' she went on hastily, observing the expression on his face. 'I decided that I would keep spies to inform me when Guttmann should next appear in London – as I do in most of the important capital cities of Europe. I am, you see, a wealthy woman. I am of age, and unmarried, and as long as I remain so I have the disposal of my own considerable property. That is my principal weapon against the creature, Guttmann . . . No, Mr Holmes! I can see what you are thinking. But it was never my intention to offer you money. You are a gentleman, and I expect you have property of your own. But, what is more important, if you regard C.P.E. Guttmann as your enemy, it is surely the result of your own love of virtue and of your Queen and Country, as I regard him so because of my love for my unhappy sister.'

'Thank you, Princess.'

He was moved. She continued, 'Fortunately, when he arrived yesterday afternoon from Dover I was here, in London, staying in my Bruton Street apartments, so I determined to introduce myself to you as quickly as possible – and, as you perceive, informally and, I hope, secretly.'

'Do you know if he is in London at this moment?' asked Mycroft.

'I'm sure he isn't. My spy' – she pointed out of the window – 'down there . . .' she added.

'The negro?' asked Mycroft.

She nodded. 'His name is Cyril,' she said. 'A name used by the nobility here, I think. Not in my country, of course, where you find it in every village. He says he is the rightful King of the Zulus, only his family was deposed by the present king . . .?'

'Shaka?' Mycroft suggested.

'I think that is the name. He is a beautiful animal – only the most terrible liar! But he sees clearly enough. And Guttmann is easily recognized. He spotted Guttmann arriving by the boat-train at Charing Cross and saw him take a cab, a four-wheeler, across the Thames to Waterloo Road Station.'

'A four-wheeler provides greater concealment than a hansom, of course,' Mycroft observed. 'Did your Zulu king learn where Guttmann was going to from Waterloo Road? Back to Godalming, perhaps?'

'No. I'm afraid he didn't.'

'But somebody at the station – a ticket clerk, perhaps, or a porter – may remember. As you remarked, Guttmann's appearance is distinctive; and quite a modest sum of money can wonderfully stimulate the memory.'

Sophie Trubetskoy rested her hand on her cane as if to rise instantly from the chair.

'Shall we go to Waterloo Road now, Mr Holmes?' she asked.

Mycroft was taken aback. 'Certainly not!' he replied, more brusquely than he had intended.

83

He saw the disappointment on her face.

'In the first case, Princess,' he added more gently, 'it is Sunday evening. It is unlikely that the railway servants who were on duty yesterday afternoon will be the same as those who are there now. In the second case, it is best that we proceed cautiously, step by step, and that each step is guided by careful consideration. I have, as yet, no firm evidence of any connection between Mme Tirard and Guttmann except that they arrived in Town at the same time, and by the same boat-train, yesterday. I therefore have no evidence that there is indeed a connection between the disappearance of Mme Tirard's gentleman-friend, Jean-Christophe Thibault, and the appearances of Guttmann in this country except for an agreement of dates. We do not want to create any stir at this juncture – to cause tongues to wag. Tomorrow will do well enough. Put your spy to it; let us try his worth. As long, of course, as you can trust him not to run off with the money you give him to stimulate the memories of the servants of the London, Brighton and South Coast Railway Company.'

'He won't do that, Mr Holmes,' she replied without explanation, but with complete conviction.

'Is your blackamoor so honest a fellow?' Mycroft asked.

'Honest?' she laughed. 'He is a stray, the leader of a pack of young gutter footpads such as you find in any great city. They are the Zulus he rules over! They caught me one night when I was out alone. They would have stripped the clothes off my back – except that I showed them that a Trubetskoy, even a woman, is not taken so easily, and that I would have killed one or two of them before they overcame me . . .' She released the catch under the handle over her black cane. Mycroft caught a glimpse of several inches of razor-thin steel before she closed it with a barely audible click.

'Cyril followed me home. He was like a stray dog; he would not be shaken off. I think he had never encountered a woman like me, you see? So he had fallen in love with me. Now he is devoted to me. Not to anybody else, of course. But to me.'

'And his tribe know every court and backyard and alley, I expect,' suggested Mycroft. 'I can see why you regard him as "wonderfully necessary".'

'A tribe of wild children, Mr Holmes,' she confirmed with a smile.

In the same way, he thought, her ancestors had probably kept packs of wolf-hounds which had only been half tamed, to protect themselves and their estates.

'When your devoted savage has found out Guttmann's destination from Waterloo Road Station,' he asked, 'will you send him round here directly?'

'Certainly, Mr Holmes.'

'And, Princess? Do you have friends in Paris?'

'Of course. It is the city of my mother's birth.'

'This Mme Tirard. She says she is the wife – probably widow – of Pierre Tirard, lately Mayor of the *Deuxième Arrondissement*. So she can scarcely be an unknown in Parisian society. Do you think we might discover all we can about her? I mean, matters of some delicacy, such as her friendship with this Jean-Christophe Thibault, silk manufacturer of Lyon?'

'I know exactly the right person, Mr Holmes. I shall send to her by telegraph first thing tomorrow morning. Mme Garcia-Viardot knows everything about everybody in Paris.'

85

'Pauline Garcia-Viardot?' he asked. 'The opera-singer?'

'Pauline Garcia-Viardot, the beloved of the greatest of our Russian novelists, M. Ivan Turgenev,' Sophie Trubetskoy replied.

'Thank you, Princess,' said Mycroft.

At the top of the stairs, as she was leaving, he said, 'My dear, I cannot thank you enough for coming to search me out. The information with which you have provided me regarding Carl Philipp Emmanuel Guttmann is invaluable – and I am sure more is to come. There is only one thing which worries me. I shall not conceal it from you. Your motives for pursuing Guttmann are most understandable. But they are in the nature of a private vendetta – you must admit. No harm in that, my dear!' – he attempted to forestall any protest on her part – 'no harm in the world! Except that it can result in enthusiasm. Enthusiasm is the enemy of enterprises such as this – the enemy of tact, caution, strategy. Do you understand me? That is why we English stand first among all other nations for moral fibre and commercial probity. The fact that we are not an enthusiastic race is the secret of our success. I only say this because if we are to catch our prey, cool consideration is of the essence. You don't mind me speaking to you like this, do you, Princess?'

She smiled up at him and shook her head very slowly and wisely, so that the ludicrous notion occurred to him that she was making fun of him.

'No, Mr Holmes. I do not mind in the least.'

From his window he watched her departure. She walked up the opposite pavement in the direction of St James's Street. The negro emerged from the shadows to follow her at some fifteen yards distance with his curious dancing, loping stride. Behind him, following at a distance of another fifteen yards or so, came two filthy, ragged children, a boy and a girl, with greasy, matted hair trailing about their thin, prematurely aged faces.

He remained until they had passed out of sight. He returned to the table beside his chair. He consumed one of the remaining muffins. When he had finished it, he picked up the fourth and last muffin. Glancing at the door as if he was afraid he might be disturbed, he wiped the muffin on the plate which had been put out for his companion's use, taking care to leave crumbs and traces of butter. Satisfied by what he had done, he sank into his armchair and consumed the last muffin in comfort.

Chapter Eight

Sophie let herself into the apartment. As usual, her fat old *nyanya* came bustling up to fuss over her.

'My pet! Pigeon! Where have you been all this time? And the *barin*, Barnaby, waiting for you all evening! And you dressed like that . . . akh, akh, akh!'

Captain Barnaby, a slim, dandified young man in the undress uniform of the Twenty-first Lancers, looking older than his years on account of his luxuriant dundreary whiskers and thick, pointed moustaches, was standing at the drawing-room door.

'I did not ask you to come here this evening, Eddy,' Sophie told the young man.

Leaving her cape in her *nyanya*'s arms she went past him, patting his cheek with her fingers as she did so.

'But Sophie deahwest,' he called after her as she disappeared into the closet. 'I always call on you on Sunday evenin's when you're in Town. It's the wegular thing, don't you know?'

He had to wait for her to reappear.

'Only on the understanding that I don't have a more

important engagement,' she replied. 'This evening, I did.'

'Oh I say!' he protested. 'What sort of engagement? And dwessed like that, too!'

'None of your business, *chéri*. And now I am very tired, and you must go away.'

'But deahwest!'

'No, Eddy.' She lowered her voice. 'You are not staying tonight. And you are not to make a fuss in front of my maids. They may not understand what you're saying, but they know what you mean. So be a good boy, yes?'

'But goin' about in Town, dwessed like that! It ain't at all the thing!'

'Don't you think it suits me?' she asked.

The ends of his moustaches twitched as his lips formed unspoken words. Finally he said in a sulky voice, 'Suits you deuced well, my dear. Too well for my liking!'

She kissed him lightly on the moustache, standing on her toes to do so.

'Oh I say!' he repeated.

'Now off you go,' she told him. 'And if you're a good boy, perhaps I'll let you come here on Tuesday night, after you've had your game of whist with your majors and your Colonel in the mess – if you keep sober, that is!'

She let him out of the apartment herself. As she secured the door behind him, she turned to her old *nyanya*.

'He's going to help me, *Nyanusha*! I knew it. I was certain he would!'

As her *nyanya* followed her into her bedroom, Sophie saw the expression on the big, round face.

'Don't frown, *Nyanusha*! I haven't done anything to make you cross. Can't you see how happy I am tonight?'

'Yes, I can, Sofya Sergeyevna! I can see it. And God can too! A young lady like you should not live the way you do.

89

You ought to be leaving that *Mistr* Guttmann to God. God sees all; it is for Him to punish the evildoer. That's what the Fathers tell us. You have your youth and your looks. For you there should be balls and the opera – and one young man at our door, eh, my dear? Not a procession of them who come and then vanish after a week or two! And we have no business to be here, in this city – it's dirtier than Moscow, and they don't fear God here, at least not properly like good Orthodox Christians. We should go back to the Princess, your mother, that's my opinion . . .'

'Hush, *Nyanya!*' Sophie told her.

'Your heart will turn to iron,' her *nyanya* persisted. 'That's what happens to people who won't leave retribution to the judgement of God, Sofya Sergeyevna, you mark my words.'

Ignoring her, Sophie went to the corner of the heavily draped and furnished bedroom furthest from the door, where hung the votive lamp under the icon of the Smolensk Mother of God. She bowed to touch the floor with her fingertips, then blessed herself.

'In the all-honourable and majestic name of the Father, Son, and Holy Spirit, now and forever, and unto ages of ages. Amen . . .'

She bowed low again, touching the floor, and again blessed herself:

'O exceedingly glorious, ever-virgin Birthgiver of Christ-God, bear thou my prayer of heart-filled thanksgiving unto thy Son, our God . . .'

And even as she prayed, in complete sincerity of heart, she could not help smiling at the thought of how embarrassed Mr Mycroft Holmes would have been if he could have seen her thus offering thanks for him.

Chapter Nine

Abigail Rodgers sat in the barn, her bare legs and muddy boots hanging over the edge of the hayloft. Her long yellow hair – of which she was quite vain – was piled roughly under her drab mob-cap; strands of it were plastered with sweat on her forehead. She had been working extremely hard, at least in her own opinion, cleaning up after the milking. It was a hot forenoon; bright sunlight shone past the great barn doors which tilted from their hinges, on to the empty waggon which stood below where she was perched, its shafts resting on the haystrewn ground. Dust from the dried hay hung motionless in the brightness.

A book of verses was spread open in her lap. Before she turned the page, she wiped her fingers on the flounced pinafore-apron bib over the now-growing curve of her bosom. She read, mouthing the words as she did so,

'A sailor with a wooden leg,
A little charity implores;
He holds his tattered hat to beg—

Some, let us join our little stores.
Poor sailor! We ourselves might be
As helpless and as poor as he.'

Beside the verses was a coloured picture of the beggar sitting on the city pavement and in front of him, feeling in their purses, two girls of about Abigail's own age, in velvet paletots, crinoline and with spotlessly white lace pantalets about their ankles.

The reverend author of the verses would have been surprised and dismayed to know the effect of his rhyme on this young reader, at least. It was the governing principle of all Abigail's imaginings that she deserved better of life than to have been born the daughter of a humble yeoman-farmer. One of the children in the illustration was yellow-haired as she, but her hair was gathered, under her 'military' cap, in a net of red cord with gold threads, and on her tiny feet were spotlessly polished boots which fitted close as gloves and were on slightly raised heels. Abigail imagined herself dressed like that girl, without a speck of dirt on her, stopping to give a penny – no, sixpence! – to a poor beggar. She imagined herself smiling very sweetly at him as he thanked her, his eyes moist with gratitude.

'Abby? Abby, where be you to!'

At first she was too far gone into her imaginary world to hear.

'Drat the girl! You come out here, child, wherever you be a-hiding, or I'll tell your fayther to take his belt to 'ee!'

Her mother's voice was made permanently hoarse with shouting – shouting at the beasts and the fowls, shouting at the stupid, sullen workhouse girls who were all they could afford as servants, shouting for the men to come in for their tea, shouting for Abigail. Abigail's real mother – the mother of her imaginings – was altogether different: she existed in a murmur of silken quiet, waited on by maids who did her bidding before they were asked, and had only the kindest, gentlest words for a daughter who was beginning to grow into as lovely a woman as she was herself.

She could hear her mother's wooden pattens clumping on the cobbles of the yard outside. She closed the book and thrust it as deep as she could into the pile of hay nearest to her. Then she dropped straight down on to the floor of the barn, beside the waggon, recovering her balance just as her mother appeared in the dazzling sunlight of the barn doorway.

'So there you be! And what you been up to, may I ask, Miss Lady-of-Leisure?'

'I bain't no lady-of-leisure!' Abby answered back. She was too cautious to add that she wished she was. 'I done a lot of work this morning! I only come in here 'cause I were looking for a clean besom.'

'Don't you tell me none of your fibs, missy! You know well as I do Billy don't keep no besoms in here. Not since wintertime. 'Sides, you got straw all over your backside, you have!'

Suddenly, unexpectedly, she slapped Abby across the face with such force that Abby tottered and had to catch on to the spokes of the waggon wheel.

'What you done that for!' wailed Abby. She put her hand to her cheek as the sharp cut of pain resolved into a dull jaw-ache.

'You knows danged well!' Her mother's voice had become a croak. 'I ain't got no more patience with your fibbing, and that's the truth. You lurk in here 'stead of working hard like the rest on us! Your fayther could get us a real farm-maid, a proper hard worker, with what it costs us to keep you in dress and victuals! I'm telling you, bain't going to give me no heartbreak if your fayther take 'ee down to Abinger, next hiring. You can stand beside old Tom's girl with the others. And if anybody'll take you – then, good riddance, I says!'

Still rubbing her face, Abby stared at her through a stream of tears.

'Bain't no good 'ee a-carrying on, neither!' her mother told her, but with just enough lack of conviction for Abby to give her a wary glance before dissolving into a noisy snivelling.

Her mother pushed her out into the sunlight in the yard. Abby felt her arm resting quite lightly round her shoulder. Her mother was incapable of remaining angry for more than a minute or two.

'Rosie's with the cutters up on Middle Field,' she said. 'So you take your fayther's dinner to him behind St Martha's Hill, and come straight back. You can give me a hand with all they churns this a'ternoon, and I'll see if I got it in me to forgive 'ee.'

She gave Abby another push, this time up the incline towards the farmhouse door. A leather-faced stable-hand was watching through the open stable door. He grinned to see the state Abby was in, but her mother noticed him and croaked, 'And you get back to your chores, Billy Lavendar, if you don't want me to have a word wi' the maister!'

Still grinning, Billy Lavendar backed into the gloom of the stable. There was a volley of aggrieved squawking and a cluster of hens came flapping and stirring up dust, out of the door and into the yard.

94

A few minutes later Abby emerged from the kitchen. She was dry-eyed; she had put on a clean pinafore and had scraped some of the dried mud from her boots; she had taken off her mob to let her her hair tumble loose down her back. She held her apron bundled up in front of her to carry her father's bread and cheese, and a bottle of cider. As she strolled across the yard to the gate, the stable-hand came out once more. He glanced up to the farmhouse to make sure Abby's mother was not watching.

'Daydreaming again, was 'ee, Abby, eh? Come in here wi' me, an' I'll give 'ee daydreams!' He leered at her, showing his broken and discoloured teeth. Abby tossed her head.

'One day, Billy Lavendar, you're goin' to call me *Miss* Abigail! You mark my words!'

And she went on across the yard as he called after her, 'Best take care as 'ee goes through Eldebury Woods, *Miss* Abigail! Or the drownded gentleman in Silent Pool 'll come a-leapin' out a'ter 'ee, and drag 'ee down wi' 'im to keep 'im company!'

'What drownded gentleman?' Abby shouted back scornfully.

'Jest 'ee go an' look – if 'ee dares!' the stablehand replied. Then he ducked back into the stable, even though Abby's mother was nowhere to be seen.

Abigail flounced out of the farm gate, to the extent that her mud-stained boy's boots permitted her to flounce. She took the ridgeway path under St Martha's Hill, below the ruins of the ancient chapel. While she carried her apron bundled in front of her, her head was in a dream of fashionable dress, of catching the admiring attention of gentlefolk in their Sunday best strolling in the park – she had only the vaguest idea of what one of the great London parks must be like, believing them to be vast fairy-tale gardens, all fountains, lakes and rides – of the Prince of Wales and his family driving past in their carriage, asking who that lovely young girl was, then, in front of all the bystanders, inviting her to join them. In the shimmering heat of a downland summer she trudged under the brief shade of the clumps of hawthorn which broke the expanses of rough meadow before skirting the ageless oaks of Weston Wood. She followed a line of yew trees down to the lychgate and footpath under the old ivy-covered parish church. When the footpath turned behind the church she cut across the unkempt graveyard and clambered over the broken stone wall into Eldebury Woods.

The woods were dark after the glare of the meadows; bushes and coils of bramble choked the ground between the gnarled tree-trunks. She trudged along a narrow path of dried mud at the bottom of a steep-sided little valley until she came to a clearing under the branches of a giant beech. In the hollow beyond, which formed the bottom of the valley, lay the still black surface of Silent Pool surrounded by a wide bank of drooping ferns. Abby regarded it with a mingling of curiosity and trepidation. She did not believe what Billy Lavendar had said about a drownded gentleman – and certainly nothing so silly as him leaping up to pull her in. But disbelief did not stop her being afraid of it. She turned aside rather than pass beside the pool, and scrambled up the wooded slope out of the valley, careless of the damage done by dried mud and the clinging undergrowth to her appearance. A shaft of sunlight struck down between the trees. In its warmth, she turned and looked back. Threads of sunlight glis-

tened across the still surface of the pool below her. A pair
of swallows darted across it, dipping so low their wings
almost touched the water. Abby smiled in relief. Gathering her bundle to her once more, she found her way out of
the woods on to the open upland.

Her father was standing on the summit of the ridge. He
was with old Tom, his shepherd, a weatherbeaten patri-
arch in a blue smock. The sheep were scattered among
the turf-glades in the thickness of the bracken. On either
side of the ridge stretched the gently-rolling open downland broken by stretches of woodland and, sheltering in
its folds, villages and clusters of farm buildings and the
occasional grand country house with its parkland. All
were held in a still, summer haze. A mile and a half
below the ridge-top, to the south, there was the only sign
of motion: a passenger train puffing its leisurely way
along the line from Dorking to Guildford, its small
clouds of white smoke billowing away to hang over the
fields before melting to nothing.

As Abby approached she saw that there was a third
man with her father and Tom. He was on horseback; a
small, lean, swart and weasel-faced man in a stained,
frayed tweed hacking jacket. He had a brown bowler hat
with frayed, nibbled brim crammed down over his
brow. His shirt-cuffs and collar needed turning, and they
were rimmed black with grime. His horse, however, was
a fine, well-groomed mare of sixteen hands – a gentleman's mount.

'Why! How big the lass is growed!' the man exclaimed.
'Pretty as a picture, eh? And become a woman, almost.'

'Make your curtsey to Mr Whettam now, girl,' her
father told her.

She bobbed, saying with a demure lowering of the

eyes, 'A'ternoon, Mr Whettam.' She did not like doing so, and she did not like her father telling her to. After all, Mr Whettam was only a servant up at the Hall, whereas her father was his own man.

'Brought your dinner, Papa,' she said. She took a gingham cloth from inside her apron, spread it on the ground, and placed the food and the bottle on to it.

' "Papa" is it, eh?' grinned Mr Whettam. 'All genteel-like! Quite the little lady, eh? Ever thought of putting her into service, have you, George? Like over at the Hall? Your Abby 'd make a right pretty little lady's maid in a year or two, I'll be bound.'

The horse started suddenly.

'Whoa, dang 'ee!' exclaimed Mr Whettam.

It backed several steps, shaking its neck and stamping its hooves into the soft turf. Mr Whettam slapped it on the neck, viciously. 'She'll have a taste o' the whip when we gets back,' he said. 'Still has to learn who's master, eh? Horses and women!'

The mare steadied up. Mr Whettam pointed with his switch at Abby.

'The mistress has her eye open for a new girl,' he said.

'I bain't been thinking of putting her into service, Mr Whettam,' her father replied. 'Not so long as her mother has a use for her 'bout the farm.'

'You knows what's best for your own child, I daresay,' said Mr Whettam. 'Still – if you sees fit to change your mind, I'll drop the word to the mistress. In the mean-times, George, if you or any of yourn should clap eyes on the poor, unfortunate gentleman, you send up to the Hall right away.'

'I'll do that, Mr Whettam,' Abby's father replied.

'Mad as a March hare, he is,' Mr Whettam went on,

'but he'll do nobody no harm. The maister 'll be greatly obliged.'

'I'll keep my eyes skinned,' Abby's father assured him.

'Day to 'ee, George. And you, Thomas!' Mr Whettam called to the old shepherd, who tugged his forelock.

He wheeled round the mare expertly. For a moment Abby thought he was about to ride her down.

'And you, missy! You be a good girl for your faither, mind!' he called down at her.

'Yes, Mr Whettam,' she bobbed, avoiding his weasel stare.

One day, when she had become a lady, or was even just halfway to being a lady, she would put Mr Whettam in his place, even if he was first coachman over at Ranmore Hall. One day, when she had caught the attention of some fine gentleman, or had become personal attendant to a real lady, Mr Whettam would have to hold a door open for her as she stepped up into a carriage. And she wouldn't even look at him.

'Hurry back to your mother, now,' said her father as he and old Tom sat down on the turf to share the victuals she had brought.

She went off down the hillside, down the turf path through the bracken. She turned off, back into Eldebury Woods. She picked her way cautiously through the undergrowth to the bottom of the steep little valley. In front of her lay the still water of Silent Pool in its wide coronet of ferns. She stood and looked at it. She felt challenged by it; it was too bad to be scared by somebody like Billy Lavendar – particularly if he were ever to find out that she was scared. Screwing her small supply of courage to the sticking point, she plunged into the waist-high ferns and pushed through them to the edge of the water.

There she sat down and pulled off her boots. Tucking her dress and pinafore about her knees, she dangled her feet in the cold pool. Gazing down into the ripples she had caused she noticed something below where she was sitting. She wriggled round into a kneeling position and peered down, leaning as far out over the edge as she dared, clutching on to the grass and fern on the verge. The water's surface, which she had disturbed with her toes, stilled to a glassy smoothness and she could see, as if in a mirror, the reflection of her own face. Below that, and staring up through it, was another face: dark hair floated above and around it, moving very slowly; the eyes were black, empty sockets; then she saw the fish nibbling at the cheek and darting away, sending fragments of flesh floating upwards from the gaping ragged hole through which she could see the teeth. Then she saw the whole figure clearly – that of a man, a gentleman by his clothes, sitting under the water as if leaning between two rocks.

She wrenched herself round so that she was staring into the fern. She felt like screaming, but somebody inside her remained quite sensible, telling her not to be foolish because nobody could possibly hear her. It did not occur to her that the gentleman would pull her in to keep him company; what she had seen was horrifying enough already. She picked herself up and, carrying her boots, ran back up through the woods and out on to the ridge to where her father and the old shepherd were still sharing their meal.

'Papa! Papa!' she called out breathlessly.

'What be the matter, child? Why bain't 'ee gone back to your mother, eh? And jest look at the state 'ee's in! What's she going to say to 'ee?'

'There be a gentleman a-lying drownded in Silent Pool, papa! He be a-caught atween the stones . . . and . . . and the fish been at him something horrible!'

'Ye knows what's wrong wi' you, my lass,' said her father, 'you been given too much imagination! That's what's wrong wi' you, and no mistake!' He turned to Tom. 'I tell her mother, I did, a farm-wench don't need no book-larnin'. Didn't pay no heed, though!'

'Aye!' Old Tom glanced up at Abby, screwing his eyes into the sunlight. 'Best be off home, my dear, 'fore you're in worser trouble.'

'But it's true!' Abby protested. 'Gospel oath, I swears it!'

'I said . . . be off wi' 'ee!' her father told her. ' 'Fore I takes my belt to 'ee!'

'Cross my heart!' Abby urged.

Old Tom put his wrinkled, walnut hand on her father's arm.

'Bain't no cause for the wench to come a-running back here if it bain't true, Mr Rodgers,' he pointed out. 'Not when theer's talk of a beltin' an' all!'

Her father stared up at her.

'The fish be a eatin' of 'im,' she said earnestly.

'He be a gentleman, you say?' asked her father.

'Aye, Papa.'

'And you bain't a-telling none o' them fibs o' yourn?' he asked. 'Cause it be a whipping matter if you be!'

'No, Papa!'

'Mr Whettam did say 'twere a gentleman gone missing, right enough,' he said.

'Aye, he did that, Mr Rodgers. He did,' Old Tom confirmed.

Mr Rodgers got on to his feet.

'By God, lass! You best be telling the truth! Now be off home to your mother! I'll be going across to the Hall, Tom. If it be the gentleman Mr Whettam was a-telling of, I daresay Mr Jenks-Robinson'll be after sending down to Dorking for the police.'

As Abby ran off, still barefoot, along the ridge in the direction of St Martha's and the farm, Mr Rodgers started descending the hill in the opposite direction. The old shepherd remained with his scattered flock grazing contentedly among the bracken.

Mr Rodgers crossed the yard of Ranmore Hall. Above him hung miniature crenellated battlements, while pinnacled turrets and twisted Jacobean chimneys reached high into the dazzling sunlight above ivy-draped walls and ornamented windows with leaded lattice panes. The Jenks-Robinson's family brougham had been dragged to the centre of the yard and was being washed and polished.

Whettam came out of the coach-house to meet him.

'Abigail see-d him, eh?' he said, when Mr Rodgers had told him what she had reported. 'Sharp little wench, that un! Best keep your eye on her, eh? You be right, though. Mr Jenks-Robinson'll want to know straight way.'

He reached up and patted Mr Rodgers on the shoulder. He went up into the house, leaving Mr Rodgers waiting. A minute or two later he reappeared, accompanied by a grave-looking and dignified manservant. 'Will you please to come this way, Mr Rodgers?' he asked.

Mr Whettam grinned and scurried off back across the yard. Mr Rodgers followed the servant into the house. They went along several tunnel-like whitewashed passages until they reached the front hall. There, beams of sunlight streaming through the great stained glass windows above the main staircase spun webs of colour on the stone flags and on the panelling. Someone in a nearby room was playing the piano – a stange sort of music, to Mr Rodgers's ears, in which cascades of notes seemed to run into one another with no hint of the robust sort of melody he enjoyed.

As the music continued, Mr Jenks-Robinson came out into the hall. His country clothes – tweed plus-fours and Norfolk jacket – hung unsuitably on his soft, slight frame. His face looked as though it had never been exposed to sun, wind or rain: it was as soft and as smooth as that of a schoolgirl.

'My dear Rodgers, so very good of you to come so promptly,' he said, wiping his fingers on a large blue handkerchief.

He listened with head tilted as Mr Rodgers repeated what Abby had said. Mr Rodgers noticed the piano-playing had stopped abruptly.

'Thought as 'twere best, a'ter what Mr Whettam tell us, to come straight over, sir. Seein' as how you might want to inform the police, and that.'

'Well done, Rodgers! Very well done!'

Mr Jenks-Robinson continued to dry his hands on his handkerchief. It seemed as though the agitation he was keeping out of his facial expression had somehow transferred itself into his fingers.

'You're a sound fellow, Rodgers!' Then he said, 'One moment, if you please,' and turned and strode off into the room from which had come the sound of piano-playing. There was a subdued sound of urgent conversation. Shortly afterwards, Mr Jenks-Robinson returned to the hallway.

103

'Quite right! Quite right!' he said. 'We're sending down to Dorking for the constabulary. We'll all go over to Eldebury Woods together, eh? If you would care to wait in the kitchen until the constables arrive here, I daresay Mrs Armitage might be prevailed upon to offer you a cup of tea or a glass of something more refreshing, what d'ye say, Rodgers? I know what I say – I say you're a good, sound fellow!'

'Much obliged to you, Mr Jenks-Robinson, sir,' Mr Rodgers replied.

But he did not really feel it. Mr Jenks-Robinson was an outsider, an off-comer who, wealthy though he might be, had no business being master of a fine old place like Ranmore Hall.

Up on the ridge old Tom pulled off his ragged straw hat, mopped his brow on the sleeve of his smock, then replaced his hat on his head in order to shade his eyes. On the road below, descending from Ranmore Common in the direction of Abinger, a dog-cart was travelling at a fast trot, sending clouds of sandy dust to hang in the quivering afternoon air. He peered down, trying to focus his sight on it. By screwing up his eyes he could just make out Mr Whettam crouched forward over the rail, clutching the reins and snapping the whip at the horse's flank. Beside him was a thick-set stableman from the hall. He saw the motion of Mr Whettam's head turning to look up to the top of the ridge. Immediately, Tom turned around and appeared to busy himself calling up his dog. When he looked back again at the road the dog-cart had disappeared behind the trees of Eldebury Woods, and the dust was beginning to settle.

*   *   *

That night at the Rodgers' farm, as the hands were having their tea round the kitchen table and were being served as always by Mrs Rodgers, Abigail and the farm-maid, the outside door crashed open. Mr Rodgers came in, his face red and sweating with exertion and fury.

'Abigail! You come here! D'ye hear me, wench?'

Abby cringed away.

'What be the matter, George?' asked her mother, struggling to keep her hoarse voice calm.

Mr Rodgers ignored her.

'Make a fool o' your own fayther, would 'ee? Make a fool o' 'im in front o' the off-comer, and Whettam, and Sergeant Parrish and the police, an' I don't know who besides!'

'I didna'!' wailed Abby. 'I never did!'

'Send us all on a fool's errand, would 'ee? You come here, you little slut! I'll larn 'ee fibs, dang 'ee!'

He wrenched down a heavy leather strap from the wall. Abby screamed.

'I never telled no fibs! I never! I did see un! I swear! In Silent Pool. Gospel truth, I swear it!'

'An hour, we was draggin' it!' Mr Rodgers shouted. He slashed at her with the full weight of the strap. Mrs Rodgers croaked out 'George!' in helpless protest. The farm-maid hid her face in her apron, but not before she had caught Billy Lavendar's eye and exchanged grins with him.

'Get across to the barn wi' 'ee!' Mr Rodgers shouted. 'Ye'll get your fill o' punishment theer.' He lashed again at Abby as if driving her like an animal.

'Billy see-d un!' screamed Abby, in one last desperate bid to stop her father. 'Billy Lavendar – he see-d the gentleman in Silent Pool! He said he did!'

Her father lowered the strap. He looked down the table at the stableman. 'Well, Billy?' he asked.

Billy smirked, more from nervousness than satisfaction. 'I never see-d nothing o' the kind, maister,' he said. 'I never see-d nothing nor said nothing.' He turned to the others. 'Couldna 'ave said nothing, could I, 'cause I didna' see nothing!'

Mr Rodgers turned again on Abby. 'You get down to the barn wi' 'ee!'

He pointed the strap at her. Abby turned and went. Her father followed her. The hands sat silent round the table listening to her crying and pleading from across the yard outside.

'Reckon as she be gettin' what's been a comin' to her for a long time past,' Rosie, the dairymaid, said in her thick voice.

'The lass were telling the truth, I reckon,' said old Tom. He looked down at his plate and spooned food into his mouth.

Nobody paid him the least attention. Billy Lavendar had been about to make some remark about how, perhaps, old Tom had seen a drowned man in Silent Pool, when he noticed what old Tom and everybody else had noticed: that Mr Whettam was standing at the door, gently tapping his boot with his switch.

Chapter Ten

Mycroft was sitting in his room in the Treasury. Although it was classified as an office, in reality it was no more than an annex to the Clerks' Room and separated from it by an open arch. The Clerks' Room existed in a state of noisy, schoolroom chaos, its occupants the younger sons of men of property who had not found their way into the lower echelons of Army, Church or Politics but were nonetheless compelled to seek a salary. They smoked incessantly so that the place was obscured in all seasons and weathers in a blue, cigar-scented fug, with ash spilling over ledgers and documents. They gathered at the windows, passing the working day by watching out for any pretty lady's maid or milliner's apprentice on the pavement below, then leaning out and calling down 'Walker!' in admiration and, on attracting the attention they were seeking, soliciting an assignation.

Mycroft was content to ignore the hubbub and to be ignored. In his deep leather padded porter's chair, he sat in comfort. Occasionally he was moved to write in one of the huge, dusty, calf-bound ledgers in front of him with a quill pen. Now and then, with podgy finger, he would flick at the wooden beads of the abacus beside him – more in abstraction than from a need to calculate figures. The work assigned to him far from tried his intellect; there was more than enough time for him to consider problems, fiscal and otherwise, and to explore solutions in mental, if not physical, seclusion.

'Holmes, my dear chap, the First Secretary presents his compliments and requests the pleasure . . .'

Mycroft surfaced from a deep, brown study unrelated to the complexities of the Government's next Finance Bill. He glanced up with a look of glassy indolence. He sighed. 'Thank you, Phillips,' he said.

The First Secretary's first secretary smiled indulgently. Three clerks, little more than boys, were observing through the arch, and smirking. 'I do believe Mr Martins means immediately,' said Mr Phillips. Mycroft twisted round to look for his stick, which was resting against the chair's wing.

'If I do not leap to my feet instantly, my dear fellow' – he grasped the stick horizontally, leant across his table and gently prodded the young man aside – 'it is because you are obstructing my passage.' He lowered his stick and dragged himself heavily to his feet.

'Obliged to you, sir,' he added, and lumbered out through the Clerks' Room with Mr Phillips taking up the rear.

The First Secretary raised his head from the papers in the despatch-box open in front of him.

'Ah, Holmes!' he said, none too pleased. 'You are sent for from the FO.' He pointed to another young man who was standing at the door of the office with Mr Phillips.

'Upon my word, Holmes,' he said impatiently, 'I wonder sometimes which office of state it is which is supposed to employ your services.'

Mycroft, his stick dangling between his fingers, spread out his hands to indicate his helplessness.

'My dear First Secretary, I do assure you that this traipsing around which seems to be my lot is none of my asking. On the contrary, I'm sure it is conducive neither to peace of mind nor health. But what can one do?'

The young man beside Mr Phillips said, 'Lord Granville in person is asking for Mr Holmes, First Secretary. He says that it is over a matter of some urgency.'

The First Secretary sighed.

'It is always over a matter of some urgency!'

Mycroft went down to the street with the young man. They rounded a corner under the shade of the trees and crossed Downing Street to enter the Foreign Office building by a side entrance. Going down a narrow passage, they reached the hall and the Great Staircase. Another young official greeted them on the turn of the stairs, by the larger than lifesize white marble statue of a naked nymph with an amphora on her shoulder. In a hushed voice he said, 'His Lordship is in the map-room.'

Mycroft followed him up to the first gallery with its wide, carpeted walks, its walnut panelled walls, brass rails overlooking the hall below, and crouched marble caryatids supporting the pillars reaching up to the glass of the roof. They turned through the lofty open door into the official map-room.

'Ah, Holmes! My dear fellow, thank goodness you're here!' Lord Granville turned to greet him. He had a semicircle of aides standing round him. Broad expanses of oilcloth maps hung suspended from their rollers against the walls. 'Can't find Ceylon, my dear chap!

None of us! We can't find it anywhere. Deuced rum thing, don't you know?'

In front of him hung a huge map of the Caribbean. One of the aides had a wooden marker, the point of which he was resting on the southern tip of Florida. 'Could have sworn it was somewhere round here, my lord,' he said. He ran the marker down across Puerto Rico and on to Cuba.

'It don't float about, my lord?' suggested another aide. 'Like one of those damned coral things, don't you know? What d'ye call them? Reefs!' He laughed vacantly. Mycroft pushed him aside, took the string on the bottom rod of the map and sent it rolling up with a clatter, leaving the aide with the marker pointing it into the air.

'Here! I say!' the aide protested.

Mycroft took a curtain-pole from the liveried attendant standing at the door. He hooked it into one of the rolled maps and drew it down. It was of the Indian Ocean. He handed the pole back to the attendant, then pointed with his stick.

'There, my lord. There is Ceylon.'

Lord Granville peered at it.

'By God, Holmes! You're a miracle!' he said. 'How d'ye keep all that stuff in your head, eh?' He gazed up at the map, adjusting his eyeglass as he did so. 'And there's Madras, by God! I've a nephew in Madras, don't you know? Deuced unhealthy climate, South India!'

He turned round to Mycroft quite abruptly.

'Given any thought to the little matter Sir James Swarthmoor spoke to you about, eh, Holmes?' he asked. He let the eyeglass fall on to his chest.

'Is that what you wished to speak to me about, my lord?' Mycroft asked.

110

'Why else do you think I'd have you brought over from the Treasury?' asked Lord Granville.

'Yes, my lord.' Mycroft cleared his throat. 'Of course, my lord.'

'My dear fellow!' Lord Granville laughed. 'You don't suppose I'd take you from your post just to ask you where Ceylon might be on the map? I'm sure one of our common clerks could have told us that! Shall we go somewhere a little more private, eh?'

He swept out on to the gallery. Mycroft watched the cortège of aides and secretaries following him. He tacked himself on to the end of it.

'Ah! Sir James!' called Lord Granville. 'We have your Mr Holmes with us.'

Sir James had been waiting, leaning against the rail and half-concealed in a thicket of giant dried bullrushes. He joined the procession being led by Lord Granville round the gallery, taking his place in the rear with Mycroft.

'C.P.E. Guttmann is in England,' Mycroft told him. 'He arrived on the same boat as Mme Tirard.'

'Did he, by Jove!' said Sir James. 'And where is he now?'

'I am hoping to find out. He took a train almost immediately from Waterloo Road.'

'It could be coincidence . . . Look, Holmes! I don't want you galloping off on one of your hobby-horses.'

'It could be coincidence that he was also seen in Godalming on the very same day that our M. Thibault arrived here and vanished.'

'Who saw him?' asked Sir James.

'Freddy Colton. One of the very few men in England who would be able to recognize him.'

'Freddy Colton is in Buenos Aires.'

'On the second of May he was in Godalming, Sir James.'

111

'Are you suggesting that Guttmann and Mme Tirard are some sort of associates in this affair?' asked Sir James.

'Or adversaries, out to thwart one another's schemes – one cannot tell at this juncture. What I am telling you is this: what you described yesterday as a bee in my bonnet and today as a runaway hobby-horse is to me a tolerable certainty: Berlin has an interest, if not a hand, in this business.'

'Lord Granville won't like it, Holmes! He won't like it a bit! He is convinced the Germans are our natural allies.'

'Carl Philipp Emmanuel Guttmann?' demanded Lord Granville. 'And who the devil may he be?'

'In 'sixty-eight, you remember, my lord. In Florence. The unfortunate business of Lady Kilgarden . . .' Sir James reminded him.

'By God, yes! And that damned priest fellow!' Lord Granville exclaimed. 'The Papal Nuncio – would have thought giving peaches on the q.t. to altar-boys in the vestry would have been more in his line, what? And somebody put the canard around that that wretched Kilgarden woman was an agent of ours, or some such nonsense! You extricated us from that awful business, didn't you, Holmes?'

'Some people have been kind enough to say so, my lord,' Mycroft replied. 'But one thing is entirely certain. It was Guttmann who acted as go-between for Lady Kilgarden and the Papal Nuncio.'

'Of course, my dear boy!' Lord Granville replied amiably. 'He's a valet. The Prince von Bismarck's *valet de chambre*. It's the sort of thing *valets de chambre* do, ain't it? Common sort of fellows, with ideas above their station!'

112

'I believe that what Holmes here is trying to tell us is that Guttmann is something more than your ordinary valet,' Sir James suggested. 'He sees him as von Bismarck's *éminence grise*.'

'That is perfectly correct, my lord,' Mycroft confirmed. 'C.P.E. Guttmann is von Bismarck's valet as Olivier le Dain was Louis XI's barber, or Père Joseph was Richelieu's chaplain. It is Guttmann who is an agent – the Prussian Minister-president's agent. And, therefore, one of the most dangerous men in all Europe.'

'My dear Holmes! Do you seriously suggest that a *valet de chambre* represents a threat to British interests?'

'He *has* already represented a threat, my lord,' Mycroft replied boldly. 'In Florence, in the summer of 'sixty-eight.'

'Only by chance, Holmes. By chance! He happened to be the messenger boy in the Kilgarden affair,' Lord Granville replied.

'I have tried to convince Holmes that Guttmann was acting in a private capacity on that occasion, my lord,' said Sir James.

'Of course he was!' Lord Granville replied.

'Very well, my lord,' said Mycroft. 'I beg you to recall the events which led up to the recent terrible conflict between France and the German Confederation. Do you remember how, in reply to a question on a matter of Prussian-French relations put by the French Government to the King of Prussia, King William drafted a reply of a most tactful, even peaceable nature? King William, you will recall, was taking the waters at Bad Ems. The telegram, despatched to Paris and the world's press from Berlin, had, by the careful alteration of one or two words, been changed to something so utterly insulting to

113

the Emperor Napoleon III that no monarch could have borne the humiliation of accepting it.'

'And what has the man Guttmann to do with this?' asked Lord Granville.

'Everything, my lord. The King of Prussia would not have stooped to secretly altering his own draft reply. Nor can we suppose the Prussian Minister-president capable of stooping to forgery . . .'

'Certainly not!' exclaimed Lord Granville. 'Prince von Bismarck is a *Junker*, a true gentleman!'

'But gentlemen in high office, my lord,' Mycroft explained, 'sometimes retain attendants who know how to anticipate their employers' wishes in such a manner as to absolve those same employers from any hint of blame . . .'

'I hope, Holmes, you are not suggesting that I would stoop . . .'

'Certainly not, my lord,' Mycroft assured him in his most honeyed tone. 'But you know better than any of us that Prince von Bismarck has publicly stated his belief in what he calls *realpolitik* and what we might call a Machiavellian approach to policy. Only one man had an opportunity to alter the wording of that telegram. When the King of Prussia went on holiday to Bad Ems he took with him a special messenger to act as *liaison* between himself and his Minister-president in Berlin. That man was C.P.E. Guttmann. It was C.P.E. Guttmann who undertook to despatch to Berlin His Majesty's pencilled reply to the French diplomatic note. It was C.P.E. Guttmann who, by the alteration and addition of a word or two, converted it from a dove of peace to an irrevocable *casus belli*.'

For a moment there was absolute silence in the huge

114

office. Then Lord Granville said, 'Damnable! Quite damnable! To think that two of the world's greatest powers could go to war because of the scribbling of some *valet de chambre*! Damn it, gentlemen, it's unthinkable! I won't believe it! That's it! I simply won't believe it!'

He slumped into silence once more. Then he began tapping the ormulu edge of the table in front of him with a pencil. Suddenly he barked a short laugh.

'Damn it, Holmes! You're a deuced clever fellow, and no mistake! But you're like all clever fellows – can't keep your ideas from running away with you, d'ye know what I mean? Good God, man! You'll be telling me next that your Guttmann fellow was responsible for the Charge of the Light Brigade!' He laughed harshly.

'I couldn't say that with any certainty, my lord,' Mycroft replied. 'I do know, however, that Guttmann was with the Prussian Military Attaché to the French Army, and that he was with General Bosquet's staff on the Sapoune Heights above Balaclava that afternoon.'

Mycroft and Sir James were walking across Horse Guards Parade towards the Mall and Carlton Terrace.

'Were you speaking the truth, just now, when you told "Pussy" Granville that Guttmann was at Balaclava?' asked Sir James.

'If he wasn't there, he should have been,' Mycroft replied. 'It was the sort of unholy mess in which he rejoices.'

'I thought as much. You have no business to be pulling the august leg of Her Majesty's Secretary of State for Foreign Affairs!'

'It is my business, for as long as people see fit to consult me, to warn Her Majesty's principal advisers of what I

115

conceive to be a very considerable threat to this realm.'

He stopped in the middle of the expanse of sanded empty space.

'Sir James,' he said with the utmost gravity at his command. 'There is nothing to be proven as yet. But there are questions – questions which strike me with fear. When M. Thiers and the French Government sued for peace last March, Prince von Bismarck ordered that the French army should be reduced to a mere thirty thousand men, with no artillery to speak of. The fortresses along the Franco-German border were, without exception, to be blown up and demolished. Four months later the French army stands at one hundred and seventy thousand battle-hardened veterans, many of them, including Marshals MacMahon and Gallifet, released from Prussian gaols, and more than two thousand modern guns . . .'

'Von Bismarck permitted the French army to reassemble in order to crush the rebellion in Paris,' Sir James pointed out. 'I don't suppose the rulers of the newly-founded German Empire were any more keen on seeing Communism triumph in Paris than were Thiers or Admiral Saisset.'

'That reassembled and reorganized army has not stood down, even though the rebellion in Paris has been utterly suppressed. It still has its two thousand guns. And the frontier fortress of Belfort still stands with its fortifications, its garrison, its guns all intact. No, Sir James! Von Bismarck has never been magnanimous in victory. He has always treated a defeated enemy with the petulant vindictiveness of the sufferer from dyspepsia which he is.'

'What you are saying, Holmes, is that the Germans must have exacted a price for allowing the French to retain its army intact.'

116

'Exactly, Sir James.'

'And what do you suppose this price to have been?'

'I don't know. Nobody knows save the High Contracting Parties. But I tell you this: a Frenchman having connections with the rulers of his country comes over here in the hope of informing "the highest in the land" of something which is "of the utmost importance" to this country, and promptly disappears. By some strange quirk of coincidence – or so you would like me to think – C.P.E. Guttmann is here the very day the man disappears. And seven weeks later, the very day after M. Thiers indicates his concern at the man's disappearance, C.P.E. Guttmann arrives here a second time.'

'In effect, you are saying that there is a secret protocol to the Franco-German treaty ending the war, which is inimical to our national interest.'

Mycroft flicked a fragment of gravel across the parade ground with the ferule of his stick.

'Sir James, I do not *know* anything – any more than you do. But if you do not dispute the data which I've put before you, what conclusion could you draw from it? Any investigation requires a hypothesis. Can you think of a better one?'

They began to walk again, slowly in the dusty heat.

'The problem, Holmes,' Sir James replied thoughtfully, 'is that the north Germans have always been our friends and allies – think of Blucher and the Iron Duke embracing at La Belle Alliance. Besides, there is no conceivable conflict of interest between our peoples. Prussia has always been a continental power, even at its most expansionist. Great Britain's destiny is imperial, dependent on our fleet. Prussia has never had a fleet worthy of the name. Britain has no conscript continental army.'

117

'Sir James, I have a favour to ask of you,' said Mycroft. 'I wish to take leave of absence from the Treasury in order to pursue a particular line of investigation.'

'For how long?' Sir James asked.

'For as long as may be necessary, of course.'

'My dear Holmes! That might turn out to be more a retirement than a furlough . . . A month, my dear fellow. Any longer and I would have trouble explaining your absence to the First Secretary.'

'Very well. I'll have to make do with a month.'

Mycroft was about to embrace the absolute calm of the Diogenes Club – in fact he had one foot actually on the step – when he was accosted by a young negro. At first he did not recognize him in his tartan suit and brown bowler hat.

'Begging your pardon, massa sir,' said the man.

Detecting the impudence in the voice, Mycroft chose to ignore him. He had reached the fourth step when he realized with some horror that the fellow was pursuing him, might indeed pursue him into the club itself.

'Bwana, sahib!' the creature said, behind him. 'If you don't mind. I got a message for you. From the Princess.'

Mycroft turned. The fellow grinned at him. 'Massa, sir?' he repeated, without the least hint of servility or even the common deference of a member of the servant class. Mycroft pointed his stick at the young man's stomach.

'The only reason I know positively that you did not steal these appalling traps you're wearing,' he said, 'is because an experienced criminal like yourself—'

'Oh, massa sir!' the young man interjected, his face a caricature of injured pride.

'– would not have forgotten to remove the tailor's card.' He flicked the label hanging from one of the sleeves with the end of his stick.

'The Princess bought 'em for me,' said the negro, ' 'cause she knows I'm down on my luck.'

'The Princess Trubetskoy bought those for you?' Mycroft asked incredulously.

'She give me the money, like.'

'You mean you stole it from her.'

'I did not! Wouldn't steal from her. She's a regular 'un, she is! She knows how to treat a feller as 'as fallen in his fortune, so as not to hurt his price.'

'Would it hurt your pride if I gave you shilling?'

'No. Not really.'

Mycroft took out his purse and handed a shilling piece to the young man.

'Now,' he said, 'what has the Princess asked you to tell me?'

'The personage you is h-interested in, like, took a first-class ticket from Waterloo Road Station to Dorking,' the negro told him.

'To Dorking!' Mycroft exclaimed.

The negro stared at him.

'Dorking. You are quite sure?'

'Sure as certain, massa boss!' said the negro.

Mycroft pointed his stick at him again.

'Enough of your impudence!' he said. 'Can you take a message to the Princess for me?'

'That's what ah is here for, massa,' sang the young man, waving the palms of his hands.

'Enough!' said Mycroft sharply, because he wanted to laugh at him. 'Tell the Princess that I am much obliged to her. Tell her that I will remain at my lodgings until eleven o'clock tomorrow morning. Tell her that she would oblige me further by calling on me. Be sure to tell her so.'

'You can count on me, boss!' sang the young man.

'Huh!' exclaimed Mycroft, disbelievingly. He changed his mind. 'No! No. I'm very grateful to you, fellow. Here's another shilling. G⟶ ⟶raight to the Princess . . . Dorking, of all places! It's hardly to be believed!'

He went on up the steps to be gathered into the palpable silence of the interior. After handing over his hat, gloves and stick, he went straight up to the library. Before entering, however, he signalled to one of the attendants and whispered to him, 'A large B and S if you please. And fetch me the most recent edition of Black's *Interesting Localities*, if you would be so good.'

Chapter Eleven

Abigail followed Mabel up the back stairs from the kitchens, then up a second flight. On the bare, uncarpeted landing where stood the huge black linen-presses, Mabel turned and started pushing Abby rudely, in the small of her back, until Abby stumbled out through the white-painted doorway on to the long bedroom landing.

'An' get on wi' it, will yer!' said Mabel, who was at least two years older than her, " 'cause if we ain't out of the bed-rooms 'fore the quality comes up from breakfast Mrs Armitage'll knock twopence off our wages, an' I'll give 'ee a black eye, so I will!'

Abby clutched at the slop bucket. It seemed enormous and had banged against her legs all the way up. The cloth, soap and hard brush kept slipping from under her other arm. She did not know what she would do when the bucket was full. The faded print gown and blue apron she had inherited from the between-maid whom she had replaced were too big for her; the toes of her boots kept being trapped in the hems so that she stumbled.

She had never been so wretched in all her life, she

decided – not even on the vary rare occasions when her father had taken a strap to her. Once upon a time she had harboured the idea of being in service at the Hall as a ladder by which she would climb to better things: she had dreamed of Mrs Jenks-Robinson recognizing a natural superiority in her pretty looks, her long yellow hair and her delicate air, and promoting her almost immediately to the rank of parlourmaid, and from thence to personal attendant with access to her mistress's cast-off but still fashionable dresses. Nothing now seemed further from possibility. Her own clothes had been taken from her by Mrs Armitage as soon as Mr Whettam had brought her over from the farm; the clothes she had been given proclaimed her a slattern regardless of how she might behave. Already, in the few hours she had been at the Hall, she had been cuffed by Mrs Peters, the plain-cook, for standing in the way, by one of the parlour-maids for daring to address her, and by Harry, the running-footman, because he happened to be passing her in the scullery passage. She wanted to cry and cry, not only from utter, hopeless misery but also from a burning sense of being subjected to lifelong punishment and degradation for something she had not done.

She set off down the bedroom passage, the bucket banging against her knees. She stopped at the first door, scratched at it as she had been instructed, listened and, on hearing nothing inside, went in. The room was empty and still, the expanse of bed between the gleaming brass bedstead rumpled and unmade. She had never been in a room so large – it was bigger even than the farmhouse kitchen. She stared at the intricate lace borders on the sheets and pillowcases and on the silken underclothes spread over the back of the settee – so different from the clumsy cotton lace her mother had taught her to stitch on her own calico undergarments. She went to the washstand and struggled to lift the heavy porcelain bowl to empty it into her bucket. It swayed in her arms, slopping soapy, dirty water on to the rug. When she had replaced the bowl she knelt down, trying to dry the rug first with her cloth and then with her apron. She went to the bedside cabinet and looked in. The chamberpot was empty.

She carried the slop-bucket out. Already it had begun to feel heavy. She scratched at the next door. Again, when she could hear nothing she opened the door and looked inside. It was little more than a cupboard, with two enamel baths, one on top of another, half a dozen chamberpots piled on top of one another and some rough shelves with Turkish towels stacked on them. She struggled over to the room on the opposite side of the passage. Again it was empty, with its wide bed lying half-stripped and unmade – a gentleman's bedroom, she noticed: a black evening-suit hung, severely pressed, on the stand in the sunlight glare of the open window, and there was a scented smell of shaving soap from the wash-stand such as she had never smelt in her parents' room.

She had emptied the wash-bowl, spilling only a little of the contents – she noticed the tiny fragments of beard in the grey, soapy water – and had just emptied the chamberpot and was wiping it dry, when the deepest, richest voice she had ever heard said in a heavy, strange accent, 'Good morning, little girl!'

She was shocked speechless. She had heard stories of bad gentlemen who waited in their rooms to catch maids at their work in the hope of making them do things with them. This one had just entered, and he was still in his shirt-sleeves. He was enormous: he stood on the further side of the bed, blocking out all sight of the door to the passage. The strange, blond straw-stubble hair on top of his heavy-jowled face, cropped to bristles like the badger-bristle on her father's hair-brush, almost touched the ceiling; the massive shoulders gleaming in the sun's rays suggested latent but cruel strength from which somebody like her could never escape; the watery grey-blue eyes which had caught her in their gaze and did not wander from her for even the fraction of a moment suggested profound intelligence, observation and calculation devoid of feeling.

Abby stood paralysed with terror, her hand still pressing the cleaning rag under the inside rim of the chamber-pot which she was holding in the lap of her apron, exactly as she had been cleaning it when he spoke. She wanted to tremble but could not, any more than she could have spoken or cried out. It was as if she were in the presence of some huge and terrible wild beast which, devoid of pity and therefore impervious to any pleading, was devoting its reason only to the method by which it might destroy and devour her.

She heard her own voice say in the cringing tone of any workhouse skivvy, 'Beg pardon, sir, I'm sure.'

Then, quite extraordinarily, the bestial, inhuman calculation in the watery eyes changed, even as she stared back at them into a wonderful, irradiating kindness which seemed to reach out to her to embrace her in its friendly warmth, so that dry-eyed terror might at any moment turn to tears.

'The fault is mine, little girl,' he said. 'I am – how do you say it? – one lazy devil!'

'Oh no, sir!' she protested in a whisper as hoarse as her mother's voice.

She bobbed a curtsey and managed to put the chamberpot back into the bedside cabinet.

The huge gentleman took a tweed Norfolk jacket off the back of a chair and drew it on over his great shoulders. She stood and watched him, still unable to move from the spot.

'I am late for breakfast,' he said. 'Such an important occasion, the English breakfast! Will your mistress forgive me? That is the question, yes?'

He adjusted the watch-chain in his waistcoat pocket. He looked at her again, as if recognizing something he had not recognized before. He smiled at her so warmly that she felt an irrational happiness stealing over her, as if all that had happened to her during the past day or so was no more than a bad dream.

'What a big bucket for so delicate a little girl!' he said. 'And such a pretty girl!'

It was the sort of thing a bad gentleman might say – she knew that very well. But she knew also, and with absolute certainty, that this gentleman was not bad; that he was simply being kind.

'A pretty little maiden like you', he said, 'should not be made to do such work. What is your name, if you please, young lady?'

'Abigail, if you please, sir.'

'Ah! The little girl who was brought here yesterday, from the farm?'

She wished she did not have to tell him. She desperately wished to retain his good opinion of her.

'The little girl who said she had seen a body in the woods?' he asked. 'In the Silent Pond?'

'Silent Pool, if you please, sir,' she corrected him.

'Of course! Of course!'

He was still smiling down at her from his towering height, holding her in the warmth of his kindness.

'I told the truth, sir!' she blurted out, unable to help herself. 'I bain't no fibber, sir!'

'*They* all say you were telling the lies, little Abigail,' he said quietly.

'I weren't!' she repeated. 'Bain't fair. What's happened an' all! Fayther giving me a right whipping, an' letting Mr Whettam bring me over here just like I were girl to one of my fayther's hired hands an' that.'

The gentleman sat down on the edge of the bed. Abby's mother had always told her that it was bad manners to sit on the edge of the bed. But she knew that this great big gentleman had done so so that he could be level with her as they spoke – another example of his understanding and kindness.

'They thought,' he said in his deep, rich, gentle voice, 'here is a little girl who likes story-books and poetry, yes?'

She nodded. 'S'pose so, if you please, sir,' she whispered.

'They thought, because she likes stories and poems, she is making up a story,' he suggested. 'That's what they thought.'

' 'Spect so, sir. Only I weren't never!'

'Shall I tell you something, little Abigail? I too like stories and poems. But there are so many people in the world who do not understand people like us. And they can be very unkind to us – like they are being unkind to you, now.'

He reached out and took one of her hands, holding it in his own great one.

'They think because we like stories,' he said to her, 'we

126

do not know what is true and what is not true. But we know better than they do!'

'Do we?' asked Abby, smiling at him through unshed tears.

'Oh yes, little Abigail! And I can prove it to you. I know that you have been telling the truth and that they are mistaken.'

He stared into her eyes, mesmerizing her. He nodded. 'Yes,' he repeated. 'You see? I understand.'

Abby said to him, 'If you please, sir. Will you say . . .?'

He shook his head and smiled sadly.

'No, little maiden. That is not possible. I cannot tell your master and mistress you have been telling the truth because they would only say, "There is that *Dummkopf* of a German again, with his *Dummkopf* notions!" That is a German word – *Dummkopf* – it means solid in the head, like wood, yes?'

He gave her hand the gentlest of squeezes.

'Poor little Abigail!' he said. 'It is very hard for you. But suppose Mr and Mrs Jenks-Robinson thought you had talked to me – a foreigner and a guest – about it. Would they not be very cross? Would they not think they must put you out before you tell other people about it? And would your father take you back if they put you out?'

He paused. Abby slowly shook her head.

'You would have to beg, little Abigail,' he told her. 'The world is not kind to little girl beggars – not at all kind . . . And now I must go downstairs because Mrs Jenks-Robinson will think I am still asleep, yes? And the kedgeree will be getting cold! What a strange English dish is kedgeree!'

He stood up once more. He put his hand lightly under her chin, tilting it upwards. He drew her faded mob from off her head.

'Ah! I knew! Lovely yellow hair! Just like one of our German maidens.'

'Mrs Armitage says I got to cut it off,' said Abby.

'Cut it off!' The gentleman sounded aghast. 'Such beautiful long yellow hair?'

'Mrs Armitage says it be too long to keep clean and tidy.'

'Little Abigail,' he stared down seriously at her. 'I cannot tell them that you have been speaking the truth. But I can speak to Mrs Jenks-Robinson and say it would be a sin for little Abigail to have to cut off her so-beautiful hair!'

'Oh would you, please sir?'

'Oh yes, little Abigail. I certainly will . . . And I will tell her that it is I who have been keeping you from your work just now, yes?'

'If you please, sir.'

'You and I are going to be friends. I alone know you have been telling the truth – that is a bond of friendship, is it not?'

'Oh yes, sir, thank you kindly, sir! Only, if you please, sir, you bain't the only un as knows I were a-telling the truth. There's Billy Lavendar.' She could not keep the bitterness out of her voice. 'It were Billy Lavendar what told me about the gentleman what was lying a-drownded in Silent Pool – or I wouldn't never have looked, and that's God's truth!'

For a moment she felt terrified once more. She was certain she had said the wrong thing. All the kindness in the gentleman's face had vanished in a moment, as if it had never been there. The watery blue eyes were filled with a vacant, bestial insensitivity. She heard his voice growl, 'Who is this . . . Billy Lavendar?'

She could hardly reply. She had to grate out the words, 'Me fayther's stable-hand, sir. On the farm.'

It had only been a moment. The kindness came flooding back over her. Perhaps it had only been her foolishness. Now the gentleman was smiling at her as before.

'And this fellow' – he pronounced 'fellow' in the strangest way, as if he were exaggerating an English accent – 'Billy Lavendar? Did he not say he had told you about the drowned man when your father punished you?'

Abby shook her head. 'He said he never told me nothin' of the kind,' she said indignantly.

'He is a very bad man, this Billy Lavendar,' said the gentleman. 'He should be punished, yes?'

Abby nodded. 'Shall we make sure that he *is* punished,' asked the gentleman. Abby nodded again. 'Severely punished?' asked the gentleman, Abby nodded even more emphatically. 'Would you like to *see* him punished?' asked the gentleman. 'Oh yes, sir,' Abby whispered, 'if you please, sir.' The gentleman put his great hand on her shoulder.

'You and I, little maiden, we shall be friends, as I have said. I know many people – important people. If you stay my friend and do what I ask, I shall look after you. Do you understand? I may not be able to say to Mr and Mrs Jenks-Robinson that you are a truthful young lady, but I can make sure you do not remain a – how do you call it? – slavey? for very long. Will you trust me, little Abigail?'

'Oh yes, sir! You bain't half a kind gentleman, and no mistake, sir!'

'We must all be kind to each other, mustn't we, little maiden? That is how we go to Heaven when we have . . . passed over – that is the English expression, yes? . . . like that poor gentleman . . .!'

He waved his hand toward the window and the general direction of Eldebury Woods.

Chapter Twelve

Mycroft was standing at his study window, looking down at the street and enjoying a sense of holiday at the sight of clerks and his fellow public servants hurrying up the pavement, their newspapers rolled under their arms, towards the War Office building. He bent over and drew up the sash, admitting the rumble of carriage wheels and the general clatter of traffic with the fresh morning sunlight. Behind him Mrs Turner, assisted by Maisie, the prematurely aged adolescent who was her general maid, was clearing the breakfast things from his table.

'Mr Holmes!' she protested.

Mrs Turner was not convinced by the new-fangled notion that open windows, even in summer, were an adjunct to health. Indeed, she adhered to the miasmatic theory of infection which taught that sickness – whether it be the common cold or cholera – was borne on the air in the form of an invisible cloud.

'My good woman,' Mycroft cut her objection short. 'The smell of Finnan haddock before a meal is a great appetizer, I'll not deny it. It is not so agreeable after the

131

meal, particularly to the person who has not had the pleasure of repasting on it.'

'What do you mean, Mr Holmes? You ate every scrap, as well as both poached eggs!'

'I was referring, of course, to my visitor,' Mycroft told her.

'Visitor, Mr Holmes!' exclaimed a shocked Mrs Turner. 'But Maisie hasn't dusted nor swept yet! And your bed's not made. I'll tell you, your staying at home this morning's put everything to sixes and sevens!'

'I think I can say that my visitor will not be seeing the state of my bedroom,' Mycroft replied. 'The rest will have to wait, I fear. The lady is already here.'

He backed into the shadow of the curtain.

'A lady visitor!' exclaimed Mrs Turner. 'At this hour? Whatever will the world come to?'

'A pretty pass if we do nothing to prevent it,' he replied. 'Be off with you, woman!' He saw the surly expression on Maisie's sallow features. 'And take your damsel with you,' he added. 'The lady is a princess – a real princess – so be on your best behaviour, mind.'

Mrs Turner gave him what she thought was an old-fashioned look. Maisie clicked her tongue in disapproval. Mycroft was too busy spying out of the window to pay attention to either of them.

Sophie Trubetskoy was stepping down from a four-wheeler on to the pavement immediately below. She was fashionably dressed in predominantly green silks and muslin with the fullness of her bustle skirts suspended from her forearm by a narrow, black, braided cord. She was wearing a small, flat, feathered hat in the sixteenth-century style, pinned at a debonaire tilt, and was carrying a parasol. The young negro had dropped down before her, but a blood whose features were hidden from Mycroft below the glossy brim of his tall, shiny hat had pushed him away in his enthusiasm to assist Sophie to dismount. Sophie accepted his arm with a dazzling smile and a charming murmur of thanks. When she was standing on terra firma the gentleman hesitated, still supporting her arm. Sophie smiled once more and removed her arm from his.

'Cyril?' she beckoned to the negro. The negro came forward again. The blood took a look at him, raised his hat to Sophie and strolled off at a smart pace in the direction of the War Office. Sophie hooked her parasol on to her wrist. She took money from her purse and gave it to the negro, then, leaving him to dismiss the cab, she stepped up to the front door.

As the sound of the doorbell rang through the house, Mycroft retreated into the room, picked his copy of *The Times* from the table, and sank into his armchair. He folded it over to the leading articles as the frou-frou of skirts came up the stairs to the landing, and settled himself to give every impression of a state of absorption in the events of the previous day. He allowed the study door to fully open before he pulled himself to his feet.

'My dear Princess! I did not mean to put you to the inconvenience of—' He broke off. 'Why! You look quite lovely this morning!'

It was obvious that Mrs Turner, who was on the landing behind her, had not recognized Sophie in woman's clothes.

'Thank you, Mrs Turner!' he called.

He folded the newspaper and closed the study door.

'Of course you meant it, Mr Holmes,' said Sophie. 'You enjoy conveying a sense of urgency. You may pretend to

133

be lethargic – so English. But you enjoy excitement like you enjoy nicotine.'

'Aha, Princess!' He wagged his finger at her. 'You've caught me out! We Holmeses have French blood in our veins. Worse! The blood of French artists! My great-grandfather was Carle Vernet, the friend and contemporary of the great David. My grandmother was sister to Horace Vernet, who shared a studio with Delacroix. It has left me with the strong conviction that miscegenation is something which should be guarded against. It can result in a man's blood and thus his entire emotional character being at odds with the society in which he lives. I see its manifestation all too clearly in the behaviour of my poor younger brother, Sherlock – whose guardian I am. I have frequently attempted to warn him, to explain that he should not place himself in situations which may prove overstimulating to the nervous system . . .'

'You do not avoid such situations, Mr Holmes,' said Sophie.

He motioned her to a chair at the table.

'I am called, on occasion, to place myself in such situations for my country's sake. One cannot turn one's back on one's patriotic duty, you know?'

'Why did you send for me to come here this morning, Mr Holmes?'

'I was not so rude as to *send* for you, I hope!'

Sophie gave a slight shrug.

'Send. Request. What is the difference? Was it my message to you?'

'Most certainly.'

'Before you explain, I must tell you that there is something else you should know – about your Mme Tirard. I

134

sent a telegraph to my friend Pauline Garcia-Viardot in Paris; I received her reply this morning. She says that Pierre Tirard who was Mayor of the *Deuxième Arrondissement* was *un mari complaisant*. He was notorious for it. And Mme Tirard enjoyed a wide circle of gentlemen acquaintances. Your M. Thibault may have been one of them, but her particular friend was the gallant Admiral Saisset.'

'Admiral Saisset! I told them that in coming here she was acting as an agent for somebody else! Oho! The game really is afoot, and no mistake! Admiral Saisset's mistress – if you'll excuse the expression! Princess! We are playing for high stakes. None higher, if my hypothesis proves correct. And our opponent is the Prince of Contrivances, the modern Machiavelli, the Arch Anarch in person, Carl Philipp Emmanuel Guttmann! Will you join me in the game? I have a month's leave of absence from my official employment to devote myself to bringing it to a successful finish.'

'I will join you on one condition, Mr Holmes,' Sophie replied.

'And what would that be?'

'That you treat me as an equal partner, whatever befalls.'

'Princess, you are a young lady, little more than a girl! C.P.E. Guttmann is the most ruthless of antagonists, as you well know.'

'I am by birth, Mr Holmes, a Siberian she-wolf. Not one of your grey English mouses – mice! Don't you know that by now?'

'Would Herr Guttmann known you if he caught sight of you?' asked Mycroft.

'He was there when I was presented to Prince von

Bismarck in St Petersburg. But I was only eight years old.'

'And though we were in Florence at the same time for a few days in the summer of 1869, I have no reason to suppose he would recognize me. That is one advantage . . . Do you know, Princess? I think our next move should be to employ your man downstairs in keeping an eye on Mme Tirard. Does he still have the following of infant criminality you told me of?'

'I think so.'

'Then let us employ them. Let us ensure their devotion by rewarding them with more than they could expect to gain by stealing. Let them keep watch over Mme Tirard's every move. Let them never lose sight of Kendall's Hotel, or of her if she moves out of it. And let us see whether she and Guttmann meet one another.'

'And what are we going to do, Mr Holmes?'

'If you are prepared to endure the rigours of a railway journey, you shall travel with me on the next Basingstoke train from Waterloo Road. We shall alight at Egham. There is a gentleman presently residing on Cooper's Hill, above Egham, who may be able to cast some light on the question of why Guttmann should have twice visited the same region of Surrey this summer. He may even be able to direct us towards the reason our M. Thibault had to be silenced.'

'I am not easily fatigued, Mr Holmes, I do assure you.'

'Of course you are not, Princess! The young have an enviable surplus of energy – I see it in my brother, Sherlock. He is always doing!'

'Then you must not be concerned on my behalf,' Sophie told him.

She rose to her feet and hitched the cord holding the fullness of her skirts up her sleeve.

'We are a partnership, Mr Holmes. My inexhaustible youth, your dazzling intelligence. It is you whom we must not allow to fatigue yourself!'

Mycroft gave her a look of utmost gratitude.

'Bless you, dear Princess!' he said with absolute sincerity.

Chapter Thirteen

Billy Lavendar never was able to understand what happened to him that fine, sunny forenoon. Perhaps if he and Liza Makepeace up at the Hall had been scholars, and she had been able to send a letter in writing to him directly, nobody would have made any mistakes. But they weren't; and so it was Mabel who came creeping round the back of the stable when Mrs Rodgers wasn't looking, to whisper the message through the broken window.

The message was that Jemima Whettam, who kept house for Mr Whettam, her father, above the coach-house at the Hall, had sent to Mabel at the farm a written piece of paper saying that Liza Makepeace wanted Billy to meet her in Eldebury Woods, in the Dell, most importantly, before the town-hall clock in Abinger struck noon. The importance of the message was made clear by Jemima's instruction that Mabel should burn the piece of paper as soon as she had read the contents; Mabel was of the opinion, so she told Billy, that it was because Mr Whettam would get into one of his terrible bates with

Jemima if ever he found she had been acting as messenger between one of the domestics at the Hall and a common labouring man.

Billy Lavendar was excited and disturbed as never before in his harsh but uneventful short life. He never saw Liza Makepeace except on Sunday, at church, and once a month when he went with Mr Rodgers to the market in Dorking. They had never exchanged more than a few words and once, after a few jugs of ale and some dancing in the coach-yard of the Bear, two clumsy kisses, one from him to her and one – miracle of miracles! – from her to him.

The physical image of Liza was with him always. There was the full, rounded ripeness of her breasts, which he longed to feel and to polish by stroking, as if they were two great apples. There was the way her backside moved when she walked, swinging the strings of her apron to and fro. All too often he went to his straw bed in the stable loft to the thought of Liza Makepeace. He couldn't imagine why she should want him to meet her most importantly in Eldebury Woods. There were possibilities, of course. Perhaps somebody was giving her grief of some sort and she needed a champion to stand up for her. Perhaps she had got herself into trouble with her master and mistress and was faced with having to apply to the union-board for relief – he knew that bunch of stony-faced beaks only too well. Perhaps – but was it really possible? – she felt about him the way he felt about her, and couldn't wait for him to pull her down into the leaves . . .

Now the yard was empty, and the clanking of pails from the dairy told that Mrs Rodgers and Mabel were fully occupied. Billy had been greasing the hubs of the

139

big wain, which meant removing the heavy, iron-rimmed wheels from the wooden axles. He would be forgiven if he said he had to go down to the smithy in the village to borrow a crow. He set off, following the same track as that taken previously by Abigail. Like her, he went through the ancient, overgrown churchyard and over the broken wall into the woods.

The woods were warm and silent. The dell was the steeply banked valley, just wide enough for a small cart, which ended on the ferny bank of Silent Pool. He had been a fool to let that Abby know he had seen the drowned man; he had only done it because of the way she had provoked him with her missy, stuck-up ways. It was the first rule you ever should learn – never tell anybody anything which might bring you trouble and grief. Let the dead look after the dead: he had heard it read from the great Bible in the church, and he didn't suppose it contained a wiser piece of advice than that. Anyway, it was clear from the trouble Abby had got herself into that somebody had taken the body out of Silent Pool, so there wasn't anything to worry about any more.

He was deep in the woods, more than halfway along the dell toward Silent Pool, when he heard the voice calling – a sweet-sounding, woman's voice, it was. It came from behind him, a little way above. He turned to search. 'Billee!' it called most musically. 'Billee Lavendar!' It transformed his very own name – the invention of some poor-law matron who had remained unknown to him – into music. The briars and undergrowth were thick all about him; they concealed the origin of the voice.

'Liza Makepeace?' he shouted back.

'Billee Lavendar?' sang the voice, filling him with a

happiness he would not have thought himself capable of containing.

The voice had moved in the long grasses and briars. It was closer.

'Billee Lavendar?'

He turned again in the enchantment.

'Liza Makepeace! Don't you josh me, mind!' he called, but with no animosity in the world.

For one moment he thought he caught a glimpse through the bushes of Abigail Rodgers, her long tresses flying like those of a wood-sprite.

Then, suddenly, he heard the clatter of a cart and the heavy drumming of hooves on the dry, compacted earth floor of the dell. It was almost upon him, the wagonette from the hall. There was Mr Whettam crouched over the reins, whipping the horse savagely, staring demonically, his lips sucked in to a thread; and the horse itself, its mane flying, its nostrils flared and dropping white foam, its albumen eyeballs starting from their sockets.

Even before he was struck down by the horse, Billy began wondering why? Mr Whettam was an angry man, but it wasn't Jemima Billy was after. Being after Liza Makepeace – even having wicked thoughts about her – wasn't a killing matter. She had been a workhouse brat like himself . . . He fell, and the iron-shod hoof burst him into a pit of fire and darkness. Almost instantly, and mercifully, the wheel went over him. He felt and heard the crack of his spine, and all pain ceased. The dell became a tunnel of light filled with music, with voices calling him, one over another, a crowd of shining ones all calling on him to join them – unbelievably, *wanting* him to join them . . .

Chapter Fourteen

'The sky is getting hazy,' said Mycroft.

They were alone in the velvet-upholstered first-class compartment. Mycroft had been staring up out of the window, above the steam from the engine which billowed into the hedgerow. Sophie had just emerged from the *en suite* closet attached to the compartment.

'There'll be thunder before nightfall,' he continued. 'I fear we should have remained at home.'

Sophie adjusted her skirts and sat down.

'Who is this man you are taking me to meet?' she asked, refusing to indulge him in his lesser anxieties.

'Colonel Sir George Chesney? One of the most perceptive intelligences in the British Army – one of the *few* perceptive intelligences in the British Army. Which is, presumably, why he has been retired from active service. The War Office does not approve of intelligent serving officers; they ask questions, you know? He is the only man I know who, if we give him the data we have now assembled, might assist me constructively in my cerebrations.'

'He must be an extraordinary fellow!' said Sophie.

Mycroft gave her a very quick glance, but she did not appear to be smiling.

'He dared to suggest publicly that we were attempting to protect the greatest empire the world has ever seen with a fleet which is largely obsolete and an army smaller than that of many second-rate powers. It was regarded by his masters as little short of mutiny. Increased expenditure on defence means higher taxes. The result was that Sir George Chesney, a soldier of proven courage and resource, was stripped of his regiment and sent to take command of a college for civil engineers. There, I suppose, he may use his brain without disturbing the dust gathering in the War Office.'

They got down at Egham and procured a pony and trap, the only equipage available at the railway station, to take them to the Indian Civil Engineering College on Cooper's Hill. They left the bustle of Egham High Street by Egham Hill and turned up Cooper's Lane, following a long high wall enclosing parkland. As they reached the top they could hear the sound of a bat striking a ball, and a ripple of genteel applause. Mycroft tapped the shoulder of their driver and asked him to pull up. He pointed to the meadowland and trees below them in the increasingly diffused sunlight.

'There you have it, Princess,' he said. 'Everything a man like Sir George would like to see strongly defended.' He pointed to the instantly recognizable mass of Windsor Castle, dominated by the Round Tower. 'It's the true heart of England down there: the monarchy under which we live in a peace and stability denied to other nations . . . And here, on the other side of that narrow lake, do you see? Runnymede, where King John was

143

compelled to sign the Magna Carta. There is the cradle of our English liberty! You have the memory of a beloved sister to fight for. This is what inspires me for the fray. And there is a storm coming up, wouldn't you say, fellow?' he asked the driver.

'Oh aye, sir! There'll be rain afore nightfall, sure enough,' the man replied.

They drove round into an ornamental gateway and up a long avenue until they reached the front of a large country house built in the perpendicular gothic style favoured by A.W. Pugin and his disciples. A turbaned syce came down the steps to greet them. He told Mycroft that the Colonel Sahib was down on the fields playing cricket. Mycroft ordered the driver of the trap to remain and asked the syce to take him round to the kitchens until they were ready to return to Egham. Offering his arm to Sophie, who opened her little parasol and rested it on her shoulder, he led her down several terraced gardens to the fields.

Sir George Chesney was seated on a folding garden chair near the pavilion, with his students, predominately English but with a sprinkling of Indians among them, squatting on the grass around him watching the game. He was a heavily built, broad-shouldered forty-year-old with a weathered face, shrewd eyes and fierce whiskers. His white ducks were rumpled about the knees and calves from the cricket pads which now lay in the grass beside his chair. There was a small yellow and black cricket cap with a tassel perched ludicrously on top of his freckled bald head.

'Holmes! My dear boy!' he exclaimed. 'How did you summon up the determination to journey so far from Town?'

He noticed Sophie and rose to his feet, scrabbling his cap from his head as he did so.

'My dear young lady! Pray forgive me!'

'This is the Princess Sofya Trubetskoy, Sir George,' said Mycroft.

'It is, by God! . . . I beg your pardon again, my dear – er – Princess,' said Sir George. 'One doesn't expect to see young Holmes in the company of attractive members of the gentler sex, don't you know?'

Mycroft cleared his throat and looked embarrassed.

'Princess Sofya Trubetskoy, eh?' Sir George continued. 'There was a Prince Trubetskoy in the Crimea, I recall . . .' He turned to Mycroft. 'Commanded the Russkies' *Corps d'Elite* against Scarlett and the Heavy Brigade at Balaclava. Devilish handsome fellow, he was – and a damned fine horseman . . .' He turned back to Sophie. 'But then all you Russkies are born in the saddle, ain't you?'

'He was my uncle, Sir George,' Sophie told him.

'Was he, by God! He was a good soldier, I'll give him that. Damn' near did for Scarlett's lads that morning! You know, Princess? You Trubetskoys must be a damned handsome family!'

'Thank you, Sir George,' said Sophie.

'Had your innings, eh, Sir George?' Mycroft intervened.

'Eh? What's that? Out for a duck, of course . . . Oh, well played, sir!'

A ball came careering towards the boundary some ten or fifteen yards away. A young Indian in a turban retrieved it from the long grass and threw it with an easy grace back to the wicket.

'Damn' good shot, sir! Sir George called across to the

batsman. 'The College – Eton, you know,' – he explained to Sophie and Mycroft – 'sends us a scratch eleven now and then, to give us a game. Whip the breeches off us every time, of course.'

'We came to consult you, Sir George – on a matter which may prove to be of some urgency.'

'What! Both of you?' Sir George smiled at Sophie.

'We are both deeply concerned with the matter,' Sophie replied.

'Sir George.' Mycroft lowered his voice. 'Certain important persons in Her Majesty's Government have asked me to undertake an investigation into what we have discovered to be a case of abduction. I believe that you are uniquely qualified to cast some light on one particular aspect of it.'

'Really, dear boy? And does the War House know you've come here to consult me?'

'Certainly not, Sir George!'

Mycroft glanced about him, his florid features creased with anxiety.

'Better go up to the house, eh?' Sir George suggested.

'Can you leave the field with honour?' Sophie asked.

'Dear young lady! Venables here will be delighted to see the back of me . . . Venables? The honour of the Indian service is in your hands!'

A moustached young man sprawling in the grass, a cigarette between his fingers, waved acknowledgement.

'Very good, sir!'

'Not that there's much honour to be had in this service, don't you know?' said Sir George, as they turned their backs on the game. 'These young empire-builders will all be dead of typhoid and dysentery before they've reached my age!'

'Nobody knows we've come here,' said Mycroft. 'Neither your masters nor mine. They'd regard it as a colloquy of Cassandras.'

'Gad, Holmes! You've a deuced clever way with words, I'll give you that! A colloquy of Cassandras. I'll have to remember that!'

Sophie gave the open parasol resting on her shoulder a whirl.

'Do you have your home here in England, Princess?' asked Sir George.

'Oh no. If I have a home, it is in Nice with my mother. My father is dead, and my mother is French, so she has returned home.'

'I've heard that now Nice is become part of France it has also become very fashionable.'

'That is probably because my mother has taken up residence there,' Sophie replied.

They walked across the gravel paths at the top of the garden terraces.

'We'll go through the side door,' said Sir George. 'It will take us straight to my office.'

The slope from the playing-fields had taken its toll of Mycroft. He was panting for breath and mopping his brow some distance behind Sir George and Sophie. They waited for him to catch up. The air was close; beyond Windsor the sky had grown heavy with cloud. Sir George led them through to his office; above his table-top desk hung a Winterhalter portrait of the Queen; on the panels of the wall were framed plans and elevations of railway suspension bridges over hatching to indicate ravines and chasms. Sir George went straight over to the the decanters standing on a tray under the stuffed head of a wild boar.

147

'Fine old tusker, eh, Princess? Took him when I was up in Simla. Jolly proud of him.'

Mycroft flopped down on to an upholstered Windsor chair.

'Question of Defence of the Realm, is it?' asked Sir George. Without waiting for an answer, he asked, 'Glass of Amontillado, Princess? or Madeira, perhaps?'

'Amontillado will suit me very well, Sir George.'

'Brandy and seltzer, Holmes?'

'Obliged to you,' Mycroft replied. 'Perhaps a question of the Defence of the Realm. We can't be certain. But what you tell me this afternoon may make it more, or perhaps less, so.'

Sir George poured out the drinks.

'So who was abducted?' he asked.

'Seven – nearly eight – weeks ago,' Mycroft began, 'a prosperous silk manufacturer from Lyon, a M. Jean-Christophe Thibault, disembarked at Folkestone from the night steam-packet out of Boulogne. By letter, he had informed an English acquaintance that he had information of the utmost importance which he wished to communicate to somebody in this country who was, in his own words, "one of the highest in the land". He was met by two men who said they were police officers from Scotland Yard who, we have since discovered, gave false names. M. Thibault has not been seen since.'

'Abducted in order to silence him,' Sir George confirmed.

He handed the glasses to Sophie and Mycroft.

'Good health!' he said, raising his own brandy glass. 'Good hunting! . . . Murdered, do you suppose?' He glanced in Sophie's direction. 'My dear! I'm so sorry!'

'Not at all, Sir George,' she replied. 'Mr Holmes will

148

tell you that I am not of a particularly nervous disposition.'

Mycroft nodded. 'We cannot of course rule out such a possibility,' he said.

'And was he a politician?' asked Sir George. 'For want of a better word.'

'He may have become one,' Mycroft replied. 'He was connected with politicians. He himself was distantly related to the French Prime Minister through marriage. In fact, only last week M. Thiers communicated with "Pussy" Granville, informally soliciting his support in searching for M. Thibault's whereabouts. That is why my services have been enlisted.'

'This M. Thibault was not the French Prime Minister's unofficial envoy, by any chance?' asked Sir George.

'By no means,' Mycroft replied. 'M. Thiers does not appear to have known that he had disappeared until last week.'

'So that the information M. Thibault came here to communicate could have been a French government secret?' Sir George asked. 'I mean *could* have been.'

'Quite so. Particularly since it would appear that he may have shared a mistress with no less a personage than the hero of the Paris siege, Admiral Saisset. Incidentally, the lady has arrived in London to seek out her missing lover, furnished with a *laissez-passer* issued and signed by the bold Admiral.'

'Phew!' Sir George whistled between his teeth. 'So this lady, rather than your Lyon silk manufacturer, is likely to be an agent of the French Government.'

'Exactly. But the plot thickens further. The Princess here has her own reasons for her interest in a certain Mr C.P.E. Guttmann . . .'

149

'A German gentleman?' asked Sir George.

'Not a gentleman!' said Sophie. 'A creature!'

'A Prussian creature,' Mycroft confirmed. 'The Princess was able to tell me that this Guttmann fellow was in England on the day Thibault was abducted. She has also discovered that he returned on the same day and on the same boat as the French lady.'

'And he is an agent – for the Imperial German Government, as we must now call it?'

'Certainly for Prince von Bismarck,' said Mycroft. 'Nor is he one of your ordinary bloodhounds. He's the best of the breed. He served von Bismarck even before he became Prussian Minister-president – as his confidential servant, his secretary, his spy, perhaps even as his assassin. Guttmann knows no law, no scruples, save the interests of his master and therefore the advancement of the Prussian State. In the words of our national poet, he could "put the murderous Machiavel to school". He performs those deeds – those extensions of diplomacy – to which von Bismarck would not wish to attach his name . . . Do you, by any chance, have a cigar?'

'Of course, my dear boy,' Sir George replied. 'But the Princess . . .?'

'If you please, Sir George,' Sophie said, 'don't refrain from tobacco on my account.'

'You are most indulgent, Princess. Thank you,' said Sir George.

He produced a silver cigar box. Mycroft appeared too deep in his own thoughts to be capable of thanking either Sophie or his host. Nevertheless, he drew on his cigar, once lit, with every sign of deep satisfaction.

'The Princess,' he said, '– and this is the part of the plot which should most attract your interest – has pointed out to me that on the first occasion – the day of our Frenchman's disappearance – Guttmann was seen in Godalming, shopping for gloves in the High Street and giving every indication of displeasure at having been recognized. On the second occasion – last Saturday – when he had arrived at Charing Cross railway station off the boat-train, he went straight to the Waterloo Road railway terminus and there booked a first-class ticket to Dorking.'

The room had grown darker. Outside, a wind had blown up and was scurrying the trees and bushes of the gardens.

'Last night, when I returned to my club, I consulted Black's invaluable *Guide to Roads, Railways and Interesting Localities*.'

'And what did you find there?' asked Sir George.

'I found a place called Ranmore Hall.'

'Fine old place,' said Sir George. 'I know it well – or I did know it before it passed into the hands of its present owner. It stands on the heights above Ranmore Common; it overlooks Box Hill across the Dorking Gap. I beg your pardon. Pray, do proceed, Holmes.'

'Its present owner—'

'Is a bounder, they say,' Sir George interrupted. 'A Johnny-come-lately . . . I'm sorry.'

'– Mr Cuthbert Jenks-Robinson,' said Mycroft. 'He's a tradesman, a Welsh coal-master who, by marrying the inheritrix of a heavily encumbered country estate, has elevated himself into the propertied classes . . . That, of course, while it may be deplorable, is not actually criminal. But this man's fortune derives from selling best-quality anthracite to Prussia. Welsh anthracite sells like gold-dust in the western provinces of the new German

151

Empire, don't you know? The guns which destroyed the French Imperial Cavalry at Sedan and battered down the ramparts of Paris were forged in Welsh anthracite. Jenks-Robinson has prospered mightily as a result of von Bismarck's continental wars.'

'War with Denmark over Schleswig-Holstein, war with Austria, war with France,' said Sir George. 'Where next?'

The three of them sat in silence. Outside there was a clap and a roll of thunder. As the rain began to fall, the cricketers ran past the window clutching bats, pads and gloves under their arms and shouting to each other as they went by.

'A secret protocol to the treaty of peace between France and Germany,' said Mycroft. 'That is my hypothesis. The price exacted by Bismarck for allowing the Versailles Government to re-mobilize its armies. And M. Thibault, who is that rarest of commodities, a genuinely Anglophile Frenchman, came here to warn Her Majesty's Government of its contents. Godalming and Dorking, Sir George. Does that mean something to you?'

Sir George nodded. 'A hypothesis to add to the hypothesis. But let us take our glasses and our cigars to my little map-room. Shall you come with us, Princess?'

'Of course I shall,' Sophie replied.

Chapter Fifteen

Sir George led them to a small door behind his table-top desk, under the portrait of the Queen. There was another more violent clap and roll of thunder. A few seconds later a lightning flash filled the room with a momentary white light.

'We have prepared maps', Sir George told them, 'of various localities hereabouts. We have photographed them on to glass plates. It is a device of my own,' he added with modest pride. 'By employing an infernal machine similar to the magic lantern one can throw a greatly enlarged image on to a white screen. This greatly assists in any examination of the features of the ground. The technique is intended to help in the preparation of engineering projects, but it is capable of other uses . . .'

He opened the door and let them in.

'Wait here until I've lit the gas,' he told them. From inside the blackness of the room he called, 'This must all seem very dry stuff to you, Princess.'

'Not at all, Sir George,' she called back.

Sir George lit the gas-mantle. The light crept up,

153

revealing the cupboards, lockers and map-rolls. Sophie and Mycroft went in. At the end of the classroom rows of tables and drawing-boards was suspended a large white sheet.

'There is nothing "dry", as you call it, about opposing the forces of evil,' Sophie told him.

'No. Of course not, Princess.' Sir George accepted the rebuke with courteous humility.

He lit the big lantern-projector as they sat down at the tables in front of him. A huge white disc of light shone on the sheet in front of them. The thunder rumbled distantly – the room was windowless.

'It feels very safe in here,' remarked Sophie.

'I'm sure we have a map-plate of the Guildford and Dorking districts,' Sir George said, fumbling in a locker-drawer. 'I have to admit, usually I leave this sort of how-de-do to others . . . Ah! Here we are.'

He turned down the gas-mantle. The disc of light on the sheet in front of them became a huge rectangular map. A ridge, its contours heavily shaded, bisected it horizontally, straight as a rule, from the distinctly drawn houses and streets of Farnham to those of Reigate.

Sir George went to the front. He held a pointer in his hand.

'The old Pilgrims' Way,' he indicated tapping the ridge, with his pointer. 'The Hog's Back – like a Great Wall of China, eh? Every military strategist knows that it is London's second line of defence after the Channel. Even William the Conqueror was forced to march round its western flank, to advance on London from the north. Today, of course, if a modern invader were to do that, what with the railway and the telegraph, it would be wasting valuable time. It would simply leave our leaders with a day or two's grace to muster men and *matériel* to resist them. To the east, where the ridge dips toward Canterbury, here, we have Ashdown Forest and the Medway Estuary to hold up any rapid advance.

'There is only one gateway through this natural barrier. It lies directly between the open beaches of east Kent and Sussex and the Mall and Buck House. Here!' He laid his pointer on the one clearly visible breach in the fiercely shaded ridge. It lay in the dead centre of the map.

'Dorking Gap,' he said. 'If ever there was a sudden invasion of this country – to take us by surprise – it would consist of a landing at Pevensey or Little Hampton, followed by forced marches through the Dorking Gap to London. Within two days the enemy would be occupying Whitehall and the Palace. If they were unopposed, dragoons and light infantry – and Uhlans, of course – could cover twenty-six, twenty-seven miles a day without difficulty.'

'Why should this – invasion? – be unopposed?' Sophie asked.

'Your friend Mr Holmes knows, don't you, my boy?'

'We have some seventy-nine thousand trained men serving with the colours,' said Mycroft. 'Most of them are in India, Gibraltar, the West Indies, Ireland. There are about three hundred immediately available for the defence of London – the guardsmen on ceremonial duties at the palaces, the Bank of England, the Tower and Windsor Castle.'

'Don't you have your Royal Navy?' asked Sophie.

'Indeed we do,' Sir George replied. 'But it is protecting our navigational paths to the China Seas, India and the eastern Mediterranean. We have no ships in the

155

Channel – and we have no iron-clad men-o'-war any-where. The only chance we could have against a surprise landing from across the Channel would be for us to rush to Dorking Gap here as many guardsmen, guns from the Tower and gentlemen and farmers and gamekeepers – men who can ride fast and shoot straight – as we could gather together in one day; to hold it until we could summon up a *levée en masse* as the French did after Paris came under siege. You see, a successful invasion would have to consist of a small advance force – one easily shipped and supplied. To the invader, time would be the decisive factor. He would need to advance on London with great speed and seize the government offices, the Palace and the person of the Monarch, the great railway termini and St Martin-le-Grand and the central tele-graph offices. If his progress on London was obstructed, even for a day or two, he would have little chance of success. He would find himself outnumbered and, with the arrival of our ships in the Channel, he would lose his lines of supply and communication.'

Mycroft emitted a heavy groan, as if stirring himself out of sleep. 'Let me see.' He pulled himself up into an erect position on his chair. 'If our . . . hypothetical . . . enemy wanted to make sure of success in penetrating the heart of England – the Palace, Whitehall, the Tower, let us say – the best thing for him to do would be for him to ensure that Dorking Gap could not be defended.'

'Exactly so,' Sir George agreed. 'If the element of surprise were so complete that the invader could send ahead a troop of light dragoons with a few trained sharpshooters or, even better, a screw-gun or two, to take up position on the heights on either side of the gap, it would be sufficient to hinder the proper disposition of our people in order to oppose his passage.'

'Or if a small detachment of determined, skilled marksmen were already *in situ* when the landing took place at Pevensey or Little Hampton . . .?' suggested Mycroft.

'Even better, of course, from the invader's point of view,' said Sir George.

'Is Ranmore Hall marked on your map?' Mycroft asked.

Sir George leaned over and scanned the Dorking district, his shadow blotting out half the rectangle of light. There was a muffled roll of thunder from outside.

'Here we are!' He moved back. Only his pointer formed a line to the summit of the shading to the left of Dorking Gap. 'As your edition of Black's *Guide* remarked: "standing on the heights overlooking Dorking Gap." '

'A handful of riflemen with telescopic sights?' suggested Mycroft. 'Perhaps a screw-gun with an experienced team . . .?'

'At Ranmore Hall, do you mean?' asked Sir George. 'Very probably they could prevent the establishment of a proper defence of the Gap for some hours. Even the lightest of artillery could sweep Box Hill and the ground between the ridges. The Reigate to Guildford railway line lies within gunshot range of the Hall; they could prevent the disembarkation of troops brought by train from London or Windsor. It would be the classic forlorn hope, of course. Our people – even the small force immediately available to us – would destroy them. But if they were desperate enough they could hold out long enough to be reinforced by a flying column of light dragoons. The end result would prove fatal to us.'

'The thought of squadrons of Uhlans riding up the Mall, just as they rode up the Champs Elysées!' Mycroft shuddered. 'Unbelievable! Can you believe it, Princess? Can you think the unthinkable?'

'Very easily, Mr Holmes. If the French Imperial Guard could leave Holy Moscow a burned-out shell and a British army could sack the Red Fort of the Mogul emperors, why should the thought of Uhlans riding up to Buckingham Palace be so unimaginable?'

'Because, my dear, it is something quite, quite different,' Mycroft replied in lofty disdain. 'It is against nature' – he paused – 'like blasphemy, don't you know?'

'Why?' Sophie demanded. 'Because you have a sea between you and the rest of the world? You English are all so certain you live in a "sceptred isle, a moated Paradise", your Admiralty doesn't even bother to keep a fleet in your precious Channel.'

'Well said, Princess!' Sir George exclaimed. 'On the other hand, I suspect that, for all his bluster, Mr Holmes has come here with you precisely because he believes it is all too possible.'

'Against nature and the will of Divine Providence, maybe,' said Mycroft. 'But possible, alas!'

'And we mustn't let the will of Divine Providence be thwarted, must we?' said Sophie. 'Do you suppose Herr Guttmann is staying at Ranmore Hall with this Welsh coalman—'

'Merchant – not coal *man*,' Mycroft told her.

'– Welsh coal *merchant*,' Sophie continued, 'who sells coal to the Prussians?'

'If he is,' suggested Sir George, 'might he not simply be negotiating for further supplies of Welsh anthracite to be sent to Prussian factories?'

'No!'

'Certainly not!'

Sophie and Mycroft spoke at the same moment, taking both themselves and Sir George by surprise.

'Why this complete agreement between you?' Sir George asked. He turned up the gaslight once more and blew out the flame in the lantern.

'Because . . . You tell him, Princess,' Mycroft said.

Sophie looked at him, suspecting that he was trying her.

'Because, Sir George,' she replied, 'Prince von Bismarck would not send Herr Guttmann if he wanted something as honest and as . . .' She glanced to Mycroft for help.

'Straightforward?' Mycroft suggested.

'Quite . . . very stupid of me . . . As straightforward as buying coal for German factories. Herr Guttmann is evil, Sir George. He only does evil things. I think von Bismarck keeps him in a cage and only lets him out when there is something wicked to be done.'

Sir George laughed. 'Really, Princess! That's taking things a little too far. Don't you think so, Holmes? After all, Prince von Bismarck is the political servant of a Christian King-emperor just like our own Sovereign Queen.'

'There are some servants', said Mycroft, 'who have a will of their own . . . Sir George, as you suspected might happen, your hypothesis has reinforced my own – and my worst – fears. We must return to Town immediately. Princess, are you prepared to face the elements and drive back with me to the railway station?'

'Of course, Mr Holmes.'

'But, Holmes,' Sir George protested, 'there's a storm

outside. You can't return to Egham until it has passed. Not when you are escorting a lady!'

'I believe we have very little time, Sir George,' Mycroft replied. 'I detest unnecessary haste above all things, as you know. But I believe the times are laying hard conditions upon us and that we must act as quickly as possible.'

They were driving back down Cooper's Hill in the premature twilight caused by the storm. The thunder had passed over them; it rumbled fitfully in the distance. Occasional flashes of sheet lightning glimmered over the downland. The rain, however, had not stopped. It was lashing down, beating on the tarpaulin covers of the trap and splashing into the rivulets which dribbled down the muddy surface of the road. They had almost reached the turning on to Egham Hill when one wheel of the trap lurched into a deep rut. It stuck; the horse, jerked back in the shafts, lost its footing and fell, its hooves clattering and skidding on the road. One of the shafts snapped. The horse regained its footing but the shaft hung uselessly and the trap stood tilted at a violent angle. The driver jumped down and went to the horse's head to calm it. Sophie followed, heedless of getting boots and stockings and petticoats muddied in the wet. She turned to help Mycroft to clamber down, holding out both her hands to assist him. Between panting and gasping, with rain streaming from the rim of his hat, he managed to utter, 'Thank you, m' dear,' several times. He stood in the roadway muttering, 'What's to be done? What's to be done?' with the rain streaming from his hat – so that Sophie did not know whether she wanted to burst out laughing at the ridiculous sight he presented or to hit him several times with her little parasol.

The driver was at the horse's side attempting to rig the broken shaft by strapping it with the harness. Sophie reached for a tarpaulin cover from the trap and held it over both her head and Mycroft's. Mycroft looked pitifully at her and said again, 'Thank you, m' dear.' Then they noticed, a few yards below, a covered wagonette being driven hell-for-leather through the rain in a southerly direction along Egham Hill.

'Perhaps they can be of assistance to us,' Mycroft suggested.

Taking Sophie's arm he pulled her with him, splashing through the puddles to intercept the vehicle before it went by. They saw, hunched under the canopy of the wagonette, a small ferret-faced man, lean as a jockey, draped in a black oilskin cape, with a stained bowler hat crammed down on his head. He was clutching the reins and lashing at the horse without compassion for the beast. On the raised, sprung seat beside him, and sitting very erect, was, by comparison, a huge, heavily built man with a square-shaped face and heavy jaw. He had a blond moustache but was otherwise clean shaven. Nor was any hair visible below the rim of his soft, wide-rimmed hat. Behind the two men, with her head and shoulders covered in a woollen shawl and the sleeves of her ill-fitting faded print dress clinging damply to her arms, was a young servant-girl twelve or thirteen years old.

'Hey! If you please!' Mycroft broke away from Sophie to lumber clumsily down the streaming road, waving his stick to attract the attention of the occupants of the cart. He saw the eyes of the bigger of the two men. They were quite extraordinary, with a pale, expressionless opacity which suggested that though the body of which they

were a part was living, temporarily it had been aban-
doned by the intellect and soul. He felt Sophie, clutching
at him, trying to drag him back with all her might.

'No, Mr Holmes!' she cried out. 'No! For God's sake!'

The driver was whipping up the horse cruelly. The
wagonette careered past them. They were near enough
for it to splash them with muddy water.

'My dear young woman!' Mycroft protested angrily.

Sophie laughed, the rain streaming like tears down her
face. 'Didn't you see who that was?' she demanded.

'Who? Who?' Mycroft shouted back at her through the
rain streaming down his face.

'You've never met him, have you?' She pointed at the
wagonette heading away along Egham Hill. She pushed
her straggling, soaking hair back from off her face with
her sleeve.

'You've never actually met your great friend, Herr
Guttmann!'

As he stared at her in stupid astonishment, she laughed
again, nodding as she did so.

'Oh yes!' she shouted at him through the rain. 'I was
only a child. But I could never forget him. Even then he
haunted my dreams like a premonition! Mr Holmes!
Didn't you realize that was Carl Philipp Emmanuel
Guttmann up there?'

Careless of the rain, Mycroft turned away from her.
He stood staring after the wagonette as it bolted away
into the premature darkness.

Chapter Sixteen

Mycroft lay in bed; he was on the frontier between dream and wakefulness. He was, therefore, partially aware of the shaft of moonlight through the open window where the curtains were only half drawn. He was aware, as if it were on the dream side of the boundary, of the black shadow moving at the window and obscuring the moonbeam like a cloud. He stirred and groaned. He murmured, 'Guttmann!' and in doing so stepped over the frontier into reality. There was no mistaking the creak of the window sash being raised from outside. He heard the clatter of a cab in St James Square below. For a moment there was silence, then the creaking began again. The shadow moved, letting the moonlight in once more. Fingers crept under the open lower sash, slipping it up very gently. Mycroft opened his eyes. He raised his head as far as he dared.

'Who's there?' he called. 'I'm warning you! I have my revolver here!'

He hadn't, and even if he had possessed one he would not have known how to use it. Staring into the darkness, he clutched the sheets under his chin.

'I shan't warn you a second time!' he called, marvelling at his own courage. 'I shall shoot!'

'Hush!' said a voice immediately outside. 'It's only me, massa sir! The Princess said as I was to come.'

Again, the moonlight between the curtains was blotted out. The negro slipped under the open window, nimble as a limbo dancer. He landed on his feet on the floor. The moonlight shone in once more.

'I don't suppose she told you to come in through an upstairs window, you scoundrel!' Mycroft protested. 'What were you proposing to do? Cut my throat by any chance? I only have two sovereigns here. Not worth a hanging.'

'I weren't going to cut no throat, sir!' the negro said, his voice turning falsetto in indignation. 'Like I says, I only come 'cause the Princess said I was to. An' I didn't want to disturb Mrs Wotcher-calls-her or nuffink. I brung Cissie, 'cause she got some'ing to tell you, see? Some'ing important. Leastways, the Princess says it is.'

'You haven't got Cissie out there on the window-ledge, have you?' asked Mycroft.

'No! 'Course I ain't! Here! You're having me on, ain't you?'

Mycroft clambered out of bed. He pulled a huge quilted dressing-gown over his nightshirt.

'Deuce take it! What time is it?'

The negro took a large turnip watch on a chain from his waistcoat pocket and examined its face in the moonlight. Mycroft lit his bedside candle and carried it over to the negro.

'You can read the time, I suppose?' he asked.

'Wotcha mean?' the negro demanded indignantly. He stared at the face. Mycroft, meanwhile, was examining the monogram inscribed on the back of the casing.

'Half past two,' the negro announced triumphantly.

He realized what Mycroft was up to. He closed his hand round the watch to conceal the inscription. Staring defiantly at Mycroft, he replaced it in his waistcoat pocket.

'It were my father's!' he whispered loudly. 'And his father's before him. And *his* father's for all I knows . . . 'Cause they was kings, they was. Only we calls 'em chiefs where we comes from.'

Mycroft pushed him toward the door into the study.

'I suppose you have a name, you young villain?' he asked.

' 'Course I have! It's Cyril. *Prince* Cyril to them as knows what's what!'

'Cyril!' Mycroft snorted.

'Weren't my bleeding fault my father were done out of his kingdom by that there Shaka, now was it?' Cyril asked. 'He named me 'cause he meant to bring me up a gentleman, see?'

'Go downstairs – quietly, you young villain – and fetch this – Cissie? – up here.'

As Cyril crept downstairs Mycroft lit the gas-mantles in the study. A minute or two later there was a whispering and mouselike scuffling outside the door. Mycroft opened it, and immediately Cyril pushed a thoroughly unsavoury, smelly, ragged little object into the room. Mycroft fixed his face into a smile of reassurance. The child would have turned and beat a retreat instantly if Cyril hadn't been blocking the doorway behind her. She was about twelve years old, dressed in the filthy remnant of what had once been the fashionable evening gown of an older, much taller woman. Over it she wore a greasy, ragged boy's jacket which could not hide the fact that the gown was slipping from her thin, narrow shoulders, while its grimy hem trailed on the floor like a wedding train. The face, under a ruined poke bonnet, was that of a prematurely aged woman. One eye had been blacked, while her mouth was sucked in between her cheeks where most of her teeth were either missing or broken.

Mycroft was on the point of reaching for her arm to draw her further into the room. He changed his mind, however, wiping his hand on his gown even though he had not touched her. Still managing a smile, he beckoned her to him.

'Come, child. Come. The Princess said you were to come here, did she not?'

The child shook her head fiercely.

'She didn't?' asked Mycroft. 'Who did?'

'Shirul,' said the child in a baritone rasp.

'So,' Mycroft continued. 'You had better sit down and tell me what it is you have to tell and . . . you shall have a new sixpence.'

Cissie still hesitated. He pointed to an upright chair by the table. Cyril shoved her towards it. Mycroft, on a sudden, second thought, snatched the previous evening's edition of the *Pall Mall Gazette* from the table, opened it and planted it across the seat of the chair. 'There you are, my dear,' he said.

Cyril prodded her to the chair as if she were a recalcitrant domestic animal. She sat down at last. Mycroft sat down on the opposite side of the table. There was a purse lying there. He picked it up quickly, then took a sixpence from it and held it up to her. 'Now, my dear,' he said.

She did not reply, but sat staring at the sixpence as

166

though hypnotized. Cyril gave her a hard thump across the shoulder with the back of his hand. 'Go on!' he ordered her. 'Tell the gentleman what you see-d.'

The girl swung round with sudden, unexpected vitality. 'Fuck off, you!' snarled the gravelly, baritone voice.

It was an expression Mycroft had never heard issuing from the lips of a member of the fairer sex. In fact, although he had never articulated it, he had believed women to be constitutionally incapable of formulating such an expression. Conquering his revulsion, however, he leaned forward and said gently, still holding up the sixpence, 'Please tell me what you have seen, my dear.'

The girl rewarded him with a dazzlingly friendly if toothless smile. She spoke confidingly to him while he struggled to understand what she was saying.

'Cab come for the 'ooer—'

'The what?' asked Mycroft.

'The grand 'ooer what live in the hotel,' said the girl, pointing vaguely in the direction of the window.

'The lady,' Cyril explained. 'The French lady's what she means.' He thumped the girl's shoulder with his fist. 'Ain't a 'ooer!' he said. 'A bleedin' lady, that's what she is!'

The child swung round on him again. ' 'Course she's a bleedin' 'ooer!' she snapped back. 'Come with a four-wheeler, didn't they? Curtains drawed an' all . . . That's how grand 'ooers get taken to all them nice places!' she explained to Mycroft. She turned on Cyril again. 'And don't you hit me again, yer black nonce!'

'Did you see who the people were who came for the – er – lady?'

'Yer, 'course I did. Two gentlemen in silk hats. One of 'em threw me a penny.'

'What happened then?'

167

'They come out with her, and get into the cab with her. One of 'em tell me to piss off 'cause he weren't going to give me anuvver penny. Shouted at me he did, the bastard!'

'You was pestering him, I bet!' said Cyril. 'Drawing attention to yourself like I said you wasn't to!'

'Did the lady come out with them immediately?' Mycroft asked, hoping to put the question before the girl, Cissie, turned on Cyril once more. But he had to wait for her to calm down.

'Were the two gentlemen inside the hotel for very long?' he asked when she had turned to face him again.

Cissie screwed up her face to indicate that she was thinking hard.

'Not *so* long,' she said. 'It weren't so long she done business with both on 'em—'she thought again – 'A bit long, though.'

'Just long enough for her to make herself ready to go out with them?' asked Mycroft. 'If she hadn't expected them this evening?'

Cissie fell silent. Mycroft realized that it was far outside her experience.

'What you have told me has been extremely interesting, my dear,' Mycroft assured her. 'Pray do go on.'

To Cyril, who was on the point of hitting her again, he said, 'My dear young man, I appreciate your concern on my behalf, but I should be most grateful if you would allow your female friend here to tell her story in her own time.'

'Yer! You bleedin' well listen to what the old gent's saying!' said Cissie. She turned back to Mycroft with the nearest thing she could manage to a sweet smile. 'Wotcher want to know, mister?' she asked.

'Would you say that the lady wanted to go with them?' Mycroft asked her.

'Yer. 'Cause business is business, ain't it?'

'Did you manage to find out where they took her?'

' 'Course I did.' She prodded her thumb in Cyril's direction. 'That's what he tell me to do, didn't he? I hanged on the back of the growler, see? 'Cause the cabbie can't see you if you're clever. And there ain't nobody cleverer 'an what I am. Not at hangin' on the back of a growler there ain't.'

'So where did they go?'

'Grosvenor Square. See? I know all the names of everywhere. They kep' the cab hangin' about outside. An' they takes the 'ooer inside. They was in the house 'bout 'alf an hour, I reckons. Bleedin' great house it were, wiv railings and steps – lots of steps – an' pillars an' all . . .'

'You can tell the time, my dear?' Mycroft asked.

'Heard the clocks chiming, didn't I?' Cissie inferred he'd asked a stupid question.

'What was the time?'

'When the 'ooer went back to the hotel, yer means? Half past eleven, it were.'

'Did the gentlemen go back with her?'

'You soft in the 'ead or somefink?' Cissie sneered. ' 'Course they didn't! Not *after* they'd done business with her. A woman see-d her back to the cab. All stiff and starchy she was, wiv a face on her like a fucking policeman.'

'And the lady went straight back to the hotel?'

'Yer.'

'Can you tell me something about this house the men took her to? You've been very helpful so far. I think you may well deserve more than a sixpence.'

'Yer mean a 'ole shilling, sir?' she asked hopefully.

'We shall see. Do you remember anything in particular about the house in Grosvenor Square?'

'Big. It were big.' She screwed up her face again. 'There were a big shiny plate on the door. Only I ain't no scholar, see. There were a flag on the watchermacallit – *you* know! – over the bleeding door, like.'

'Can you describe the flag?'

'Nah! 'Course I can't. It were dark, weren't it? Only, it were a big flag, and there were somefink like a bleedin' great bird stuck on the end.'

'Of the pole, you mean?'

'Yer. The stick – the pole. You knows what I mean!'

'These two gentlemen and the lady. Were they speaking in English? I mean, could you understand what they were saying?'

'Yer, when one of 'em give me a penny, I could. Only, they talked funny when they was talking to each other like.'

'They were talking to each other in a foreign language?'

'Yer. 'Course they was.'

Again she made it sound as if Mycroft was impenetrably stupid.

'An' then there was another thing. Don't signify nuffink – but the Princess said I'm to tell you. Leastways, that's what he says!' She jerked her thumb in Cyril's direction.

'What is it?'

'The 'ooer were a-crying her bleeding eyes out when she come back to the four-wheeler. I mean, there weren't nobody to see it nor nuffink, 'cept me o' course. Stupid, it were. She weren't even trying to wipe 'em. Just come

170

down the steps – not hurt nor nuffink – letting the wet run down her face like a bleedin' baby, an' all! Anyways, soon as she were back in the hotel I went round to his bleeding majesty here, at the Princess's ken, like he tell me to. An' he brung me straight round here.'

'You have done very well, Cissie. Very well indeed. You shall have your shilling.'

Cissie's face was grimily radiant.

'No . . . no!' Mycroft changed his mind. 'The labourer is worthy of her hire. You shall have half a crown.' He took the coin from his purse and gave it to her. She gazed at it. Her face turned wistful.

'There won't be no penny-gaffs open now,' she said. 'Could've slept snug and warm in a real bed tonight, I could.' Her fingers closed over the broad coin. She looked at Cyril; her eyes narrowed fiercely. 'An' you ain't goin' to take it off of me, neither!' she snarled.

'Most certainly he must not!' Mycroft agreed.

'Don't I get nothing for my trouble?' Cyril demanded.

'A prison sentence for breaking and entering, if you're not careful,' Mycroft told him. 'But if you return to the Princess and ask if she would do me the favour of permitting me to call on her tomorrow morning, I shall give you the sixpence I was going to give to your young friend here.'

'Yer!' said Cissie. 'Give 'im the sixpence. He don't deserve no more.' She uttered a deep, rasping cackle. As she headed for the study door, clutching her half-crown, she announced, 'I'm going to Leicester Square. There's a stall what sells hot sausage rolls in Leicester Square. Prime, they are!'

Opening the door to see them out of the study, Mycroft put his finger to his lips. Cissie gathered her straggling

171

skirts in the fingers of one hand, as she had observed the fine ladies doing. Her feet were bare of all save dirt. Cyril and she tiptoed out silently. Mycroft closed the door after them. He paused, listening, but they made not a sound. He went to the chimney breast to turn down the jets in the gas-mantles. As he did so he whistled the first phrase of the *Marseillaise* softly through his teeth.

Chapter Seventeen

The following morning Mycroft walked across Piccadilly to Sophie's apartment in Bruton Street as early as he dared. There was a thin drizzle; vapour rose from the streets. The porter at the front door let him in with some reluctance, but as Mycroft furled his umbrella and began to ascend the stairs there was a clatter of boots on the flight above. Cyril's face appeared over the banister. He called down, 'Why, bless us, massa sir! Me and the Princess thought as you was never going to come!'

Mycroft stopped halfway up the first flight. He leant on his stick, clutching the brass rail, and waited to recover his breath.

'You're a jackanapes, sir!' he gasped.

He climbed to the landing. The door to the apartment was open. He pushed Cyril aside with his stick and entered. Sophie advanced on him, both hands outstretched to take his.

'Dear friend!' she exclaimed. 'Thank you for coming so soon.'

She drew him inside. Once again she was dressed for

walking out, this time in a pale blue promenade gown and paletot trimmed with sealskin and a tiny sealskin 'military' cap with a fine black veil. Russian maids in cotton sarafans and smocks were bustling to and fro. A fat old Russian nurse was standing in the vestibule muttering and shaking her head in generalized disapproval.

'Now,' announced Sophie, 'you see what a useful partner I am? As soon as Cyril's spies report, I am in touch with you. So! We shall walk out together, you and I . . .'

The old nurse came up to Mycroft to take his hat, stick and gloves. Sophie babbled at her in Russian, too quickly for Mycroft to follow what she was saying. The nurse babbled back at her, but beat a retreat.

'Cyril?' Sophie called over Mycroft's shoulder. 'You are to come with us. Fetch the large umbrella.'

She turned to the icon in the far corner of the room, bowed low and signed herself with the cross three times. Mycroft was surprised and slightly shocked by the profundity of her obeisance before the image of the Virgin and the Slavic emphasis with which she blessed herself. It was so very un-English and oriental in someone whose command of both the English language and English manners was so complete. He wanted to rebuke her for indulging in such flamboyant behaviour.

She returned to him and took him by the arm.

'I thought it best that Cyril should take the child to you last night, even if it meant you had to be woken,' she told him as she led him downstairs. 'One can never tell what will become of such creatures, even in an hour or two. They will be arrested for picking pockets; somebody will give them half a crown so they think they will never need to earn money again . . .'

174

'Princess!' protested Mycroft. She had managed to make him feel guilty.

'Or they die in the street,' Sophie shrugged. 'One can never tell what will happen to them.'

The porter opened the hall door to let them pass. Sophie did not so much as look at him. They stepped down on to the pavement. Cyril opened the big umbrella and held it over their heads.

'We shall walk,' Sophie pronounced. 'It is not *so* bad, and it will do us good.'

'Where are you taking me?' Mycroft demanded.

'To Jermyn Street, of course. To Kendall's Hotel. That is where you wish to go. And you cannot speak to Mme Tirard *tête à tête* without a chaperone.'

She had set course for Bond Street. Mycroft found that he had to trot to keep under the umbrella with her.

'Why do you think I want to speak to Mme Tirard?' he demanded, struggling for breath.

'Because you want to know why she was taken to the French Embassy last night . . . I mean, of course, that you have already guessed why. Like I have already guessed why. Neither of us is stupid, after all. But you long to hear what *she* has to say. Am I right?'

Mycroft glanced over his shoulder. Cyril, holding up the umbrella, gave him a broad, impudent grin.

'She knows, all right,' he said, pointing at Sophie's back.

'*Who* knows?' Sophie asked severely, without turning her head.

'Her *Highness* knows,' Cyril corrected himself, still grinning.

Mycroft stopped abruptly. The small cortège stumbled into one another.

'Perhaps, Princess,' he said, 'you'll tell me what it is that you and I have guessed?'

Sophie looked up at him anxiously. It occurred to her that she had angered him. He saw her anxiety and was instantly mollified.

'The reason she should have been taken to the embassy?' he asked. 'The reason why these official gentlemen could not have said what they wanted to say to her in a private drawing-room in the hotel?'

'Because they were taking her to see somebody too important to come to her?' Sophie suggested.

'And what do you suppose was being communicated to her which caused her to weep "her bleeding eyes out", as your messenger so inelegantly but tellingly put it; to be so taken with distress that she couldn't summon the energy to wipe the tears from her cheeks. This man's' – he jerked his thumb in Cyril's direction – 'little spy is very observant – worth cherishing in fact. She certainly shouldn't be left to die in the street for want of a half-crown piece.'

He had not been able to resist saying it, but Sophie ignored it.

'Mme Tirard has been told either of the Thibault man's death,' she suggested, 'or of his arrest – as a traitor? But she has also been given instructions of some sort. Is that right?'

'Quite right, Princess. Well said!'

Sophie looked pleased.

'Otherwise,' Mycroft continued, feeling flattered by her pleasure, 'there would have been no need for her to have been taken – under guard, as it were – to the embassy. As you say, she has received instructions. And it is for us to discover what they are. You see? I agree with your diagnosis entirely.'

Arm in arm they crossed Piccadilly and went down Duke Street to Jermyn Street. At the corner they had only to cross Jermyn Street to reach the hotel. But they stopped abruptly. There were two four-wheelers and a brougham in front of the hotel, with their coachman. There were also four uniformed police at the door of the hotel. On the pavement stood Sir James Swarthmoor, with the hotel's head porter holding an umbrella over his head. Standing beside him was the familiar figure – at least to Mycroft – of the Metropolitan Police Commissioner, Sir Philip Doughty.

Mycroft took Sophie's arm. 'Too late now,' he said. 'We've been observed. What the deuce is happening?'

They stepped off the pavement, leaving Cyril and the umbrella behind. Feeling the rain on their heads, they both turned round.

'Don't like it,' Cyril admitted, and for once he was not grinning. 'All that law and that standing about waiting for trouble!' He made as if to retreat back up Duke Street. Mycroft pursued and grabbed him by the arm.

'Don't you run off, my boy!' he said. 'Making fools of your mistress and me. You're supposed to be a respectable servant now. So behave like one!'

They crossed the street more or less sedately. Sir Philip Doughty greeted Mycroft.

'You may be pleased to hear, Holmes, that your little problem has solved itself.'

'Indeed, Commissioner?' Mycroft said with as much enthusiasm as he could muster. 'That is very good news!' He looked at Sir James.

'It seems so,' Sir James agreed. He glanced at Sophie.

'Princess?' Mycroft said. 'May I have the pleasure of presenting to you Sir James Swarthmoor and Sir Philip

Doughty. Gentlemen, this is the Princess Sofya Trubetskoy.'

Presenting her gloved fingers for them to bow over, Sophie said, 'Mr Holmes told me that Mme Pierre Tirard is staying here at the hotel. I do not personally have the pleasure of being acquainted with Mme Tirard. But in Paris we have so many acquaintances in common that I decided it would be proper for me to leave my card. Two strangers in a foreign land, you know!' She uttered an apparently artless little giggle.

A swarthy, pock-faced man with a thick black moustache, wearing a caped, oilskin coat and a brown bowler hat, was standing at Sir Philip Doughty's shoulder. Sir Philip turned to him. 'Well, Grimes?' he asked. 'What do you say?'

'I say it may be a merciful Providence has sent this lady, sir,' the man replied. 'It could be Mme Tirard might have need of a friend. Distressing business, you know!'

Sir James explained to Sophie, 'Princess, this is Inspector Grimes of the Metropolitan Detective Police.'

'Honour to meet you, madam.' Inspector Grimes raised his bowler and held it up over his head. 'The fact of the matter is, these gentleman and I have just had the painful duty of communicating very bad tidings to Mme Tirard. We've had to tell her that we've reason to believe the body of a dear friend of hers – a very dear friend – has been found drownded.' He cleared his throat.

Mycroft said, 'Jean-Christophe Thibault?'

Sir James replied, 'It is quite possible. There was a shoemaker's label stitched on the inside leather of one of his boots. It was very indistinct – the thread of the letter-

178

ing was almost gone, but it was sufficient to tell us that it was in French.'

'The problem is, madam,' continued Inspector Grimes, 'we have no alternative but to ask the lady to accompany us to see if she can positively identify the body – the *corpus delictus*, if you see what I mean. I fear it will prove a most distressing experience. The presence of a friend of the same sex—'

'But I'm not a friend of Mme Tirard. I haven't even introduced myself to her yet!' Sophie protested.

'It would be a Christian act,' Mycroft told her.

She glanced up at him with considerable suspicion.

'Where is the body at present?' Mycroft asked.

'The Holy Cross Hospital mortuary, Staines,' said Inspector Grimes. 'It was pulled out of the Thames just a few yards above Hythe.'

'We have chartered a train to take the Inspector and Mme Tirard from Paddington,' said Sir Philip. 'It will be more merciful than a prolonged drive by horse and carriage. The morning should see this unhappy matter through.'

'Staines is no more than a mile or two from where our wretched conveyance almost took a spill yesterday, Princess,' Mycroft told Sophie. 'The Princess and I drove out from Egham yesterday,' he explained to Sir James. 'The Princess was most anxious to see the place where Magna Carta was signed,' he added.

Sophie stared at him. But she knew better than to ask the question which had formed on her lips.

'M. Thibault, if it is indeed he, did not die yesterday,' said Sir James. 'The doctors examining the body say that it has been in the water weeks rather than days. It will not prove a pretty sight – if you'll forgive me, Princess.'

179

'I think perhaps I should go in and make myself known to Mme Tirard,' Sophie said. She turned to Cyril. 'You may go home. Give the umbrella to Mr Holmes. Go on! Be off with you!' She clapped her hands. 'You can't come to – wherever it is. You will only give poor Mme Tirard a fright!'

As Cyril stood looking surly, refusing to give up the umbrella to Mycroft, she turned her back on him, smiled charmingly at Sir Philip Doughty and said to him, 'Will you take me to this so unhappy lady, sir? I am ready to accompany her during her ordeal, if it is her wish.'

'That is extraordinarily kind of you, Princess,' Sir Philip told her. 'Is there anybody here in Town whose consent we should seek for your making such a journey of mercy? Husband, for instance? Father? Guardian?'

'Oh no!' Sophie told him. 'Mr Holmes is my protector in London.'

'Indeed!' exclaimed Sir James. The note of surprise came involuntarily from his lips.

Once Sir Philip and Sophie were inside the hotel, Mycroft turned to Cyril, who was still sulking.

'You heard what your mistress said. Give me the umbrella, and be off with you.'

Cyril glanced at the policemen standing by the carriages. He handed over the umbrella and slouched off, glancing back and muttering to himself as he crossed the street.

'Surly devil,' observed Sir James. Then he said, 'I imagine this must be the Russian girl you spoke of the other morning. And is she really the young Princess Trubetskoy?'

'I have every reason to believe so, Sir James,' Mycroft replied, somewhat stiffly.

'Deuced pretty, whoever she is!' said Sir James. 'Why do you suppose she came spying after you? You did suggest she had been spying on you, you know.'

Mycroft managed to force a laugh. It sounded more like the honk of the seal he sometimes resembled. 'Did I?' he replied. 'I was mistaken, of course. She had called on me earlier in the day, not knowing that I was passing – *hoping* to pass – the weekend in Oxford.'

Sir James grunted and said nothing.

'Of course it was entirely natural that the poor girl felt she should make her presence in London known to me.' Mycroft airily waved one hand.

'Really?' asked Sir James.

'We are related, you know. Oh yes! Through my French grandmother. Princess Trubetskoy – Princess Sophie's mother – is a Frenchwoman. We are cousins.'

'Ah! I didn't realize the Yorkshire Holmeses were so well connected,' said Sir James. ' "Of sturdy, respectable yeoman stock", is the description given in the *County Proprietors' Register*, as I recall.'

Again Mycroft preferred to let it pass.

'So I have undertaken to accompany her during her stay in Town – as far as my duties permit.'

'And your duties – not to say the leave of absence you wheedled from me – permitted you to drive with her out to Egham and Runnymede yesterday . . .?'

Sir James broke off his questioning as Sir Philip Doughty came out of the hotel. Behind him came Mme Tirard and Sophie, their faces concealed under their black veils. Sophie had her hand under Mme Tirard's arm, supporting her. Sir Philip spoke in a low voice to Detective-inspector Grimes; Grimes called to one of the coachmen. The coachman held open the door of his four-wheeler as, holding up an umbrella, Grimes guided Mme Tirard and Sophie to the carriage and helped them up the step.

'I shall be returning to Number 10, Sir Philip,' Sir James called, waving his stick at the second carriage. 'Let me know what transpires. Holmes? May I carry you as far as Whitehall and the Treasury?'

'The Treasury, Sir James?' Mycroft asked, taken aback.

'Of course. The man, Thibault, has been found, however unfortunate the circumstances. It is most regrettable that poor Mme Tirard is required to identify the body, but it is no more than a necessary if unhappy formality. We have no reason as yet to suppose that there was any other reason for Thibault's death than misadventure . . . Balance of mind disturbed, perhaps. One of the unrecognized casualties of a terrible war. You have to admit this story of his coming rushing over here, demanding to speak to "the highest in the land", puts his state of mind in some doubt . . . Yes, Holmes, my dear boy, I'm sure you have your own theories on the matter, and that they are as ingenious as always . . .'

'Absolutely no call to put yourself to the trouble of going to Staines, Holmes,' Sir Philip Doughty confirmed. 'Matter for the Coroner's Court to sit on now.'

'Tell me,' said Holmes. 'At what time, more or less exactly, was Thibault's body fished out of the river?'

'Why do you wish to know?' Sir James asked suspiciously.

'Natural curiosity,' Mycroft replied.

'It was at sunrise this morning,' said Sir Philip. 'A boatman found the body. He was on the river bringing in a nightline.'

Sir James smiled slightly. 'Up and about before the waterkeepers, eh?'

'Something of the sort, I expect. Honest fellow, though,' Sir Philip replied. 'Reported the matter. We'll try to persuade the Middlesex Constabulary not to press poaching charges.'

Mycroft hesitated. For once he did not know what to say. Just then Inspector Grimes jumped down from the carriage and came over to them. He held the rim of his hat in salute.

'Begging your pardon, gentlemen. It's the Princess; says she don't think it'd be proper for her to go all the way to Staines unless this gentleman accompanies her. She says the Princess, her mother, wouldn't like it at all!'

They looked round at the carriage. Sophie's head was round the door. There was an anxious expression on her face.

'Mr Holmes!' she called. 'You will come with us? Oh *please* do, Mr Holmes!'

It was a plea so heartfelt that even the passers-by on the pavement turned to see what was the matter.

'Very well, Holmes!' Sir James said, less persuaded than resigned to the fact that he had been out-manoeuvred. 'I daresay we must let you do what your charming young cousin asks.'

'Thank you, Sir James,' Mycroft replied with grave sincerity. He went with the inspector and mounted the carriage. Inspector Grimes clambered in after him, stumbling over himself in his anxiety to avoid the ladies' skirts. The two men sat squeezed up side by side, opposite Mme Tirard and Sophie.

Inspector Grimes called up through the hatch to the coachman, 'To Paddington, Williams. Platform Fifteen.

Soon be there,' he added in Mme Tirard's direction, as if it were a consolation.

They moved off. Sophie turned to Mme Tirard.

'*Pauvre Madame! Quel malheur!*' she said, her voice only just audible to Mycroft above the growl of the wheels on the street. '*Ça va bien, ma chère?*'

Mme Tirard gave her a little nod, and sniffed. Sophie took a handkerchief from her reticule and placed it in Mme Tirard's hand.

'Oh! *Tu es très, très gentille, chérie!*' Mme Tirard replied, her voice trembling.

Sophie glanced at Mycroft and pulled a face. Mycroft shook his head, warning her not to let Inspector Grimes see. But Grimes was too busy gazing with kindly concern at Mme Tirard.

Chapter Eighteen

They were standing in the main chamber of the Holy Cross Mortuary, Staines, Mme Tirard with Inspector Grimes on one side and Sophie, still holding her arm, on the other. Mycroft, and a young doctor in the ill-fitting, second-hand black frock-coat which he clearly regarded as the uniform of his profession, stood facing them. Between them was the open sluice to which the tiled floor gently sloped from all four sides. Above them, on an iron coronet, hung a ring of gas-jets. They remained in silence.

The clatter of trolley wheels began at a distance, and came nearer. Mme Tirard glanced at Sophie who, all scepticism gone, put her arms round her. An elderly attendant, a tall, gaunt-faced starveling wearing a soiled white apron, pushed in the trolley and wheeled it into position over the sluice. He reached up and drew down the coronet of gas-jets so that the shape of the body under the grey, patched sheet lay under its full glare. The doctor turned to Mme Tirard.

'Madame?'

At first she did not seem to hear, or if she did, was unaware of what was expected of her. Sophie gently eased her forward to the side of the trolley. Inspector Grimes drew the sheet off the face. Mme Tirard gazed down at it as if it were something which was not of the least interest to her.

'This man did not die of drowning,' said Mycroft.

'You fool, Figgis!' the doctor exclaimed. 'This is the fellow who was brought in late this morning.' He drew the sheet off the body. 'See? He hasn't been fully laid out, he's still clothed!'

Sophie led Mme Tirard a few paces away.

'A vagrant – some poor fellow looking for casual labouring work such as stone-breaking perhaps. He was found on the Hythe road. A cart went over him by the look of it: ribcage smashed in; spine snapped. It's always the same – knocked down, you know, then the horse's hoof, then the cart-wheel' – he imitated the noise of cracking by clicking his tongue.

'My dear sir!' Mycroft protested. 'Have some regard for the ladies' sensibilities!'

The doctor shrugged. Mycroft added, 'Nor is the poor chap a vagrant. He was in regular employment. Notice the mud on the boots and gaiters? There, you have loam from fields well prepared for cultivation of crops – harrowed and ploughed. And these marks on his breeches? They are obvious to anybody who looks at them. They are made by the charring on horses' hooves when they are being held up in a smithy, for shoeing – work only done by a man whose master regards him as responsible. If this fellow was on the road, he had only very recently been turned off; if not, there's a farmer looking for a missing hand.'

He reached over and replaced the sheet over the young man's face. As he did so, he saw the expression on it.

'I'll tell you something else,' he said to the inspector. 'The poor chap knew what was about to happen to him.'

The inspector nodded. 'He knew right enough,' he agreed.

They stood back as the attendant wheeled the trolley away again.

'I'm sorry, gentlemen,' said the doctor. 'We don't often have two bodies come in here the same night and early morning – not unless there's been a derailment on the Brighton and South Eastern.'

Mycroft noticed that Mme Tirard had begun to tremble quite violently. Sophie was looking at him pleadingly, as if he could have done something to hasten the process. Perhaps she thought he should not have demonstrated his powers of observation over the first body; in his heart he would have agreed, even if he was silently rehearsing the excuse that it had been in order to assist the Middlesex Constabulary in their investigations.

There was the clatter of a trolley returning. Although Mme Tirard's and Sophie's faces were concealed behind the net of their veils, Mycroft felt that their distress was palpable on the chill cellar air. As the attendant wheeled in the trolley, he heard Sophie say, *'Courage, chère amie!'*

Once again the inspector drew back the sheet.

'If you would be so kind, madame,' he said.

Sophie led Mme Tirard to the side of the trolley. The black mesh of her veil was particularly fine. The glare from the gas-jets penetrated it so that Mycroft could see the expression of appalled disgust on her face. He wondered if she rather than Mme Tirard was about to collapse. He saw Mme Tirard's small mouth twitch. The lips parted. Barely audibly, she whispered, '*Mais oui! C'est lui.*'

'She says that it is M. Thibault,' said Sophie.

Mme Tirard let out a deep groan. Suddenly, quite violently, she tore herself from Sophie's comforting embrace. She walked up the floor a little way from the group round the trolley. She groaned again, and heaved. Head stooped, she vomited twice on to the open tiles. Sophie waited for her to finish then went over to her and put her arms round her to support her once more. Mme Tirard stood shivering in her embrace. The doctor went over to them.

'Perhaps madame would care to come to my office to rest for a moment?' he suggested. He led her away. Inspector Grimes hesitated, then followed. Sophie looked back. Mycroft was with the attendant, beside the trolley. He motioned to her to remain.

'How can you, Mr Holmes?' she asked.

'To what are you referring, Princess?'

'How can you stand there, looking at . . . that?'

'She recognized him,' Mycroft said.

'Yes. She did. And I must go to her!'

'Wait!' Mycroft commanded. Then he noticed the condition she was in. '*You*'re trembling,' he said.

'Of course I'm trembling. It's cold in this place!'

'Would you have recognized this? Even if it had once been somebody you were supposed to know well?'

'Perhaps. If I had loved him.' She paused, still trembling. 'No,' she said.

'*She* recognized him because she already knew it to be him,' said Mycroft.

Sophie stopped trembling.

'Of course! That's what she was told yesterday evening, at the French Embassy in Grosvenor Square.'

'You are a very bright girl, Princess,' Mycroft told her approvingly. 'Now! Who do you think told them at Grosvenor Square that Jean-Christophe Thibault was dead?'

'The government in Paris? . . . No.'

'Think back to yesterday afternoon. Perhaps you do not understand the geography of southern England well enough to fully appreciate what we saw.'

'We saw Guttmann,' said Sophie. 'We saw him driving' – she turned and pointed away from her as if she were visualizing the scene – 'we saw him driving . . . away from the Thames?' she asked.

'We saw him driving away from Egham – only two miles from here – and therefore away from the Thames; in a wagonette, heading in the direction of Leatherhead, and therefore Dorking.'

'So *he* put . . .' she pointed gingerly at the trolley.

'Yes, Princess.'

'He put the body in the Thames, *away* from Dorking?'

'Well done, Princess! As far away as an afternoon's drive in a light vehicle could take him. Now you must go to poor Mme Tirard. Her distress is so clearly evident, I fear I may have been unjust in my judgement of her . . . It is the mark of a strong and balanced mind, you know, to admit to one's minor follies.'

When Mme Tirard had recovered her composure somewhat, Inspector Grimes and Sophie assisted her up to the mortuary yard and the carriage which was to take them back to the railway station. Mycroft lingered in the cellar to speak privately to the doctor.

'Mme Tirard will come to no harm?' he asked. 'I refer to the rigours of the journey back to Town.'

'I have administered a mild sedative,' the doctor replied. 'She may feel slightly drowsy, but she will remain quite calm for two or three hours.'

'The body, Doctor. The deceased did perish by drowning, did he not? I mean, you do not suppose that injuries were inflicted on him and then his body was committed to the deep, as it were?'

'We have no reason to suppose he died of anything except drowning, sir. Of course, given the state of decomposition, it would be impossible to take one's oath upon it. He had been in the water a great while.'

'A great while, Doctor?'

'You saw for yourself, did you not?'

'How great a while?' Mycroft asked.

'Certainly weeks rather than days.'

'Mr Holmes, sir!' Inspector Grimes called down into the cellar. 'I think we ought to see the lady back to London and her hotel quick as we can, if you don't mind me saying so, sir!'

'A moment, Inspector, if you please!' Mycroft called back. 'Forgive me, Doctor, but you say he was in the water a great while . . . I hope this doesn't sound ridiculous to you, but he would not have had to remain in the *same* water all that time, would he?'

'You are not a police officer, are you, sir?' the doctor asked with a slight smile.

'Simply curious,' Mycroft replied.

'Perhaps a practitioner in forensic science would be

190

capable of answering your question. But not a humble sawbones like myself. All I can tell you is that in what remains of that poor fellow, there are no marks to suggest any violence or damage of any sort which might lead one to suppose anything other than that he fell into the Thames and drowned.'

'Mr Holmes! If you please, sir!' Inspector Grimes called down.

Chapter Nineteen

The next morning, as Mycroft was having his breakfast, Mrs Turner knocked at the door of the study to let him know that Sophie was below.

'Well? Show her up, Mrs Turner!' he told her impatiently, but she just stood there in the open door, holding aside the faded tapestry draught-excluder.

'Well?' he demanded.

'Mr Holmes, I never expected to have to say this, truly I did not, you being as nice and quiet a gentleman in your habits as anybody could wish for – at least until this last week!'

'And what has happened this last week?' Mycroft asked.

'I can't permit it to continue, Mr Holmes. I mean, I've got to think of Maisie – and Lizzie when she comes in. It isn't a good example to set the servants, sir. I'm sorry, sir – but it isn't! And I've always kept a regular, well-behaved home for Mr Turner, and nobody can say any different . . .'

'Mrs Turner, am I to take it that you are referring

to Princess Trubetskoy and her visiting me?'

'Yes, sir! It isn't proper, as I'm sure a gentleman-born like you very well knows – her visiting a single gentleman's study unaccompanied, and with the door shut! It don't set a good example, sir!'

Mycroft rose with an effort from the table. He laid down his copy of *The Times*. He dabbed his lips with his napkin, as an afterthought.

'Mrs Turner, I think you should know that, in Russia, there is no family nobler than that of Trubetskoy – except that, perhaps, of the Tsar himself. Princess Sofya Trubetskoy is a true princess. And I'm sure you recall the words of William Shakespeare, "Nice manners curtsy to princesses . . ." '

'Did he really say that, Mr Holmes?' asked Mrs Turner. 'Or are you making it up?'

'Mrs Turner! May heaven forgive you, madam! Let me tell you something else. If ever you should be seeking another gentleman to make his diggings here, in Mr Turner's delightful house, and you were able to tell him that the Princess Sofya Trubetskoy used to visit here and partake of your excellent hospitality – think of the impression it would make!'

He inclined his head and said softly in her ear, 'And now, please request the Princess to come upstairs.'

'Of course, Mr Holmes.'

When Sophie was installed, sitting at the opposite side of the table, with Mrs Turner hovering over them, he said to her, 'May I recommend some of Mrs Turner's inestimable scrambled egg and kidneys?'

'Oh, I'm so sorry!' Sophie smiled up at Mrs Turner. 'I have breakfasted already. And Mr Holmes has told me about the magnificent breakfasts you cook for him, Mrs Turner. It is a real shame!'

For a moment Mycroft was afraid that she would lay on the compliments too thickly. But Mrs Turner did not notice anything amiss.

'A cup of coffee, your highness?' she suggested.

'If you please, Mrs Turner.'

When Mrs Turner left them alone, Sophie said, 'I had breakfast with Mme Tirard. I have spent the whole night with her. She is greatly distressed, as you saw for yourself.'

'Nausea is not easily assumed,' Mycroft agreed. 'But it can be caused by a number of things. Sheer physical disgust, for instance, unrelated to the person she thought she was looking at. Or apprehensiveness endured over a prolonged period of time.' He pushed a kidney thickly coated in scrambled egg into his mouth.

'She has been weeping all night,' Sophie told him. 'She kept on saying, "Why did they have to kill him? Why did they have to kill him?" She said it over and over again.'

'Did you ask her who "they" were?'

'No, Mr Holmes. I did not.'

She looked darkly into his face.

'Do you imagine,' she asked, 'that because I was born in a Siberian penal colony I have no womanly feelings?'

'The thought never occurred to me,' Mycroft replied.

'Besides,' said Sophie. 'I thought that if I did not ask directly, I might learn more.'

Mycroft pointed his fork in her direction.

'You, my dear young lady, are "a lass unparalleled". I'm glad you have elected to be my friend. I feel almost sorry for Herr Guttmann!'

'She also said that "they" had promised her that M.

194

Thibault would come to no harm. She said that several times, as well. With great bitterness. But I'm afraid I have to admit, despite your compliment, Mr Holmes, that I did not discover who "they" were. I suppose I assumed that "they" were Admiral Saisset or M. Thiers.'

'Or those directing her from the French Embassy in Grosvenor Square,' Mycroft suggested. 'Princess? Would you forgive me if I were to smoke a cigar? The action of a good cigar does help to galvanize the brain into activity.'

'It is rather early in the day, isn't it?' Sophie asked. 'But if it is necessary – and if you open your window – I shall permit it.'

'Obliged to you, Princess. Greatly.'

He took his place by the open window. He smoked in silence, letting the bluish cloud curl from his lips out to drift away over the noisy traffic in the street below.

'The French Embassy staff summoned her to tell her of Thibault's death – we may be tolerably sure of that, if only from the alteration in her behaviour *after* she had been summoned there,' he said, at length. 'So why was she sent to England in the first place? It could be that Admiral Saisset, and even the French Prime Minister himself, hoped that she might find him and persuade him to return to Paris *before* he gave away any secrets to our government. That would be the most plausible reason for sending his lover – if that is what she was.'

'I'm convinced that she was,' Sophie said. 'After yesterday.'

'A merciful Providence saw fit to reveal Guttmann on the road, yesterday,' Mycroft went on. 'We cannot be absolutely certain that he had been carrying the body to place it in the Thames, but it is the only reasonable hypothesis we have to work on. Thibault had been dead weeks rather than days. So what has Guttmann been about? Only he could have told the French that Thibault was dead. If the secret Thibault was carrying was one which neither the Prussians nor the French Government wanted our people to discover, why didn't Guttmann inform the French that Thibault had been silenced weeks rather than two days ago?'

Again silence fell between them as Mycroft smoked.

'Unless,' Sophie began, and then stopped.

'Please. Continue,' Mycroft told her.

'Unless Guttmann himself didn't know that he was dead. Perhaps Guttmann wanted him alive, not dead.'

'I suppose it is possible. I'm afraid we are going to have to investigate Herr Guttmann's activities in Surrey more closely.'

'I have promised to keep Mme Tirard company on her return journey to Paris,' said Sophie. 'We shall leave this afternoon.'

'Will you, by Jove!' Mycroft exclaimed.

'I shall return tomorrow by the afternoon boat-train into Charing Cross. I may have more to tell you then.'

'And I', said Mycroft, 'shall take the down train to Oxford. Where's the confounded Bradshawe? Ah! Here we are! My young brother Sherlock is a profligate young fellow – intelligent enough in his way if he did not abuse his brain by engaging in fisticuffs and fencing and such like. However, since he is my brother, he is naturally endowed with certain talents which I hope to make use of before his chosen mode of existence causes them to waste away entirely. I shall employ him as our spy in the Dorking area.'

'Mr Holmes?' said Sophie. 'You must give me your most solemn promise.'

'And what might that be?' Mycroft asked.

'You will make sure that I am – how do you say it? – At the kill?'

'*In* at the kill, Princess,' he corrected her. 'I shall see to it, so far as it lies within my power.'

He had begun to experience an occasional, irrational sense of euphoria which was entirely foreign to him. It was a feeling which came over him, albeit fleetingly, in her company or when he entertained thoughts of her. The dreadful possibility occurred to him that it could be the first symptoms of what lesser intelligences – those given to a vulgar turn of phrase – would call 'falling in love'. In the same way that Providence had provided the sense of pain as a warning to protect the physical body from damage, so this feeling was sent as a warning to him to protect that mental stability and calm which was necessary for the proper exercise of his intellect.

Chapter Twenty

'You have brought the piece of raw steak, I trust?'
Sherlock called from his bedroom.

'Indeed, sir,' replied the elderly scout whose ragged
white locks and ancient morning-coat were crusty
enough to suggest he had been laid down in the college
cellars with the wine. He placed the tea things, including
the glass-covered plate of sandwiches and the chafing-
dish with toasted tea-cake, on the table. A saucer contained a shining fragment of red meat. 'Will that be all,
sir?' he called.

'Yes, thank you, Driffield,' Sherlock called back.

Mycroft was in the window-seat of Sherlock's rooms in
Brasenose. He looked out past the noble Carolingian
dome of the Radcliffe Camera to the pinnacled facade
and baroque-ornamented gateway of All Souls. The spec-
tacle filled him with longing. He could be safe within
those cloistered walls and silent quadrangles; a word to
Sir James Swarthmoor, a favour to Her Majesty's ministers safely accomplished, and he had little doubt that a
fellowship would be his, a *laissez-passer* to a lifetime's

tranquillity of body and soul. Come the four quarters of the world in arms, nothing would ever disturb the stillness of All Souls:

> Hierusalem my happy home,
> Would God I were in thee!
> Would that my sorrows were at an end
> Thy joys that I might see . . .

He sighed. Sherlock came out of the bedroom. He had bathed and changed after an afternoon of sporting activity. The Grecian regularity of his features, the gimlet penetration of his gaze, was distorted by the increasingly yellow and black colouring of the swelling about his right eye.

'Oh, my dear Sherlock!' Mycroft protested. 'Apart from the damage done to your eyesight, have you the least idea of the effect of that blow on your central nervous system?'

Sherlock gave him a grimace. He reached over to the saucer and dabbed the fragment of raw steak under his damaged eye. He winced.

'And for heaven's sake put down that gory relic!' Mycroft continued. 'It cannot do the least good to damage already inflicted. Even if you have deadened your finer human feelings by indulging in sports of the more barbarous kind, I assure you *I* am still the possessor of a finely-tuned sensibility!'

Sherlock lowered the piece of raw steak, if only to the level of his chin.

'My reply to the request you are about to make, Mycroft, is a definite and decided negative.'

'I haven't put any request to you,' said Mycroft.

'Not yet. But you didn't make the tedious railway journey here to ask my advice on the case on which you are currently employing yourself. Here. Take a cup of this excellent Darjeeling. And help yourself to the tea-cakes; I ordered them entirely on your behalf. I may be deficient in "finer human feelings" but I am not a stranger to a proper sense of humility. Neither would I pretend to be able to cast light on a problem over which you had difficulties, nor would you expect me to do so. Our methods, like our tastes in music, are too divergent. No! You want me to scout for you – to act as your runner. That is why you are here!'

Mycroft reached over to the table. He took a plate and placed two rounds of sandwiches and two tea-cakes on it.

'But you will permit me to recite the facts of the case, will you not?' he asked.

'I should be greatly interested to hear them,' Sherlock replied truthfully.

Mycroft hesitated. 'Might as well,' he said. He reached over and took a third tea-cake and piled it on to his plate.

Between large mouthfuls, and even during them, he explained to Sherlock what had occurred till then. When he had finished, he reached over and rewarded himself with a fourth tea-cake. Sherlock had listened intently, holding the steak to his eye with one hand and taking the occasional finely-cut triangle of sandwich in the other.

As Mycroft started to consume the last tea-cake, Sherlock said, 'So, what you wanted of me was to go crawling all over the Surrey hills in pursuit of this Carl Philipp Emmanuel Guttmann – while you sat in rapt contemplation in your favourite chair in the Diogenes Club . . . Pray, don't deny it, Mycroft. There's guilt written all over your face! I do know that a painstaking accumulation of data is not precisely your *métier*, but this time you are going to have to do your own detective work, I'm afraid. And please refrain from pointing out how much I am supposed to be indebted to you for your care of me as your younger brother!'

'I think you might give it a little consideration,' said Mycroft in a pained voice. 'Particularly in view of the fact that the half is, to all intents and purposes, over. I don't suppose you intend to pass the entire Long Vac frowsting in your rooms here.'

'Certainly not! My neighbour, here on these stairs, has invited me down to his family's place in Norfolk.'

'Not the fellow whose bull-terrier froze to your ankle when you were on your way to morning chapel!' said Mycroft.

'The same. Victor Trevor,' Sherlock replied. 'I'm going with him to Donnithorpe at the weekend.'

'I hope the Dean read prayers of commination over the beast for obstructing you on your way to worship,' said Mycroft. 'There is, I recall, an appropriate form of words provided in the Book of Common Prayer.'

Sherlock ignored the observation.

'We are the best of friends,' he said. 'He and his beast. Trevor is a good sound fellow. He inflicted this on me to prove it.' He pointed to his black eye. Mycroft shuddered.

'His father', Sherlock continued, 'has a small but serviceable library. It contains, amongst other rarities, a set of folio volumes of music printed in Florence for the household of Duke Cosimo II. I wish to consult them with regard to the paper I'm delivering to the Aeolian Society next term.'

'Ah yes!' Mycroft replied. 'The paper on Orlandus

201

Lassus. I remember . . . However, I would have thought a proper sense of obligation toward an elder brother . . .'

'The paper is on Don Carlo Gesualdo,' Sherlock interrupted him.

Mycroft stopped. His jaw dropped. Then he said, 'I was certain, Sherlock, we had agreed that Lassus, not Gesualdo, was to be the object of your inquiries.'

'*You* had agreed,' Sherlock replied. 'Not I. I'm pretty certain what I shall be telling the Society in Magdalen next term will have repercussions well beyond the walls of the University. I'm on to something big, Mycroft!'

Mycroft raised his eyebrows.

'I believe,' Sherlock continued, 'that I am on the verge of being able to assert beyond all doubt that Don Carlo Gesualdo was innocent of the death of his wife and child.'

'I suppose that nothing I shall say', Mycroft told him gloomily, 'will dissuade you from following the path to neurasthenia and a pathological morbidity of intellect?'

'Certainly not the offer of having me spend the Long Vac crawling behind the Surrey hedgerows on your behalf!' replied Sherlock.

He accompanied Mycroft out of Brasenose College. They strolled past the Camera and into the deserted quadrangle of the Bodleian Library.

'There's no great mystery attached to these secret protocols drawn up between the Prussian High Command and the Versailles Government, of course,' Sherlock observed. 'But you don't need me to tell you that!'

'No, of course not!' replied Mycroft.

He stopped. 'Perhaps, my dear Sherlock,' he said, 'you would care to explain your conclusions on the matter, and how you arrived at them. And, my dear boy! Would you oblige me by not holding that repulsive piece of meat to your damaged eye one single moment longer!' He had only just noticed that Sherlock had brought the fragment of raw steak out with him.

Sherlock lowered it.

'The method is simply that of Okham's Razor,' he said. 'One has only to pare away what is impossible, what is irrelevant, and finally what is only barely probable, and observe what remains.'

'And what remains in this case?' asked Mycroft.

Sherlock looked at him curiously. 'You are putting me to the test,' he said.

His mouth twitched slightly. He dabbed the meat to his eye. Mycroft prodded his chest with the end of his stick.

'Tell me, you young pup!' he said.

'There really is only the one possibility to be deduced from what you have told me – one thing detrimental to the interests of this country which the French Government could have ceded, back in April, to win consent from the Prussians for the restoration of their armies: that is that the Prussians and their German tributaries should have unimpeded use of the Channel ports.'

'Of course!' exclaimed Mycroft involuntarily. He lowered his stick.

'One may presume', Sherlock continued, 'that this would necessarily involve some similar arrangement regarding the railways in north-eastern France which feed into those ports – Boulogne, Calais, Dieppe, Le Havre, and the rest. We saw, last year, how in the north German states the railways were cleared to allow the unobstructed passage of trains carrying troops and *matériel* to the frontiers. This would now apply to railways linking the German frontiers to the French Channel ports. In the eventuality of a Prussian assault on our south coast, von Moltke and von Roon would only have to give the word and railways and harbour quays would be cleared instantly. Prussian forces would move to embarkation in northern France within a matter of a few hours – probably under cover of darkness.'

'And we would have nothing – neither fleet nor army – with which to oppose them!' exclaimed Mycroft. 'It is too frightful to contemplate!'

'It is frightful enough for a dedicated French anglophile to consider taking his life in his hands in order to warn Her Majesty's Government!' Sherlock replied.

He dabbed at his eye with the raw steak. Mycroft had not the heart to protest.

'There is one other possibility,' Sherlock observed.

'What is that?'

'That your friend, Jean-Christophe Thibault, was stark-raving mad.'

Sherlock's thin lips curved into a grin.

'If so,' said Mycroft, 'a number of important people have gone to a great deal of trouble to silence his ravings.' He shook his head. 'It is not possible, I fear,' he added.

'By the by, Mycroft,' said Sherlock. 'I suggest you consult your *Continental Gazeteer*. You will find there a railway junction in the Grand Duchy of Pfalzel-Buckelburg. It is called Drei Jungfrauen. You should draw the attention of your masters to it. It is there that the railway lines from all the major western German states converge. It is also the point from which one may travel directly to the major Channel ports in north-eastern France.'

On returning to Paddington Station Mycroft took a hansom directly to the Diogenes Club in the hope of obtaining an hour or two's tranquillity of spirit. Scarcely had he sat down in his favourite chair by the library window than one of the attendants crooked his finger in order to attract his attention. He came over to Mycroft's seat; in his hand he bore a piece of white card on which a scrawled message had been inscribed in pencil. Mycroft snatched the card from him. He rose; the moment he reached the library door he said aloud, 'Tell the porter to fetch my hat and gloves immediately!'

Although he had not spoken particularly loudly, until that evening it had been unknown for a founder-member of the club to speak audibly upstairs. Other members came to the doors of various rooms leading out on to the first-floor gallery. Some were rubbing the sleep from their eyes; not a few were clearly irritated by the disturbance. Somebody whispered, 'Where's the fire, deuce take it? Eh, what?' One or two leaned over the wrought-iron balustrade as Mycroft hurried downstairs. Whispered voices followed him like the wings of pursuing Furies: 'Disgraceful behaviour!' . . . 'Founder-member – fellow should know better, by God!' . . . 'Report the young bounder to the committee!'

In the vestibule he snatched his hat, coat and gloves from the waiting porter and ran out, down the steps and across Pall Mall. He trotted as fast as his girth permitted along the pavement. The negro was propped against the wall of Number 73a, but Mycroft ignored him. Mrs Turner came out to him as soon as he opened the front door.

'It's the Princess, Mr Holmes! She's waiting for you upstairs.'

'She's supposed to be in France!' Mycroft exclaimed.

'She's been waiting all afternoon,' said Mrs Turner. 'I

went over to the club, sir. I hope you don't mind. I wrote you a message.'

'I received it, thank you, Mrs Turner.'

'Her Highness is ever so condescending, sir. She's been no trouble at all.'

'*Thank* you, Mrs Turner!'

He pulled himself up the stairs by the banisters at a speed which left him at the top gasping for breath. Sophie came to the study door. He noticed that she was dressed in a long yellow duster-coat as if for a long journey. She came on to the landing and took his arm solicitously.

'What has happened?' he croaked.

'I will tell you when you are sitting down comfortably,' she replied.

There was a tea-tray on the table.

'I see Mrs Turner has been looking after you,' he said.

'She has been looking after me very well,' Sophie replied. 'We have quite "taken to each other" – that is what you say?' She lowered him into his chair.

'You are supposed to be with Mme Tirard in Paris,' he said in a tone almost of rebuke.

She sat down opposite him, across the table.

'When I went to Kendall's Hotel,' she said, 'Mme Tirard was already gone. I came straight here to tell you as soon as possible.'

'What has happened?' he asked.

'It was only half past midday when I put down in Jermyn Street. Mme Tirard had suggested I take a light lunch with her at the hotel before we set off, but they told me she had left for Charing Cross Station two hours earlier. They said she had left in a great hurry and had asked that her boxes be sent after her. There had been two gentlemen, the manager told me – French

206

gentlemen – come to fetch her in a closed carriage.'

'From the French Embassy, I dare say,' said Mycroft.

'One of the porters told me that she had tried to pass a sealed envelope to him, but one of the French gentlemen spotted it and took it from her, and put it into his own pocket.'

'Did anybody see her face? Was anybody able to observe her condition?' asked Mycroft.

'They said her face was veiled all the time she was leaving. I asked for a cab to be called and drove straight to Charing Cross. There was no sign of her, however. She must have left by one of the ordinary trains to Dover or Folkestone. So I came back here. Was I right to do so?'

'Of course, Princess. You have done very well.'

To his surprise she looked pleased, even flattered.

'There is nothing for it, you know,' he said. 'I shall have to go into Surrey myself. We shall achieve nothing unless we can discover precisely what Guttmann is about.'

'May I come with you?'

'No, Princess. I'm sure you would not be deterred if I were to tell you that it might prove a dangerous enterprise. But if we were together we should be too conspicuous. It would give rise to talk in a small place like Dorking. I dare say the presence there of any stranger would be a matter for conversation. The news of a couple such as you and I would reach Ranmore Hall almost instantly. I suggest you allow me to take your negro follower to act as messenger between us.'

'Nobody would be more conspicuous than he!' Sophie objected.

'He would be so conspicuous that nobody would dream that he or his master were up to any sort of trick. What spy would ever dream of having a blackamoor servant in tow? Everybody will see a gentleman intent on spending a few days on holiday viewing the ancient Pilgrims' Way to Canterbury, accompanied by his negro valet.'

'But you will remember your promise, Mr Holmes?' Sophie said. 'You are not to make an end of the affair without sending for me?'

She sounded quite crestfallen.

'If it is humanly possible, Princess, I shall send Cyril to fetch you.'

Later that same night Mycroft went across to the Carlton Club to ask to speak with Sir James Swarthmoor. Sir James took him up to the library, which was almost deserted due to the lateness of the hour. They sat in the seclusion of one of the alcoves, in the comfort of deep leather upholstery. Sir James ordered Scotch whisky and sodas.

'My leave of absence from my official duties must be extended, Sir James,' Mycroft said.

'Really?' asked Sir James with a slightly sardonic smile.

'I believe I've hit on the burden of the message the unfortunate M. Thibault wished to convey to Her Majesty's Government.'

'Indeed! And what might it have been?' asked Sir James.

'It is remarkable', said Mycroft, 'how certain things come to one – like a great melody to a composer. It suddenly occurred to me, as plain as a pikestaff.'

'What is as plain as a pikestaff?'

'That there could only be one concession the French could offer the high command of the German Confederation in return for the re-mobilization of their armies – one, that is, which would be detrimental to the interests of this country.'

'Yes? Go on.'

'A secret protocol attached to the Versailles armistice which cedes to the Prussians discretionary control of the Channel ports, thus providing what has now become the German Imperial General Staff with the capacity to mobilize men and *matériel* within the frontiers of Germany for an attack on this country.'

'You know perfectly well, Holmes, what "Pussy" Granville would ask – and with justification, I may add! Why, in God's name, would Prince von Bismarck and the German peoples wish to attack a natural friend and ally?'

'Let me ask a question, Sir James. Why should an anglophile Frenchman risk his life – and lose it, as it turns out – in an attempt to warn Her Majesty's Government, if the substance of his warning was not an extremely serious matter?'

'The poor fellow may have been an anglophile,' said Sir James. 'I don't doubt it. But he was not a politician: he was a manufacturer, a tradesman with, no doubt, a tradesman's axe to grind. Just because his wife's family and that of the French Prime Minister are connected in some way is no proof that a wily old serpent like Alphonse Thiers is going to confide in him – not at least some grandiose scheme by which the French Republic is going to aid and abet its Prussian foes in a treacherous attack on this country!'

'I am not suggesting Thibault was told of this arrangement by M. Thiers,' Mycroft replied. 'I believe it to be a case of what our transatlantic cousins call "pillow-talk". I have discovered – and it is fact, I hasten to add, Sir James – that Mme Tirard has been, for some time, sharing her extramarital favours between M. Thibault and Admiral Saisset.'

'My dear Holmes!'

Sir James burst out laughing, then glanced somewhat sheepishly out of the alcove.

'I have it on extremely good authority,' Mycroft continued severely. 'It is a reasonable hypothesis that Mme Tirard learned in an unguarded moment of the arrangement from one lover – the second most important figure in the French War Ministry, after all – and in true womanly fashion she was unable to keep the secret to herself. So she confided it to her other lover. I believe Mme Tirard came here, to London, in part due to her distress at what she felt she had caused to happen but also acting as agent for M. Thiers and Admiral Saisset, to discover how much damage Thibault had already done, or, if it were possible, to prevent it being done at all.'

'Have you found the least shred of evidence for this extraordinary theory?' asked Sir James.

'I believe we were on the very verge of discovering it,' Mycroft replied. 'After we had returned from Staines, yesterday, Princess Trubetskoy kept Mme Tirard company all through the night. Mme Tirard asked the Princess to accompany her back to Paris this afternoon. The Princess agreed, believing that Mme Tirard was about to confide something of importance to her. Two hours earlier than the time the Princess had agreed to meet Mme Tirard at Kendall's Hotel, two French gentlemen with a closed carriage came to escort her to Charing Cross Station. They left with her so quickly that, though her boxes were packed, they have had to be sent on to Paris after her.'

'These French gentlemen would, I suppose, be from the French Embassy,' said Sir James. 'The Foreign Office has informed M. Thiers of the discovery of Thibault's body. It would be perfectly proper for officials of the

French Embassy to assist Mme Tirard to return to her native land . . . No, Holmes, despite all your ingenious theories, the fact remains that as far as HMG is concerned, the affair of the unfortunate M. Thibault is now a matter for Scotland Yard and the Detective Police.'

Mycroft pulled himself out of his deep armchair and sat forward.

'Sir James, the night before the discovery of Thibault's body, two men came from the French Embassy to Kendall's Hotel and took Mme Tirard back with them to Grosvenor Square. An hour later she returned to the hotel in a state of deep distress. It is my opinion that she had been informed that Thibault had been killed, some ten or eleven hours before the recorded discovery of his body in the Thames.'

'Had *died*, Holmes! Not was *killed*! There is not a scrap of forensic evidence to lead us to suppose his death was anything other than by misadventure. Not even the French authorities have suggested otherwise.'

'The "misadventure" bearing the appellation Carl Philipp Emmanuel Guttmann!' said Mycroft.

'Holmes! Holmes! I wish we had never dragged you away from your weekend at Oxford,' groaned Sir James.

'Mme Tirard kept saying to the Princess all last night, after her return from identifying the body, "Why have they killed him?" and, "They swore they would do him no harm!" In any case, *killed* or *died*, it seems to me that the poor lady was informed of his death before his body was fished out of the river.'

'Like all your other theories, Holmes,' Sir James told him, 'it is supposition. If officials at the French Embassy were able to tell her of Thibault's death before the discovery of his body, who do you suppose told them?'

'That', Mycroft replied, 'is all too simple! The man who killed him, of course.'

Sir James buried his face in his hands. Mycroft, however, continued without pity.

'It is possible that M. Thiers would have preferred Thibault to have remained alive, though Admiral Saisset would have had no regrets at his rival's departure from this vale of tears – crimes of passion are, after all, a French speciality. But all this is entirely consistent with both German and French Governments wanting the man silenced.'

Sir James raised his head from his hands and stared at Mycroft.

'You know, Sir James,' Mycroft said calmly, 'if you do not wish me to exercise my intellectual powers, you should not call on me to assist you in inquiries such as this.'

Sir James Swarthmoor took a very deep breath.

'Holmes, my dear fellow! You have one more day, plus the weekend, to provide some evidence to corroborate your theories – this extraordinary conjectural edifice which you have been pleased to erect. And that is all! Thibault has been found. How he met his fate is, officially at least, a matter for a coroner's jury and the police. I could not possibly justify your absence from your desk at the Treasury one day longer. You have until half past eight o'clock on Monday next!'

Chapter Twenty-one

Mycroft sat alone in the dining-room of the White Posts Hotel in Dorking. He was at a table by the window. Outside, in the yard, Cyril was leaning against the stable wall, clay pipe dangling from his lips. Three very young women – hotel chambermaids – who had begun by looking at him in giggling wonderment, had plucked up the courage to talk to him. As he regaled them with tales of life on London streets, something like adoration had crept over their faces. A gentlemen and lady who had just left the dining-room crossed the yard to a waiting family brougham into whose shafts fresh horses had just been harnessed.

The waiter, a sallow-faced, hollow-cheeked, elderly man with a stoop, was no advertisement for the food he was serving. Ever since he set eyes on him Mycroft had kept his ears open for any sound of a consumptive cough. As the man placed the dish of mutton chops and potatoes on the table, Mycroft eyed them carefully. He prodded them with his fork.

'Is everything to your satisfaction, sir?' the waiter asked anxiously.

Mycroft gave him a watery, grey look. He nodded.

'Your wine, sir?' The waiter picked up the bottle of claret to pour it into Mycroft's glass. Mycroft nodded again. He helped himself to a mouthful of chop.

'You're kept fairly busy here, I dare say?' he asked with his mouth full.

'Oh yes, sir. This is a particularly quiet evening, sir. We was lucky here when the railway was built – not like some of the old coaching inns. Being near the station we became a railway hotel, as you might say.'

'Passengers stepping down from the railway come here for refreshment before travelling on by cart or carriage, eh?'

'That's the way of it, sir.'

'Since you only have myself to attend to,' said Mycroft, 'perhaps you would care to take a glass of wine with me.'

'That is very kind of you, sir. Very kind indeed, if I might say so.'

Mycroft waved his hand in the direction of a glass on a nearby table.

'Help yourself.'

'Very condescending of you, sir. There! I'll drink to your very good health if I may.'

'I expect there's a fair amount of traffic here for the houses of the gentry hereabouts,' Mycroft suggested.

'I was going to say, sir. There's a number of what you might call "noble seats" hereabouts, if you're one for fine buildings. There's Wotton Place – that's Mr Evelyn's mansion. And there's Abinger Hall – that's the property of Lord Abinger, of course. And then there's Ranmore Hall, up on Ranmore Common. If you're one for the picturesque view, sir, then the prospect of Ranmore Hall, looking over the Gap from the slope of Box Hill, hasn't its equal in the whole county, so they say.'

'Really? And who is the proprietor of this – er – Ranmore Place . . .?'

'Ranmore Hall, sir. The gentleman is in trade, sir. A Mr Jenks-Robinson. In coal, I believe – a very necessary product.'

Mycroft looked up at him, alerted by the note of contempt in the man's voice. He put down his knife and fork.

'One of the props on which the industrial wealth of our great nation is founded,' he said sententiously.

The waiter sensed his disapproval.

'I've heard nothing against the gentleman, sir, I do assure you! Nothing in the world! It is only that Miss Cornwallis-Herbert, as *Mrs* Jenks-Robinson was before she was married, was so much admired by everybody here in Dorking, sir. She was a *real* lady – a true Christian gentlewoman, if it don't sound presumptuous in talking so of my betters, sir.'

'Who was this Miss Cornwallis-Herbert before she was married? Have a drop more of this excellent claret.'

'Oh thank you, sir. This is a red-letter day for me, to be sure!'

Mycroft picked up the bottle and refilled the waiter's glass. 'Miss Cornwallis-Herbert?' he reminded him.

'The Cornwallis-Herberts were the owners of the Ranmore estates, and the Hall, of course, as long as anyone hereabouts can remember. But the estates fell on hard times, as you might say. And then Miss Cornwallis-Herbert – she was past her first youth, sir, and still an unmarried lady when she inherited the property on old Mr

215

Cornwallis-Herbert's death. If I dare say as much, I suppose, seeing as how she was no great beauty and how she was the proprietor of an encumbered estate, she weren't likely to attract the attentions of the sort of gentleman-born, if you take my meaning, who could have saved the property. So when Mr Robinson come on the scene, as you might say – he didn't become Mr *Jenks*-Robinson till after they was betrothed, if you'll excuse me saying so – she grasped at the opportunity.'

'So things have changed up at the Hall?' asked Mycroft.

'Oh yes, sir! They have, and no mistake. Old Mr Cornwallis-Herbert and even Miss Cornwallis-Herbert kept open house up there: balls and house parties at the weekend and I don't know what besides – there was always something going on up at the Hall! But Mr Jenks-Robinson keeps his self to his self most of the time. A very quiet gentleman, you might say.'

'So you wouldn't say there was a constant stream of guests travelling up to the Hall?' Mycroft asked.

'Why, bless you! No, sir,' the waiter laughed. 'There's the Prooshian gentleman. He comes and goes as he pleases, by all accounts. They do say he's something to do with the coal-mining business, like Mr Jenks-Robinson his self. No, it's quiet as the grave up there , most times. Except – now there's a funny thing! If you were to come just two weeks from today, sir, I dare say we wouldn't be able to accommodate you. It's the one time Mr Jenks-Robinson does throw the grounds open to the public. I expect it's because he's a manufacturing gentleman, sir. He has open house to all the Mechanical Institutes of Reigate and Guildford and Godalming, and here at Dorking, of course. And everybody is allowed, for one penny piece, to go and see the traction engines, and the electrical machines, and to try their skill with the telegraph. And there's a beer and ale tent for the menfolk, and a tea-and-cake tent for the ladies, and roundabouts driven by steam-engines for the children . . .'

Mycroft raised his flipper-like hand to interrupt the flow of this account. 'The Poet-Laureate describes it perfectly!' he said.

> 'Sir Walter Vivian all a summer's day
> Gave his broad lawns until the set of sun
> Up to the people: thither flocked at noon
> His tenants, wife and child, and thither half
> The neighbouring borough with their Institute
> Of which he was the patron . . .'

'Exactly so, sir! Precisely so; Lord Tennyson has it exactly,' the waiter told him.

'But why could I not be accommodated by the White Posts Hotel?' asked Mycroft. 'You have a large establishment here.'

'Because, sir, this year there is to be a German band, sir. I except it has been arranged by the Prooshian gentleman. And the musicians are to be accommodated here, with their instruments!'

'Are they, by God!' said Mycroft. 'In a fortnight's time, you say?'

'Yes, sir.' The waiter was quite surprised by his reaction.

'How many of these musicians?' Mycroft asked.

'Some twenty of 'em, I believe. With their conductor. And with the guests who come regularly for these occasions, sir, it won't leave much room for anybody else. And they say the Germans are great trenchermen.'

'I wonder if you would be so good as to send in my

servant – the black fellow out there,' said Mycroft.

'Very good, sir.'

When Cyril came in, Mycroft said to him, 'I trust you can keep yourself from falling into the clutches of the local Circes long enough—'

'Local whats, Mr Holmes, sir?'

'Don't be impertinent, man. And don't interrupt me when I'm giving you an order.'

'Sorry, sir, your honour,' he grinned unrepentently. 'Didn't know you was giving me an order, see?'

'I shall write a letter to the Princess as soon as I've risen from the table. I want you to take it to the railway station and make sure it is sent by tonight's Royal Mail. It is most urgent. Do you understand?'

Cyril nodded. 'Take it as done, sir.'

Mycroft grunted. 'Don't know why the Princess ever took you into her service,' he said.

'She didn't, Mr Holmes, sir. I took myself into her service, 'cause I wanted to.'

'You took yourself into her service?' asked Mycroft.

'It was when we was trying to rob her, sir—'

'Rob her?'

'At night, sir. On the pavement. She were on foot, wearing her boy's duds, like you seen her, sir. She showed more spirit than I ever see-d in a lady afore! I tells you, sir: if I was still a Zulu Prince, I'd ask the Princess to marry me, and that's the solemn truth!' Then he added in utmost seriousness, 'Know what I mean, sir?'

'You're an impudent, lying rascal,' said Mycroft. 'And if you've ever been prince of anything, it is the Cut in Lambeth . . . But I understand what you mean.'

He paused. 'Just make sure my letter to her goes to her by the Royal Mail, tonight,' he said.

Chapter Twenty-two

The following morning, during the breakfast hush,
Abigail came up the back stairs to the bedrooms once
more. This time, however, she was not struggling with
a slop-bucket. She was in some measure transformed:
the clean print dress she was wearing fitted her; her
starched, flounced apron was a spotless white and she
wore a blue protective apron over it; and her mob was
muslin, with a frontlet of starched calico. In fact,
following Liza Makepeace's sudden departure, she had
been promoted to Liza's position as chambermaid.
There was a deal of silly talk about Liza having run off
with Billy Lavendar. Abigail knew better. Abigail
knew that Mr Guttmann had arranged for Liza to go
to London town to become parlourmaid in a house
belonging to some grand friends of his. She knew
that Bill Lavendar was in no condition to marry anybody – and serve him right, he'd always been nasty to
her.

She stepped through the door leading on to the
carpeted, first-floor bedroom passage. In the sunlight at

the far end, on the oak-panelled landing, the giant figure of Guttmann was standing gazing out of the window. Abby smiled even though he wasn't looking in her direction. The sight of him filled her with a delight she could not have put a name to – the joy, perhaps, one was supposed to feel about Jesus, but never did.

'Mr Guttmann!' she called softly. 'Good morning, Mr Guttmann!'

As he turned to look at her she smiled flirtatiously at him.

'Why, if it isn't little Abigail!' he called to her.

He eyed her up and down.

'How do you like your new situation, my dear?' he asked as she came up the passage. 'You will give satisfaction, I trust – no grounds for complaint from your mistress, eh?'

'I hope not, if you please, Mr Guttmann,' she smiled.

She knew who was responsible for her rapid promotion. She knew that it had been greeted by the other maids with deep dissatisfaction, but that they would not dare to show it openly, knowing who her patron was.

'I've got to wait for Annie to show me my duties,' she explained.

'Do you see what I have here?' Guttmann asked.

He smiled down at her, and she bathed in his approval. She hoped that a few afternoons previously, on that strange, fearful drive in the wagonette to Staines and back through the storm, she had proved herself worthy of his friendship. She had not exactly believed, but had felt nonetheless, that he had conjured up the darkness, the rattling, drenching curtains of rain, the electrical javelins of light which had struck at and fractured the cloud – that he had designed it to protect them in their dreadful but ordained task. By demonstrating her devotion she had earned her reward. In return for her continued service he would surely see to it that she achieved the place in the world her looks and natural gentility merited.

'Do you know what this is, little Abigail?'

Resting on his arm he had a brass-and-leather naval telescope.

She shook her head. He opened it and raised it to his eye, pointing it at the window.

'It is a telescope – the kind ships' captains use at sea,' he told her.

'It makes things look closer, doesn't it, Mr Guttmann?' Abigail said.

'It does. You can point it at things which are quite far away and they look very near.'

'I 'spect Lord Nelson had a telescope like that,' suggested Abigail.

'I am sure you are quite right,' Guttmann replied. 'But do you know, little Abigail? Ah! I should not call you *little* Abigail any more, should I? Not now that you have become my helper. I know that really you are very grown-up . . .' He put his arm round her shoulder. Boldly, she reached hers round his waist, still smiling up at him.

'I *was* very grown up when we went to Staines, weren't I, Mr Guttmann? And I never told nobody where we'd been, even though the others downstairs was jealous – 'cause they thought as you'd taken me out for a treat, see. And I didn't tell them no different.'

'I hope you didn't. It is very important you shouldn't, you see.'

'Mabel says as I'm your sweetheart,' Abby told

221

him. 'She makes it sound really nasty, she does!'

'Perhaps it's because she is jealous of you, eh?' He patted her on the cheek. 'You see, little Abigail, you are not only a very grown-up girl for your age. You are also very pretty . . .'

'Prettier 'n Mabel?' asked Abby.

'Much prettier!' He bent over to whisper in her ear. 'Which is why, when I go away, I shall give my little sweetheart this telescope for her very own.'

'Oh, Mr Guttmann! Will you? Honest?'

'Of course, *liebchen*. But now you must look at something most amusing.' He removed her arm from around his waist. 'You must look through the telescope,' he told her, 'and tell me what you see.'

He held it pointing at the window as she put her eye to it.

'Can't see nothing,' she said in angry disappointment. 'It's broke!'

'What does it look like?' he asked her.

'Like it's all foggy.' She looked up at him. 'Like somebody gone and made me cry,' she told him.

'Put it to your eye again. Now turn it here – just here – until you see something.'

'Oh! Oh my!' Abby gasped in amazement.

'Now you can see something?' Guttmann asked.

'Oh yes! It's like I can reach out and touch the grass – the other side of the Gap! Well I never! And the box trees. They ain't half close!'

Guttmann bent down and whispered in her ear, 'Look up nearer to the top of the hill. What do you see?'

Abby raised the barrel of the telescope.

'Oh!' she exclaimed. She laughed. 'Well I never!'

'Tell me, *liebchen*.'

'It's a funny, fat man. And he's got a black nigger-boy standing behind him. The black nigger-boy is holding an umbrella to keep the sun off of the funny fat man.' She laughed even more. Guttmann laughed with her. She said, 'Now the funny, fat man's trying to do something with his eyes, only his hat's so big it's in the way . . . Now he's had to take off his hat . . . Oh lawks! He's looking at me. Here! Do you know what? He's got a telescope his self and he's looking at me!'

'What's that you say?' The smile vanished from Guttmann's face.

'It's only a little one, Mr Guttmann. Not a nice big one like ours. And he's looking straight in here, he is!'

'Give it to me!'

Guttmann seized the telescope quite roughly. He put it to his eye, trying to focus it as he did so.

'You snatched it!' Abby protested. 'You should have asked nicely.'

'Silence, you little fool!'

His sudden anger shocked and hurt her.

'It's very rude to snatch!' she answered back, though even as she did so she knew she was being foolish.

He lowered the telescope from his eye. He glared down at her with a glowing demonic intensity. In uncontrollable terror, she stepped back, putting out her hand to fend him off. 'I'll tell the mistress on you!' she said hoarsely.

He stared down at her. His angry glare turned to a sneeringly incredulous smile. Out of the appalled confusion of her fear, she whimpered, 'I'll tell her all the things you get up to.'

His smile grew more terrible. The tears began to pour down her face, but they could not extinguish her terror. Solemnly Guttmann shook his head.

'We would never tell, little Abigail,' he said softly. 'Not you and I. Not on one another. Not unless we wanted to betray our true destiny by having to scrub steps, and empty chamber-pots, and polish shoes, and press suits for ever and ever! And you and I were not meant for that, were we, little Abigail?'

She heard herself whisper, 'No, sir. Very sorry , sir! I am indeed!'

As she stood staring at him through her tears as if in a trance, he raised the telescope to his eye once more. From a coloured blur, Mycroft and Cyril came into sharp focus. Mycroft, in striped blazer and white trousers, a wide-brimmed straw panama hat on his knees, was sitting on a folding stool. Beside him, to the front, a portable artist's easel and board was set up. Behind him stood Cyril, looking distinctly awkward and surly in a crumpled, ill-fitting linen suit, holding a coloured umbrella to keep the sun off him. Mycroft was holding a small black spy-glass to his eye. It was pointed directly at Guttmann.

'I know you from somewhere, my friend,' Guttmann said to himself quietly.

Abigail stared at him.

'Oh yes, *liebe Mann*,' he said softly. 'It will come back to me, never fear!'

He snapped the telescope shut. He turned to Abigail. He smiled more gently.

'Do you still want us to be friends, little Abigail? *I* want us to be friends.'

He held out the telescope just far enough to remind her of the promise of rewards to come. She dropped her gaze to look at it. Her fingers clutched at her apron. She nodded.

'There!' he told her. He chucked her under the chin. She flinched slightly. He said, 'Come, *liebchen*! I'm not going to hurt you . . .' He stroked her cheek with his thumb.

'Oh Mr Guttmann!' she whispered back hoarsely, staring at him with a face smeared with tears.

'Show me that we are still friends,' he said to her.

'Show you?' she asked, fearful of what he might want of her.

'Yes, *mein liebchen*. Put on your boots and shawl. Tell the good Mrs Armitage that I have asked you to run an errand for me, yes? Then go across to Box Hill to that funny, fat man and his black savage. Be the sweet, pretty *kleine Mädchen*; find out what you may about him, and what business he does here, yes? Gentlemen never object to pretty *kleine Mädchens* asking curious questions – *you* have found that out, I am sure . . .'

He gave her cheek a pinch so that it hurt. She rubbed it.

'See?' he said, 'I will give you a sixpence. Come back with what I want to know and I shall give you a whole shilling. You will like that, eh?'

Abigail nodded fiercely. Then she said with a recovered boldness, 'You going to give me the telescope if I'm a good girl for you? Honest?'

Guttmann laughed robustly.

'Pretty girls can get anything they want if they are as clever as they are pretty . And you *are* a clever little girl, are you not?'

He pinched her cheek again. She gave a little gasp of pain, but she whispered, 'Yes, if you say so, Mr Guttmann.'

'I say so, little Abigail. I certainly say so.'

*   *   *

Mycroft had put his straw panama back on his head. He leant forward toward the easel, sketching in with charcoal the contours of Ranmore Heights opposite and, on the crest, Ranmore Hall. He had sent Cyril down to Dorking to fetch up some dinner and a bottle of ale. Abigail had reached the crest of the hill. She remained for a moment in the shelter of the trees. Then she came across the sloping meadow, approaching cautiously. She stopped at a discreet distance, watching Mycroft and twisting a lock of her long yellow hair between her fingers.

Mycroft glanced sidelong at her. 'Good afternoon, young woman,' he called, his voice quite severe.

'Afternoon, sir,' Abigail replied shyly. She moved in closer to him.

'And what are you doing up here at this hour of the day?' Mycroft asked. 'A young woman like you should be at her work.'

'Finished my morning work, if you please, sir. So I'm let out for an hour.'

'You must have a very kind mistress,' Mycroft observed.

'Oh yes, sir. She's very good to me, sir.' She edged nearer, and stood looking coy.

'What do they call you ?' Mycroft asked.

'Abigail, please sir.'

'Very well, Abigail. Who might your mistress be ?'

'Mrs Jenks-Robinson, if you please , sir. Only really it's Mrs Armitage, sir, 'cause it's Mrs Armitage what sees to us.'

'Mrs Armitage being the housekeeper, I take it.'

Abigail breathed in deeply. 'Yes, sir.'

'So you're in service over there – at Ranmore Hall?'

'Yes, sir. The Hall.'

She put the lock of hair hanging between her fingers into

her mouth, then remembered herself and took it out again. She came near enough up to Mycroft's shoulder to see what he was drawing.

'It's the Hall,' she said.

'I'm very relieved you are able to recognize it, Abigail,' Mycroft replied.

Abigail looked at him. She giggled at him. Then she said, 'If you please, sir? You one of them artists, sir?'

'Why, bless you, no, Abigail!' Mycroft exclaimed. 'If I had to live by making pictures, I fear I would very soon starve.'

'Why are you making a picture of the Hall then, if you please, sir?'

'For my own amusement, young woman. Because it is a beautiful house with a very fine prospect – one of the finest I have ever seen.'

'You ain't from these parts then, please sir?'

'No. I live in London. I thought I'd come here for a few days of fresh country air and sunlight, don't you know? And to try my hand at some sketching. I expect you have a great many visitors come to look at a fine place like Ranmore Hall. I dare say there'll be guests from abroad – from foreign countries – come to stay, eh?'

Abigail was unsure of herself. She scratched at the flank of her apron.

'Not that many,' she said. 'Not what you'd call many.'

'But one or two, eh? I expect you've managed to pick up a word or two of foreign tongues, have you, Abigail?'

She looked down shyly at the toes of her boots.

'French, eh? *Bonjour monsieur?*' Mycroft suggested. 'Or German, perhaps: *Guten tag, mein Herr?* What do you say?'

Abigail looked embarrassed – almost guilty. 'Dunno,' she whispered. 'Don't understand them foreign words.'

'I believe you are going to have a great many visitors at the hall in a fortnight's time – when Mr Jenks-Robinson throws open his grounds to all the neighbourhood. Or so they tell me in the town. And then there'll be a few *mein Herrs*, I'll be bound! A whole musical band from Germany, eh?'

'Yes, sir.'

'I expect there'll be tents and stalls with sweets and favours, and ribbons and lace, eh?'

Mycroft watched her face keenly.

' 'Spect so, if you please, sir.'

Her gaze wandered past him. Her mouth opened slightly. He turned to see what she was staring at . Cyril had returned. He had appeared over the top of the ridge. Mycroft smiled at Abigail.

'Oh, my dear child! There's nothing to be alarmed about. He's as black as soot, I know. But he doesn't eat people any more; at least, not when he's with me.'

Cyril pulled a sour face.

'Here,' Mycroft said to Abigail. 'You're a bonny wee thing, as our Scotch friends would say.' He took out his purse. 'Here's sixpence for you . Only you must promise to keep it so that you may spend it at your master's garden party.' He dropped it into her outstretched hand. Her fingers closed over it.

'Thank you kindly, sir,' she said. Then she added, 'If you please, sir. Will you be coming to the Hall?'

'Why? What should I do there?'

'Dunno. There'll be races and such . . .'

'What! Me? Run races?' Mycroft smiled. He noticed the grin on Cyril's face, and glowered at him.

Abigail did not notice. She was now in a confiding mood.

'And they say the master's got a real cannon, and he and Mr Whettam is going to run the Union Jack up the flagpole and let off the cannon, and everybody's got to shout "God save Her Majesty!" And the gentlemen'll all have to throw their hats in the air! If you please, sir,' she added as an afterthought.

Mycroft looked sadly at her.

'That sounds very fine, my dear – very fine indeed. But, alas, my duties will keep me in London that day, I fear. Most disappointing . . . isn't it, Cyril?' He looked at Cyril.

'Oh yes, sir,' Cyril replied. He rolled his eyes. 'Ah sure would jest love to see all them hats a-flyin' in de air!' he announced. Then, in his own voice, he added, ' 'cause you never knows where they're going to come down, do you?' He winked knowingly.

They watched Abigail going off down the slope. Mycroft took off his hat and fanned his face with it.

'The impudence! The damned impudence! They're so deuced sure of themselves, they think they can make fools of Englishmen the same way they made fools of the Danes and the Austrians and the French. They think the best way of hiding what they're up to is to tell everybody about it. They let the whole of Surrey know they're bringing in twenty or more bandsmen – and that they have a gun over there, "to fire a salute to Her Majesty!" '

'Are we going back to London?' Cyril asked hopefully. 'To warn people and that?'

Mycroft shook his head. 'They'd never believe it,' he said. 'They'd accept what those people told them' – he pointed in the direction of the Hall. 'An innocent German band! A blank wad shot off in Her Majesty's honour! They'd believe every word of it! Oh no, my friend. We have to stay on here, alas, until we can take back hard evidence of treason!'

Chapter Twenty-three

Guttmann was on the landing at the same time next day, scanning the slope of Box Hill with his telescope. But there was nobody there. He slammed the telescope shut with the ill-temper of a child deprived of a treat. For a short while he remained on the panelled landing, looking from window to window like a giant, crop-headed Minotaur who could scent his prey without being able to see it.

He turned abruptly and strode down the passage. The door to Mrs Jenks-Robinson's bedroom was half open. The chambermaid, Emily, was inside changing the sheets. She stopped the moment he entered.

'If you please, sir. You can't come in here, sir!' she protested. 'This is the mistress's room, sir.'

When she realized that Guttmann was paying no more regard to her than if she had not been there at all, she threw the top sheet back over Mrs Jenks-Robinson's discarded linen, which was lying on the clothes-chest at the foot of the bed.

'Begging your pardon, sir! But you shouldn't be in here,' she tried once more.

It was a situation she had never previously been faced with, and one she had never dreamt she would have to deal with.

'Be quiet, stupid girl!' Guttmann told her.

Emily wondered whether she should continue protesting: then she saw the terrible anger in his face – the vacant, mindless anger of a wild beast. She stood at the bedside, clutching at the sheet, paralysed with fear. Even when he took his eyes off her and went to the window she felt she could not move.

'Mr Guttmann's allowed to go where he likes. Ain't you, Mr Guttmann?'

Abby was standing in the doorway clutching the clean linen for Mrs Jenks-Robinson's bed to her small bosom.

'That is right, little Abigail,' Guttmann replied.

To Emily, it was as if he had split himself into two coexistent beings: a kindly, avuncular one for Abby and a bestially angry one for herself.

He opened the telescope and lifted it to his eye. Abby dropped the folded linen on to the bed in front of Emily and went over to join him at the window. Guttmann examined the rolling crest of Ranmore Common behind the house. As he swung the telescope round in an arc, Mycroft and Cyril came into sharp focus – Mycroft sitting at his easel, spy-glass in hand, Cyril in attendance behind him.

'Aha!' Guttmann exclaimed. 'So there you are! You are thorough, my friend . . . painstaking – as if you had all the time in God's sweet world.'

Abigail gazed enviously at the telescope.

'Is the gentleman up there?' she asked.

'He is, *liebchen!* He most certainly is!'

'He didn't tell me much about his self,' she said.

232

'Oh yes he did!' Guttmann replied, without lowering the telescope. 'The questions he asked – they told enough. Oh yes!'

'He weren't half interested when I tells him 'bout the cannon what the master's got for the garden party!'

'I'm sure he was!'

'I think as he'd 've liked to come to the garden party. Only he's got duties in London, he said.'

She wanted Emily to bear witness to her friendship with Herr Guttmann.

'Perhaps we shall make him change his mind, eh, little Abigail?' he asked.

He lowered the telescope. Abby stepped back, afraid that he was about to tweak her cheek again. Guttmann laughed at her. Then he noticed Emily staring as if transfixed from where she was standing by the bed.

'Well, girl?' he demand. 'You surely have not completed your matutinal duties?'

'Don't know what that means, if you please, sir,' said Emily in a terrified whisper.

Guttmann laughed. He imitated her for Abigail, in a small falsetto voice: ' "Don't know what that means, if you please, sir!" Don't know your own language, child! That's what it means!'

Abigail laughed delightedly at Emily's discomfiture.

Guttmann raised the telescope to his eye once again.

'Oh yes, my friend. I remember you now,' he said. 'I remember you very well! And I can see right into your skull – I can see that brain of yours, calculating away like a money-lender's abacus, click, click, click! My friend, we are going to break that machine! When we are through with you, it will still go click, click, click! But no result will come from it except nonsense, poor Mr

233

Holmes! It will calculate and calculate, but it will pro-
duce no result.' He turned and looked down at Abigail.
He ran his knuckle gently down her cheek. 'Except that
little Abigail shall have her telescope, eh?'

'Oh yes please, sir!' Abigail said, staring up at him in
greedy admiration.

'I think', declared Mycroft, 'that the hour has come . . .'

'Oh yes, sir?' asked Cyril.

'To send you for our lunch. What do you say, sir?'

'I say it's a prime idea, sir!'

Cyril lowered the umbrella with which he had been
shading Mycroft from the sun, and massaged his arm.
Mycroft put down the stick of charcoal with which he
had been sketching the back of Ranmore Hall.

'Why, man!' Mycroft exclaimed. 'You're never tired!'

'What do you mean, sir?' Cyril looked indignant.
' course I'm tired! Holding that thing, all morning!'

'My dear fellow,' Mycroft informed him, 'if you were
still in Africa, you'd have to hold one of those things over
your chieftain's head all day – and it would be made of
leopard skin and be very heavy, I dare say.'

'If I was in Africa, I wouldn't be holding no umbrella
over nobody, not even myself, 'cause we Africans – we
ain't afraid of the sun!'

Mycroft ignored the remark.

'You will procure us some bread and cheese – and
some more of that excellent bottled beer from Wellings's
ale house.'

He gave Cyril a shilling.

'Hot baked pies is prime,' Cyril suggested, somewhat
wistfully.

'Bread and cheese is better for the digestion. You

never know what goes into meat pies,' Mycroft insisted.

Cyril shrugged. 'Suit yourself,' he said.

He laid the umbrella on the ground and swaggered off down the Common in the opposite direction to Ranmore Hall. Making his way down the trodden way through the bracken, he passed the old shepherd from Rodgers' Farm with his flock. Old Tom raised his staff in salute. 'Afternoon to you,' he said, looking Cyril up and down. 'Don't see many of your sort round these parts, to be sure.'

'Don't see many of your sort round the parts where I comes from,' Cyril replied loftily.

'And where might that be, son?'

'Africa,' Cyril replied with unaccustomed brevity.

'You don't say!' the old shepherd exclaimed. 'Now I has heard as you've come from London with the fine gentleman what's staying down at the White Posts Hotel.'

'Didn't say as I'd come *straight* from Africa, now did I? I've had my misfortunes, like some people do.'

'What sort of misfortunes would they be?' asked old Tom.

'Like I should have been a king – King of the Zulus.'

'Oh yes? Like I should be Prime Minister if it weren't for that old Mr Gladstone pipping me at the post, as you might say,' old Tom nodded philosophically. 'Don't suppose Your Royal Majesty could spare an old man a bowl of 'baccy?' he asked. He held out a foul clay pipe. Cyril shook his head.

'Sorry, grandad. Smoke cheroots myself. More genteel in the company I keeps . . . However, since us nobly-born folks has what you might call a h-obligation towards the likes of you, I'll tell you what. Them sheep look happy grazing round here, so you just stay where you are, grandad, and I'll bring you a pipeful of 'baccy

when I'm on my way back to my gentleman up there.'
And he set off down the track, waving to the old shepherd without looking back over his shoulder. Old Tom watched him in astonishment, then hawked and spat.

Mycroft went on sketching even though, with the umbrella lying some distance off where Cyril had dropped it, he was now sitting in the full glare of the sun. He removed his straw hat and mopped his forehead with his handkerchief. As he did so, a dark shade moved between himself and the sun and fell across the white sketchboard. He felt a clutch on his shoulder like that of a hook. He looked round to find there the handle of a stick, an ornate dragon's head with bared teeth carved in ivory. He lowered his handkerchief from his face.

'Guttmann, Mr Holmes,' Guttmann introduced himself. He removed the handle of his stick from Mycroft's shoulder and moved round to face him over the easel. 'Carl Philipp Emmanuel Guttmann.'

He pronounced each name as if he was savouring it.

'We have not been formally introduced,' he continued, 'but I recognized you. A man of your intellectual stature is not easily forgotten. Three years ago, almost to the day, was it not? July, 1868? The unfortunate matter of Lady Kilgarden and the Papal Nuncio to the House of Savoy, as I recall. You couldn't see me, but I was watching you, in the courtyard of the Bargello: Signor Ricasoli was offering you his heartfelt thanks, thanks which were richly merited, if I may say so. Your interpretation of the affair was absolutely correct, of course, even if neither your government nor the Italians were prepared to act on it. I do assure you, Mr Holmes, I felt for you. I too know what it is to be treated as a Cassandra.'

236

Mycroft glanced behind him to find there the weasel-like figure of Whettam, Jenks-Robinson's head groom, and two other ill-disposed-looking stablemen.

'And I, Herr Guttmann, have seen you,' Mycroft replied. 'On a somewhat more recent occasion.'

Guttmann tried to hold him with his eyes. Mycroft was careful not to look directly into his gaze, to avoid it just so slightly that he would not realize.

'The moment I saw you sitting there, up on Box Hill,' Guttmann told him, 'I knew I had seen you before. And when I remembered *where* I had seen you, I knew *who* you were, and – what is more to the point – why you had come. You see, Mr Holmes? The game is over already. You know what I'm up to. And I know what you are up to. So it has become boring again! And already, I am sure, you have told your masters what is going on – but they don't believe you, of course! You see? I do understand! So you decided you would have to put your head in the dragon's mouth to find some further proof before you could convince them. That is right, eh?' He pushed his finger between the teeth of the handle of his stick to indicate what he meant. He paused as if thinking for a moment. Then he pointed his finger at Mycroft.

'Do you know? I do believe it would be much more satisfactory if you and I were to left entirely alone – to play chess one against the other without interference . . . without having to try to convince our wooden-headed masters where the pieces were on the board. What do you say, Mr Holmes?'

'I say, Herr Guttmann, that I am very surprised to hear you suggest that you regard Prince von Bismarck as a wooden-head.'

For a moment he thought Guttmann would strike out

at him. He tried to pull himself to his feet. Guttmann nodded peremptorily to the grooms. Once more Mycroft turned his head to look at them. Whettam pulled a carefully-wrapped wad of lint from his pocket. In it was a small blue-black bottle. He removed the stopper and sprinkled the contents on to the lint. The two other grooms rushed forward and grabbed at Mycroft to secure him.

' "Bind fast his corky arms!" ' Mycroft quoted.

'I do not not know what that is,' said Guttmann. 'But I should tell you, Mr Holmes, that you are trespassing on Mr Jenks-Robinson's land . . .'

'It is common land,' Mycroft replied. 'According to the ancient liberties of this realm . . .'

Whettam had come up behind him. He pushed the lint pad over Mycroft's face.

'Minimum force, my friends,' said Guttmann. 'Minimum force to remove the trespasser from your master's land.' He raised his foot, and with sudden viciousness ground his heel into Mycroft's crotch. Mycroft doubled over in pain and, in so doing, pushed his own face into the chloroform pad . . .

Cyril walked across the Dorking High Street to a tobacco shop. He carried a parcel of bread and two bottles of ale under his arm. Women and children stared at him. One small boy let his hoop fall into the roadway. A passing cart trundled over it, smashing it, but the small boy was staring so intently at Cyril's face that he didn't notice. Cyril went into the shop.

'Afternoon, miss,' he said politely to the plump middle-aged woman who had come out of the back to serve him. He even raised his cap. The woman stared at him, wide-eyed with horror. She retreated backwards into the store-room, unable to take her eyes off him.

'Mr Fredericks! Oh, Mr Fredericks!' she called out. 'It's the heathen nigger-man! That gentleman's nigger-man from the White Posts!'

'I ain't nobody's nigger-man!' said Cyril. 'I'm black – and I'm my own man! And I ain't no heathen, neither!'

But he did not wish to make too much of a point of all that. Instead he waited until she had disappeared into the back, then he removed the lid from one of the tobacco jars on the counter, clutched at a generous handful of shredded tobacco, and stuffed it into the pocket of his linen jacket. He replaced the lid on the jar and was carefully picking telltale shreds of tobacco from the lapel of his pocket when the shopkeeper came in, apprehensive but brave as befitted an old soldier.

'How can I serve you?' the shopkeeper asked. There was a note of challenge in his voice.

'One of your twopenny cheroots, h-if you will be so kind,' Cyril replied in the grossest imitation of a genteel accent.

The shopkeeper stared at him as if he should have been a ventriloquist's dummy rather than the source of his own voice. Then he looked down at the twopence which Cyril had placed on the counter as if he had not expected to find Christian money placed there. Cyril added a further halfpenny to it.

'H-and a box of vestas, h-if you please, my good man.'

The shopkeeper nodded. 'Very good, sir.' As the man turned to take a cheroot from a jar on a shelf behind him, Cyril glanced at the tobacco jars, wondering if he dared to make another raid on them while the shopkeeper's back was turned. He decided against it.

Before leaving the shop he lit his cheroot from the gas-jet on the counter. He stepped out on to the pavement, smoking in debonair style and coolly ignoring the stares of passers-by. He left the town behind him and climbed up through the woods to Ranmore Common. The sheep scuttled away through the bracken at his approach – all except a single black one which stood its ground staring at him.

'Hullo, friend,' Cyril said. 'Have a cigar?' He pointed the tip of his half-smoked cheroot in the sheep's direction. As it trotted towards him, however, he hastily took it back. 'Better not, eh? Stunt your growth.'

He went on up to where the old shepherd was sitting under the shade of a hawthorn tree.

'Got a pouch for your 'baccy, grandad?'

The shepherd pulled a small oilskin bag from his breeches' pocket, under his smock. The neck was untied; the bag was flat and empty.

'Hold it open, then,' said Cyril.

The shepherd pulled open the neck with his thumbs, holding it up as if he were a beggar. Cyril stuffed it with the tobacco from his jacket pocket until it was as tight as a bladder. The shepherd looked up at him in amazement. ' 'Ere! I can't afford that much,' he exclaimed. 'Not in one go, like!'

'Ain't costing you nothing, grandad. Just you consider yourself one of them lilies of the field what toils not, yet the good Lord give 'em all the 'baccy they can smoke.'

'There was one o' your sort', old Tom said, 'over at the Hall – back in Mr William Cornwallis-Herbert's day . . .' He pulled out his clay pipe and filled it, his fingers trembling with his longing for a smoke. 'Him as was Mrs Jenks-Robinson's fayther,' he continued. 'He was a witty fellow just like you.' He pushed stray wisps of tobacco into the clay bowl.

'What sort, grandad? Here! Thought you might need these . . .' He dropped the box of wax vestas into the shepherd's lap. 'Cost you a 'alfpenny, them will.'

'Blackamoor, like you,' the shepherd replied. 'Coal black, he was. Blacker 'an you, I reckons . . . He were Mr Cornwallis-Herbert's tiger – rode on the back of the family coach and that . . . Here! Why's it costing me a 'alfpenny?'

' 'Cause I paid a 'alfpenny for 'em, o' course. From my own pocket, an' all.'

'What about . . .?' The old shepherd pointed to the tobacco.

Cyril looked at him, opened and closed his eyes several times, and said nothing.

'You be a card, an' no mistake!' said the shepherd. He lit his pipe luxuriously and puffed deeply several times. Then he reached into the pocket under his smock and gave Cyril a halfpenny from the handful of coppers in his hand.

'Good master, is he?' Cyril asked.

'What? Farmer Rodgers? He be a fair man as masters go.'

'I means Mr whatsit-Robinson. At the Hall.'

'Thinking on seeking a situation there, be you?'

'P'raps. Change is as good as a rest, they say,' Cyril told him.

'Funny place, the Hall these days. Funny goings on, they do say . . .'

Old Tom sat and smoked thoughtfully. Cyril waited,

leaning against the trunk of the tree, in the shade.

'My maister's little wench, Abby. She be in service in the Hall,' said old Tom, at length.

'She tell you there's funny goings on, did she, grandad?' Cyril asked.

The shepherd shook his head. 'Abby Rodgers be a talkative little thing – ay, and one for giving herself airs and graces at that! The maister says it's on account of her allus having her head in one o' they story-books. She only been working over at the Hall these past two or three days, so I reckons they be keeping her busy-like. The maister were all agin her going into service, short while back. Reckon he decided he and his were too good for service. Danged sure little Abby thought so! Heard her say it. Summat changed the maister's mind on that score danged quick, I can tell 'ee! Only a few days past, it were, like I said' – he paused to draw on his pipe again, and to relight it. When at last it was going satisfactorily, like a steam-engine, he continued – 'there's the maister looking over the hoggets here with me when up come little Abby bringing his dinner, and she tells 'im this tale 'bout how she's see-d this poor drownded gentleman lying in Silent Pool – down there, in Eldebury Woods.' He pointed down into the trees. 'The maister, he sends little Abby straight back to the farm, and then he's off to tell Mr Jenks-Robinson 'bout what she's said she's see-d. They get the constables from Dorking, and the keepers, an' danged if I knows who else besides, an' they're off to drag the Pool. Only they don't find nothing; it be little Abby making up a story like what she's read in one o' they books. Leastways, that's what they says. And the maister give 'er a thrashing to make 'er see sense, an' says he'll take her down to the next hiring in Abinger. Only –

'twere a funny thing, I reckons – that very moment 'e's took his belt to her, Mr Whettam – what's head groom at the Hall – come an' says as Mrs Jenks-Robinson wants little Abby for one o' they 'tween maids, up at the Hall. Only she got to go with Mr Whettam up to the Hall that very same night . . .'

There was silence between them for a moment or two. Cyril remarked, 'They do say as Mrs Jenks-Robinson's a kind, forgiving sort of lady. Leastways that's as what my master's been told.'

The shepherd drew on his pipe. 'That poor lady,' he said, 'ain't got a word to say for herself. Not since she got herself hitched as you mught say to Mr Jenks-Robinson . . .' He spat into the bracken beside him. 'An' neither on 'em got anything to say while that Prooshian gentleman's a guest at the Hall. Leastways, that's what I been told. It's that Prooshian gentleman rules the roost . . . Any road – an' this only be my opinion mind, nobody else's – there weren't nothing to forgive! The little wench were telling the truth, even if she do stick her little nose in the air.'

'What makes you think that, grandad?' Cyril asked.

' 'Cause her didn't have nothing to get out of telling no lie, that's why. She got a 'ead on her shoulders bright as a new farthing! Her knew sure as dang it they'd drag the Pool . . . An' I'll tell 'ee something else – only don't you go telling nobody, 'cause I'm an old man, an' I don't need no trouble in my old age . . .'

'A brick wall ain't as silent as what I am, grandad – when I've a mind to be.'

'If Abby Rodgers were making it up about how she'd see-d a drowned gentleman in Silent Pool, she didn't get it from no story-book.'

243

'Who'd she got it from, then?' Cyril asked.

'She'd got it from Billy Lavendar. That's who!'

'And who might he be, when he's at home?'

'The maister's stableman. Abby said he'd telled her when the maister were taking his strap to her. 'Course, Billy were proper frit, by then! Wouldn't say nothing. And now, he bain't at home, 'cause he's a-run off an' disappeared like wi' Liza Makepeace – maid, over at the Hall. And that's a danged rum thing, I tell 'ee! 'Cause Liza Makepeace – she had all the lads from Chilworth to Mickleham arter she – and Billy Lavendar weren't no great catch!'

'No accounting for taste, grandad!' said Cyril, with a mighty air of human understanding.

'You never did set eyes on Billy Lavendar, son!' said old Tom. 'And there's another rum thing. It were after my maister had gone over to the Hall like, to tell 'em what Abby said she'd see-d; an' it were afore the constables and the keepers had been got together; I seed Mr Whettam with two of them as what passes for stablemen at the Hall, only I says they're old lags more like. They was in one o' them dog carts, driving down toward Eldebury Woods and Silent Pool. Going hell for leather, they was! Fast as you like, like the devil were after 'em!'

'Or like they wanted to get there *afore* the police?' asked Cyril.

'Now I didn't say nothing 'bout that, did I?' the old shepherd asked back. 'Can't help what folks think for they selves. But I didn't say nothing 'bout it.'

He pressed the tobacco down into the bowl of his pipe. He drew on it again.

'Tell you something else,' he said. 'They do say as the Prooshian gentleman's taken a great shine to little

Abby – gives her bright new sixpences to run errands for him, and that. Mind you, it's maids' gossip. And Abby allus were a comely little lass, so I 'spects as they're jealous on her.'

'This Abby,' asked Cyril. ' 'Bout so high, is she? With long yellow hair? 'Twixt being a child and being a woman as you might say – an' uncommon pretty?'

'Ay. That's Abby Rodgers,' old Tom agreed.

Cyril threw away the stub of his cheroot. He gathered up his parcel of bread and cheese, and bottles of ale.

'Best be off. Master'll be a-wondering where I got to.'

He bade the old shepherd goodbye, and set off up the Common. As soon as he thought he was out of the shepherd's sight he started running. When he reached the summit where he had left Mycroft only to find him gone, he thought he must have mistaken his way. Worried, he searched the ground all about him, kicking down the bracken more in anxiety than in hope of finding anything. Then he saw the umbrella, still open, but half-hidden in the tall ferns. He heard voices calling. Looking down the Common towards Ranmore Hall he saw Whettam and several men with him. Shouts came echoing up the hill: 'There he is! There's the nigger!'

He dropped the parcel and the bottles of ale. Then he changed his mind, picked up the bread and cheese and one of the bottles and thrust them into his jacket pocket. He started running as fast as he could down the opposite slope, and bolted for the cover of the woods.

Chapter Twenty-four

Midnight had already struck when Cyril finally arrived back in Bruton Street. Sophie was preparing for bed; she was in her nightdress, sitting at her dressing table. Her old nurse was brushing her hair, scolding her in Russian all the while. The object of the *nyanya's* scolding was sitting on the side of the bed, where no gentleman was ever supposed to sit. Moreover, he was wearing nothing but a white linen shirt. The rest of his uniform – the mess kit of the Twenty-first Lancers – was draped over the sofa at the foot of the bed, with his black peaked cap perched on the top.

There was a penetrating whistle from the speaking-tube out in the hallway; it was connected to the porter's office in the vestibule downstairs. A moment later Sophie's French personal maid came in.

'Forgive me, Mademoiselle. The *concierge* he say Cyril is downstairs – with a policeman! The *concierge* he say the policeman will take Cyril to . . . Savile Row? . . . and put him in prison if you do not . . .' She fluttered her hands. Sophie took her *nyanya's* wrist and moved her hand and hairbrush from her head.

'Tell the *concierge* to send Cyril up here with the policeman, if you please, Jeannine,' she ordered the maid.

She rose from the dressing table and took down her *peignoir*, which was hanging beside the mirror.

'You will have to excuse me just a little longer, Eddy, *mon chéri*,' she told the young cavalry officer on the bed.

'Do I have to, weally my deahwest?' he complained. 'Dash me! There's always something happenin' when I come heah! It's that fwightful blackamoor, ain't it? Night in the pokey wouldn't do him any harm fwom what I've been told.'

Sophie went over to him, kissed him lightly on the lips and patted his cheek.

'*Chéri*, I shall not be away a moment longer than I have to. I promise.'

'That's what you always say!' he complained.

He tried to put his hands round her waist but she turned away too quickly for him.

'Oh, it's too bad!' he protested as she skipped to the door and closed it behind her.

Cyril was standing just outside the hallway door. There was a scratch across his cheek which had been bleeding. His light summer suit was badly creased and thickly smeared with coal-dust. Beside him was a burly police constable with a large bull's-eye lantern suspended from his belt.

'Beg pardon, milady,' said the policeman. He was clutching his helmet under his arm. 'I found this man here prowling up the back entry in what you might call a suspicious manner. He says as he's a servant o' yours, milady, come home with a h-important message for you . . .'

247

'Back from the country, see?' Cyril nodded, as if that was sufficient to explain his battered appearance.

'Thank you, officer. He is my servant,' Sophie replied. 'Come inside, Cyril,' she added with a note of severity. 'Thank you, officer,' she told the policeman.

The policeman hesitated. 'Begging your pardon, milady. But 'e was h-acting suspicious-like. I mean there h-ain't no charges nor nothing. But h-if it ain't out of place, I'd h-advise you to keep a close eye on him. H-it's my h-experience, milady, them negroes is naturally sly, as you might say. Slyer than most men-domestics –'cause of 'em being closer to the h-animal world than what we is, I h-expect.'

Sophie smiled. 'Thank you again, officer. And good-night to you.' She closed the door. 'Well, Cyril?'

'They got Mr Holmes!' he replied. 'They got Mr Holmes, an' they're putting it about as I done it!'

'I was afraid that might happen,' she said calmly, 'when Mr Holmes asked me if he might take you with him.'

'Why didn't you tell him, then?' Cyril demanded.

'Because, dear soul, Mr Holmes believes himself to be omniscient. And I did not think it the appropriate moment to tell him anything different.'

'Don't know what om . . . whatever it is . . . means, I'm sure!' said Cyril sulkily.

Sophie turned to her maid and said in French, 'Jeannine, go and make sure there's some hot tea. And bring out the brandy for the poor *coquin*.' To Cyril, she announced, 'We shall go into the kitchen. You can have something to eat and drink, and at the same time you can tell me what has happened.'

'Mademoiselle!' Jeannine exclaimed in French. 'Cook

248

won't like that! She won't like that at all!'

'Bah!' Sophie replied. 'Do what you're told. It's not your place to worry about what Cook likes!'

She took Cyril through the length of the apartment, to the kitchen at the back. She told him to sit down at the table. She put a knife and plate in front of him and bustled about finding bread, butter and cold meat. Jeannine, meanwhile, muttered protests at her mistress's behaviour with much tut-tutting, shrugging of the shoulders and *moues* of the lips, until Sophie finally lost patience and snapped at her, 'Jeannine? *Tu voudrais faire un tas d'histoires, ce soir, hein?*'

'*Mais non, mademoiselle!*' the maid replied indignantly. She slapped a glass of tea down in front of Cyril as hard as she dared to without spilling it.

Sophie sat at the angle of the table, close to Cyril. He looked pleased with himself.

'And now, my dear rascal, tell me.' Her tone was deadly serious. She rested her elbows on the table, and cupped her chin in her hands. 'Tell me everything that has happened.'

Cyril talked rapidly, between mouthfuls.

'We was on the hill, 'bove the house – Ranmore Hall, you know? Watching for what was going on an' that, an' pretending as what he were drawing it like one o' them gentlemen artists. An' he sends me to fetch his dinner from down in Dorking. An' when I comes back, he's gone. An' I'm standing there, wondering an' that, when these men start coming up the hill. An' they're shouting at me, an' pointing an all. So I runs away down through the woods. They comes after me, but I'm too fly for 'em. Then I makes my way back to the hotel. Only they're there afore me. They're in the yard, talking among

249

'emselves, like. So I dodges behind the wall, an' I listens to 'em. An' they're telling the hostlers an' that, that they suspects it's me what's made away with 'im – me being a heathen cannibal an' I don't know what besides. I legs it to the railway station. Only there's a pair o' coppers standing at the entrance keeping watch. So I dodges into the goods yard, an' I jumps a ride in a coal waggon to Redhill. An' then I gets on a passenger train to Charing Cross, an' I drops off on Hungerford Bridge in the dark, an' legs it straight here to tell you.'

'You did quite right, Cyril,' said Sophie. 'You are' – she hesitated for a moment – 'a sound fellow,' she concluded.

She reached across the corner of the table and gave his hand a squeeze.

'They will come after you, of course,' she told him. 'But that won't worry you because they have been after you many times before. In any case, we must rescue Mr Holmes and resolve all this before they catch up with you.'

Jeannine slammed down the brandy decanter and glasses in front of Sophie. They rang with the shock. Sophie poured a stiff glass and pushed it across to Cyril. She looked up at the maid.

'You may go to bed now, Jeannine,' she said. 'Out of my sight – quickly!'

Jeannine bobbed a curtsy while retaining the sulky look of her mouth.

'*Bonsoir mademoiselle.*'

Sophie waved her hand impatiently. She asked Cyril, 'Did Mr Holmes find out anything – about . . . Ranmore House – Hall? . . . for instance? Is Herr Guttmann there?'

250

Cyril told her that he was. He told her about the garden fête which was to be held there, and the German band, and the cannon. Sophie became more and more excited, questioning him more and more as he went on. Cyril was telling her how, from what the old shepherd had told him, he had reason to believe that the young maid who had spoken to them on Box Hill had been sent across the Gap to spy on them, when Captain Barnaby appeared in the kitchen doorway. He had put on his blue and light blue regimental jacket over his shirt, but his legs were bare under his shirt-tails. Standing as close to attention as his cavalryman's bandy legs permitted he screwed his monocle into his eye and surveyed the kitchen.

'Oh I say!' he exclaimed. 'Weahly, Sophia, m'deah! This is beyond the pale, don't you know? – to keep a gentleman hangin' awound on account of your negwo-footman!'

Cyril looked up, but his face revealed nothing except the blood on his cheek. Sophie rose from the table. She rested her hand lightly on Cyril's shoulder for the briefest of moments, to let him know that he was to remain there. She went out to Captain Barnaby.

'You will have to learn to trust me, Eddy,' she told him. 'Surely you must know by now that if I keep myself from you at this hour of the night . . .' She paused, standing close to him, looking up into his face as if she might kiss him at any moment. His monocle dropped from his eye.

'Oh, I say!' he murmured, as if she wasn't treating him fairly.

'. . . it must be for a very important reason.'

She rested her outspread hand on his chest, caressing

251

one of his regimental buttons with her forefinger.

'My servant has just returned from Surrey to tell me that something rather dreadful has happened to a dear friend. Not a friend like you, Eddy; a friend whom I care about in quite a different sort of way. But he is important to me. Do you understand, my darling?'

'You mean, like a bwother?' Eddy asked suspiciously.

Sophie shook her head. 'More like an uncle,' she told him.

He smiled with relief. 'Do you wish me to leave?' he asked.

'No, Eddy, by no means!' she told him. 'I shall need your help, desperately, I am sure.'

'Weally, Sophia? I mean, you wouldn't be pullin' a chap's leg, would you?'

'No, Eddy. I'm very serious. Never more so,' she told him. 'I believe I shall have to go down into Surrey tomorrow morning.'

'And you'll need my pwotection?'

'Yes, Eddy. I will need your protection.'

'You know you have only to command me, my deahwest!' His face shone with pleasure. 'What is this dweadful thing that has happened to your fwiend? Fallen fwom his hoss and bwoken something? Been shot by some silly young arse what don't know his stock fwom his muzzle? That's the sort of thing usually happens to people in the countwy, don't you know?'

'It is nothing like that. I believe he is being held against his will.'

'A pwisoner, you mean?'

'Perhaps. Go and wait for me, like a good boy, until I've found out all I can from my man. Then I'll tell you about it, and you can give me your advice as to what I should do. I must talk to my servant alone. He is afraid of you, you know? The uniform and your natural authority . . .'

'The blackamoor didn't seem in the least afwaid!' Eddy told her. 'Impudent looking wogue, if you ask me!'

'You don't know him the way I know him,' Sophie replied. 'That's only a pretence. It's his pride. Now you go to bed and wait for me, you dear, good boy, and I will return to you as quickly as I can – I promise.'

'Darkies are like childwen. They ain't supposed to have pwide. Ain't good for 'em!' said Eddy.

But Sophie had left him to return to the kitchen. Sitting at the table once more she listened intently as Cyril told her what he had heard from the old shepherd about the young maid who said she had seen the body in the Pool, and the stableman who, she said, had also seen it, and who was supposed to have run away with a chambermaid.

'So the girl was taken away to the Hall,' Sophie said. 'And the stableman vanishes . . .'

She stopped. She clenched her fingers, pressing them to her lips.

'Mr Holmes said that the man in the morgue – the one that was not M. Thibault – was a farm-hand who had looked after horses! Did they kill him *because* he said he'd seen the body in the Pool?'

She looked at Cyril as if hoping that he would confirm what she was saying.

'This girl tells her father she has seen the body in the Pool. Her father goes to Ranmore Hall and tells *them*. Then the groom and two of his men go down to the Pool and fetch poor M. Thibault's body to hide it before anybody else sees it. And then, at the first opportunity, Herr

253

Guttmann and the groom take it to the Thames and drop it in so it will be found far away from Dorking. And they take the body of the poor labourer and drop it on the road, after telling everybody that he has run away . . . *Bozhe moy!*' She made the sign of the Cross, then clutched her hand over her mouth. 'They will kill him!' she said. 'Mr Holmes!'

Cyril drank some of the brandy and pulled a face. He stared at her. As if trying to reassure herself, Sophie said, 'But it was you found this out, wasn't it? Mr Holmes didn't know about the body in the Pool. So what was it he knew – what was it *they* knew he knew – which made them take him?'

'Dunno, to be rightly sure,' said Cyril. He took another sip of brandy, more cautiously this time. 'He's asked questions of the little maid 'bout this German band. The one what's a-going to play at this 'ere garden whatsit up at the Hall. The waiter at the hotel tell us about that. And then he got all excited like, 'bout a real cannon what they're agoin' to shoot off to Her Majesty's good health at that there same garden whatsit. The little maid tell 'bout that – an' she said 'bout the German band an' all.'

Sophie sat silent again for a moment or two. Then she asked, 'When is this garden thing you're talking about?'

'Couple of weeks, I s'pose. Some'ing like that.'

'How many men will there be in this German band? Do you know?'

'Mr Holmes he asked very particular 'bout that. Twenty men or so, they said.'

'Dorking Gap can be held by a few skilled sharpshooters and a light cannon. That's what Sir George Chesney told us.' She was thinking aloud. 'It could be held long enough to prevent proper defences

254

being prepared against an invasion from the sea.'

'What's all this 'bout an invasion?' asked Cyril. 'And who's this Sir George Whatsit, then?'

'Never you mind . . . So this maid could have told them at Ranmore Hall that Mr Holmes had found out about the Germans and the cannon?' she asked.

' 'Course she could,' Cyril replied. 'It were her tell us, weren't it?'

'Cyril, you are to take a bath and have a good night's rest. Tomorrow you are to go on a journey for me. You will put on clean, respectable clothes – do you understand? You are to take a letter for me to Colonel Sir George Chesney at the Indian Civil Engineering College. It is near a place called Egham; you will go by train from the Waterloo Road railway station. And Cyril? You are to tell Sir George Chesney everything you can remember about your visit to Dorking. He will be extremely interested, I am sure. You will stay with him and obey his orders . . . That way the police won't find you and arrest you for the murder of Mr Holmes.'

She went back to her bedroom. Her old nurse intercepted her in the passage and came fussing after her. Sophie stopped outside the bedroom door. 'Give me your blessing, *Nyanya*,' she told her, 'and go to bed.'

She bent her head to prevent any further talk. After a muttered grumble of disapproval, the nurse signed the Cross over her with her thumb and bustled away.

'An aunt of mine was made prisoner, just like your fwiend, I dare say,' Captain Barnaby remarked as Sophie joined him in bed. 'Seized by a cousin of mine. Thowoughly bad lot, my cousin Seb – held a cornetcy in the Cherrybums, don't you know? He and a couple of chums kept her prisoner in some dweadful old place up in

Yorkshire. Twying to get some countwy-bumpkin of a sawbones to say she'd lost her marbles so he could get his gweedy fists on her twust-fund. The pater wescued her in the nick of time. Cousin Seb was cashiered. Took to dwink, so we packed him off to Canada. Is that the sort of thing what's happened to your fwiend, do you think?'

'I believe that something of the kind has happened to him,' Sophie replied. 'Pray God it be nothing worse.'

She turned and put her arms round him.

'Oh I say!' he sighed with pleasure.

'Eddy? Will you help me to rescue him?' she murmured. 'You know? "In the nick of time"? That is what you say, isn't it?'

'You know I'd do anything for you, Sophia, my deahwest!'

Chapter Twenty-five

Mrs Jenks-Robinson sat by the empty hearth fiddling with her embroidery frame. With the rain which was rattling and streaming down the high drawing-room windows had come an ominous twilight. She had rung for Jemima-Anne, who was now clumsily leaning over where she was sitting, lighting the gas-mantles. Ordering the lamps to be lit and fires to be laid were among the few responsibilities she was still permitted, independent of her dear Mr Jenks-Robinson.

She heard the sound of the dining-room doors opening. So soon? she wondered, ashamed of her sense of disappointment that she could not have had a few more moments in peace. Mr Guttmann and Mr Jenks-Robinson had finished their after-dinner cigars. Jenks-Robinson called to the butler, his voice unnecessarily blustering, 'Wotner! Herr Guttmann's coat. Sharp, if you please!'

Herr Guttmann's friendship was so important to Mr Jenks-Robinson – he was just about the only man for whom he had any real admiration – that Mrs Jenks-

Robinson wished she could have liked him. Because of that she got up from her chair, whispered anxiously to Jemina-Anne, 'Oh do be quick, girl! You don't want the master to find you in here!' and went to the drawing-room door.

'Oh Herr Guttmann! You're never going out in this downpour.'

Guttmann bestowed on her his most oleaginous smile.

'No, *liebe Frau*. You may rest assured.'

He thrust his arm into the topcoat the butler was holding up for him. Mr Jenks-Robinson took his wife's arm and led her back into the drawing-room.

'My dear, it is none of your business what our guest wishes to do. I wish I could prevail on you to understand that!'

She gave him an anxious glance. She thought of one or two of the young women she knew – ten, even twenty years younger than herself – who would have turned their husband's irritation with a pretty, childish coquetry. All that had been granted to her were the babyish tears which were starting and which would alienate dear Mr Jenks-Robinson's affections, so unsuited were they to her heavy-browed, rather masculine features.

'I was concerned for him,' she replied. 'Truly, I was, my dear. Please don't say I was being impertinent.'

Jenks-Robinson smiled. 'A little impertinent perhaps, my dear. But I know you are trying to improve your behaviour.'

It was wonderful – like the forgiveness of God.

'Oh yes, my dear,' she replied. 'Indeed, I am.'

'I will keep no secrets from you, dear lady,' Mr Guttmann called to her from the hall. He came to the drawing-room door. 'I am going downstairs to inspect your husband's wine cellars,' he told her. 'I believe the structure is as interesting as is his excellent taste in wine.'

'They are very ancient,' said Mrs Jenks-Robinson doubtfully. 'I have never been down there myself, of course. But I believe they date from the original keep, which is fourteenth century, you know. And there is a well below them, I am told.' She laughed nervously, afraid that she was talking too much but unable to prevent herself. 'Though I don't think anybody has taken water from it since my ancestor held the house for the king against Parliament, in the Civil War, you know?'

'My dear, I'm sure Herr Guttmann has better things to do than to listen to your somewhat uninformed account of the history of my house.'

'Not at all,' Guttmann said. 'I should be fascinated to hear all that Mrs Jenks-Robinson has to tell me about it. History is my passion – after music, of course. But for the moment, *liebe Frau*, you will have to forgive me . . . See! I have my coat on.'

He made his last remark sound as if he were displaying kindness to a mentally-subnormal child. He bowed stiffly, then went down the hall.

One of Whettam's stablemen was standing by the low door under the staircase. He was holding a lantern. Guttmann turned to Jenks-Robinson. 'Stay with your wife, Mr Jenks-Robinson,' he told him. 'That is your place.'

The stableman shone the lantern through the open door. Guttmann stooped under the lintel. On the top step inside he turned and took the lantern.

'You will remain there until I return,' he told the stableman. 'I do not wish to be disturbed.'

259

To Jenks-Robinson he added with some impatience, 'Go and look after your wife, man! She is hungry for your affection. Affection makes a good housewife, they say! Why don't you discover it for yourself?'

He closed the door behind him and descended the long flight of stone steps, the light from the lantern shining on the ragged rock-face which formed the inside wall. At the bottom he passed down an aisle formed by wine racks and the necks of bottles chained together like galley-slaves with dusty, cobweb meshes. Above him the roof, dimly lit by the passing flame, was vaulted like the crypt of an ancient church. At the farther end a flight of steps led to another low, arched door. Guttmann drew a monstrously heavy key from his topcoat pocket, and unlocked it. Beyond was a small, low-vaulted chamber. A pile of straw covered in a ragged tarpaulin lay against one of the walls. He examined it, holding the lantern before him. A rat the size of a large kitten scuttled out of it. Guttmann kicked at it and it vanished into the blackness, emitting a piercingly shrill squeak of fear. Guttmann stared down into the straw. The corners of two ammunition boxes were just visible. He put down the lantern and carefully rearranged the straw and the tarpaulin to ensure that the boxes were perfectly covered. Then he opened a trapdoor in the centre of the floor. A heavy wooden ladder dropped down into the blackness below.

He lowered himself down on to the ladder with an agility surprising in so big and heavily-built a man. In the blackness the lantern in his hand shed an aureol of light around him and the rungs immediately above and below. He continued the descent, on and on. Once, he called, 'Hallo, down there!' and his voice echoed, ringing into oblivion, so that it seemed he was descending into apparent nothingness.

When at last he reached the foot of the ladder the pool of light spread on a rock floor. All around were dim shapes of rock, like the interior of a deep cave. He held up the lantern. A rope reached up into the blackness above, to an invisible pulley. At its lower end it disappeared into a large round hole in the cave-like floor – a well without a parapet. On the lip of the hole stood a water jug and a loaf of bread on a pewter plate. A large rat sat unafraid, eating at the loaf. Guttmann shooed it away. It left behind it a litter of crumbs and thick, black little droppings.

Guttmann carried the lantern over to where the other end of the rope stretched down from the pulley far above in the blackness and was secured by a wooden drum with cogs and a ratchet and a wooden wheel and handle. He put down the lantern and, with a considerable effort, began to wind the handle, drawing the rope up out of the well. Eventually Mycroft's bulky, bulging shape arose out of the well. He was strapped into a canvas breeches buoy, suspended at the end of the rope. He hung slumped to one side as if he might, at any moment, turn over to hang upside down.

Guttmann carried the lantern over to the well. He stooped down, broke a piece of bread from the loaf and held it out to Mycroft.

'Eat, Mr Holmes. We do not want you to starve.'

He stood with his arm outstretched over the edge of the well. Mycroft watched him from the rope's end like a spider at the end of its thread. Suddenly he reached out. Guttmann stepped back quickly, with a laugh. The rope above Mycroft's head vibrated like a taut harp-string. Guttmann wagged his finger at Mycroft.

'Naughty boy! Very naughty! You were going to snatch my sleeve and pull me over, weren't you? Here.' He held out the bread again, just far enough for Mycroft to take hold of it without being able to touch his hand. Mycroft took the bread.

'I meant to send you on the same road to black Avernus that you sent poor Thibault,' Mycroft told him.

'The Frenchman?' asked Guttmann. He sounded puzzled. Then he let out a hearty laugh. 'Do you think I threw him living down there? Shame on you, Mr Holmes! I took you for a more intelligent fellow!'

'Where else would you have drowned him?'

'*I* drowned him? Oh my dear old chap! *I* have never drowned anybody. Nor – before you become pedantic – have I had anybody drowned. I did not kill M. Thibault any more than I shall kill you – or have you killed, if it comes to that!'

'How then did he come by his death?'

'He did drown. You know that. Down in Silent Pool. But he was not drowned. You are very slow, tonight.'

'Silent Pool?' Mycroft asked.

'Ah! You don't know this district very well. It is a pool in the woods on the other side of this ridge. They are thick woods where a man might lose his way easily. Perhaps he lost his way and fell into the water, in the dark. Or perhaps he killed himself – suicide, you know?'

'Why should he have done that?' Mycroft growled.

'Perhaps just enough of his brain remained to him – his thoughts? – to know he had gone mad. And perhaps he did not like going mad. Yes! I think that is why he did it. He did not like going mad . . . as I am quite sure, Mr Holmes, you will not like going mad.'

He paused for Mycroft to say something. But Mycroft would not oblige him. Instead, the rope turned him gently. Guttmann followed him, round the circumference of the well.

'You see, Mr Holmes, I did not intend the Frenchman to die. I am sorry he died. I would be even more sorry if you died. A death is so inconvenient. There is always fuss if somebody dies – police, examining-magistrates, *juges d'instruction* . . .'

He continued to pace round the well as Mycroft's rope swivelled.

'Now, madness. That is quite different. And, in a way of speaking, a mad man is even more silent than a dead man. Take your own case, for example. You are a Cassandra. Up until now nobody has believed what you told them. So who will believe you when we release you from here and you are quite, quite mad . . . Let me give you a drink of water.'

He poured liquid from the jug into a tin beaker. He stretched his arm out and cautiously gave it to Mycroft. Still clutching at his bread, Mycroft put the beaker to his lips. With a cry, he spat out the water. He coughed and spat again.

Guttmann shook his head. 'Not nice?' he asked. 'We must be thankful for what we can get when we are in difficulties.'

Mycroft threw the beaker at him, ineffectually; it clattered into the blackness across the rock floor.

'Now what will we do?' asked Guttmann. 'That was foolish. And anger will not help to keep you from going mad. But I'm sure you realize that.'

He picked up the lantern. As he took it back to the drum and the wheel, intending to lower Mycroft down into the well once more, Mycroft called to him, 'A small thing, Guttmann – but I should like you to satisfy me on one point.'

Guttmann paused. Affably, he asked, 'What is that, Holmes?'

'The reason my masters will not believe what I tell them is that they cannot see any reason for conflict between your new empire and our own.'

'That is because there is no reason, my dear Holmes. Not yet. But the time will soon come when we shall need possessions in Africa and Asia for precisely the same reasons as you do: like yours, our industry will require cheap raw materials and unprotected markets waiting to be exploited. And when we do seize our overseas possessions we do not want to find native hordes armed by the British waiting to resist us, and we do not want to use sea routes only by kind permission of the British Royal Navy . . . Look at it from our point of view – from a Berlin point of view. At the moment Russia is still angry with you because of the Crimean War, Austria has become little more than a shadow, a dependency of Hungary, the King of Italy is at war with the Pope and France is a conquered nation. If we wait until there is a true rivalry between our two empires – a genuine *casus belli* – as, in the future, there is sure to be, it is most unlikely that we Prussians will enjoy the unique coming-together of the advantages we enjoy now: a fully-mobilized army hardened in battle, its morale high with victory, and no Grand Alliance to ensure that the balance of power is maintained in Europe. On top of that we have all the advantages of complete surprise: the narrow seas lie open and undefended and your shores are unprotected; and you scarcely have any army here on your island. No, my dear fellow – we shall never have another golden opportunity like this.'

He pointed upwards at the rope on which Mycroft was suspended.

'Old chap,' he said, 'I should eat your bread if I were you. There are others who have their eye on it.'

Mycroft writhed round to look upwards. The dark shape of a rat, its head downwards, was descending the rope in rapid, jerking movements.

Guttmann laughed. He released the brake which held the winch and let the handle slowly unwind. Mycroft disappeared into the blackness below the lip of the well. The movement of the rope shook the rat from its grip; it fell squealing shrilly into the depths of the well: some moments elapsed before the final splash echoed from far below.

Guttmann picked up the lantern. Before he went over to the foot of the ladder, he looked back down into the well.

'It is where you find Truth, they say – in a well,' he called down, his voice echoing against the walls. 'Think of this, Holmes, old fellow – that is, while you are still capable of rational thought. It will be a very short campaign – it will all be over within a few weeks. But it will also be an abiding mercy. There will be little bloodshed and, after all, our royal masters and mistresses are all members of the same imperial family, are they not? They will deal kindly with one another. But supposing we were to permit our two great empires to grow in rivalry – think what would be the result – what terrible bloodshed would ensue, what destruction! It would be Armageddon: the Apocalyse. The continent of Europe would be devastated. Yes, my friend! Europe would become that vacuum which nature abhors, eh? And imagine what would rush in to fill that vacuum! From the east, Mongol and Cossack hordes. From the west, the mercenary buffalo soldiers – the cretinous descendents of the sweepings of our own cities, despatched by the levantine rulers of the cities of the New World in their insatiable lust for gold. Think of it this way. We are saviours, old chap. I by the sharpness of my strategic vision, you by your descent into lunacy. There is something wonderfully complementary about that, wouldn't you say? So we are, in our opposite ways, saviours of our European civilization, to the world's lasting benefit.'

He set foot on the ladder and began to climb. From the well came Mycroft's voice, first as a croak and then clear and full. He was singing, *'Deutschland, Deutschland über alles – Deutschland über all' die Welt!'*

'Something like that,' Guttmann called down into the blackness. 'Sing on, my fine fat bird!'

Chapter Twenty-six

Guttmann stepped out of the low door under the stairs as a maid hurried past along the hall from the kitchen, carrying a tray to the drawing-room. Another maid was going upstairs, a lady's soaking fur-trimmed mantle draped over both arms. The butler, Wotner, was shaking the rain out of a scarlet-lined military cloak over the stone flags of the hall floor. In the drawing-room, Sophie was on the sofa beside Mrs Jenks-Robinson. Her dark curls clung to her forehead where her face had been unprotected by hood and bonnet from the storm, and the hem of her skirt and the lace edging of her petticoat against her boots were sodden and mired. Captain Barnaby was standing with Mr Jenks-Robinson by the window, looking out at the rain-swept evening. His boyish curls had been flattened by the rain; his undress uniform was soaked round the shoulders and cuffs; his tight trousers, strapped under his boots, were smeared with thick mud to the knees.

'Oh Herr Guttmann! We have had such an adventure while you have been downstairs,' exclaimed Mrs Jenks-

Robinson, her wan face displaying something like animation. 'Poor Mademoiselle . . .'

'De Montegaillard. Sophie de Montegaillard,' Sophie prompted her brightly. 'And this is Captain Edwin Barnaby.'

Barnaby clicked his heels and inclined his head slightly in Guttmann's direction.

'Twenty-first Lancers,' he introduced himself.

Guttmann nodded in acknowledgement, but his eyes were on Sophie. Sophie gave him a look of surprise, as if she was unable to understand why he should be inspecting her face so carefully.

'Herr Guttmann?' she asked, making it clear from her tone of voice that she was rebuking him ever so gently for his rudeness.

'We have met, mademoiselle?' he asked. 'Forgive me, but . . .'

'*Mais non, monsieur*!' Sophie laughed girlishly. 'We have not met. But I know who you are. Everybody knows who Herr Guttmann is!'

' 'Pon my soul! Deuced if I know who Herr Guttmann is!' said Barnaby. 'But then, I don't know about anything vewy much – except about hosses, eh?' And he let out a strangulated laugh from the back of his throat.

'Then I shall tell you, Eddy, *mon chéri*,' Sophie said, 'and if I am wrong, I shall seem *tout à fait imbécile, n'est-ce pas*?' She spelt out each word on her fingers. 'Herr Guttmann is *le Prince de* Bismarck's' – she paused just long enough to discomfort Guttmann with the thought that she was about to say valet – '*secrétaire particulier? Oui? C'est exact?*' She laughed vacuously. She reached up and patted her curls as if to reassure herself that they were drying out in their correct positions.

At the window, Mr Jenks-Robinson stood looking embarrassed, even guilty.

'Miss de Montegaillard and Captain Barnaby have met with an unfortunate accident,' he explained to Guttmann, as if he were a bad boy making excuses. 'The wheel has come off their carriage.'

'Entirely my fault, I'm afwaid,' drawled Barnaby. 'Takin' Mademoiselle de Montegaillard to stay with my mother at her place in Farnham, don't you know? Certain the weather was goin' to stay fine. Meant to dwive Miss de Montegaillard up along the widge – deuced pictuwesque, the Hog's Back on a fine summer's evenin'. Bwought the governess-car over. Too light for bad weather, eh? Wheel caught in a wut – snapped off like a twig, spokes all smashed. Poor Mademoiselle de Montegaillard spwained her foot in the fall – deuce near dwowned in all this wet, I dare say! Cawwied her in my arms to the neawest civilized-lookin' establishment, don't you know?'

'Captain Barnaby is so strong!' said Sophie admiringly.

'Mademoiselle de Montegaillard must stay here tonight, Captain Barnaby,' Mrs Jenks-Robinson declared. 'Mustn't she, Mr Jenks-Robinson?'

'Of course,' Guttmann intervened. 'If she is injured, she must stay. Captain Barnaby can come with his mother's carriage to fetch her tomorrow . . .'

'Of course,' echoed Mr Jenks-Robinson. He decided to assert himself. 'Forgive me, Captain Barnaby – but your mother does keep her carriage, does she not?'

'She does, Mr Wobinson. It would be twemendously obligin' of you both if Mademoiselle de Montegaillard could enjoy your hospitality tonight. Her foot, you know – needs west. And I can twavel on to the mater's place by twain, and weturn tomowwow with the mater's cawwidge, just as you say.'

Sophie breathed a sigh. She lifted one foot slightly off the ground. 'It is feeling a little better,' she said. 'But oh! Madame! It would be wonderfully kind of you. *Vraiment!*'

'Then you shall most certainly stay,' said Mrs Jenks-Robinson.

Sophie said sweetly, 'How kind of you to speak for me, Herr Guttmann. Even though our two peoples have so recently been at war.'

Guttmann bowed to her.

'I am sure, mademoiselle, if you feel no restraint at staying under the same roof as myself, I can only feel relief, gratitude and pleasure in equal measure.'

Sophie laughed and clapped her hands delightedly.

'Oh Herr Guttmann! *Bien sûr, vous êtes très gentil!*' She pointed to his coat. 'But I am keeping you from going out?' she asked.

'Herr Guttmann has been down in our cellars,' said Mr Jenks-Robinson hastily. 'He expressed a wish to inspect the wine we have laid down.'

'It was my dear father . . .' began Mrs Jenks-Robinson. She broke off as Mr Jenks-Robinson glared at her.

'You keep a cellar, monsieur?' Sophie asked Mr Jenks-Robinson, as if it was the most wonderful thing in the world. 'With *French* wine?'

'Mr Jenks-Robinson is very fond of a good claret.'

The manner in which her husband looked at her made Mrs Jenks-Robinson put her fingers across her mouth.

* * *

After the rain had eased off Barnaby went off down the hill, back to the road and the broken carriage. A stable-man went with him to light the way, to bring the horse into stable and to fetch in Sophie's valise while Barnaby went on down to Dorking railway station to take a train to Farnham. In the Hall, candles were brought. Sophie asked Guttmann to assist her upstairs to her room. When she showed signs of discomfort trying to climb the stairs, she allowed him to pick her up and carry her. 'You will permit me, perhaps, to look at your foot?' he asked as he put her down. 'I have some experience in treating such injuries.'

'Oh no, Herr Guttmann!' Sophie exclaimed, as if somewhat scandalized by the suggestion. 'I could never allow it! It is a small thing, *je vous assure*. Madame will let me have a maid to bathe it for me. That will be quite sufficient.'

She noticed the slight smile on Guttmann's face.

'You are all so kind!' she exclaimed, endeavouring to turn the conversation. 'And it is so embarrassing – not only because I impose myself on you like this, but also because, do you know? I have never met Mrs Barnaby, and now I shall not be arriving at her house! Captain Barnaby and I were introduced at Lady Silverdale's; in London, Lady Silverdale has been my protectress. And now, the first time I am in Captain Barnaby's company without the chaperone – *voilà*! What will his mother think of me?'

'I'm sure that, as far as you are concerned, the Captain will explain everything to her satisfaction, my dear,' Mrs Jenks-Robinson told her. Holding her candle in one hand, she offered her arm to Sophie to assist her into the guest-room which had been made ready for her. Mr

Jenks-Robinson was with Guttmann, standing a little way apart. Sophie, on Mrs Jenks-Robinson's arm, noticed, behind the two gentlemen, the presence of the young maid framed in the doorway leading to the back stairs at the end of the passage. She looked like some small, domestic seraph with the lamplight making a shining halo of the yellow hair piled under her starched cap. She was standing still, watching; but her eyes were not fixed on Sophie. She was looking at Guttmann with something approaching adoration. Sophie had no doubt that this was the child Cyril had told her about.

She went into the guest-room with Mrs Jenks-Robinson. The bed was ready, the room lit. The maid, Emily, was just removing the warming-pan from between the sheets. She came over to help Sophie to limp to the chair beside the bed. Guttmann, outside the door, called down the passage, 'Abigail, child. Fetch hot water from the kitchen. And then you may assist in helping mademoiselle to bed.'

Emily knelt down and took Sophie's boot in the lap of her apron to unlace it.

'I will come back, my dear', Mrs Jenks-Robinson told Sophie, 'when you are in bed, to see that you are quite comfortable.'

'Oh madame!' Sophie exclaimed. 'I cannot tell you how grateful I am.' Then she added, 'I shall not require another maid to help me, I'm sure.'

Mrs Jenks-Robinson looked anxiously over her shoulder, then again at Sophie.

'My dear,' she said, 'we do prefer to take Mr Guttmann's advice, dear Mr Jenks-Robinson and myself. If he thinks it best that Abigail help you to bed . . . I mean, I know she is very young . . . but the experience is so good for her . . . Oh! I do hope you have no objection!'

'Of course not, madame.' Sophie reached forward from her chair to take Mrs Jenks-Robinson's hand.

'And there is another thing, my dear.'

'Yes, madame?' asked Sophie.

'Mr Jenks-Robinson *does* prefer people to address him by his full name. It's a small thing, I know. But he is so particular about it. He suspects that people who address him only by his second name do so' – she glanced round at the door again, then dropped her voice almost to a whisper—' to mock at him because they know he was in trade.'

'I shall remember, I promise, madame.'

'Bless you, my dear.'

When Sophie was alone with Emily she leant forward to where the maid was crouching before her, drawing off her unlaced boot. 'Does Mr Guttmann *live* here?' she asked.

'No, miss. He be a guest, like.'

'But he gives orders,' said Sophie.

The maid looked up. She smiled to herself and then quickly looked down again.

'As if he's the real master?' Sophie persisted.

The maid pretended to concentrate on unlacing Sophie's second boot – the boot on the foot that was supposed to be injured.

Sophie leant further forward.

'Well?' she asked.

The maid chuckled without looking up.

'Durstn't say, miss,' she murmured.

'It is so very odd,' Sophie observed, as if to herself. 'Downstairs, one would not have known he was just a guest here.'

Suddenly, the maid did raise her head.

'Please miss, mustn't say nothing. Least, not in front of Abby, miss – the one bringing up the water.'

'Why not? You can tell me. I shall repeat nothing, I promise.'

'She be a little tell-tale, miss. She be a great favourite like wi' Mr Guttmann, an' she tittle-tattles to him. An' he tells the master, an' then there be frightful ructions 'cause of how the master pay great heed to what that Mr Guttmann says, miss.'

'So it is as I thought, is it?' Sophie lifted the girl's chin between her fingers to look into her face. 'Mr Guttmann rules this house, does he?'

'So he does, miss, worst luck! So he does. Him an' Mr Whettam, the master's coachman.'

'Has it been like this all the time you have been employed here?' Sophie asked.

'Oh no, miss, 'tweren't like this at all. Not 'fore the mistress married Mr Jenks-Robinson. 'Twere him made all the changes wi' the outdoor staff – after Mr Guttmann's first visit, a year last spring. Old Mr Wilkins that were the mistress's coachman an' her father's afore her – he were turned away, and all the men. They're a nasty, dirty-mouthed lot in the stables now. Never gives 'em a word if I can help it!'

A sound outside prevented the maid from saying any more. She drew off Sophie's second boot. Sophie pulled up her petticoat and untied the garter on her supposedly hurt foot.

'Take my stocking down carefully now,' she said in a voice raised sufficiently to be heard in the passage outside. 'Do not hurt me . . . Ah! I expect that is the little girl with my hot water.'

274

She smiled very sweetly at Abby as she came in with the steaming water jug wrapped in a towel.

'What a very big jug,' she said, 'for such a small girl! Thank you very much, my dear child.'

Abby stood waiting and watching as Emily bathed Sophie's foot.

'I expect it will be all bruised and swollen tomorrow,' Sophie sighed. 'Do you think so, my dear?'

'They do say bathing a sprain in hot water takes away swelling,' Emily replied.

'Oh I do hope so!' Sophie exclaimed. 'I would not wish to be a burden on all your kindness another day.'

'My mother twisted her ankle,' Abby began.

'Did she?' Sophie asked, all solicitude.

'Yes. An' she wrapped un up in hot towels, an' the swellin' were gone by morning.'

'That is most interesting,' said Sophie. 'So perhaps it will be the same for me, *hein*? We shall hope so. You will open my valise, if you please. You will find my nightgown and my toilet case on the top. Bring them to the bed.'

Abby opened the valise.

'You have not been in Mr Robinson's – Mr *Jenks*-Robinson's – employment for long?' Sophie asked.

'Only for this week, miss, if you please.'

Abby lifted out the white, lace-edged nightgown and laid it on the satin eiderdown. She took out the polished leather toilet-case.

'You may open it,' Sophie told her. She added, 'I can tell that already you "give satisfaction" – that is how you say it in English?' she asked Emily.

'Yes, miss,' Emily replied.

'Particularly, you give satisfaction to Mr Guttmann,'

275

Sophie said. 'He is a very strong man, that Mr Guttmann; he picked me up as if I was – pouf! – nothing at all!'

But Abby was not listening. She was staring at Sophie's brushes with a look almost of gluttony on her face. Sophie laughed. 'You think they are pretty?' she asked.

'Yes, miss,' Abby whispered.

'I expect you would like to be a real lady's maid, one day – almost a lady yourself.'

'Yes, miss,' Abby giggled.

'Would you like to start your education tonight – by brushing out my hair?'

'Oh yes, miss. If you please.'

'Then you shall. When your friend here has helped me to undress,' Sophie told her.

She noticed the look of studied nonchalance on Emily's face.

'And then I shall be able to tell your mistress – and Mr Guttmann, of course – what a clever child you are, won't I?'

Abby giggled again: 'If you please, miss.'

Emily stood on a stool and struggled to draw Sophie's dress up over her head. Abby picked up one of the hairbrushes. She examined the carriage-clock, and then the calf-bound book lying beside it in the case. Sophie finally emerged from her skirts. As Emily spread her gown tidily over a chair, Sophie, with one hand on the brass bedrail for support, untied her petticoat ribbon and let the garment fall about her feet. She noticed that Abby was eyeing the book.

'That is my prayer-book,' she told her. 'I expect you have a prayer-book, don't you?'

'Yes, miss. It ain't nothing like that one though.'

'Probably we do not belong to the same church.'

'The writing ain't half funny,' said Abby. She had lifted the flyleaf.

'Abby! Don't be so rude!' Emily rebuked her. She had noticed the alarm on Sophie's face, and had taken it for mere displeasure.

'It is quite all right,' Sophie said, but she took the book from Abby and closed it. 'Do you know your letters?' she asked.

'Yes, miss. My mother taught me to read and write – and add up.'

'You are a clever girl, then!' Sophie told her. 'Have you brushed a lady's hair before?'

'No, miss, if you please.'

Sophie remembered to slump down into her chair. She emitted a low groan of pain. Then she sighed bravely, and said to Abby, 'But you have beautiful hair of your own. I expect you brush it often to keep it beautiful.'

'Yes, miss.'

'You shall brush mine while your friend bathes my foot.'

'Yes, miss.'

Sophie recalled the look of adoration which had been on the girl's face when she had been looking at Guttmann. In a bid to make Abby forget the book and its curious lettering, she said, 'Perhaps, if you are very good and clever at brushing, I shall give you one of my hairbrushes. Would you like that?'

'Oh yes, miss!' exclaimed Abby.

Abby went down the passage carrying the empty water-jug.

'Have you anything to tell me, little Abigail?'

Guttmann was waiting in the shadows close to the back stairs. She was startled.

'No, sir. If you please, sir.'

'There is nothing strange – nothing peculiar – about our new guest?'

'No, sir.'

'You were a long time with her, little Abigail.'

He sounded threatening. Abby shivered.

'It were 'cause she made me brush her hair, sir.'

'Was that all? Did you hear and see nothing else?'

He was whispering, but the sound of his voice, angry and sneering, exploded through her head, terrifying her.

'Abigail! Child! Did you see nothing else?' He caught her by the arm and squeezed it. She whimpered as the pain shot through her. 'You do wish to please me, don't you, little Abigail?'

'Yes, sir!' she whispered. 'She has a prayer-book, sir.'

'A prayer-book?' He squeezed her arm again so that she cried out aloud. 'Hush! Little fool!'

'Oh, please, sir!' she whimpered. 'Please, sir. Don't hurt me no more! Please, sir, it were written all funny.'

'What do you mean, funny? You mean it was in Latin. The lady is French, you little fool. She is Roman Catholic.'

'The letters was all funny, sir. Not like our letters, sir.'

'Come here!'

Still gripping her arm, he forced her down the dark side passage.

'Mrs Armitage ain't half going to be cross with me, sir, if I bain't be downstairs soon!' she pleaded tearfully.

He pushed her into his bedroom. He took her to the table by the window. He sat down, picked up a pen and opened the inkwell.

278

'Did the letters look like this?' He wrote a few words in Greek.

'No, sir.'

'Like this?' He wrote a few words in Cyrillic.

'No, sir.'

'Fool!'

Abby's face puckered up in frightened misery. Desperately, she said, 'It were a bit like that, sir' – she pointed to the Cyrillic – 'On'y, the letters were all thin, like . . . an' long up an' down. Like worms.'

'Of course!' Guttmann slapped his forehead with the heel of his hand. 'Old Slavonic!' he said.

'Please, sir?' Abby whispered. 'Am I a good girl again?'

'You are worth' – he drew out his purse – 'another sixpence.'

Sophie lay in bed, in the dark, with her eyes open. The sound of scuffling outside the door was so faint it was possible she might have been mistaken. She waited, listening to a silence which was palpable. She heard something, she was sure of it. Could one actually detect the sound of carpet-pile being pressed underfoot, she wondered? Then, almost with relief, she heard an unmistakeable click. She pulled aside the bedclothes and got up. With no trace of a limp, she went silently to the door and tried the latch gently. As she had supposed, she had been locked in.

She went straight to her valise at the foot of the bed. Burying her hands under the garments inside, she pulled out her small, double-barrelled pistol. Returning to bed, she placed it just under her pillow, so that she was able to sleep with her fingers resting on its butt.

Chapter Twenty-seven

Sophie awoke to a fresh, sunny morning. She heard once more the faint scuffling at the door. Slowly, carefully, she drew the pistol from under her pillow. She listened as the faint sound of footsteps went away down the passage. She pushed the pistol back under the pillow, and got up. Outside, the lawns and the gravel carriage-drive were steaming after the storm of the previous night. She replaced her pistol under the clothes in her valise and got back into bed. Shortly afterwards Emily brought in her breakfast tray, and Abby a jug of hot water to bathe her foot.

Later that morning she sat with Mrs Jenks-Robinson in the morning-room. She reclined in the window-seat alcove, her foot resting up on a cushion, one of Mr Jenks-Robinson's walking sticks lying within reach beside her. Guttmann came in, a morning newspaper tucked under his arm.

'You passed a comfortable night, I trust, Mademoiselle de Montegaillard; nothing to disturb your repose?'

'I was as comfortable as the best considerations of good friends could make me. If I was afflicted by some slight pain – in my ankle, you understand – it was not for want of kindness.'

She lifted the edge of her skirts to show her boot unlaced and the dressing under her stocking.

'Herr Guttmann, you must join your voice to mine,' said Mrs Jenks-Robinson. 'I have told Mademoiselle de Montegaillard she should not travel on to Farnham today but should stay here for at least one more night. We can send a groom over to Mrs Barnaby's seat, can't we?'

'It is my opinion that Mademoiselle de Montegaillard should remain here, *gnädige Frau*. I think, however, we must consult Mr Jenks-Robinson,' Guttmann replied.

'I'm sure Mr Jenks-Robinson will always follow your advice,' Mrs Jenks-Robinson told him.

'I think you overestimate my influence with your husband, dear lady,' Guttmann rebuked her.

'I'm sure I don't!' she replied, then realized how the remark could be misinterpreted. She clamped her hand over her mouth. Sophie noted the extent to which she was clearly terrified of Guttmann.

'For us poor men, I must say that the presence of so lovely and lively a young lady as Mademoiselle de Montegaillard is an unalloyed pleasure,' Guttmann said. 'I shall do what I can to persuade your husband. But there is also the young lady's fiancé, the brave captain, to be considered.'

'Captain Barnaby will comply with my wishes, Herr Guttmann,' Sophie told him with a smile. 'He will be happy for me to stay here another night – knowing, of

281

course, that I am perfectly safe. He is concerned only with . . . *mon bien-être*?'

'Your safety, mademoiselle?' Guttmann asked. 'I hope neither you nor your handsome young follower feel the need to fear for your safety while you are under the protection of Mr and Mrs Jenks-Robinson – and myself.'

'I'm sure I need not,' Sophie replied, still smiling at him.

'Visitors! We have not had so many visitors at the Hall for as long as I can remember. I'm sure it is Mademoiselle de Montegaillard's presence here,' Mrs Jenks-Robinson exclaimed, later that same day.

'I cannot believe Sir George Chesney has ridden over from Egham because of our delightful guest, my dear, charming though she may be,' said Mr Jenks-Robinson.

'From Egham?' asked Guttmann.

'Sir George is Director of the Indian Civil Engineering College on Cooper's Hill—' Mr Jenks-Robinson began to explain.

'Colonel Sir George Chesney,' Guttmann interrupted him, 'is a man with strong views regarding the strategic defence of Great Britain. Eccentric views in the opinion of your government.'

'Then you know him, Herr Guttmann?' Mrs Jenks-Robinson asked brightly. She appeared to have remained unaware of the coldness in his voice.

'Know *of* him, dear lady,' Guttmann replied. 'It is our country which Sir George regards as the Enemy in his writings. Our military academicians in Berlin have read his *feuilletons* with considerable interest – and some astonishment.'

Sophie was sitting on the drawing-room sofa with Mrs Jenks-Robinson, her stockinged foot resting on a stool. Sitting somewhat stiffly on upright chairs opposite were Captain Barnaby, now in civilian dress, and his mother, a pretty, middle-aged woman in widow's black taffeta. Guttmann stood at the fireplace, in front of its large bouquet of freshly-cut garden flowers. Beside him, and growing ever more evidently uncomfortable, was Mr Jenks-Robinson. His mouth twitched nervously.

'It appears Sir George has come to offer his services for your charity garden fête,' he said.

Sophie glanced at Guttmann, and was pleased to observe that he had been completely taken by surprise. He could not help showing it, however fleetingly.

'In what way?' Mrs Jenks-Robinson asked. She looked to the Barnabys: 'I do not know how the Colonel could possibly have heard of our little fête,' she declared. 'I'm sure we never advertise so far as Egham.'

'I'm afraid we had never heard of it at Farnham,' Mrs Barnaby agreed. 'Not until we were speaking of it just now.'

'Just now?' asked Mr Jenks-Robinson.

'I was explaining to Mrs Barnaby, dear,' said Mrs Jenks-Robinson, 'how we hold it on behalf of the Society for the Provision of Bibles to Lascar Seamen . . .'

'Such a good cause!' said Mrs Barnaby. 'What are Lascars, by the way? I suppose they are natives of some kind?'

'Sort of Indians, dear Mama,' said Captain Barnaby.

'Not the sort who burn widows, I trust!' Mrs Barnaby laughed. 'If so, we must certainly provide them with Bibles!'

283

'I expect the Colonel's intewest has been awoused by the connection with India and Indians,' Barnaby suggested.

Sophie was quite surprised by his sudden display of cunning.

'I do wish my darling boy wouldn't talk in that silly way,' said Mrs Barnaby. 'His poor dear Papa never did.'

'My poor dear Papa was never in the cavalwy,' Barnaby replied stiffly.

His mother ignored him. To Sophie, she said, 'You must try to make him talk properly, Sophie dear. You French are so *good* about pronouncing your Rs!'

'I try, madame, *je vous assure*,' Sophie replied.

Mr Jenks-Robinson asserted himself through the chatter.

'Sir George has offered to bring a team of his college-men. He has suggested they might demonstrate their skill by building a temporary rope bridge across the gap below Ranmore Farm.'

'Oh dear!' Mrs Jenks-Robinson exclaimed. 'Overlooking the railway? But that was where you were going to place your little cannon, was it not?'

'It *is* where I am going to place my little cannon, my dear,' Mr Jenks-Robinson replied. 'I have told him so. But he has pointed out that he can place his bridge-builders below the place I had in mind for the cannon. He is down there now, carrying out a survey of the ground, as he puts it.'

'Do you know?' declared Barnaby. 'It is the most extwaodinawy thing' – he glanced at Sophie – 'I was on the point of offewing my services to Mrs Jenks-Wobinson's garden party! I was just about to say, if Herr Guttmann here is pwoviding a Pwussian band, I could bwing my twoop down fwom Camberley. A musical wide, don't you know: always goes down a tweat with the ladies, God bless 'em all!'

Mrs Jenks-Robinson clapped her hands. 'That would do famously!' she exclaimed. 'Oh! This will be the best garden fête there has ever been at the Hall!'

'The vewwy least I could do in wepayment for your kindness to my dear Sophie,' Barnaby told her.

'I think we should give the matter further consideration,' said Mr Jenks-Robinson. 'I have already pointed out to Sir George that your party, my dear, is only a very modest affair – scarcely worth the very trying organizational difficulties with which he will be faced. I mean, the transport of men and materials from Egham. The return on the investment would scarcely be worth while. As for the organization involved in bringing down a troop of horse from Camberley and stabling them and feeding them – it would be wholly disproportionate to the sums we might expect to receive for my wife's little Bible Society.'

'Don't think of expense, my dear fellow!' Barnaby told him. 'My fwiends and I will be glad to bear the cost. As for the twouble involved – do my men good to pwactise twoop movement and supply. They're gettin' bone idle like all gawison twoops. Won't do any harm to get the quartermaster corpowal-major off his bum—'

'Edwin!' his mother protested.

'Sowwy, Mama!' he said instantly. 'Anyway—' He was about to carry straight on but Guttmann stopped him.

'You must forgive me, young man. I know that it is the custom in this country to regard us Prussians – even, perhaps, all Germans – as warriors. It was

285

mademoiselle's compatriot, de Mirabeau, I recall, who said that most states were a people protected by an army, whereas Prussia was an army supported by a people.'

'A wawwior wace. Yes,' Barnaby agreed. 'Nothin' wong in that, I hope. Deuced fine twadition, what?'

'Nothing wrong,' Guttmann smiled. 'If it were true.'

He must have realized by this time, thought Sophie. He must see the pieces being moved across the board. He must suspect – may even have suspected from his first discovery of her in the house – that she herself was not what she claimed to be. And yet his self-control was exercised with the same massive ease as that which contained his impressive, handsome physique.

His smile touched on her for a moment, as if he understood her agreement with him over the absurd stereotyping by English people of anybody whose misfortune it was not to be one of their compatriots. For one moment he made an ally of her. And in that moment she knew that the same combination and alternation of self-control and power in those heavy features, which intelligence and amusement made attractive, were the indisputable outward signs of someone who would prove to be a superb lover if she offered him the chance – the strongest, the most potent, the best lover ever to pleasure her . . .

The warning in her head came so suddenly it caused her to start. He had felt the need to continue with what he had been about to say to the others and had therefore taken his undivided attention off her. She knew – knew for certain – that he had been seducing her. He had not needed to say anything. There had been a moment when she had thought of him as being on the defensive and had lowered her own guard. In that moment he had introduced his spirit into her to seek out her most vulnerable point. He had not been able to exploit what he had found out – but he had found her out.

She felt strangely – because unnaturally – exhausted, as if drained to the pit of her stomach. It was fortunate that he was addressing himself to the others, and that they would have to reply to him.

'You see, my dear friends?' he was saying. 'We north Germans are a nation of landowners, merchants and manufacturers, just as you are. The band which I have arranged to come here is not a military band. It is simply twenty or so men who earn their supper by making music. I am quite sure, *Herr Kapitän*, that you would not find their playing suitable for your troopers' musical ride.'

'I'm sure they are able to play a quick march,' Mrs Barnaby said, 'or a waltz. That is all your men need, isn't it, Edwin?'

'Quite wight, Mama,' Barnaby replied. 'Or a *galop*, of course, haw-haw-haw! Anyway, as I was goin' to say, it's deuced fine cavalwy countwy you have up here. Even if you don't feel a musical wide would help your chawity, you'll have no objection, I hope, to our settin' up our lines an' bivouacin' on the Common.'

'Oh, but Captain Barnaby, you must let your men perform their musical ride!' Mrs Jenks-Robinson told him, clasping her lace-mittened hands in front of her in an attitude of prayer. 'I'm sure it will be quite delightful, and you and your fellow officers must dine here, with us, afterwards. And Mademoiselle de Montegaillard, of course!'

'Deah lady, your kind invitation is most gwatefully

accepted,' Barnaby told her. 'By this party at least, haw-haw!'

Sophie looked at him in wonder and gratitude. She heard Mrs Barnaby say to her in exasperation, 'I can't imagine why he feels the need to put it on so!' But her attention was drawn away by Mr Jenks-Robinson's angry cry of, 'My dear Isabella . . .!' and the sight, seen from the corner of her eye, of Guttman touching his arm to urge restraint.

Chapter Twenty-eight

Jenks-Robinson was hardly able to wait for the ladies to leave the table after dinner, so nervous was he that night. The maids, under Wotner's eye, had scarcely lifted the used savoury dishes from the places when he called down to Mrs Jenks-Robinson, 'Isabella, my dear? I'm sure Herr Guttmann is looking forward to his cigar!'

Mrs Jenks-Robinson was talking to Mlle de Montegaillard with an animation he had rarely observed in her since the first days of their marriage. She glanced up the table at him with that look of startled bewilderment which never failed to drive him beyond endurance. But he did not dare reveal his annoyance. Not only was Herr Guttmann watching him with the bland expressionless stare which frightened him more than any positive demonstration of anger would have done; but Mlle de Montegaillard was looking at him with a contained but pert amusement, as if she understood what was in his mind.

Mlle de Montegaillard's eyes were a clear blue, but they were strangely slanted above her high cheekbones, as if there were more than a touch of the oriental about her. The thought had occurred to him that she might be the product of some well-born French officer's *Tonkinoise* by-blow.

To bring Mrs Jenks-Robinson to her senses, he called across to the butler, 'Wotner! The decanters and cigars, if you please!'

The butler nodded, 'Very good, sir,' and withdrew to the pantry adjoining the dining-room.

Mrs Jenks-Robinson looked thoroughly flustered. She put her fingers to her mouth then lowered them in what, to Sophie, was becoming a familiar gesture of unease. She said, 'I'm so sorry, Mademoiselle de Montegaillard! It does seem as if we have been keeping the gentlemen waiting!' She rose from her place without waiting for Wotner to assist her with her chair, and so pushed it further back from the table than propriety decreed, crushing the taffeta ruching of her bustle-train as she did so.

'I assure you, *gnädige Frau*,' said Guttmann, also rising, 'the pleasure your presence confers on us makes it quite impossible for you to keep us waiting.'

'Oh, Mr Guttmann!' Mrs Jenks-Robinson simpered nervously. 'You are a true courtier!'

Sophie reached round for the walking-stick she had hung from the back of her chair. Guttmann came round the table to assist her.

'Permit me to offer you my arm to the drawing-room, mademoiselle,' he said.

Sophie rose with what she hoped was a convincing grimace of pain. She accepted his arm, thanking him as she did so. As she and Guttmann left the room together, followed by Mrs Jenks-Robinson, Mr Jenks-Robinson remained sitting alone, at the end of the table, like a child in disgrace. Not so long ago his partnership with Guttmann had made him feel as if he were assisting in the moulding of a national destiny. Now terrors prowled and prowled in the shadows of this appallingly large and ancient house in which, from the outset, he had been made to feel a stranger, a usurper.

As schemes for self-aggrandizement began to crumble, he knew Guttmann would do nothing to save him. The spiritual void, the monstrous absence of all human compunction behind the mask of affability, which previously he had seen as a weapon to be used on others, would be turned on him the moment he uttered the least cry for help or pity. He would be deserted, betrayed, whenever it should suit Guttmann's convenience or that of the potentates and powers he served: he would be left to be dragged down into a traitor's subterranean cell in the Tower, to await the dawn when, in a damp Thames-side mist, he would face a firing-squad.

Guttmann returned to the dining-room. He closed the door leading into the hall and stood with his back to it, waiting until Wotner and the last of the maids had withdrawn through the pantry to the kitchens.

The great room was clamped in silence. Unable to bear it, Jenks-Robinson said, 'I fear I have failed to break my dear Isabella to a proper wifely obedience. I can't tell you how sorry I am for the way things have turned out.'

Even as he spoke he understood the futility of apologising to a being like Guttmann.

To his astonishment, he saw Guttmann smile.

'My dear fellow, there is no need to distress yourself,' Guttmann told him. 'No harm has been done. Nothing has been lost by this venture.' He returned to his place at the table. Without seeking his host's permission he selected a cigar from the box and rolled it between his fingers. Still holding it, he poured himself a glass of port.

'I shall insist Isabella postpones her garden fête,' blurted Jenks-Robinson in an attempt at decisiveness. 'That mindless young fool's cavalry squadron can't wait about forever up on the ridge. And a party of student-engineers – half-castes, most of them, I daresay – will be no match for your people.'

'Oh, my dear chap!' Guttmann laughed heartily.

He regarded Jenks-Robinson with amiable amusement, rolling his cigar between his fingers. He kept him waiting as he clipped the end and lit it from one of the candles with every evidence of enjoyment. When finally he had sat back in his chair and was smoking comfortably, he said, 'How long do you suppose our General Staff can keep troop trains marshalled within reach of Pfalzel-Buckelburg and Drei Jungfrauen in order to move an expeditionary force across north-east France? How long do you think we can keep Rhine barges and Dutch sloops clustered in the bays and creeks around Boulogne and Dunkirk before even your Lords of the Admiralty "get wind of them" – that is what you say, isn't it?'

He let the cigar smoke curl from his lips and watched as it wreathed and spiralled upwards into the gloom of the old, panelled ceiling.

'You see, my dear friend,' he continued as if talking to himself, 'you have been found out.'

Jenks-Robinson felt a tightening in his bowels.

'Found out?' he asked. He hardly managed to hear his own voice, but Guttmann caught it.

'Mademoiselle de Montegaillard is not Mademoiselle

de Montegaillard,' he replied. 'She is not lame. And she is not French.'

'What is she?' Jenks-Robinson's voice cracked.

Guttmann laughed again. He gazed at him with amusement through the drifting cigar smoke.

'My poor fellow!' he said. 'There's no need to be so anxious! She is Russian – I would stake my life on it . . . Ah! I should not make such a joke, should I? "Stake my life"? . . . I rebuke myself for not realizing it sooner – her features, you know? They are typical of those of her race who are native of Moscow and Kazan. Besides, your angelic-looking little maid – invaluable creature! – discovered that she keeps a book of religious devotions in Old Slavonic, the language of Russian Orthodoxy.'

'She is a spy?' Jenks-Robinson whispered.

'The lady would be insulted to hear herself so described, I daresay,' Guttmann replied. 'But in effect, yes.'

'But why should a Russian wish to spy on us?' Jenks-Robinson whispered.

Guttmann shrugged his shoulders. 'Perhaps she is a personal friend of Mr Holmes?' he suggested. 'Perhaps she bears me a grudge. There are such persons,' he added, making it sound as if anyone but himself would find such a notion well-nigh incredible.

'What will you do with her?' Jenks-Robinson asked.

'I? Nothing. My Emperor and the noble Prince, my master, presently enjoy the best of relations with the Russian Tsar-emperor. I must do nothing which might . . .' He spread out his hands to indicate his helplessness.

'But you can't simply let her go, Herr Guttmann!' Jenks-Robinson cried.

293

'Does the thought alarm you, old chap?'

Guttmann put an unnatural emphasis on the 'old chap'. Jenks-Robinson saw the chill emptiness of the eyes above the smiling mouth and knew that Guttmann was playing with him in his terror as a cat would a mouse.

Guttmann drew on his cigar several times. He gazed up at the ceiling once more.

'We shall use this lovely young Russian lady to achieve one objective out of this affair.'

Once again he sounded as if he were talking to himself.

'A very considerable objective – though whether the rulers either of my country or yours will appreciate its significance is another matter . . .'

'What?' asked Jenks-Robinson. The palms of his hands were drenched in sweat. 'What is it?' he asked.

Guttmann turned his head and stared lazily at him. Then he looked back up into the gloom.

'The destruction of Mycroft Holmes,' he said dreamily.

'The darkness hath bay windows transparent as barricadoes, and the clerestories toward the south-north are as lustrous as ebony – and yet complainest thou of obstruction?'

The words echoed unwelcome in Mycroft's head. He wanted to tell whoever was inserting them into his brain that he was not Malvolio – he had never born the least resemblance to Shakespeare's 'sort of Puritan'.

He was swinging slowly in an anticlockwise direction: at least, in the pitch darkness, he thought he was. In the void one had to make such acts of faith in order to retain one's sanity, he consciously decided; to which, 'Hast thou all of thy five wits?' asked the visitor in his brain, unpleasantly.

If he opened his eyes there was nothing; a palpable, moving nothing. If he closed them again there was light; light in the blackness against his lids, shaped like the light of Paradise in Gustav Doré's illustrations to Dante's *Divine Comedy*: a great sphere of white light towards which spiralled processional arcs of light. If he kept his eyes clamped shut the processional arcs became, as in Doré's drawings, myriad upon myriad of winged figures. They were singing in strange voices which seemed part of the air itself, and if he listened carefully he could hear in the echo mounting on echo the words of the anthem mounting to the reverberate heavens. They were singing, *'Guttmann, Guttmann, über alles – Guttmann über all' die Welt!'*

The multitudinous sound was so beautiful he was compelled to join in in his own dry, cracked, jarring voice: *'Guttmann, Guttmann über alles . . .'* As he did so he realized that staring down at him, as if through a trapdoor set in the white orb of Paradise, were Guttmann's immense features. The next thing he realized was that his eyes were not shut after all. Guttmann would hardly be convinced of his final drift into insanity if he thought that he was mocking him. Immediately he reverted to, *'Deutschland, Deutschland über alles . . .'*

The angelic host dispersed into the cold, damp air, their silver wings fading fast in the raw flame-light of the two lanterns which were being held over the edge of the pit. As he swung slowly round he recognized Guttmann's huge bulk, his bootcaps on the coping stones looking disproportionately large in comparison with his face so far above. Behind Guttmann, half-obscured by the gloom, were the narrow, weasel features of the groom, Whettam. Mycroft closed his eyes as if by doing so he

295

could dismiss them. The lantern-light kept blinking between his clenched eyelids as he turned, like the light from a lighthouse.

'Poor Turlygod!' he whined, not insincerely. 'Poor Tom!'

'How are you, my friend?' he heard Guttmann ask in a voice heavy with assumed compassion.

'Poor Tom's a-cold!' he replied. He raised his voice. *'Deutschland, Deutschland über alles . . .!'* he croaked as lustily as he could manage. Then he added in an informative tone of voice, conversationally, 'I'm the foul fiend Flibbertigibbet.'

He half-opened his eyes. Guttmann had begun to follow him round the edge of the pit, observing him closely.

'Did you eat the bread we left you, this time?' Guttmann asked.

'I have dined, thank you, my good sir,' Mycroft replied. 'I thank you, I have dined.'

'That is good,' Guttmann told him.

A glimpse of sanity, Mycroft decided, would add conviction to the madness.

'I know you don't want me to die, Herr Guttmann,' he said meekly.

'Ah!' exclaimed Guttmann. He crouched down on the coping stones, watching even more carefully as Mycroft circled.

'I swallowed the old rat,' said Mycroft as if he were beginning to itemize. 'I drank the green mantle of the standing pool . . . I would eat cow-dung for my salad, if I were in a meadow.'

The possibility occurred to him that there was nothing to prevent Guttmann leaning out and cutting the rope on which he was suspended – except that he might reach up to take him with him into 'the green mantle of the standing pool' and the broken stones which, no doubt, lay below the miry surface. As he swung round again he saw Whettam's rodent face grinning at him from under Guttmann's arm. He whimpered and pointed, as if terrified at the sight of him. 'Herr Guttmann!' he cried. As Guttmann rose to a standing position once more, Mycroft continued as if accusing Whettam, 'He puts knives under my pillow and leaves rope halters on the cushions of my pew in church. He puts rat-poison beside my porridge. He wants me to kill myself, Herr Guttmann! *You* don't want me to kill myself, do you?'

Guttmann smiled. He followed Mycroft round.

'No, Mr Holmes. I don't want you to kill yourself.'

He signalled to Whettam, who retreated into the darkness. Suddenly Mycroft found he could think of nothing further to say. It was as if his brain had gone dry. Desperately he began to chant, '*Deutschland, Deutschland über alles . . .*'

'Those were not the words you were singing as we came down the ladder, Mr Holmes!' Guttmann wagged his finger at him as if he had been a naughty boy. Mycroft heard the creaking of the winch in the darkness, and the squeak of the pulley above his head. He felt the pressure of the canvas breeches in his groin. He began to rise up, out of the well.

'Those were the other voices,' he said.

'What other voices, Mr Holmes?'

'All the other voices. They mock us, Herr Guttmann. They never stop. They laugh and sing and make fun of us, on and on and on!'

Mycroft waited. He felt afraid. If they were pulling him out there would be a moment when he was on the

297

very edge of the well, and what would they do then?

Whettam came out of the shadows carrying a long boat-hook. He reached out, caught the rope, and drew Mycroft to the stone floor. Mycroft lolled as Whettam unbuckled the breeches buoy; he did not have to pretend the weakness in his legs.

'Herr Guttmann?' he asked. 'I want you to promise me something.'

'Why, what would that be, Mr Holmes?' Guttmann smiled.

Not to push me back into the well? thought Mycroft. It would be easily done, given his physical state.

'Herr Guttmann, let not the creaking of new shoes on a lady's feet, nor the rustle of silken petticoats, cause you to betray your heart to a woman.'

'Why, Mr Holmes!' exclaimed Guttmann. 'Do you *know* that a lady betrayed you to me?'

Mycroft nodded. 'Samson in Gaza,' he whispered. He did not say 'eyeless', having no wish to put ideas into Guttmann's head. Nor did he have any particular idea of what he himself meant; he was aware only of the need to keep up a tolerably convincing babble of meaningless phrases. So he was completely astonished when Guttmann said, 'A Russian lady. That was foolish, was it not? Russians are no friends of yours – of England.'

Mycroft knew he must make some response, but he was as much at a loss as he had ever been. Nor could he avoid looking into Guttmann's eyes. He put his finger to his lips, as if urging Guttmann to silence. He glanced from side to side as if afraid of being overheard, but also to avoid being transfixed by Guttmann's stare.

'She is never here?' he whispered.

Guttmann nodded. 'She is in the house,' he said. 'She

has come to – what is the word? gloat? – over the way she has deceived you.'

Mycroft felt Whettam's hand on his shoulder propelling him toward the foot of the ladder. They were going to let him go, he thought. But why? Why so soon? Guttmann could not be entirely certain his wits were irrevocably overturned. There was one possible reason, however: that they were in danger of being found out. Cyril had not been there when Whettam and his fellow lackeys had taken him; Cyril would have guessed what had happened and returned to London to tell his mistress.

He whimpered, leaning against the rungs of the ladder. He turned about as fiercely as his physical weakness allowed. Whettam was just behind him. Mycroft grabbed at his throat with both hands.

'This is what I'll do to her, the Russian bitch!' he sobbed.

It was Whettam's turn to be surprised – so surprised that for a moment or two he let Mycroft clutch at his throat without offering any resistance. Guttmann pulled Mycroft off him and turned him toward the ladder once more.

'When you are outside, Holmes,' he said, his voice coaxing, 'I shall send her to you. I shall tell her that there is a sight out in the meadow to make her laugh and triumph . . . Outside, under the stars, my friend . . .'

His voice was like an embrace, thought Mycroft. He heard himself echo, 'Under the stars . . . Oh yes!'

'You may ask the lovely lady why she betrayed you into my hands,' coaxed Guttmann.

His arm was round Mycroft's arm. He was holding something for Mycroft to look at. The mesmerist's bauble? Mycroft wondered. His eyes were closed again, he realized. He opened them. He saw the dull, bone object clasped in Guttmann's fist. He heard the click and the scrape of metal and saw the wide, sharp-pointed, serrated-edged steel blade gleam spotlessly clean in the lantern light.

Guttmann let him take it from him.

'I shall send her out to you, my friend,' he murmured in Mycroft's ear. 'Under the stars, eh?'

'Yes! Under the stars!' Mycroft whispered again.

Chapter Twenty-nine

That night Sophie dismissed the maids as soon as her gown had been removed. The child, Abby, said, 'Bain't you wanting your hair brushed, miss?' in an aggrieved tone. She had replied, 'No, dear,' rather more abruptly than she had intended, since she was certain Abby would go straight to Guttmann the moment she had left the room.

She went to bed and snuffed out her candle, then lay waiting in the dark. She heard no noise at all in the passage outside, not the least whisper to tantalize her imagination. She rose from the bed in the dark and drew off her nightgown; under it she was still wearing her camisole, bodice, drawers and stockings. She went to her valise in the dark. From underneath the clean linen on top she took out her boy's tartan trousers and pulled them on. She sat down on the edge of her bed and pulled on her boots and laced them. She buckled a wide leather belt round her waist. Into it she slipped the double-barrelled pistol she had concealed once more under the pillows. She pulled on a short coat, then went to the door to try it. It was unlocked. Very slowly she drew it open, just wide enough to glance round it. Standing by the entry to the back stairs, and silhouetted against the moonlight coming through the window on the turn of the stairs behind her, was the small, motionless sentinel-figure of Abby.

Carefully, Sophie closed her door again. She crossed the room to the window. Kneeling on the seat she opened the latch and looked out. The window was in shadow but the moonlight was bright on the garden terrace below. One of the stablemen was standing there with a gun in the crook of his arm. She closed the window with the greatest possible care, but the man turned and looked directly up at her. In the moonlight she saw his features: he had the low, bony forehead, sunken jaw and fixed grin of the congenital cretin. She felt fear crawling inside her, like some giant insect in her bowels.

There was a scratching at the door. She retreated into the shadow in the corner of room, where she could see the door dimly across the bed. There was a further slight scuffling at the door. She drew her small pistol from her belt and cocked both hammers; she levelled it at the door, resting her right hand holding the pistol on the palm of her left hand. The door handle turned. The door opened very, very slowly. The tall, burly shape of Guttmann obscured the dim light from the passage. In a desperately calm, low voice, Sophie said, 'Don't dare to come in any further, Herr Guttmann!'

'So you *are* awake,' Guttmann said. 'My little Abigail has sharp eyes.'

There was a moth-like flutter of pleased laughter out in the passage close to the door. Guttmann was carrying a bull's-eye lantern. He raised it and opened the shutter.

The circle of light from it embraced Sophie. She blinked, but held her pistol steady.

'You had better not frighten me, Herr Guttmann,' she told him. 'I may kill you.'

'Are you costumed for the English pantomime, or our German Mozart?' he asked her. 'Whichever it is, I must compliment you. You look quite charming in boy's dress! I wonder, my dear, if you would permit me to light the gas. Then we can talk more comfortably – without disturbing anybody, you know?'

'You will stay precisely where you are, Mr Guttmann – or I shall certainly kill you.'

'If you are going to have to kill me, my dear young lady, you had better do so quickly, before your arms grow tired. I expect they are beginning to feel a little stiff already . . .'

His voice soothed her.

'There is no quarrel between us,' he continued. 'Are we not, both of us, strangers in a strange land? Objects of curiosity to a people whose firm conviction it is that beyond their shores there are only barbarous tribesmen – white tribesmen and black tribesmen?'

Sophie could feel him smiling at her, could feel the warmth of him all about her.

'Why should you take up their cause, my dear, to oppose somebody who wishes you no harm in the world?' The voice spoke murmuringly in her ears, like a welcome guest entering her mind and lulling her into a wonderful calm. 'Why should a lovely, intelligent young woman insinuate herself into this house as a spy – to risk who knows what? We are neither of us fools. I respect your intelligence as I have been charmed by your looks. I have seen from your face that you have respect for me.

303

Perhaps you have been afraid of me a little, though that is so unnecessary! Let us be friends as from this moment. I reach out in the dark to take your hand in friendship, my dear . . .'

The small shape of Abby appeared behind him.

'She won't kill 'ee, sir!' she said in a penetrating whisper. 'She durstn't do a wicked thing like that!'

Sophie could hear the sneering laughter born of envy in the childish voice. It broke off instantly as Guttmann turned on Abby. He growled and swore at her, and thrust her away from him with a movement of his open hand. Sophie heard her stumble and gasp out a slight cry, and knew she had fallen.

Guttmann ignored the whimpering in the passage. He held Sophie in the circle of light from his lantern. But they both of them knew that the spell had been broken.

'Are you going to tell me who you are?' he asked. 'Before you disturb the entire household by shooting off your little pistol?'

He took one step into the room.

'I have warned you!' threatened Sophie. But her hand was beginning to shake, and the muzzles of the pistol to droop.

'I wish only to close the door, my dear. For a little necessary privacy, you know? A gentleman coming to a maiden's bedroom at the dead of night . . . We know it is only for a little harmless chat. But our host and hostess . . .?'

He closed the door without actually shutting it.

'Now, tell me who you are. You are not Mademoiselle de Montegaillard, of that I am entirely sure. I am curious, you understand. Why, when you chose to smuggle yourself into this household, did you decide to call

304

yourself by a name I'm sure you knew I'd recognize – the name of King Louis Philippe's captain of spies? Was it part of the excitement of the game? To let me know that you *were* playing a game?'

'You have left your *petite amie* outside, Herr Guttmann,' Sophie pointed out.

The significance of the French words was not lost on Guttmann.

'Please do not attempt to distract me by taunting me with petty insults. In my profession – which I take to be your profession also – one quickly finds that there is use even in garbage. It is allowed to stand, you see, until it is time to sweep it away. People prefer not to examine it closely. That, I fear, was something your friend, Mycroft Holmes, did not realize.'

'Who is this friend of mine?' asked Sophie. '. . . Holmes?'

'Please, mademoiselle!' Guttmann rebuked her. 'Wasting time will not be of use to either of us. And your arm is now most certainly growing tired. Will you not tell me your name – even now when we are alone? I shall not betray your secret to your poor deluded hosts, I promise you.'

He moved to the fireplace. She swung round her aching arms.

'If you will not let me light the gas, at least let me put this down.' He placed the lantern on the mantelpiece, still holding Sophie in its beam. The muzzles of the pistol were drooping again. She had to make an effort to level them at him. She wondered if she should not shoot him before her hands and wrists became too cramped to do so.

'If you come any nearer to me,' she told him, 'I *shall* kill you!'

He was clearly visible now, in the moonlight. His eyes, unblinking, were watching hers.

'My dear, gallant, young lady,' he told her, 'there is no need. You have won, you see. At this very moment your friend, Mr Mycroft Holmes, is returning from the underworld into the night. That, in fact, is what I came to your room to tell you.'

'I don't believe you,' she told him.

'It is true, I assure you. Do you think I came to murder you? I never kill. It is against my principles. I am a man of thought, of intellect – of peace and the arts. Just as was your friend, Mr Mycroft Holmes. I came to you like this because you and I have one thing in common: we both have concealed our true purposes and activities from our hosts. Will you come downstairs with me – since, I take it, you regard yourself as adequately dressed to do so? I will walk well in front of you . . .' He pointed at the drooping barrels of her pistol.

'What about M. Thibault?' Sophie demanded. 'You say you never kill?'

'Oh my dear! I did not kill the wretched M. Thibault any more than I have killed Mr Holmes. I am no more certain than you how the poor man came by his death. Like you, I suppose, I only know that he drowned. In fact I don't mind telling you that his death was precisely what I did not envisage. It is what has put us all to so much trouble. Now let us go downstairs and outside very quietly, so that you may satisfy yourself that I have told you the truth. And then, perhaps, you can call off your small private armies of brainless young cavalry officers and Indian engineers?'

Again Sophie raised her aching arms to level the pistol at his head.

306

'I think, Herr Guttmann' – her voice betrayed the physical strain she was feeling – 'that Sir George Chesney and Captain Barnaby may have their own reasons for bringing their men to Dorking Gap.'

'Reasons suggested by Mr Holmes, eh?'

Sophie remained silent. Guttmann laughed.

'I suspected, when I learnt of Sir George Chesney's visit here, that perhaps I had left my *tête à tête* with Mr Holmes until too late . . . By the way, are you sure you will not tell me who you are? You are Russian, are you not? You speak French too well for a Frenchwoman – I suspected that from the start. And your English is fluent – but then young Russian ladies are invariably instructed by English governesses, are they not? You are not one of those lady revolutionists whose families have settled in Munich or Geneva, are you? Ah well, if you won't tell me . . .!'

He picked up the lantern and went back to the door. He did not even take the trouble to hold her in its beam. With his hand on the latch, he said, 'I hope one day you will grant me the privilege of a second game against you. I would hate to think of us never having a chance to meet again . . . But of course, if there is a return match it will just be you and me; you will not have the advantage of partnership with Mycroft Holmes. His intellect is not what it was, I fear. He has overdone things, this time – a slight brainstorm. But come, you shall see for yourself.'

He held open the door. She came round to the end of the bed then stopped, levelling the pistol at him. He bowed slightly. 'Of course, *liebe Mädchen*,' he said, and went out into the passage.

She followed him silently downstairs. She trod carefully; the house was lit only by the moonlight shining in through the great window above the stairs and there were shadows everywhere in which an enemy might lurk waiting to forcibly disarm her. Abigail, ignored by both of them, followed them as an unconsidered, solitary and bewildered spectator. Guttmann led them across the draughty spaces of the main hall where the moonlight was filtered darkly though stained glass to the front doors. Sophie stood in the centre of the hall as he opened them. She followed him down the steps on to the broad carriage-drive. All around in the stillness the Surrey hills stretched away in folds of moonlight and shadow. Below, in the mouth of the Gap, a scattering of flickering, pin-prick lights among the matchbox houses of Dorking showed where people were still awake.

The coat slung over his shoulders gave Guttmann the look of a giant, black *revenant* as he stalked across the drive to the parapet at the edge of the terrace. He turned and beckoned Sophie to join him. He stretched out his arm and pointed down the hill. She saw, on the slope of the heathland scrub in the elbow of the winding carriage-drive below, the round figure of Mycroft weaving to and fro aimlessly among the shadows.

'I think, *liebchen*, Mr Holmes is going to need the help of a dear friend,' Guttmann told her.

He glanced down at her arm. The pistol hung at her side, against her trousered leg.

'It is perfectly all right, my dear,' he told her as if he were granting her permission not to point it at him. 'You have no need of it now.'

He pointed over the balustrade once more.

'You know?' he said. 'One of Whettam's men used an English idiom I had not heard before. I wonder if you

308

have heard it. "Five sticks short of a bundle" – that was it. Quite charming!'

Sophie turned to face him. With a considerable effort, she lifted her arms and levelled her pistol at his head.

'I should kill you!' she told him.

'Did you really like him as much as that?' he asked. There was regret in his voice. 'It is not easy to understand.'

He breathed in deeply, then sighed. He said, as if he were returning to being practical, 'You had better shoot me at some other time, *liebchen*. You would hardly be able to look after your friend if they had to imprison you and hang you for murder.'

'Perhaps I hate you more than I care about Mr Holmes,' she replied.

'*Liebchen*! How have I ever injured you?'

'You have not done *me* any injury,' she told him.

'Why should you hate me, then? You are neither a Frenchwoman nor an Englishwoman. If you are a Russian, as I suspect, you should know that I, as a son of Imperial Germany, feel nothing but the warmest regard for your Emperor and nation.'

Sophie realized that he was genuinely taken aback. For a moment she forced herself to go on aiming the pistol at him. Then, acting on a decision, she lowered it and thrust it into her belt. She turned and ran away from him, down the drive. When she had left the upper gate behind she climbed over the fence which skirted the drive and dropped down into the meadow. Plunging through the furze, taking no heed of the broom which plucked and tore at her sleeves, she ran, stumbled and slipped down the slope. Once she tripped and fell, slithering forward in the dank dew of the unkempt grass. The pistol in her belt bruised her ribs; she was thankful it had not gone off. She picked herself up, knowing that Guttmann would have seen her fall, but did not look back.

Mycroft did not turn to see her running to him. He was wandering up and down abstractedly, as if he had lost and was searching for something without actually knowing what it was. As she approached him she could hear him singing to himself, *'Deutschland, Deutschland über alles, Deutschland über all' die Welt . . .'*

She saw that he was hobbling around, picking long blades of grass and forming them into a bundle as if they were flowers. He looked at her over his shoulder and announced, to her astonishment, 'Poor Tom's a-cold.'

When he saw that the quotation was lost on her he started singing again, this time in dreadful imitation of Cyril's imitation of a southern Negro accent:

'All dem darkies am a singin',
Singin' to de ol' banjo . . .'

Sophie stood watching him. She shook her head at him. In her relief, she wanted to burst out laughing. Instead, she remarked, 'Mr Holmes, *tu es profondement dégoûtant.'* She sniffed. *'Répugnant. Je n'exagère pas!'*

Mycroft threw down the bundle of grass. He wiped his hands together.

'My dear Princess, if you had been hung down a well in absolute darkness for three days and nights even you, delightful though you are, would appear, feel, smell *répugnante.'*

'A well?' Sophie asked.

'A well. The sort of place Truth is supposed to dwell

in – as our Teutonic friend was delighted to remind me. Below the cellars. The house was originally built to withstand a siege. I daresay there's also a torture-chamber.'

He reached his hands out toward her, his face beaming.

'Were you aware, Princess, that you addressed me as *tu*!'

She stepped back, keeping him at arms' length.

'No! No, Mr Holmes. I beg your pardon! It was most impertinent of me!'

From the drive far above them, at the top of the steep slope of the meadow, there came a clattering of wheels and horse's hooves. It came nearer by the minute, until a light two-wheeled carriage careered round the bend. In the moonlight they could see Whettam crouched over the reins, lashing at the horse. Beside him, looming over him and clutching at the narrow seat-rail, was Guttmann, his face concealed beneath his wide-brimmed soft hat. As the carriage dashed along below the meadow, lurching and leaping over potholes, Guttmann turned in Sophie's direction and raised his arm in salute.

'One has to admit, don't you know,' said Mycroft, 'the fellow has a sense of style.'

But Sophie had pulled the little pistol from her belt. She levelled it at the retreating carriage. Mycroft grasped her wrist. 'You won't hit him at this distance,' he told her.

Sophie twisted her wrist out of his grip. She did not attempt to raise the pistol again, however.

They watched the carriage disappear behind the woods.

'He believes he has driven you mad,' she said angrily.

'That was his intention,' said Mycroft. 'He told me you

311

had betrayed me' – he held the knife out to her unopened in his palm – 'He wanted me to kill you, my dear, and so procure my own incarceration as a homicidal maniac. The trouble was, I have made no special study of madmen – I leave such fields of research to my young brother, Sherlock. For myself, I could only think of the mad scenes in *King Lear*. My performance, however, appeared to be received with a measure of satisfaction, though I fear I disappointed him in its conclusion.' He put the knife back in his pocket. 'My limbs are dreadfully cramped. You will have to assist me back up the hill, dear Princess, repugnant though I may be.'

Sophie offered him her arm. 'I shall attempt to endure it, Mr Holmes,' she told him.

'Mind you,' observed Mycroft during one of their many pauses for breath as they struggled back up the meadow towards the drive, 'the fact that he believes me not to be entirely myself – in the head, that is – might be of inestimable advantage at our next encounter.'

'There will be a next encounter?' asked Sophie. The moonlight caught her face. On it there was a look of fierce eagerness.

'Oh yes! You have truly met the man now, haven't you? And can you doubt it? He is a stayer, wouldn't you say? His vanity alone – disregarding his master's inclinations – will compel him to succeed where, on this occasion, he may have failed.'

As Mycroft hobbled up the drive, leaning on Sophie's arm, they encountered Abby by the front door. She was sitting on the step, sobbing.

'Well?' Sophie asked. 'Did he promise to take you with him?'

Abby shook her head. 'Wish he had!' she said. 'Dunno

what's to become of me, now!' She sniffed loudly. 'He promised to give me a telescope, so he did – 'long as I did what he said, like.' She sniffed again. 'A real big one, like sea-captains have!' she said.

'But he didn't give you a telescope?' asked Sophie.

Abby shook her head. 'An' I did do everything he told me, an' all!' she said. ' 'Tain't fair!'

'He will reward you,' Sophie told her. 'You wait and see. If he has not destroyed you, he will reward you. Men like him look after their own, you know. And you are his own, aren't you, Abigail?'

Abby stared up at her, her face silver white in the moonlight.

'That's what they says 'bout the Devil, bain't it?' she asked. 'That he looks arter his own?'

'Yes, Abigail,' said Sophie. 'And now you had better go and wake up your mistress and tell her that Mr Guttmann has had to leave – how would you say it?'

Mycroft had propped himself up against one of the pillars supporting the portico roof.

'Like a bat out of Hell?' he suggested. 'That is the expression favoured by our American cousins, I believe.'

Chapter Thirty

The weather was perfect for the afternoon of Mrs Jenks-Robinson's garden party. There were a few fleecy clouds to break the azure of the sky, and a gentle breeze to keep the air fresh and the temperature comfortable. Mycroft, with Sophie and Sir George Chesney, sat with Sir James Swarthmoor in his landau to watch Captain Barnaby's Twenty-first Lancers performing their musical ride. Mr Jenks-Robinson stood below them, at the carriage step. From the moment of their arrival he had displayed an embarrassing and sweaty anxiety to ingratiate himself with them.

The band was not German, but that of the Guildford and Bramley Mounted Yeomanry. They were playing a suitable patriotic medley – 'Hearts of Oak', 'The British Grenadiers' and 'Rule Britannia' – which they followed with *galops* and waltzes from 'The Bohemian Girl', 'Maritana', and 'The Lily of Killarney'. When the ride was finished, and had been enthusiastically applauded by the assembled company, Captain Barnaby rode over to Sir James's carriage. They all dismounted and went down the slope of the grounds to where the screw-gun had been unlimbered. It was mounted on the edge of the ridge where it commanded Dorking and the Dorking and Guildford railway line. Nearby, Colonel Chesney's men – predominantly English but with a sprinkling of Sikhs – were constructing a rope bridge, watched by a clutch of gawping ragamuffins.

One of the gun crew – a veteran sergeant-of-gunners who was proudly wearing his uniform and campaign medals – came running at a slow, rheumatic trot up to Colonel Chesney. He came to attention and saluted. Then he turned to Jenks-Robinson and reported in a stentorian voice that the gun was laid, ready to fire the Royal Salute.

'A word in your ear, sar'nt,' said Captain Barnaby.

Mr Jenks-Robinson began to display anxiety more and more uncontrollably as Captain Barnaby took the sergeant's arm and they went together down to the cannon. For some minutes they talked together as enthusiastic connoisseurs might discuss some rare exhibit. Then they came back up the grass. The gunnery-sergeant was just about to speak to Mycroft when Mr Jenks-Robinson intervened, his voice shaking with nervousness.

'The children have been playing with it all morning,' he said. 'We have made it perfectly safe for them, you see? The good sergeant here will tell you. We have blocked the muzzled somewhat . . .'

'And does that makes it safer?' Mycroft asked, enjoying Jenks-Robinson's discomfort. 'I would have thought it would make it more likely to explode.'

Mr Jenks-Robinson struggled on.

'It is light enough for them to wheel into position, you see, and to lay. They particularly enjoy laying it on to

315

Dorking railway station. I tell you, gentlemen, it is a joy to see their pranks!'

'The deuce it is!' Mycroft observed quietly.

'It's an old friend, sir,' the sergeant told him, 'the old Elswick screw-gun. Combines the first Armstrong breech mechanism with touch-firing with fuse and lanyard. Crewed 'em when we was with Sir Hugh Rose's column, sir, at the time of the Great Mutiny. Against the Maharanee of Oudh.'

'It's not a Krupps gun, then?' Mycroft asked.

'Bless you, no!' laughed the sergeant. 'From what I've heard, sir, them Prooshians would take this 'un for an antique! And the gentleman's right; it's perfectly safe for the kiddies to play with. Just enough calibre for a ceremonial firing with black powder, sir.'

'Perfectly cowwect, Holmes,' Barnaby confirmed. 'No gainsayin' it.'

Mycroft made his way down to the gun. Sophie gathered her skirts over her arm and followed him.

'What!' Jenks-Robinson laughed, too loudly. 'Is the Princess Trubetskoy also an expert in ballistics?'

Sophie turned and stared coldly at him.

'I have eyes, Mr Jenks-Robinson. And behind them, a perfectly good brain.'

'That's twue,' Barnaby agreed enthusiastically. 'Never a twuer word was spoken!'

Mycroft took a small penknife from his pocket. He opened it and scraped the surface of the metal obstructing the gun's muzzle. Sophie crouched down with him to examine it. Their heads were almost together, the rim of her flat hat touching his cheek. The patch he had scraped clean shone almost silver. She looked at him; he shook his head, warning her not to speak.

'Sergeant!' he called. 'Another moment of your time, if you please.'

The sergeant limped over to join him. He bent down with some difficulty to look at the part of the muzzle which Mycroft had scraped.

'The barrel was obstructed recently?' Mycroft asked in a low voice.

The sergeant nodded. He ran his fingers round the circumference of the exposed area. He lifted it to his nose.

'Very recently?'

The sergeant nodded again.

'Tell me what you make of it, there's a good fellow,' said Mycroft.

'Black powder, sir. Smeared over it and ignited to give the appearance of age.'

'Molten lead poured about the inside of the muzzle?' Mycroft asked.

'And zinc, sir. In a compound.'

'Sometime during the past two weeks?'

'Possible during the past few days, sir. 'Tis recent work, sir.'

From the terraced lawns in front of the Hall came the sound of the band playing and a robust baritone voice singing, 'Let me like a soldier fall.'

Mycroft said in a low voice to both Sophie and the sergeant, 'Let us discuss this at another time. We do not want to embarrass Mrs Jenks-Robinson on this, her own very particular day of the year. For the moment let us do everything to reassure the master of the Hall.'

He led them back to the others.

'Mr Jenks-Robinson, I hope I have not given any impression of harbouring unworthy suspicions. If so, pray accept my most devout apologies!'

Jenks-Robinson's face beamed with effusive relief.

'It is I who should be making my apologies, Mr Holmes, after all you have suffered in my house – even though it was never through any wish of mine. It is no defence, I know, to plead the latitude one permits a guest who is a visitor from a foreign land and who is acting as the representative of several valued commercial clients in his own country. But it is the only excuse I can offer. I do not know how I shall ever make amends, Mr Holmes.'

'By permitting us to enjoy this most delightful day as your guests, Mr Jenks-Robinson. Pray give me your hand in friendship, my dear fellow.'

'With all my heart, Mr Holmes!'

As they shook hands Sophie could scarcely control her look of surprised distaste.

They strolled back towards the garden. A crowd was standing around a traction engine decorated with fluttering pennants, waiting for it to get up the necessary head of steam with which to drive four roundabouts nearby. The band was by now accompanying a soprano – her pure, sweet voice carried the limpid melody and the words of Eily O'Connor's lament from 'The Lily of Killarney' across the lawn.

Mycroft asked Mr Jenks-Robinson, 'What has become of that little between-maid who ran errands for the man Guttmann?'

'Ah! Abigail Rodgers, you mean. We have had to dismiss her, of course. Her behaviour was most surprising. Her parents are very decent people – her father is a respectable, solid yeoman farmer. I'm afraid she has come close to breaking both their hearts. Mrs Jenks-Robinson thought it best, and her father agreed, that we should place her into the care of the Wantage Sisters.

318

They keep a place of refuge for young Magdalens – if you will pardon the expression, Princess – to which Mrs Jenks-Robinson has been a subscriber; my wife is, you will understand, the very soul of charitable generosity. The sisters there will ensure she has no access to the wrong sort of books and poems and that her training and further upbringing is that suited to a female domestic of the humbler rank.'

'So,' Mycroft remarked, 'effectively, she is as much a prisoner as if she were formally convicted?'

'Indeed, sir,' Mr Jenks-Robinson replied. 'We must pray that the nuns will know best how to rid her of that lying deceit which seems to have taken possession of her and so brought her mother to despairing tears.'

'Ah yes! We must pray indeed!' Mycroft agreed.

Two nights later Mycroft and Sir James were dinner guests in Sophie's apartment. The meal was finished. A Russian maid removed the dessert plates.

'My compliments to your cook, Princess,' said Sir James. 'I have not enjoyed such a meal even in St Petersburg on the several visits I have made to your beautiful capital city.'

'He is French,' Sophie replied. 'But he spent five years in my mother's home in "Peter" . . . Please feel free to take tobacco, gentlemen – so long as you do not expect me to retire. Cyril, you will fetch the cigars. And you need not pretend you don't know where they are!'

'No, Princess,' Cyril answered.

'I'm considering quite seriously putting him into Cossack dress,' she announced.

Cyril came to a dead halt on his way to the door. He looked back in utter dismay.

319

'To be attended by a negro Cossack would be quite unique,' Sophie said. 'There hasn't been a truly black Cossack since the grandfather of our great Pushkin served under Peter the Great.'

'It will certainly cause a splash in London society,' said Sir James.

'Don't you think it will cause the most delightful stir when he accompanies me riding in the Row?' she asked.

Cyril caught Mycroft's eye. He shook his head, appealing to him.

'Be kind to the poor fellow, Princess,' Mycroft pleaded. 'He is really very worried, you know.' Then he asked, 'Were you attended by Cossack servants as a child?'

'We were *guarded* by Cossacks when I was a child,' Sophie replied.

'Of course, Princess. Forgive me.' Mycroft turned to Sir James. 'Talking of servants – if you will take my advice, you will rescue the Jenks-Robinsons' little between-maid from durance vile in Wantage.'

'Why should we? I would have thought she well deserves to be where she is.'

'There is nobody better qualified to give evidence against Jenks-Robinson,' Mycroft urged.

'Jenks-Robinson is in no position to do this country any damage,' Sir James replied. 'He knows very well what a damn' close-run thing it was for him, and how near he came to dancing at the end of a piece of hemp.'

'But he's a traitor – and he helped to murder that poor M. Thibault!' exclaimed Sophie.

'What would be his fate in your country, dear Princess?' asked Mycroft.

'He would be taken out into Senate Square and broken

320

on the wheel – for everybody to see!' she replied.

'Lord Granville has called both the French and German ambassadors to the Foreign Office,' said Sir James. 'He has apprised them – I tell you this in confidence, naturally – that Her Majesty's ministers are perfectly informed as to the secret protocols attached to the Versailles Accords, and will be taking appropriate measures.'

'But what about justice!' Sophie demanded. She looked to Mycroft. He shook his head wearily.

'If Jenks-Robinson were to be arrested and tried – even if we had sufficient proof to secure a conviction either for his being an accessory to the murder of Jean-Christophe Thibault or on a charge of High Treason,' said Sir James, 'the Government of this country would be faced with considerable embarrassment. There would be a public outcry about how such a situation had been allowed to develop unchecked; about the state of our national defence. Do you realize? As a result of uninformed pressure by the more radical and irresponsible public organs – I'm thinking of *The Northern Star* and *The Pall Mall Gazette* in particular – we could find income tax being forced up to as much as ten pence or a shilling in the pound! This administration is confronted with enough difficulties in the field of foreign affairs as it is. Your countrymen, for example, Princess, are rebuilding a fleet in the ports of Odessa and Sevastopol which is almost certainly intended for deployment in the Mediterranean. I'm not saying that the Russians haven't a perfectly valid stake in the Mediterranean, mind you. But sections of the press here will kick up one deuce of a stink demanding to know what Her Majesty's Government intends doing about it. Then there is the question of the reparations the United States Government is demanding for losses in shipping caused by Confederate raiders operating out of Liverpool. That'll provoke another unholy row. Mr Gladstone really can't afford another crisis in foreign affairs. Not just at the moment.'

'So HMG prefers to take no action whatever?' Mycroft demanded.

'Oh! I didn't say that!' Sir James replied. He paused as Cyril brought in the cigars. He took one and rolled it under his nostrils before removing the band and clipping the end. 'May I compliment you on your choice of smokes, my dear Princess?'

'My father taught both my late sister and myself a certain discrimination, Sir James,' Sophie replied.

When Mycroft's and Sir James's cigars were alight and Cyril and the maids had withdrawn from the drawing-room, Sir James continued, 'There are unofficial channels open to the Foreign Office, don't you know?'

'But no steps will be taken actually to improve the defences of this country?' asked Mycroft. 'There is no question, in the light of our recent experience, of building up an armed force capable of withstanding a success-ful landing by an enemy expedition?'

'It is a question of what the tax-payer will stand for, don't you see?' Sir James replied. 'He wants this country defended on the one hand, but on the other he would rather invest his money in commerce than in armed forces which, of course, pay no annual dividend. It is as simple as that. You may not approve, my dear Holmes – Treasury man though you are – but we have in this country what is essentially, I would say, a tradesman's government. Moreover, there are fields other than that of Dorking Gap in which the new German Empire may well prove a dangerous foe. I refer, of course, to the field of industry and commerce.'

'It would come to the same field in the end,' Mycroft said gloomily. 'I have heard Guttmann himself say so. He prophesied a commercial rivalry that can only end in war.'

'Oh my dear Holmes! There you go again! The new German Reich will soon realize that between our two High Powers there is no real point of conflict. Unpleasant though this little business has been, I'm sure that we will find that it resulted from a passing anxiety on the part of the Prussian masters of the new Germany – a fear that our traditional policy of maintaining the balance of power on the continent would mean us opposing them, by military means if necessary. As soon as Prince von Bismarck has assured himself that we entertain nothing but the friendliest feelings toward himself and his Emperor, I am sure there will be no more such episodes. That, at any rate, is the view Lord Granville prefers to take.'

'Episodes!' exclaimed Sophie.

'Allow me to offer you one small piece of advice, Sir James,' Mycroft told him. 'Release Abigail Rodgers from the convent-reformatory just the same.'

'Why?' asked Sir James.

'Guttmann is shrewd enough to know a useful and intelligent employee when he sees one. My guess is that in a few years time, you may find pretty little Miss Rodgers the most demure and properly-behaved basement slavey – employed in the household of some important minister of state or lord of the Admiralty . . . What I am suggesting is, instead of leaving her for C.P.E. Guttmann to take up again, train her to become an agent of our own secret service. I am sure that if you took the trouble to give her the limited education required of such a person she would in time become a perfectly acceptable governess in some high-ranking Prussian establishment.'

At the words 'secret service', Sir James took the cigar from his lips in astonishment.

'My dear Holmes!' he protested. 'What in the world possesses you to think that we, in Great Britain, employ a secret service! It simply is not the English way! If we were to lend ourselves to such underhand methods we should lose that moral superiority which marks us as separate from other nations – forgive me, Princess, but it is true, you know!'

When Sir James and Mycroft were out in the vestibule putting on their hats and gloves before walking together back to Pall Mall, Sophie drew Mycroft aside.

'Such dreadful complacency!' she whispered. 'What can you do?'

Mycroft put a plump finger to her lips.

'I shall do nothing. I shall leave matters in the very capable hands of Sir George Chesney.'

'Why? What will he do?'

'We shall see.'

Epilogue

As he walked from the Diogenes Club, where he had
lunched, back to Whitehall, Mycroft made what was for
him a considerable detour. Crossing Trafalgar Square,
which he had always regarded as a frontier beyond
which lay lands as remote and as exhausting as Tibet, he
went up the Strand all of a hundred yards, to Charing
Cross Station. On the rooftops there was a white frost.
There was also a winter fog descending on which the
smoke from the railway termini would rest and accumu-
late until it achieved the necessary density to qualify as a
pea-souper, a London Regular.

Having acquired a halfpenny platform ticket – which
he regarded as a form of larceny peculiar to railway
companies – he went straight to the boat-train. He
arrived at the gate just after Sophie, wrapped in sables,
had passed through, followed by her old *nyanya* – who
was, as usual, muttering prayers or imprecations to
herself – two Russian maids who were giggling between
themselves when they weren't glancing wickedly at any
and every passing male, Jeannie, Sophie's personal maid

who was almost as pretty as, and rather more lady-like than, her mistress, and finally Cyril, wearing a neat, clerkly suit and top coat. Behind the small cortège a longer cortège of porters followed wheeling trollies bearing some forty or fifty pieces of baggage. Two uniformed attendants waited to greet her at the door of her private carriage.

'Princess!' he called.

A host of other passengers with their friends and relatives were watching from the platform and the carriage windows, the steam from their breath mingling with the smoke from the engine and the steam from the pipes under the carriages.

'Mr Holmes!'

She opened her arms to him. He was compelled to let her embrace him.

'I did not think you would come!' she told him. 'I did not think Sir James would let you! Or is it Mr Gladstone?'

'Hush!' he told her, embarrassed by her public display of affection toward him. Then, ashamed at his own embarrassment, he said awkwardly, 'I couldn't allow you to leave London without making my adieux. But I haven't told anybody I was coming.'

'I am so pleased,' she said.

Her old nurse was trying to make herself understood by the carriage attendants.

'*Nyanya moya* says that nothing is done properly in this heathen land,' Sophie told Mycroft. 'She says it doesn't even snow properly.'

'Isn't it cold enough for her?' Mycroft shuddered.

'*Nyanya moya* will tell you that when the frost is hard, it is the snow that keeps you warm.'

'Nannies talk nonsense in every language,' said Mycroft.

'Not at all,' Sohpie replied. 'What she says is perfectly true.'

She turned to her *nyanya* and spoke to her in Russian. Her *nyanya* replied in an indignant tone of voice; she bowed deeply and signed herself with the cross three times.

Sophie smiled at Mycroft. 'She says it's a godless country,' she explained.

Nyanya entered the carriage first in order to satisfy herself that it was comfortable enough for her mistress and thus for herself. She squeezed her bulk through the door. One of the uniformed attendants led the two giggling maids to the servants' compartment.

'You are leaving your black Cossack behind?' asked Mycroft.

Cyril nodded. Mycroft was surprised by the sadness in his face. It showed a gentleness he had never realized was there. Sophie stroked Cyril's cheek.

'I could not take him from London,' she said. 'He thinks he's sorry to see me go . . .'

'I *am* sorry!' Cyril protested vehemently.

'But I couldn't take the King of the Zulus away from his subjects,' she added. 'Any more than I would take Captain Barnaby from his beloved Lancers. To know that I leave friends behind me – who will be there to welcome me when I return . . . That is good.'

Still smiling, she put her hand to her heart. Then she reached for Mycroft's hand. Holding it, she said, 'I know that you would never seek to be more than a friend, Mr Holmes. So it would make me happy if you came to Nice – for a holiday, to escape your English winter, you know?'

Mycroft shuddered.

'The rigours of such a journey, and at this season of the year! A sea-passage in this weather! Princess! It's hard to know how you bring yourself to contemplate such an ordeal!'

'The sea, Mr Holmes, will certainly be as calm as a mirror, and my cabin quite warm, I do assure you. As for discomfort – how could it possibly compare with what you endured during your terrible imprisonment in Ranmore Hall?'

'It was not *so* terrible, Princess. There was nobody to disturb a fellow's sense of peace, don't you know? It put me in mind of my club. In fact, I don't mind telling you as I hung there in that perfect quiet I actually thought of one or two amendments to the rules I'd put to the committee. For instance, that we should have our journals and newspapers printed on silk: don't rustle, d'ye see.'

He glanced from side to side to ensure that nobody would overhear him. He drew closer to her, and stooped his head.

'You see, my dear Princess,' he told her, 'it was then I realized what had happened to poor old Thibault. That devil Guttmann had driven him mad so that nobody would pay the least attention to anything he said; only instead of trotting around raving like the lunatic he was supposed to be, he simply disappeared. Nothing could have been worse, both from the Prussian and the French point of view. The French authorities, we must presume, realizing that Thibault had left for England but being too late to prevent him landing on these shores, informed the Prussian authorities at their army's general headquarters in Reims. Guttmann was, as it happened, in England, engaged in making preparations for the very business Thibault was coming to warn us about. The

Prussians must have regarded it as a stroke of luck, having their best agent *in situ*, as it were, to take immediate action to silence Thibault. I dare say they would have expected Guttmann to have killed him, while Thiers, being connected with Thibault's family, might have been merciful enough to have wished him abducted and returned to France. But murder demands investigation, and all too often news of abduction – by its nature, a clumsy business – gets out and is whipped up into a political and even an international scandal by the radical press. Hence the method of silencing him – at least to all intents and purposes – which Guttmann struck on. But the one thing Guttmann could not take into account was the possibility of Thibault's vanishing from the face of the earth. Prussian and German authorities alike must have become deeply alarmed. Where was he? Had he been found? Were our people holding him secretly – and if so, was he as lunatic as Guttmann supposed? They had to try find out for themselves. So by the time Thibault reappeared, albeit dead, the bloodhounds – meaning me and you, Princess, I wasn't forgetting you – were already sniffing around. Which was, of course, the very thing Guttmann had worked to prevent. Worse still, the body was seen at the very last spot in England to which Guttmann and his masters wished to draw attention, so he had to take steps to prevent its discovery there.'

'Including the murder of that poor farm labourer?' Sophie asked.

'Certainly. Rightly, he judged that the removal from this world of a poorhouse boy without family or home of his own would not provoke too deep an investigation by the Detective Police.'

329

'And what about the girl – Abigail? She saw the body, but he didn't murder her.'

'Abigail Rodgers has a home and family,' Mycroft replied. 'Her father is not a rich man, but he's a hard-working yeoman – the sort of fellow we've always liked to regard in this country as the backbone of the nation. Her death would have caused a stir in the neighbourhood – just as the murder of Maria Marten, another humble yeoman's daughter, caused a stir. But I'm sure there was another reason . . . Do you believe in Evil, Princess? I mean, a Spirit of Evil?'

'Do you mean Satan, Mr Holmes?' Sophie asked. She signed herself with the Cross.

The old nurse appeared above them, squeezed in the doorway of the carriage. She called chidingly down at Sophie, telling her to climb on board to take her seat before the train started to move. Sophie told her not to fuss, and that she would climb on board very soon.

'She is always afraid that if we are still standing up when the train moves, we'll all fall over and break our bones,' she exclaimed to Mycroft. She added, 'Yes, of course I believe there is a Spirit of Evil.'

'You see, Princess,' Mycroft told her, 'it is my opinion that the moment he set eyes on the child Abigail Rodgers, Guttmann knew she was subject to the same Prince as himself. And I do not mean the Prince von Bismarck. You see? He was not permitted to harm her.'

Sophie stared up at him.

'You are serious, aren't you, Mr Holmes?'

'Quite serious, my dear.' Around them was the rising tumult of the train's imminent departure, doors slamming, people calling out to one another, leaning from

330

open windows, standing, fluttering handkerchiefs in the drifting steam.

Sophie mounted the step. She turned around and once more reached for his hand and took it.

'I am paying an allowance to our King of the Zulus and his people. They are to keep watch and to tell us if Herr Guttmann returns to London,' she said.

'Not "if",' Mycroft replied, ' "when". As Shakespeare has it, "We have scotched the snake, not killed it." '

'Very well, my dear. And "when" he comes, you will send for me?' she asked. 'You will telegraph immediately, mind! Nice. Or even St Petersburg. You must promise never to fight Herr Guttmann without me.'

'The moment the situation arises, I shall inform you, my dear Princess. I shall inform you straightaway, I promise.'

'And, Mr Holmes? You are to . . . to keep an eye on? Is that what you say? . . . my dear Zulu king. If it had not been for him, you know, I would not have been able to call on our friends to come to your rescue. So – now it is *au 'voir*, dear Mr Holmes.'

She leant down, kissed him lightly on the lips, then disappeared into the carriage without looking back. The attendants jumped in after her and closed the door behind them. The guard whistled and waved his flag. The train began to pull away from the platform. Mycroft was about to go off down the platform when he noticed Cyril standing there looking quite desolate. At first he intended to walk past as if he had not seen him. He changed his mind and instead patted him consolingly on the shoulder. They walked back together through the station to the concourse outside.

'Should you or any of your spies catch sight of Mr

Guttmann in London again,' Mycroft told him, 'you are to come straight to Number 73a, Pall Mall. If I am not there you will leave a message. I shall communicate with Princess Trubetskoy straightaway.'

He was sure the instruction was unnecessary, but it was some slight alleviation of their sense of loss.

Alone, Mycroft crossed the Strand, holding up the traffic – omnibuses, cabs, drays – with an imperious wave of his stick. The fog was closing in, filtering and obscuring the frosty sunlight in an increasingly greeny-orange swirl. Once he was safe on the far side he walked a short distance up the pavement and paused outside a bookshop. He peered in at the window. Then he went outside, down a couple of steps. The alteration in temperature made him cough. The bookseller emerged from a back-shop behind the gaslit counter.

'Can I be of assistance, sir?'

Mycroft rested his stick on his shoulder. He lifted it and pointed to a book on a nearby table.

'Ah, yes, sir!' said the bookseller. '*The Battle of Dorking* by "Sabretache". A chilling tale, if I might say so, sir – for a chilly time of the year. They say that the *soubriquet* "Sabretache" conceals the identity of a distinguished military gentleman.'

'You have read it yourself?' asked Mycroft.

'Oh yes, sir. It is frighteningly convincing – everybody is talking about it, as I'm sure you know. It made me wonder if such a thing could really happen. A Prussian army landing at Little Hampton; a traitor making sure it can pass unopposed through Dorking Gap – rather like the Battle of Thermopylae in a way, sir. And only two days later Field Marshal von Moltke leading his Uhlans and Potsdam Grenadiers up the Mall to occupy Buckingham Palace! Do you believe it could really happen, sir?'

'It cannot happen if enough honest men read this book and heed its lesson, I daresay,' Mycroft replied. 'I'll take it,' he added.

'You're lucky, sir,' the bookseller told him as he wrapped it. 'This is my last copy. I ordered fifty, believe it or not. They were gone in a day and a half – all except this one, which I kept back for my own reading. You may have it for half-price. Mind you, if you prefer a new copy I have ordered a further hundred copies from the publishers . . . You'd be surprised how many gentlemen have been in here asking for it. I expect some of them have come from their offices in Whitehall, round the corner, wouldn't you think so, sir?'

'Let us hope so, eh?' Mycroft replied.

He took out his purse and paid for the book.

'Quite right, sir,' the bookseller, glancing down at the money. 'Let us hope so indeed,' he added, looking up again. 'Thank you very much, sir. Much obliged.'

Mycroft walked back up the Strand, the slim parcel dangling from his finger on its string. The station concourse had become barely visible except where flares had been lit on either side of the main entrance. Lamps on the sides of cabs rattling in and out were like floating orbs of orange in the general obscurity. Through the traffic on the street Mycroft could just make out the figure on the pavement opposite. It had its back turned to him and was gyrating in a strange, slow dance. The voice, nasal and high-pitched, came singing over the growling of metal-tyred wheels and the clatter of horses' hooves.

333

'All dem darkies am a singin',
Singin' to de ole banjo.
All de bells in Heaven am ringin'
To hear dem darkies singin' so.
Chicken in de basket,
Chicken in de pot,
Oh, all dem darkies am such a happy lot!'

Postscript

The impact of the publication in November 1871 of *The Battle of Dorking*, written by Sir George Chesney under the pseudonym 'Sabretache', caused as much of a sensation as Sir Mycroft Holmes could possibly have wished. (*Vide* I.F. Clarke, 'The Battle of Dorking, 1871', *Journal of Victorian Studies* Vol. VIII [1965] pp. 322 ff). Immediately prior to Parliament's Christmas recess that year, Gladstone felt impelled to assure the House of Commons personally that the charge contained in the novel – that Britain had no means of defending itself against a German attack from across the Channel – was utterly without foundation (*vide* J. Morley, *Life of Gladstone* [1903] Vol. II, pp. 507 ff). Despite this assurance, however, immediate steps were taken to reorganize the armed forces so that all regiments of the British Army should be split into two battalions, one for service overseas and one to defend the British Isles, and that the Dover Patrol should be established by the Royal Navy to keep permanent watch over the Channel. Far

from being disgraced as an alarmist, Sir George Chesney
was restored to the Army's active list and promoted to the
rank of full general.

Editor, *The Mycroft Holmes Papers*

THE END